Aifric Campbell was born in Ireland. As a convent schoolgirl in Dublin, her greyhound won the Irish Derby and a hymn she co-wrote won a national TV song contest. She moved to Sweden where she worked as an au pair, completed a Linguistics degree and lectured in semantics at the University of Göteborg. She spent thirteen years as an investment banker in the City of London before leaving to study psychotherapy and creative writing, most recently at the University of East Anglia. She now lives in Sussex with her husband and son.

The Semantics of Murder is inspired by the life and work of Richard Montague, a brilliant and controversial professor of Philosophy at the University of California at Los Angeles who was murdered in 1971. The crime remains unsolved.

For more information on the book and the author, please visit **www.thesemanticsofmurder.com**

THE · SEMANTICS · OF · MURDER ·

Aifric Campbell

A complete catalogue record for this book can
be obtained from the British Library on request

The right of Aifric Campbell to be identified as the author of this work
has been asserted by her in accordance with the Copyright, Designs
and Patents Act 1988

First published in 2008 by Serpent's Tail,
an imprint of Profile Books Ltd
3A Exmouth House
Pine Street
Lodon EC1R 0JH
website: www.serpentstail.com

ISBN 978 1 85242 996 6

Designed and typeset by Sue Lamble

Printed by Clays, Bungay, Suffolk

10 9 8 7 6 5 4 3 2 1

To Mac

I don't claim that my novels are truth – I claim that they are fiction, out of which a kind of truth emerges. And I keep in my mind specifically that what I am writing is fiction because I am interested in truth – absolute truth – and I don't pretend that what I'm writing is more than an imaginative extension of the truth – something inventive... But simply because one puts it out as a work of fiction then one is not a liar. I do think that this ought to be recognised by people. People get very annoyed if you say, look here, Goldilocks and the three bears is a pack of lies.

Muriel Spark

• PART ONE •

• ONE •

When Jay opened his front door, Cora slunk past him down the hallway like a sleepwalker groping through a familiar terrain. Rainwater dripped from her coat sleeves onto the wooden floor. She sank into the couch as if falling backwards from a great height, head bowed, chin almost touching her breastbone. Jay could smell her despair.

A fierce hail rattled the windowpane. Cora tensed her shoulders, her coat fell open and he could see how rapidly she was losing weight, as if evaporating. He wondered if she had stopped eating entirely, if it was simply becoming too onerous a task. Just yesterday she'd confessed to a new-found fear of chewing, she was taking only soft liquid foods, the kind given to babies, feeding a growing suspicion about the dangers lurking in a piece of toast, a breast of chicken, terrified of the traps her body might spring.

Jay crossed the room and took up his usual position in the brown leather Corbusier whose geometric frame seemed to hold out the promise of a structured aesthetic. Solutions. Orderliness. Clients – although he referred to them privately as patients – could choose between a matching armchair and the low-slung velvet couch where Cora now sat, arms splayed by her side.

'Tell me more about Christopher,' he said.

A muscle spasm nagged at her left eyelid, one of the new symptoms she had acquired since they first met, a steady accumulation of stigmata that advertised her deteriorating condition. The tip of her tongue probed a cold sore. A crop of insistent pimples advanced along the underside of her chin. Her fingernails were uncomfortably short and there were livid streaks of pink rawness where she had stripped off the cuticles.

'Tell me about Christopher,' he repeated.

'I can't,' she said and rammed a knuckle into her mouth, teeth sinking into the bone, leaving trace prints on the skin. Since the mention of her baby godson two weeks ago, Cora had been chronically tearful, nostrils flared red at the tips, crumpled tissues heaped on her lap. 'This is not me,' she sobbed. 'It's like I'm leaking,' and for a moment, Jay saw her slumped in a blue rowing boat, oarless and bobbing on the winter Serpentine.

'Tell me.'

'I held him just after he was born,' she whispered, her voice barely audible against the roar of the rain. 'Christopher never cries when I hold him,' she sniffed and Jay heard a pink-lipped wail, saw a wrinkled newborn swaddled in blue flannel. 'When he was five months old I was in the garden. Amy was upstairs and he was wriggling in my arms, pounding his little fists. At my breast. I felt like I could do it, you know. I felt like I could feed him... and I knew if something happened to Amy—'

'What is it you think might happen to Amy?'

Cora swallowed, her panicked eyes darted around the room. 'Nothing. Nothing. She's my closest friend. We... we were always going to do everything together.'

The air was thick with frantic secrets. Closing his eyes, Jay caught a fleeting glimpse of a red silk scarf flapping through a car window, heard the sound of swift, light footsteps receding in the night – it was the hurried press of Cora's story unfolding just out of earshot, but when he listened, it fell silent. For five weeks now he had watched her scuttle round the fringes of her past while he sat in the armchair, a textbook arrangement of attentiveness in the fifty-minute hour. His body language had been successfully deflated years ago, during long sessions in front of the full-length mirror in his studio room, head swivelling between an oblique view of the Bay – all he could afford of San Francisco in those early days – and a honey strip of afternoon light sliding across the back wall. He'd studied his reflection, monitoring the gradual erosion of his identity into a pared-down expression of alert neutrality that would reassure his clients that he could listen without judgement, without pity, shock or horror; that he could take the story of a life and help them to rewrite it, give it a sequence and consequence it didn't have, make it a better story.

Cora was a referral from Ralph Laekin, one of the first doctors that Jay met when he arrived in the UK twenty years ago. A GP who had fled the National Health Service and invested his wife's inheritance in a private surgery for the Kensington elite, Laekin's compassion for the mental health of the privileged led him to joke more than once that he should have gone into psychiatry. Jay had taken up Cora's case with enthusiasm, believing that she would be perfect for his requirements. Now he wondered if he might be losing his touch.

Finding the right candidate was a delicate process but over the years he'd learnt that voice pattern was a reliable indicator. He needed to hear a prospective client speak, to know this was a frequency that engaged him. Cora's recorded voice, during her 28-second phone message, had started out in the hesitant lower range of a youngish woman testing the first notes of an ascending arpeggio and eventually stumbling into the upper limit of her register, so that it was no longer music at all, but a brittle shard of neutered sound on the verge of extinction.

'Mr Hamil – *ton*,' she had begun, with a curious emphasis on the last syllable of his name as if she was reading aloud from an unfamiliar text. Jay heard the muffled insistence of a car alarm and he pictured a darkened room, imagined her face scanned by passing headlights through a window. There was a sudden gasp of air, like a child who had been holding its breath and then she gave her first name – slowly, as if it might be difficult to pronounce. 'If I could see you,' she muttered, or so he thought, for even after six replays Jay could still not be certain that his interpretation was correct. But he was convinced he'd found the right material, he had a nose for these things and chose not to waste time evaluating instincts that were useful, so he removed the tape, placed it in a envelope and stored it in a box file labelled 'First Encounters'.

Cora had been three minutes late for her first session on a windworn November afternoon. She'd hesitated in the open doorway, head half-turned away as if she might change her mind and flee. A straggle of blasted leaves whipped about her legs and she brushed past him, found her way unbidden to the safe space. Jay could already detect a drained resolve in the pinch of her lips, the sense of someone getting thinner and fainter, losing definition and slipping away out of reach. A woman in her late thirties, with a pale round face and small nocturnal eyes set wide beneath unplucked brows. Her hair was fading out of an experimental auburn into an undistinguished brown and lay lank and matt on her shoulders. There was a suggestion of disarray in the accumulated fluff around the lapels of her suit jacket, the missing cuff button on her left sleeve. A loose thread dangled from the hem of her skirt. She wore a silver chain with a tiny solitaire diamond around her neck that had since disappeared, as if she'd decided that adornment was no longer appropriate.

On that first session, Cora sat propped like a marionette on the Corbusier, arms draped over the sides. Jay wondered if she would speak at all, if the effort of showing up for the appointment had exhausted her resources. Although he had never forgotten his humiliation at the hands of Hal Metzling, chief analyst at the San Francisco School of Psychoanalysis, who once unleashed a vicious and public attack when Jay pierced a client's stubborn silence, he had decided to resolve the professional debate about therapeutic interventions by eliminating silence as an opening strategy. These days he preferred to speed up the process and so he always started by saying: 'My name is Jay Hamilton. I am a psychoanalyst. Perhaps you could begin by telling me why you are here.'

Cora began predictably enough, as if she were in a doctor's surgery, with an outline of physical symptoms that he suspected were somatically motivated.

'It feels like croup. Dr Laekin told me I was hyperventilating. He said to breathe into a paper bag, but the attacks are getting worse. Before it was always just at night but then it started happening at work.'

She had struggled to keep a low profile in the office, trying to excuse her increasingly sporadic appearances with a host of minor ailments. Then, some weeks ago, she startled the receptionists by bursting into tears, stood beached in the lobby unable to contain her distress. Cora was like a mid-air explosion scattering debris everywhere and she guessed that people were already talking, gossip gators snapping at her fleeing heels. At night she'd lie watching the green digits count out her insomnia until dawn sneaked around the edge of the window blind and the bedroom walls towered over her, threatening collapse.

'I used to always read in bed,' she said. 'Maybe I should start again tonight.'

'Perhaps you are suggesting that you should read a book instead of coming here,' said Jay. 'Perhaps you think that some writer might help you become your own therapist?'

Winching both arms back into the chair, Cora had lapsed into a prolonged silence, suddenly broken by the announcement that she held an administrative position at one of the leading corporate law firms in London – a fact that she articulated with emphasis, as if by advertising the pedigree of her employer, they could both be reassured that whatever misfortune had brought her to Jay's door, it would surely pass. And then she lifted her head and from the repeated insistence of her life's completeness, her desperate assertion of sanity and self-possession, her fleeting mention of her five-year marriage to Larry, Jay understood that Cora would be talking about childlessness and that she was here to stay.

Nine desultory sessions had since come and gone, but he had yet to break the code. Each time she left he lingered in the still room casting about for the plot and, although there were moments where he sensed its darkroom image slowly forming beneath the surface, when he turned his head it vanished without trace. Outside he could hear the distant rumble of the street cleaners' cart and the slow wet hiss of passing tyres. Cora stirred on the couch, her hand moved upwards to brush a lock of hair from her cheek and Jay was struck by the exertion that this gesture seemed to require, as if the entire structure of her limbs was on the verge of collapse.

'I knew this was a bad idea,' she whimpered.

New clients, he reminded himself, think the big effort is to come here at all, not realising that the real challenge will be walking away. He had no time for those analysts who encouraged clients to become their own religion; like Narcissus drooling in his lake, they were seduced by their own minutiae, the way they held a coffee cup, the feelings aroused by certain department stores. 'You have to keep a sense of humour, otherwise you'd go mad,' said a near-hysterical group therapist to him one night, her naked breasts pressed against his chest as she offered herself up for a post-coital kiss. But there were many professionals willing to endure monotony in return for a healthy fee. 'I'm doing society a favour,' a well-known London analyst once confided over dinner. 'Do you know how many husbands pay me to see their wives just so they don't have to listen?'

Cora lifted her head.

'You never ask about my dreams,' she said.

'Are you saying you have a dream you want to talk about?'

'Isn't that what you are supposed to do?'

Jay smiled over steepled fingers. 'Perhaps you're suggesting that we are not discussing the important things? That you feel the core issues are not emerging in this space. Maybe you want to say you are disappointed in me?'

'Three times now and it's always the same dream,' she said. 'I'm in an underground car park with Amy. She's loading shopping into the boot of her car and I'm holding her handbag, when this guy appears out of nowhere and snatches it right out of my hands. Amy screams. She's always said that she carries her whole life around in her bag, so I run after him down the ramp into the darkness. I know it's a waste of time, I can't even see him anymore. Behind me I can hear her wailing, it's a horrible screeching sound, but I can't go back, I just keep on running.' Cora stared down at her clenched fist. 'I never stop.'

'So you want me to tell you what the dream means?' Jay asked.

'Yes.'

'What do you think it means?'

'Why do you always answer a question with another question?'

'Perhaps you think it's unfair that you should have to try and help yourself, Cora. Perhaps you are angry with me for not making your pain disappear.'

He let the silence settle, expecting that she would not speak again but she leaned forward and opened her palm to reveal a small blue birthday candle with a blackened wick. 'Fourteen years ago today, I had an abortion.' She held her breath to punctuate the aftershock of her words. 'It was way before Larry, he doesn't know. Amy came with me. She was the only one who knew.'

Cora burrowed down in her coat and a faint stench of wet wool filled the room. Jay curled his hand over the arm of his chair and stroked the soft leather. Timing therapeutic interventions was a tricky business and it was often a difficult judgement call, he reflected, when to speak, when to remain silent. Clients clamour for dream interpretation, only to recoil in horror from the hidden truths that burst forwards to greet them like some slathering primitive.

'Fourteen years ago you aborted your baby,' he began, squeezing the warm leather. 'You believe Amy gave you her blessing. You suspect that she may even have encouraged you. You say that both of you were supposed to do everything together, but Amy went on to have a baby when you could not.'

Cora pawed at the cushion, she was breathing only in instalments as if rationing the air. 'You believe that your infertility is a punishment for your abortion,' he continued. 'Your hands feel numb and useless because they are not nursing a baby. You imagine that Christopher is yours. Sometimes you even believe he needs you more than his mother.'

'Noooooo,' she moaned and flung herself forwards, jack-knifed on the couch. Jay nodded, releasing his grip.

'This is what you are dreaming about, Cora. This is what you wish for: that Amy will disappear and her baby will become yours.'

She howled, a long thin desolate wail and staggered to her feet, fingers clutching at her stomach as if she might be sick. Jay followed her into the hall, watched her scrabble at the latch and bolt across the street where she stumbled on the kerb and fell to her knees, spilling the contents of her handbag on the pavement. He thought she might sink prostrate into the wet stone, but she clawed her belongings back into the bag and hauled herself upright, foot plunging into a puddle of slick black water as she rounded the corner and disappeared. Jay bent down to retrieve a sodden leaf from the matwell and closed his front door, retreating down the hall to the space that Cora had just fled.

• TWO •

Eighteen years ago, on his first viewing of number 19 Edwardes Square, Jay had known immediately that the ground floor double-depth living space would be perfect for his needs: north facing, with no distracting views, its 13-foot ceiling managed to create the illusion of airiness in the tall narrow house. He had paid careful attention to the interior design and a deliberate absence of personality filled the room. Sailcloth curtains skirted the sides of sash windows whose lower halves provided a shuttered privacy from the street. The plaster half-breasts of six uplighters receded into the white walls, illuminating each corner in a soft overhead glow. Floor to ceiling shelves flanked a lustreless marble fireplace with a display of professional books. Alphabetically ordered, regularly dusted. The more startling titles were kept in his first-floor study: *Sexual Orientation in Self-Mutilating Adolescents*; *Choice Behaviour in Rhesus Monkeys: Cocaine Versus Food*; *Hungry for Love: Mothers Who Starve Their Children*.

Jay had considered the appeal of a blank interior, for art would always be a gamble, but he eventually decided on three pictures. On the wall by the door and in the peripheral vision of seated clients hung a generic Picasso print – a disembodied fish head with its triangular suggestion of female. Above the couch was an unsigned water-coloured horizon he'd bought in Santa Monica from a dark-haired salesgirl who stifled a yawn while murmuring tourists shuffled their summer feet across the gallery floor. The third picture, suspended directly over the mantelpiece, was a muted print of the Natural History Museum – Jay's favourite London façade – a delicate blend of sandstone and blue that had inspired Cora's only question during her first session.

'Do you like stuffed animals?' she'd said, staring up at the frame.

'Why do you ask?'

'All those animals in the museum gathering dust.'

'Is that how you see yourself?'

'It's just the picture,' she murmured and Jay opened her casebook and wrote:

Taxidermy.

It was rare for his clients to comment on the artwork, in fact most of them seemed oblivious to the detail of their surroundings, an observation that was supported by a recent study in *The Journal of Psychoanalytic Practice*, which revealed that eighteen out of twenty clients who had attended the same analyst for more than fifteen months failed to notice when a coffee table was removed from the room. But the Picasso had fulfilled its purpose within the first year. Jay had been just seven months into his Kensington practice and already aware of a shift in his accent, a slight flattening of the vowels, when a trust fund academic with a contemptuous quiff arrived ten minutes late for his first session and lounged restlessly on the couch before announcing that he was in the early stages of recovery from a deep depression. Turning his head towards the door, he scowled at the Picasso and mumbled, 'So utterly predictable.' He slipped a furtive hand into his pocket and, with sly pleasure, began unwrapping a Tesco's bag. A light spray of sweat crept across his brow as he tilted the peeping glint of a blade.

'They use this for disembowelling. Fish or something,' he said, lips curled in awed disgust.

'Perhaps you feel the need to demonstrate that you can defend yourself against me?' said Jay.

'Aren't you afraid that I'll go mad and start slashing you?' said the quiff with a desperate giggle.

'Do you want to hurt me or hurt yourself?' said Jay, looking away in a calculated gesture of unambiguous boredom, so that the quiff sprang out of the couch, holding the knife in an awkward grasp in front of his stomach. 'Are you going to just sit there?' he screamed, but Jay didn't reply, did not even move until the quiff lunged and Jay leapt to his feet, disarming his client with a hand chop.

'Why'd he do it?' asked the arresting officer after he escorted the sobbing client outside to the waiting vehicle.

'All anger is ultimately self-directed.'

'I never knew therapy could be a dangerous line of work,' joked the constable.

'Keeping the peace, just like you.'

Jay reached down for the casebook that lay on the floor by his feet: tan softback, American quarto, only available from a legal supplier on Chancery Lane. At fifty-one, he understood how easily whimsical preference could blossom into a rigid eccentricity, but he had never acclimatised to the metric dimensions of A4, the oversized rectangle always seemed to exaggerate the blank slate of a beginning. He turned the cover to the first page where his client's name was inscribed in large and hopeful letters.

Cora Miller

Jay shook his head, sighed. It was infuriating to have made such a poor selection, particularly when she'd been hand-picked from the long list of potential candidates that clogged his ansaphone with tentative introductions from doctors who knew the demands on his time and reputation. The luxury of choice was one he exercised to the full, for when he'd started out in San Francisco back in the 1970s, he had to take what he could get, had to scrabble for referrals, all those hours wandering down the blind alleys of other people's lives, all those tears, rages, confessions, threats, promises; clients using him as a medium to communicate with the living and the dead, mothers and fathers and siblings and lovers and bosses and children and neighbours and friends. But the phenomenal success of his first book had changed everything. *Psychoanalysis: Science or Art?*, first published in 1978 (now into its seventh printing) and still a core text on the syllabus of most teaching colleges, was described by an eminent Maudsley psychiatrist as 'an engaging, fascinating and witty account of the tensions between psychoanalysis and medicine'. The book had strategically positioned Jay in neutral territory, that no-man's-land between psychiatry and psychotherapy and was surprisingly well-received in the UK. It was this unexpected response, followed by an invigorating lecture tour, that had first prompted Jay to consider emigration.

The fact was, by 1981 he'd had it with barking seals and cable cars and was ready to close the door on his West Coast chapter and the first thirty-three years of his life, so he packed up and took a plane to London where the flatness and rigorous respect for personal space had a definite appeal. His timing could not have been better. In those days it was virgin territory, professionally speaking, just before the British public discovered their urgent need for therapeutic life-support. All through the late seventies, a torturous battle had raged between competing fiefdoms of therapists and medics. The British Psychoanalytic Society lobbied for the regulation of the disordered tribes of psychotherapists who, when they weren't squabbling with each other over tiresome theoretical differences, were fending off the psychiatrists who trumpeted the results of their definitive studies on the effects of medication. These turf wars and shrill dissent meant that the Secretary of State for Health could comfortably ignore the lot of them and refuse to allow the issue of regulation to be brought before parliament. Despite his book, Jay remained consistently apolitical on its core issue, a position that endeared him to the psychiatrists but antagonised some analysts, who accused him of breaking ranks like some unruly cleric. Privately he believed that the argument about art versus science was a red herring, a legacy of Freud's obsession with proving the scientific status of psychoanalysis, which Jay believed to be far more revealing about the great man's insecurities than anything else.

Two decades on, the mutual antipathy still festered in the great Drugs versus Therapy debate. Last year at a launch party he attended for the publication of an anthology of contemporary psychoanalytic essays, a psychiatrist with a bearded sneer raised his glass to the table and bellowed: 'Where does the therapist go to unwind after a hard day's work? Why, to another therapist of course.'

As a rule, Jay preferred to maintain a polite distance from his peers. His first few months in London – his silent tussle with the clinging tentacles of the BPS whose members were distrustful of his growing celebrity, his youthful American otherness – persuaded him to avoid the psychoghetto of Hampstead where analysts jostled for space with writers. Expanding his search southwards he found himself standing one morning in front of the black railings that marked the perimeter of the communal gardens on Edwardes Square while the estate agent struggled with the front door of number 19, chattering through the property's advantages that Jay had already identified: 1389 square feet of Kensington backwater evenly distributed over three levels and a first- and second-floor view of the gardens. The house was on the southern side of the square, a narrow street flanked at either end by pre-war mansion blocks. A flat-fronted late Victorian in a terraced row of six, it was squashed between a whitewashed mews and a small converted warehouse where the corners of large canvases were visible though high crescent windows. The French windows on the first floor were framed by decorative wooden shutters that seemed superfluous, but Jay took the architect's advice and left them intact. He supervised a meticulous transformation that removed all traces of the previous owner, a cardiganed widow whose right hand convulsed in a constant twitch. Six months later, on 22 June 1982, he sat on a packing crate in the hallway inhaling the scent of fresh paint, the smell of optimism and new beginnings, and it seemed to Jay as if this renovation might erase the memory of all the other places that had cluttered up his life.

It was nearly twenty years now since he had stood on the threshold of his safe space trying to view the arrangements through the eyes of his first English patient. He wondered if he would discover some sort of cultural variance, but it turned out that his clients would always be the same, all looking to make sense out of chaos, none of them seeing that meaninglessness is liberation. They seemed, however, to take comfort in Jay's foreignness, as if his alien status was in keeping with the exoticism of a therapeutic relationship. For some, like Cora, it had a particular resonance. In the closing minutes of her second session she told him that her husband was American. '*East* Coast though,' she added with emphasis. In the old days Jay would have made a client explore this type of remark, dwell on *what it meant*, encouraged her to see that there are no innocent conversational gambits, but he'd long since abandoned the rigour of his formal training in favour of a more individual approach. In a sense, as a client once peevishly complained, Jay wasn't really an analyst at all.

'Larry's a banker,' Cora explained. 'He's back working in New York at the moment. Comes home at weekends.' And for a moment Jay had a vision of Larry backlit on a Hampton shoreline, white surf licking the curve of his blanched toes. He picked up his pen and wrote:

Therapy as adultery

Cora's simultaneous confirmation and denial of his connection with her husband was, Jay believed, an expression of her discomfort at being on the brink of a secret intimacy, but he left this obvious intervention unsaid. 'Yes, I am from the West Coast,' he nodded and as he uttered the words, he was reminded how surprising it was that even after so many years in London, there were still mundane sensual pleasures he missed: the dry crumble of Hershey's chocolate, the warm feel of a dime, the mournful bellow of a fog horn over the mist-thick Bay, the clinking lap of water underneath the weathered pier boards. Most of all, he missed the sea, a whole geography of sea. For Jay had discovered years ago that London had the landlocked quality of Moscow when his first southbound crawl through the shocking ugliness of the city's boundaries led him to England's dismal coastline, where the old flee to count out their days in the bleak seaside towns of Eastbourne, Littlehampton, Worthing, Bexhill-on-Sea – names with the ring of finality about them, all those clipped vowels that the English stifle, as if an open mouth could unleash some monstrous slack-jawed passion. He drove slowly along the coast, through towns connected by a continuous loop of bungalows whose dormer eyes reflected the invisible view to France. Couples picnicked in the safety of their cars, staring in wordless communion through the windscreen at the watery

Mediterranean parody; men sat on park benches, their pink skulls shiny in the cold spring sun as they gazed out on a bifocalled view of the rolling swell while, behind them, vacant B&B signs creaked in the incessant wind and trains spilled hopeful weekenders into a terminus of pedestrianised streets where Poundstretchers offered a refuge from the rain until evening fell and frightened visitors high-tailed it back to the city's comforting embrace, away from the horrors of the senior citizen future that awaited them. Throughout the eighties there had been a steady stream of women who were determined to prove the beauty of the English countryside and dragged Jay on misguided day trips that ended in a red sweep of taillights stretching out through the motorway darkness that enveloped them.

He was fascinated by the charmless reality of England, its embarrassing lack of majesty.

A streetlamp sputtered into fragile life outside the window. It seemed the rain had ceased; Jay could hear a surge of water gurgle in the drain and the cleaners brushing a slow receding sweep along the footpath. Turning to the next blank page in the case book he wrote:

9th session
Flight

Cora was not the first client to have fled from an unpalatable truth. There were always trauma risks involved in the premature unveiling of the unconscious and, in other circumstances, Jay might have held out for longer. Today, however, frustrated by lack of progress, he had felt that it might be a gamble worth taking, but now his client had gone, leaving him with an empty stage. He looked over at the Picasso and a certain symmetry between the mutilated female body and Cora's panicked departure. Seventy minutes of unscheduled afternoon stretched out before him, plenty of time to trawl her case notes for inspiration, but there was the intrusion of this evening's appointment whose imminent approach resonated through his day with the persistent hum of a tuning fork.

Turning his head to the mantelpiece, he considered the source of his unease. Dana Flynn's letter had lost its crisp surprise, the paper was soft and malleable from overuse, for he had been shuttling it back and forth between his study and the safe space like a dog unable to find a suitable spot to bury his bone. Since its arrival three weeks ago, Jay had found himself continually ambushed by reminiscence which presented as a sort of arrhythmia that disrupted the familiar beat of his days. Only this morning he'd caught himself holding his breath on awakening and lay suffocating between the sheets, wondering if his autonomic responses had failed for his chest was bursting with noxious gas and he had to force himself to exhale.

'In the course of my research into a group of European scientists and philosophers who settled in the United States during World War Two,' wrote Dana Flynn, 'I came across some correspondence with your brother Robert, during the period when he was a student of the famous logician Alfred Tarski at Berkeley.'

Standing in the hallway, the envelope crushed in his palm, Jay was overwhelmed by a startling rush of recall, like a sudden and exhilarating change in temperature. It was May 1970 and he'd slipped into the back of a lecture theatre where Robert Hamilton, Professor of Philosophy at the University of California at Los Angeles and Jay's dead brother, stood in the centre of the sunken podium. The blackboard behind him was a jungle of calculus.

'Einstein,' he declared, 'was one of the two great frauds of the twentieth century.'

The transcribing students raised their heads. Robert grinned, ran a hand through his thinning hair, his unbuttoned collar revealing an unshaven neck and a new flabbiness about the chin. A girl sitting in the front row raised her hand.

'Professor Hamilton, who was the other one?'

'Now that would be Freud,' said Robert, rubbing his chalk-smeared hands, 'but my younger brother up there in the back row might disagree.'

The audience looked round but Jay had already turned away, left the double doors swinging in an air rush behind him and strode out into the campus heat. He sat down in the speckled shade of a massive oak whose grey trunk was scarred with leprous scabs and watched a gaggle of students trail behind a lone protest banner, heading across the lawns towards Dickson Plaza. It was the beginning of the end, America's ignominious retreat from Vietnam.

'Hey,' said Robert, tapping him on the shoulder, 'don't take it all so seriously.'

Jay rose and followed him along the path, past a grove of myrtle trees that peeped out from the side of Dodd Hall like a troupe of ballerinas, their slender torsos stretched uniformly upwards. He reached out to stroke a scarlet blossom, its soft bottlebrush spikes coating his palm with a sticky citrus scent.

'But you know what?' said Robert, stopping to polish his glasses on a shirttail. 'I'm still waiting for you to give up that psychobabble and get into real science.'

Jay thrust a gummy fist deep into his pocket. The eighteen-year age gap between the brothers had created a lingering relationship ambiguity which he had long since understood to be rooted in the absence of a paternal experience and his own childish attempts to endow Robert with the crown of a father who had been somehow lost when Jay was about two years old, in circumstances which were never satisfactorily explained by their mother.

'That's life,' she said, as if this could cover it, as if hoards of fathers were abandoning their families every day.

As a young child Jay had studied the wedding photo that he found hidden face-down in her bedside drawer, a sepia representation mounted in flimsy brown card where the bride appeared like a silhouette in an ankle-skimming skirt, her face obscured by a cloche hat, a fringed shawl draped over her shoulders. It seemed as if, already on his wedding day, the groom had realised his mistake, for Frederic Hamilton stood beside her, his moustache drooping above a wild grin that smacked of panic, even to the six-year-old observer. A chain sneaked out from the pocket of an oversized waistcoat and disappeared underneath his jacket. 'That watch was loaned,' his mother sniffed. 'Everything was borrowed just for the day.'

Although he could not truthfully claim any personal recollections of his father, Jay sometimes noticed that the smell of stale tobacco jarred inexplicably. He had a memory of a shadowy presence by the screen door on 1152 Woodward Street and a rough-palmed grip that was looser than a two-year-old was accustomed to. There was a fingerprint in the fine film of dust gathered on the shoulders of a black suit jacket that hung from a peg at the back of his mother's wardrobe, brown strands of fossilised tobacco sweetening the pocketed air. But Jay could not be sure if these were memories at all, or if it was just the absence of presence that he remembered, all the things that didn't happen, walking scrub-kneed to church on Sundays alongside the click of his mother's unaccompanied heels, past other families who made a perfect set, when the Hamiltons had a missing piece, a father who wasn't dead, only unaccountably absent. A deserter.

He understood early on that there was some sort of hard-coded weakness in his father's genetic script. No backbone, no staying power. Frederic Hamilton just wasn't up to it: the wife, the family, the neighbourhood, the business of carving out a hard little life and eventually the yoke of responsibility slipped off like eager tumbleweed and he drifted along a path of increasingly casual labour that snaked across the state line and ever eastwards, wiring money back home to stave off his discomfort and hold open the possibility of return. This was, as far as Jay knew, the pattern that had been established in the earliest days of his parents' marriage and one to which his mother quickly became accustomed. In fact, it was doubtful if Frederic's absence even bothered her at all, for there were compensations. There was Robert to look after, an ever-present husband would have used up the energy that she preferred to lavish on a more rewarding emotional investment. Over the years Frederic's homecomings became more infrequent, although they could not always have been unwelcome, for Jay was, of course, conceived during one of these visits – a fact of which Frederic Hamilton remained apparently unaware until sometime in 1950, when he showed up unannounced at Woodward Street and found a new son in diapers on the front porch. Robert came high-tailing back from Berkeley as soon as he heard and their father turned obligingly on his heel, the door slammed in his face by his own son and his own shortcomings. But it worked, scared him enough to stay away for good, save for the odd card from nowhere in particular, with nothing memorable to say. Jay remembered a black-and-white photo of a bridge and a postmark from Boston. 'Lot of big bridges out East', his father had written in careful capitals and his mother read it aloud over and over again, laughing until she cried, while Jay traced his finger over the meticulous pencil.

Even as a thin-legged youngster Jay had sensed how paternal abandonment could deal a crippling blow to a child's self-esteem, how the mere suspicion of rejection might throw a life off its natural trajectory and trigger a slow slide into a quagmire of self-loathing and delinquency. So he devised his own survival strategy, became a fearless climber, the fastest runner on the block. At six years old, he began to explore the inland waterways of Northern California, the eighty-mile suck from Stockton to the ocean, wondering if his father had one day started following the delta's homeward flow and just kept on walking. Which turned out, in fact, not to be the case, he would later discover, because Frederic Hamilton had surfaced briefly in 1956, in Green River, Utah, one thousand miles in the opposite direction, like a gasping seal coming up for air. This time his departure was final, the silence punctuated only by the occasional card, until his premature demise in December 1969, (a heart attack in a hostel in Minneapolis) and the abandoned family found an opportunity for closure in the curious satisfaction of death.

Looking back, Jay congratulated the Hamiltons on handling it all so well. His mother had been remarkably sanguine under the shade of a cedar in Oakwood Memorial Park. 'I guess he didn't have a clear picture of where he wanted to be,' she murmured, scooping up a handful of earth and drizzling it over the open grave. 'Let's go,' said Robert, scraping a heel on the grass. None of them guessing that in fifteen months time Jay and his mother would be standing there throwing clay on Robert's grave; or that nine months after that, she would succumb to the cancer that suddenly emerged to gorge itself on her breast, her stooped body dragging itself between the chair and the bed, fiercely resistant to Jay's suggestions that she should move up to San Francisco so that he could look after her more in the hours between his practice. But she stonewalled as he knew she would and so he drove the 800-mile round trip to her Van Nuys duplex every weekend, fed her chicken soup, coaxed her to walk, sat in a hospital armchair and watched her slip through his hands and fade away.

In December 1971, at the age of twenty-three, Jay found he'd buried his entire family in the space of two years.

• THREE •

Jay placed Dana Flynn's letter on the mantelpiece and sat down, only to immediately stand up again and wedge it in between two journals on the top shelf of his bookcase. Such fretting was out of character, these days subverted by the relentless assault of memory, but a biographer would be looking for colour, something that might give flesh to the subject and it was undoubtedly this reflexive scanning that has unsettled him, triggered a reluctant hunt through buried landscapes and unleashed a flock of hidden remembrance, like a wetlands beater raising startled fowl for the waiting guns.

He had immediately recognised Dana Flynn as the author of an acclaimed biography of Alan Turing. 'Still in the top ten,' said the assistant at Waterstone's on Kensington High Street, pointing to the central display table where copies of *The Enigma* were piled high in anticipation of Christmas interest, its consistent sales reflecting an insatiable appetite for sexual intrigue and conspiracy theories. She had captured the public imagination with an accessible treatment of the young British mathematician who had predicted that the computer would one day rival the brain, the man who had invented a machine to decode German intelligence during the second World War, only to be abandoned as a security risk by MI6 upon discovery of his homosexuality, and who wound up dead at the age of forty-two, with a cyanide-laced apple on his bedside table. Although Dana Flynn wasn't by any means the first to throw suspicion on the suicide verdict, her – in Jay's opinion – rather dubiously presented closing chapter had triggered a frenzied newspaper debate which he had followed with some interest.

The Enigma's dust jacket was frustratingly light on biographical detail but he concluded that the author was in her early thirties, born in Massachusetts, with a PhD in History (Penn State). There was no mention of family. She had lectured in various undistinguished universities in the US and won a couple of research fellowships to second-tier institutions. Turing was her first book. Turning the opening pages, Jay was irritated to find the inscription: 'To M.E.' for he disapproved of dedications, all these books hijacked by cryptic messages, secret declarations of love that can only destabilise the intimacy between author and reader, as if the entire work was written for an unidentified audience of one.

But despite his reservations about Dana Flynn's credentials, he believed it fitting that his brother was finally receiving some attention. The lack of public tributes after Robert's death had been extraordinarily disappointing for Jay had expected a flood of posthumous testimonials acknowledging the pioneering nature of his brother's research in logic. After all, Robert had been on the verge of revolutionising semantics by providing a scientific account of linguistic meaning, applying mathematical techniques to natural language and thus explaining what philosophers had grappled with for centuries. The sceptics crouched, sniping from the sideline, but, even now, thirty years after his landmark publication, Robert's theoretical framework remained the classical paradigm in the study of formal semantics.

Dana Flynn had not been at all forthcoming about the specific nature of her interest and her response to Jay's email had been frustratingly evasive. If Alfred Tarski – Robert's teacher in the Philosophy Department at Berkeley in the early

1950s – was the primary focus of her attention, surely one of his many pupils would scarcely warrant more than a footnote in a biography. But a nagging curiosity prompted Jay to agree to a meeting during her visit to London. Since Robert's death in 1971, he had been contacted by two other researchers, which he presumed was due to the fact that all of his brother's papers had been bequeathed to the Special Collections library at UCLA. The first enquiry was a phone call from a mathematician at the Massachusetts Institute of Technology looking for any unpublished material that might have escaped the archives. The other was from an Oxford professor working on a biography of some minor British mathematician who was an occasional house guest of Robert's in Los Angeles in the early sixties, but the scrawled request was so gracelessly composed that Jay didn't respond, although he vividly recalled an evening in the summer of 1964, when the mathematician in question had argued with Robert about his theoretical claims.

It had been Jay's first visit to the city and he was sixteen years old when he boarded the rumbling Greyhound at Stockton in a dry and dusty dawn. Rolling southbound along the I-5, through the flatlands of central California, endless miles of irrigated pastureland, his chin lolled on his chest and he drifted into sleep, waking with a start as the interstate rose out of grey scrubland into the first promise of beauty. Afternoon shadows slid over the crinkled ridges of the San Emigdio Mountains, thumbprints of vegetation clung to the rocks as they circled upwards towards a view of some sort of Steinbeckian utopia and, in the distance, Los Angeles erupted out of the cracked skin of the desert as the terminus of dream.

Jay's first glimpse of 3840 North Beverly Drive was from the window of his brother's Mustang after they took a slow northeast route from the campus, stalling somewhere on Sunset, Robert squinting over the arc of his big white wheel, oblivious to the tooting cars as they cruised through the manicured opulence of Beverly Hills. They sailed along the boulevards of palm and jacaranda and big leaf maple where stuccoed mansions hid behind the huge wrought-iron gates that advertised their exclusivity, where the distant splash of concealed pools was screened by impenetrable hedges and dogs and guards patrolled the neuroses and torments of the stars. The creeping spread of celebrity was already like a choking vine. Up, up they climbed into the lush seclusion of the foothills and it felt to Jay like falling into a dream, Robert's enthusiastic monologue spilling out of the open windows into Coldwater Canyon where the houses were carved into mesas and orange-tipped poppies bobbed in rocky ledges. The buildings petered out long before the intersection with Mulholland and they slowed down, turned a sharp right into a little drive bordered on both sides by jagged walls of greyish stone. A steep slope led up to a small brown two-storey with a low-slung pitched roof and a white door bearing the number 3840.

'This is home,' said Robert, opening the car door and Jay marvelled at the choice of location. Robert shrugged with that older brother smile of his, possessing not just great intellect but now also apparently great wealth, which was how it seemed to Jay. He stood for a while on the drive underneath the alders in this little oasis tucked high above the city, never dreaming that he would find himself standing in that very spot seven years later, wedged in by the police cars that blocked the mouth of the drive.

Later that night a handful of Robert's colleagues from the Philosophy Department sat in the backyard and sucked on warming beer while Jay lurked in the shadows, bemused, confused and very drunk, struggling to disguise his youthfulness from the jaded eyes of his brother's friends. A man appeared in front of him wagging a finger, 'You look soooo like him, you know, so like,' he mumbled and lurched away.

'What I mean is this,' Robert said to a slender figure in a brown shirt who leant unsteadily against the wall of the house. 'Any four-year-old child is already a linguistic genius, OK? So let's not worry about how or why this happens, let's leave that to the others for the moment. The question I'm asking is: how do you *describe* that competence?' His voice had reached a hectoring pitch that brought a lull to the small group. 'What is our theory of language?' he continued. 'Build me a model that shows how it works. Explain what's going on.'

'I beg your pardon, but isn't that exactly what Noam Chomsky has done up at MIT?' said the brown shirt in a clipped English accent. The group tittered.

'No,' barked Robert. 'He has done nothing of the sort. Everyone's saying that he's brought science and method to the study of language, but his only interest is in syntax. This so-called Chomskyan revolution has no rigour, no adequacy, and it is unforgivably inelegant.'

'Yeah right,' quipped a voice from the deck.

'Chomsky leads nowhere,' Robert continued impatiently. 'He thinks semantics is a branch of psychology! But linguists are not capable of answering the really important questions. The analysis of language properly belongs to mathematics and *that* is what I intend to do: solve the mystery of meaning.'

'An explanation of humanity,' sneered the brown shirt, wiggling a beer can in front of his face.

'Why not?' said Robert, throwing his gleeful arms skywards. 'Perhaps there is no theoretical difference between natural and artificial language.'

The Englishman laughed, swayed briefly in the centre of the yard and folded into a corner. Jay lunged down the steps to throw up in the midnight foliage and collapsed into an aching sleep, only to be woken hours later by a hot plunge of anonymous wetness in his ear and Robert's high-pitched giggle cutting through the post-party silence. 'For Chrissake leave him alone, it's my kid brother,' and they rustled away sniggering in the dark leaves.

Jay stood up abruptly and the casebook slipped from his lap onto the floor. This exhumation was surely the source of his difficulties. It was as if a lid was creaking open on his vaporous past and old unwelcome phantoms were slipping out to invade the present. His resuscitated brother was gliding towards him, gathering up the years. Every time he sat down in his study to write, Jay experienced a peculiar breathlessness as if he had run some great distance. In his armchair attending to a client, he noticed an uncharacteristic restlessness that he associated with vigilance, like the twitching ears of a dog who senses some far-off storm.

He picked up Cora's case book, tucked it under his elbow and stepped into the hall. Perhaps, he thought, a certain order and focus would be restored after tonight's meeting. He would find out what Dana Flynn wanted and then, when his duty was expedited, he would be able to resume his work.

He turned his key in the lock and placed it on the top of the narrow ledge of the doorframe, for the room was strictly off-limits to anyone other than clients, there was a risk of contamination, of the professional spilling into the personal. Years before, Jay had discovered the pitfalls of inadequate delineation when a woman he took home, emboldened by a night's champagne, had thrown herself on the couch and swept a wrist across her brow in mock anguish, as if what unfolded in this place was some sort of charade, while Jay stood with a clenched jaw, unable to move lest he grab her flimsy shoulders and hurl her out onto the street.

• FOUR •

Jay's study was a small but perfect square, expertly carved out of the drawing room that spanned the entire first floor of the house. The herringbone parquet had been restored to a high gloss varnish and an original fireplace removed to accommodate the wall of customised cupboarding that housed his casebooks behind lockable sliding doors. French windows to the front overlooked Edwardes Square gardens that lay now submerged in the darkness of late afternoon.

Jay sat down in a high-backed leather chair and rolled into position at his desk. The printed manuscript sat squat and expectant under a halo of lamplight.

TALES FROM THE SAFE SPACE
by
J. Merritt

He slid a hand over its pristine body, considering its spareness and then placed Cora Miller's casebook beside it so that their edges were abutting, as if she might be encouraged by this abundance, find the plot that awaited her and burst into life. Cora was, of course, unaware that she had been chosen as model and muse for the centrepiece story in the collection that would follow the two highly acclaimed novels by J. Merritt: Jay's literary alter ego and one of the best-kept identity secrets in the London publishing world. His agent and publisher had expressed some reservations about this change in tack, citing the English public's lack of enthusiasm for short stories, but they were prepared to indulge as long as J. Merritt's second novel, *White Space*, was firmly entrenched in the bestseller lists.

As a nineteen-year-old psychology major at Berkeley in the late sixties, Jay had figured out what Freud might perhaps have thought but never actually said, that the clinical practice of psychoanalysis generates ideal material for the creative writer. It was art, Jay believed, to which Freud had truly aspired, his lifelong passion for literature fused so exactly with his scientific ambition and a wistful longing to unite the two in a feverish embrace. Although his essay on creative writers and day-dreaming was a personal favourite, Jay had long ago concluded that Freud was, in the end, both failed writer and analyst, torn between the conflicting strictures of two camps. The reluctant doctor spent his entire life stubbornly insisting on the scientific basis of psychoanalysis, so blinkered was he after fifteen years studying the central nervous system of fish. And so, while Jay could successfully treat his clients in a therapeutic environ-ment, he felt that by incorporating them into his fiction, he could reach a far wider audience and might even succeed where Freud had failed in the integration of science and art.

J. Merritt's first two books had been expansive, rich and luxuriant. But lately he had come to find the sprawl of the novel unseemly, endless pages of dissection and narrative, flesh picked over and laid bare. Now, mindful of the dangers of increasing age and having too much to say and convinced, as he was, that most books, films, conversations and, without question, *all* therapeutic alliances were far too long, Jay planned to raise the tension with eleven short stories based upon selected case histories. Rigour and discipline, he had decided, with plenty of silent space for the readers to do some work. He sought brevity and restraint, stories so aggressively minimalist that the reader must strain to fill in the gaps and so *live* the

story, shape the life. *Tales from the Safe Space* would have none of
the pomposity of a novel, it would be a series of tight vignettes,
loosely connected by the theme of maternal neglect, which he
hoped would provoke some controversy in the literary pages.

Like bloated bodies rising to the surface, Jay's clients
emerged from the pages of his casebooks and stumbled onto
centre stage in his collection of stories. There was Lola, for
example, a client from way back in San Francisco whose chronic
addiction to douche bags had so disrupted the bacterial culture
of her vagina that she developed severe recurrent thrush and,
eventually, amenorrhea. On page 67 of *Tales* she appeared re-
incarnated as Ruth, whose hygiene obsession was part of a
regime of self-harm designed to blot out the emotional bruising
left by an abusive mother.

Sometimes Jay would find himself confronted by a character
who had featured in his clients' dramas, a mother or father or
husband who might have strictly a walk-on role, a soundbite of
colour, the silver flash of the underside of a fish. Like Cora's
husband, for example. Larry had been carefully excised from
her life and repositioned on page 117, at the moment before he
met her. It was the image of a pair of salt-stained Docksides on
the Hamptons shoreline and the screech of wheeling gulls that
made Jay see Larry as he believed Hopper would have presented
him – half-formed, waxen, emblematic – to an audience
scouring their backyards for a sign of pathos.

In the mid-nineties, just before the publication of J. Merritt's
second novel, Jay had toyed with the idea of creating what
might amount to a new literary genre, the invention of a
psychoanalyst to rival the crime sleuths, those amateur
detectives who satisfy the populist desire for explicable motive.
For months he had laboured with a mulish energy but the voice

of an impostor mocked him from the page and he was forced to admit defeat when he found himself mired in the kind of narrator dilemma that he associated with creative writing classes, where sensitive undergrads groom the shabby disguise of their autobiographical disasters like primates checking each other for lice. But he did discover an extraordinary talent for reproducing the client. It seemed that he could effortlessly tune into the frequencies of the distressed, sounds inaudible to another ear and it was this quality that quickly built J. Merritt's reputation. Jay had therefore kept his writing safely client-centred until fifteen months ago when he opened his laptop one evening and the voice that had eluded him years before strutted across the screen: *Tales from the Safe Space* had arrived from nowhere. For a year, Jay worked on his anonymous analyst, flexing the writing muscle just as he might fine-tune another part of his body, it was like twisting a long-wave radio dial, minute precision movements until he finally hit perfect pitch. He took out his casebooks and set himself the exhila-rating challenge of nailing each life in 1,500 words. It was a warming-up exercise for his collection, he never wrote the full story until he was ready and then did so in one final burst of as many hours as it took.

Jay turned to page 39 of the manuscript and smiled down at 'Homo Erectus', the story of Brian, who nursed a desperate nostalgia for all that had been lost the very first time a hominid climbed down from a tree, stretched out a prehensile limb and, finding the sensation so pleasing, forgot he was a quadroped and stayed erect forever. For weeks, Brian sat hunched in the Corbusier, although Jay suspected that he was sneaking around on all fours at home, terrified of the fearfulness that had never left him since the day his mother had stood up after Christmas dinner with the tearful promise, 'I won't be back.' She had been as good as her word for twenty years. In a later session, Brian suggested coyly that he might be more comfortable on the floor, but Jay refused to entertain this idea and watched him lope off northwards through Edwardes Square with the long-armed looseness of his ancestors. The transference was working, accelerating even, and within weeks, Brian had locked onto Jay as the mother object, the focal point of his affection. He was inching closer, looking hungrily at Jay's lap and eventually confessed to a dream of sitting right there in his maternal embrace, being lovingly caressed and de-loused. But Jay knew that Brian's rage would soon be unleashed with all the vengeance of the spurned child, that he would need to crush his mother's windpipe until she became silent and submissive in death and could never, ever, abandon him again. So Jay referred. Brian was put on anti-psychotics and, in the process, he found another therapist willing to hold his paw and start the tape all over again, so that he could stall any forward momentum and stay cocooned in his nursery pain.

The neon eye of his sleeping laptop pulsed in the shadowy outreaches of the desk. Jay opened Cora's casebook. During his psychoanalytic training, Metzling had encouraged the class to make detailed notes straight after each session, like how a suicide fantasist sat in a chair, or how a depressive avoided eye contact. Jay used to fill pages with his clients' free associations, tracing the footprints of their childhoods, the forgotten tastes and sensations that lingered between the shadowlands of memory and imagination, until he realised the futility of it all, the stunning irrelevance of truth. After all, even Freud had admitted that it was the imagined past he was seeking, that biographical truth could be left to the historians. These days Jay's notes were outline sketches, a series of fragments, sometimes just single words that blossomed into the stories they might later become. An impressionistic starting point was all he needed to begin. The light sharpened, a plot slowly emerged and then he could stop listening to the client and simply select what suited. Occasionally, he might intervene and lead the story where he wanted. If historical truth was already an impossible concept, who could be a reliable witness to their own life? So when the patient started to deviate from the plot, Jay steered them back with the suggestion of unexplored feelings, repressions they never knew existed. It only took a little prompting to unleash a fury over the dim past – an explosion of retrospective anger is a wonderful sight, the northern lights of a therapy session.

He recalled how Metzling would sit stroking his squirrel-red beard while he scanned the windowless room, inviting his fledgling analysts to consider the dramas that would unfold when they became the witnesses and collaborants, the architects of other peoples' futures. It was an elaborate game play, this business of containing one another's pain when they congregated for afternoon group sessions, seven plastic chairs arranged in a little circle of hell. Jay was astounded at the depth of his classmates' engagement, it was a compulsion to seek out and endure the pain that had so nearly crushed them, like enthusiastic terriers with their noses stuck in a rabbit hole. He used to wonder if their stock of empathy would ever run out, or was it like myosis, could they simply grow new cells? Month after month they rummaged about in the past, looking for something that might assuage their boundless appetite for distress. 'Physician heal thyself,' he whispered at the end of his first year and that is what Jay would always see in every analyst he met. Years of practice had convinced him that the mining of the past was generally useless in the business of learning to be happy and he didn't believe it was empathy or containment that patients needed, or even very much attentive listening, it was solutions and practical advice. But no one at the SFSP was interested in talking about coping strategies or the possible value of defence systems, they were all hooked on repression, believing that everything must be forced into the open and that all paths lead back to the infant at the breast.

In his own analysis, which was mandatory as part of his training, Jay learned to manage the transference and the counter-transference. It seemed there was little to stir up and what *was* there, he could control in a carefully calibrated editing process, although Metzling got close once and looked him in the eye. 'You make me uneasy in a way I can't quite explain,' he said. Jay could have told him it was like shouting in a soundproofed room where all the noise is absorbed by the containing walls.

He reached for *Tales* and flicked a thumbnail backwards and upwards through the crisp manuscript. A searing white abyss glared back at him from the blank pages where Cora's story should be and as the paper gunned past, he felt a dizzying sense of motion, a slight lurch, like a corner taken too fast and he thought he heard a moan outside. He pushed back from the desk and stood up, stepped over to the French windows where the pavement below him glistened under the street lights. Headlights flared around the northern corner of the gardens, it was a procession of nocturnal parkers fleeing the sea of stalled traffic on the High Street, barging their way into the square like wild boar thrashing about for truffles. The convoy was already eight cars deep at six o'clock. All week the square had been packed – it was the countdown to Christmas and Kensington had been transformed into a retail paradise where spotlit consumables twinkled in the windows and gridlocked nightshoppers swarmed the wide pavements. It was the tranquil affluence of Edwardes Square that had attracted him twenty years ago, its polite absence of neighbourliness, the illusion of community. The genteel residents preferred their private business to be discreet – 'For Sale' boards were frowned upon by the Committee, as was the practice of opening up the gardens to an annual public viewing. But a tide of investment bankers had kick-started its eighties renaissance almost immediately after Jay moved in. He witnessed the slow exodus of the natives as old English money surrendered to the lure of the new and the eastern and western flanks were prised from the reluctant clutches of owners who could no longer argue against the preposterous logic of profit. They finally buckled at the shrill insistence of City boys who roared into the square in their sports cars for dashabout viewings at inconvenient times, bounding up the stairs and dispensing with any attention to detail. Jay watched it all from his French windows, imagining the straight-backed lady owners fiddling with flower arrangements on their dining-room tables while the scrubbed young men strode out through the front doors to collar estate agents on the pavement with their outrageous bids. The ladies fingered their brooches, eavesdropping through the letterboxes that shielded them from the thrilling vulgarity of price and the young men rolled up their shirt sleeves and sped off eastwards to scream down the phones at other young men in New York and Tokyo, leaving the ladies to linger in the dark hallways long after they were gone, running their hands over the chipped dado rail, the scuffed gloss of a skirting board, the worn carpet that led along the hallway through the three-hundred-year bowels of the house and out into a world that was being completely re-evaluated. No one knew what anything was worth anymore and it was all very unnerving, these deep currents in the smug waters of wealth.

All through the eighties Jay watched builders' vans clog the narrow one-way system in the early morning, as a procession of skips carted away the entrails of the past to make room for a more robust future. Nannies lolled on tartan picnic rugs while their charges explored the gated lawns. Fleets of SUVs revved their impatient engines on Friday afternoons, like a herd of stampeding buffalo departing for weekend homes in the West Country. In springtime the houses were swathed in wisteria, front gardens bloomed with magnolia and cherry blossom whose white petals showered the uneven flagstones. Jay came to savour the August solitude when the square shimmered empty and abandoned in the heat, while the absent residents lay gasping at their rental view of the Tuscan hills, or nibbled lobster in Nantucket, or hurled a cabriolet along the cliff road to St Tropez and the gardens sighed, a sanctuary in the heart of the city.

The convoy stalled on the street below him as the first car reversed into a parking bay, the smell of exhaust from the throbbing engines seeping into the room. Jay stepped away from the window, a little chagrined for the quiet streets and a certain authenticity that had vanished.

He turned back to the desk and closed the open casebook, imagining Cora teetering on the edge of Kensington High Street, washed by a wave of traffic spray. Perhaps she had fled to Laekin, perhaps the doctor would call Jay tomorrow with his nervous assessment, confess his natural squeamishness in the face of emotional distress and admit he'd written out a prescription for some anti-depressants that would take two weeks to have any effect.

'You know you must see your doctor for that,' Jay had replied when Cora asked about drugs in her third session. 'Perhaps you are asking for my approval?'

'I thought maybe taking something... that it could give some relief.'

'Perhaps you think it might help you forget everything that you are bringing up in this space?' he said, for Jay believed in medication only in extremis: lose the alertness and you often lose the battle. Clients bellowed for the heavy fog of SSRIs, desperate to insulate themselves from raw emotion, to be relieved of the burden of living. Lately, he had developed a particular interest in the delicate precipice of breakdown, he was captivated by the profound clarity of the disturbed mind, how a tangled ribbon of distorted logic could lead, for example, to the most eloquent argument for suicide. He found himself increasingly engaged by the immediacy of suffering, the agony of being perpetually on the edge of disintegration. It was a fascination with the critical moment *before*, when the trembling edifice of those elaborate defences that barricade the conscious from the unconscious, besieged for a lifetime by the slow build-up of relentless pressure, finally collapses under the spectacular weight of flood water and the client is swept away. He was intrigued by the unpredictability of outcome: a client could swim to shore and be saved; she might perish, succumb to the comforting embrace of oblivion, or she could plunge into an un-medicated freefall, retreat into the limbo of diagnosable illness, and Jay would lose interest. Switch off. Refer.

The fact remained that medicated patients quickly became dull. It was a faustian exchange that left them pliable and incurious, trading human experience for the frozen wastes of a numb monotony. In 1997, towards the tail end of his socialising tolerance, Jay had attended a dinner in the River Room at the Savoy where a well-known psychiatrist had slumped into the chair beside him, chewing on a plump cigar. 'You're an American,' he slurred, knocking over the water glass. 'Your lot started this love affair with Prozac, opium for the masses and all that. Depression, scourge of modern man,' he prodded Jay with a belligerent hiccup. 'You chaps think you invented it. Bet you didn't know that there was a paper written here in London by an English doctor a hundred and fifty years ago about the explosion in the so-called democratic disease. Blamed it on the pressure of modern life: too much travel, too fast, too much choice. Hah! *Plus ça change,*' he concluded and a heavy hand crashed down on the tablecloth between them.

• FIVE •

In the centre of the ensuite stood a cavernous cedarwood tub that Jay had chosen for its angular minimalism but never used, for he was unable to feel comfortable with the idea of soaking in his own filth. Instead he showered, screened by a sheet of clear glass that spanned the length of one wall. His refurbishment of the house had revealed the inadequacies of the English plumbing system where the unpressurised hot water output delivered a niggardly dribble and, insisting on a flow rate of seventeen litres per minute, Jay arranged for a five-bar pump to be imported from the US, where the business of personal hygiene was accorded due importance. It was true, he thought as he plugged in his shaver, that the bathroom had the opulent austerity of a Japanese hotel. 'Very impersonal', a transient redhead once remarked when she strayed in to finger the tub in that louche manner of hers that was reminiscent of a feral child.

Female guests were always invited to use the second bathroom and although this request left them initially surprised and sometimes even a little wounded, any reluctance was transformed when they inspected the arrangements – a vast white oval Spoon bath sculpted from a resin composite, whose deep matt curves sloped downwards to rest on the sandstone floor and a row of glass-fronted cabinets with soaps and shampoos and bath emollients from L'Occitane, deep-pile towels in nutmeg and freshly laundered white kimonos.

Jay leaned over a shallow ceramic trough and examined his

freshly shaven jawline in the mirror. Over the years he had monitored the gradual emergence of a striking resemblance to his brother and now, as he progressed through middle age, it seemed as if Robert was coming alive in his face. They shared the same perfect oval and a certain dark intensity in the wide-set stare – brown eyes flecked with amber, their father's only visible legacy. But lately, what had once appeared like critical distinctions between them had disappeared. For example, Jay's chin, which had always been broader and more assertive, seemed to have collapsed into his brother's pinched afterthought; his nose, once straight and patrician, was expanding into an excessive fleshiness about the nostrils; a faint scattering of wrinkles marked the side of his forehead, the kind of deterioration that was commensurate with a much younger man and he remembered how Robert's porcelain skin had been curiously unlined at the time of his death, as if he had managed to remain untouched by the frantic business of his existence. Jay tugged at his hairline, once a mahogany brown, now evenly flecked with grey. At least he wasn't going bald, a process that had begun very early for Robert, a rapid and definite retreat that exposed the broad flat plane of his skull.

He straightened up into the comforting reminder of height advantage. At fifteen, Jay had already been a good five inches taller than his brother, approaching six feet with wide shoulders and strong capable hands. 'Look at you, you're twice the man I'll ever be,' Robert had joked, with a mock stomach punch that was puny, almost girlish in contrast. Once, when he was seven, Jay surprised him with a baseball bat, dragged him out to the backyard where Robert fumbled with the mitt and bowled an awkward underarm before recoiling in skittish apprehension when his kid brother whacked the ball over his head.

Jay closed the wardrobe door and checked his reflection in the full-length mirror. He was lucky to gravitate effortlessly

towards a healthy diet and regular exercise and he understood
the impact of his physical presentation, could read the covert
glances of admiration from women at other tables in restau-
rants and bars – and most especially, he found, at the theatre.
But the art of looking good required more rigorous vigilance in
midlife, he reflected, pinching a thin fold of loose skin on the
back of his hand. It was the loss of elasticity that he mourned
most of all, as if the epidermis was announcing the steady
inevitability of a progressive internal decay. For some months
after Robert had died, Jay experienced a disproportionate
interest in biological trivia, a compulsion which he had
subsequently observed in many bereaved clients and which he
recognised as one of the myriad responses to a violent or
sudden death. Graphic images of internal organs – the lungs,
the liver, the intestines – mocked him from the pages of medical
textbooks, their lurid reds and blues underscoring the
cartoonish mechanisms upon which his fragile life depended.
He read on, nauseated by physiological specifics and the
saturated colours that leapt out from the illustrations. It was
his astigmatism, of course, that caused the circulatory system
to hover above the page like a field of bluebells. In the furtive
quiet of the library, Jay monitored the secret pump of his heart,
closing his eyes on a pulsing starburst of veins that called to
mind an unexplored moment dredged from earliest history,
when he and some unidentifiable companion swung over a
battered half-door gawping at the disembowelled viscera of a
freshly butchered beast, until a man in a brown workcoat
stained with recent slaughters picked up a handful of steaming
entrails and flung it at the boys who fled shrieking from the wet
slap of laughter that pursued them all along the waterway.

Now, as Jay squared up to his reflection, framed by the
white shroud of the bedspread behind him, the accelerating
resemblance to Robert struck him as a sort of theft, as if he was

being burgled of his own identity by the grasping fingers of an indomitable presence who refused to be bludgeoned into oblivion. 'How the dead struggle to be remembered,' Marina had sighed on her first session with Jay after the unexpected death of her thirty-five-year-old husband. She'd taken to spending her nights in a bus shelter on Kensington Gore, comforted by the view of Prince Albert who sat alone on his refurbished throne watching carloads of black ties arrive for a night's entertainment in his concert hall across the road. Marina shivered inside the chilled wrap of her coat, soothed by the thought of Queen Victoria in her little black dress, distraught with grief and laudanum, caught in the grip of an unreasonable longevity for it would be forty long years before she could follow her beloved into the ground. 'They are looking for something of substance,' Marina insisted, 'a white cross, a street name, a snatch of song that never dies,' and she lapsed into silent contemplation of the honours lavished on the departed, tributes hurled out over open graves, all the things that were never said when hearts were still beating, words thudding like clumps of clay on dead ears.

Jay remembered Robert's memorial service at UCLA as a rather shabby affair. The College's choice of Kinsey Hall as a venue had seemed inappropriately ironic, for it was the scene of Robert's triumph two years before when he delivered his keynote lecture on semantic theory to an audience of international scholars. Their mother had insisted that Jay and herself sit in the front row where the delegates took side-swipe views of her incongruousness, her neatly coiled henna hair crammed into a pillbox, her low-cut blouse revealing a dejected expanse of worn cleavage. Earlier that day Jay had glimpsed her through a slit in the bathroom door savagely rooting out grey hairs.

'Caesar will die,' Robert had declared. 'This sentence cannot be considered true or false independently of the context of use.'

Their mother had smiled knowingly, as if his lecture was a private joke, as if she understood everything.

'I shall not apologise for the fact that my talk will contain only proofs, statements and theorems. As a matter of fact, one might regard this as a virtue akin to purity.' A humorous ripple spread through the audience. Robert, of course, took knowledge very seriously, something that Jay later realised was rarely found, even in those at the top of their game. Robert believed in limitless possibilities, obstacles were simply plot beats or opportunities for lateral thinking, a brief pause for breath. Once on Santa Monica beach in the fading light, he had flung himself backwards as the evening sand chill crept along their legs and said, 'Everything can be explained. This is a physical world.' He was always full of ruthless advice on how to live, a model for the kind of uncompromising home truths that Jay sometimes meted out to clients who found themselves buried alive under a mountain of their own rubble. Little pricks of motivation, journalistic sound-bites on how to achieve fulfil-ment, like: get up off your ass and stop whining.

An hour before the Kinsey lecture Jay had called round to Robert's office in Dodd Hall and seen the scathing remarks scribbled across an abstract of the speech. Apparently Robert's colleagues were not convinced that he could deliver on such radical claims. Natural language was far too unwieldy to be subjected to formal analysis they said and warned him against flying in the face of a philosophical tradition that went all the way back to the Vienna Circle. But Robert rejected all that, parting company in happy defiance. At the time, Jay had been only peripherally aware of the linguistic wars that had raged across America all through the 1960s. It was nothing short of a revolution that saw what had previously been considered to be a dull backwater emerge at the heart of an epistemological battle triggered by Noam Chomsky, whose interest in language had developed as he studied the finer points of Hebrew grammar at his father's knee.

'I regard the constructions of a theory of truth as the basic goal of serious syntax and semantics,' said Robert, looking round the hall, 'and the developments emanating from MIT offer little promise towards that end.' He paused, leaning forward on the lectern. 'I have what I consider to be a more hopeful way of approaching ordinary language than the attempt of Chomsky. I believe the kind of model-theoretic work I will present to you tonight has considerably more relevance to philosophy and ordinary language than many of my critics would grant it.'

A hush fell on the stunned audience as they gophered through pages of voluminous notes, scribbling clarification in the margins, staring aghast at Robert's proofs until their pencils lay defeated and they abandoned the pretence of even keeping up. He shone brighter and bigger than they could ever imagine, he was leaving them all behind in a trail of incomprehension. 'Nothing can be done to make easy reading of Hamilton's writings,' a mournful reviewer would later conclude on the posthumous publication of Robert's landmark book. 'They must be studied slowly and with care. There is little concern for the uninitiated reader as well as a notational sophistication that makes his fragments of English forbidding to non-mathematicians.'

After Robert's lecture had ended the delegates spilled out onto the steps as dusk stole across the cropped grass. The campus sidewalks were littered with lilac jacaranda blossom and a woman in a white dress bent down to scoop up the long tubular bells, like crushed silk in her delighted palms. Jay stood on the kerb staring up at Kinsey Hall, a 1920s block of elaborate sandstone and red brick on the eastern side of UCLA's central quadrangle. It was a pared-down version of the heavyweights,

Royce Hall and the Powell Library, whose monumental bell towers faced each other in mutual regard. A trickle of students streamed between the vast arched entrances, hounded by the inscriptions that pursued them everywhere, each building offering up some rebuke, urging them to transcend their grandest dreams. 'Open thou mine eyes, that I may behold things out of thy law', his mother intoned and Jay followed her gaze to the words carved above the doors to Kinsey, where Robert stood shaking hands with a cluster of colleagues, his thin lips stretched wide by an eager smile. She repeated the inscription as if committing it to memory. The light was fading away, a startled moon pressed against a dirty rose sky, the neat rosebushes glowed a brilliant white garland all around the building perimeter, a burst of backslapping laughter erupted around Robert and a thick damp roll hit the back of Jay's throat as the temperature inched lower, dragging a heavy fog in from the ocean.

Two years later, on 12 March 1971, he had shepherded his mother into the front row for Robert's memorial service, disheartened by what he perceived as a lack of dignity in the proceedings. Kinsey Hall seemed smaller than he remembered and the lecture theatre format lent a voyeuristic feel to the occasion. Jay was disappointed at the shuffling attendance and put it down to some combination of the unusual circumstances of his brother's death, academic rivalry and plain bad manners, the insensitivities of a nation that doesn't appreciate protocol. A couple of graduate students stood at the entrance distributing a single-sided page with a distinctly unflattering head-and-shoulders shot of Robert taken from the department yearbook, his face barely visible behind ludicrously large frames. A stark announcement was laid out in grotesque calligraphic script.

March 12 1971
In Memoriam
Robert Merritt Hamilton, 1930 – 1971

Jay prised the paper from his mother's trembling grasp. Montgomery Furth, Chairman of the Philosophy Department, made his way towards the podium and stood blinking at the lectern.

'As chairman and colleague,' he began, 'I should like to express on behalf of the entire intellectual community at UCLA, the terrible loss that we have suffered through Robert's premature death. Not only did we value his inestimable brilliance and creativity as a scholar and his dedication as a teacher, Robert's work went beyond anything but the most rarely encountered.' He paused, looked up at a point somewhere above the audience's heads. 'A person with his gifts turns up very seldom,' he continued and Jay immediately recognised that the text was borrowed from testimonials written ten years before to the Selective Services department for the purpose of securing Robert's exemption from military service. Jay had found these documents the previous day, buried in the paperwork at 3840 North Beverly.

One letter began:

Professor Robert Hamilton is in a critical occupation and is of more value to the nation's defense effort in his current position than as a draftee in the armed forces. The field of mathematical logic in which Professor Hamilton has distinguished himself so brilliantly is one that has many applications to issues that arise in the higher levels of planning for national defense. Such technical talents are of great importance in resolving problems in systems development and weapons design. This is evidenced by the fact that several of the young men who have done their doctoral work under Professor Hamilton's direction are now employed by industrial and research agencies involved in a broad range of applications that include the Polaris program as well as development projects in artificial intelligence, such as voice-controlled weaponry. I would specifically highlight the collaborative research that Professor Hamilton has performed for the United States Air Force...

The Chairman touched his brow with a clenched knuckle. A restless silence fell on the proceedings, broken only by his mother's slack-jawed breathing, short snatched gasps accompanied by an occasional shudder. 'Robert's research,' he continued, 'was of the highest possible calibre in a field characterized by the most exacting standards. His students and colleagues regarded him with awe. He advanced into full professorship at UCLA in the highest degree of acceleration ever known. Our loss is both terrible and irreparable.' Furth cleared his throat and tugged at his tie. The whole business was taking its toll. 'Finally, let me repeat here what I have already communicated to Mrs Hamilton and Robert's younger brother Jay. It is hard to find consolation at such times. But I can assure you that Robert's work, which had already won him international renown, will long outlive him and will continue to furnish foundations on which others can build for many years to come.'

Jay wondered if it was the unwelcome scent of scandal that had unsettled Furth or if he might have seen Robert's letter of protest to the Chancellor just a few weeks before. 'The Chairman's understanding of the word consensus is not the same as mine, which corresponds to the dictionary definition: *a collective unanimous opinion of a number of persons*. Because experience has taught me the imprudence of allowing views to be attributed to me which are not my own, I find I must set down the items with which I disagree in the Chairman's recent report.'

'What do you think of that?' Robert had asked Jay, waving the letter with a flourish as they drove up through Coldwater Canyon after a late pizza in Westwood.

'I think you just like stirring it up,' Jay had replied and Robert shook with a laughter that Jay could still hear, a vivid windrush that split the humid night with its tireless enthusiasm. Their headlights trapped the sparkling eyes of a racoon in the darkness while Robert quoted cheerfully from a reference he had written on a colleague looking for a lecturing position at Princeton. 'The candidate represents the very worst not only in philosophy but in scholarship in general. I should call him a charlatan if that were not an understatement.'

'You make enemies lightly,' said Jay. Robert laughed and dropped him off at the end of the driveway. 'I only tell the truth,' he said.

Jay hesitated in the open doorway. A warm breeze blew wisps of cottonwood catkins in an aimless drift to the ground. 'I'm not coming in,' said Robert, with that look of wild anticipation on his cheeks, eyes glittering behind his thick lenses. 'You want to come with me?' he asked with an ugly leer and Jay slammed the door on his brother's snigger, stood watching as he revved the engine and turned the car round, headed for Downtown and his private underworld.

After the memorial service Jay had thanked Furth for his eulogy and stood at the head of the receiving line as a human shield against his mother's crumbling performance. The amplified bells chimed out across the campus as they emerged under a high blue sky and she pointed a quivering hand at the towers above Powell. 'No, no,' Jay whispered, 'it's not for Robert, they always ring on the hour.' She slumped forwards with a hideous moan and a neighbour from Van Nuys drew her firmly to one side.

The mourners shuffled down the steps, muttering

condolences. Jay shook their dismal hands, deflecting the unasked questions in their eyes. A colleague of Robert's whom Jay had never met flung herself at his neck and sobbed, 'Oh, it's all so awful,' but when he prised her loose he saw that she too was looking for an explanation and, although he knew that distance insulated him from the poisonous gossip that accompanied his brother's sensational death, Jay could already hear the creaking rumour mill, the campus whispers, the seamy undertow of sordid suggestion. He could see the spreading stain, the ghost of a smirk on Detective Green's lips as he stood off to the side, sucking on a cigarette.

• SIX •

At 6:47pm, Jay settled into a wing chair at the Berkeley Hotel in Knightsbridge and watched a stiff-shirted waiter approach him, one hand folded behind his back. He murmured a greeting and as Jay looked up, the words 'Kir Royale' unexpectedly sprang to his lips, prompted by a vision of pink bubbles so vividly alluring that he wondered if he had discovered a new-found longing for an aperitif that he despised. 'The Chardonnay,' he said and the waiter bowed and turned away.

At a nearby table, a middle-aged American presented a detailed account of his day's business meeting to his wife's glazed contemplation of her champagne. The man crinkled the cellophane wrapping of a panatella, the unbroken drone of his monologue cutting like a metronome through the sporadic bar hum. The woman fingered a pearl necklace around her throat and shot Jay a flickering glance.

The lobby bar at the Berkeley was not a fashionable venue, but Jay had chosen it for the generosity of the seating arrangements, the luxury of defining space that facilitated private conversation. It was also, he guessed, exactly the kind of choice that Dana Flynn would predict for a man of his age – she would have done her homework for this meeting and Jay did not always favour a strategy of confounding expectations. He wondered now if a biographer with a research interest in a brilliant scientist might be curious about fraternal difference and what, if anything, she thought about the brothers' divergent careers. It had recently occurred to Jay that Robert and himself had far more in common than might appear, in fact – unlikely as it might seem – the two of them shared a similar purpose. Although, of course, that wasn't how Robert saw it at all in 1966 when Jay announced his long-term intention to study psychoanalysis.

'I beg you to rethink your decision', Robert had written in urgent reply to Jay's letter.

> Don't waste your talents in this field when there are so many other worthy possibilities. It is my belief that psychoanalysts are charlatans. I cannot endorse an occupation that is devoid of intellectual rigour, whose practitioners cultivate vulnerability and encourage patients to celebrate their own fragility, so that they become afraid to experiment, afraid to live, but most of all, afraid to take responsibility for their own lives, preferring to blame others for their own shortcomings. If your chosen profession continues to exercise the public imagination – and sadly I believe it will – you will create a generation that spends their whole life bleating about imagined misfortunes that have befallen them in childhood, trapped in an unhealthy confusion between fact and fiction. Who will be the heroes in this new world, where good and evil are no longer held to be matters of choice, where grown men and women dedicate their lives to idle contemplation of their navels?

It was, of course, typical of Robert to commit his uncensored opinion to the mailbox without a thought for the consequences. 'You mustn't be too disappointed in this letter. I simply have to tell you what I believe to be true.' Jay had folded the notepaper into a tight square and pondered the ruthless-ness of honesty. Who was it for exactly, this precious gift?

'Weigh this great truth in your hand,' he sometimes urged his clients. 'Who benefits from this venomous dart that masquerades as treasure?'

'You think your wife wants to hear about your little fling?' he'd once asked Alex, who had spent three sessions wallowing in the throes of guilt after a month of frantic sex with his colleague's PA. 'Who needs the truth here?' Jay demanded when Alex protested the need to unburden himself to his wife. 'We always said there'd be no secrets,' he whined. 'That was your first mistake,' said Jay. 'Secrets are meant to be carefully guarded. They conceal the ugly frailty of our humanity.'

Alex shook his head, 'No, no, it's never been like that between us.' Jay leaned forwards, 'You think your wife wants to hear from your lips what she already suspects? And what should she do with that knowledge? You want her to choke on her humiliation and then beg you to stay so that you can feel forgiven? The truth is always for the teller. We spill our guts for absolution, so we can sleep easy. We tell the truth because we cannot bear to be locked in the vault with our own weakness. We tell the truth so that we can slip from under the yoke of guilt.'

Alex hung his head.

'Don't kid yourself,' said Jay in the forty-ninth minute.

For four long years, Jay had endured the weight of his brother's disapproval. Robert had mounted an aggressive campaign to dissuade him from his psychoanalytic ambitions, and, in the summer before he graduated even hijacked a weekend visit to insist Jay attend a Saturday seminar in formal semantics at UCLA, in the hope that some exposure to rigorous scientific method might change his mind.

'The proper application of our labour and effort is in the natural sciences,' Robert had announced, dropping his jacket over the back of a chair. He pushed the heavy frames over the bridge of his nose and glared up at the audience, a group of postgraduate linguists who had heard he was some sort of genius who sat up in his room in Dodd Hall constructing a great theory of language that would change everything.

'"Every man loves a woman",' he declared. 'Is this sentence ambiguous?' The students nodded uncertainly, wary of stumbling into a logician's trap.

'So where does the ambiguity in the sentence arise? Is it in the interpretation of the words "man" or "woman" or "loves"?' The class held its collective breath and sank a little lower into their seats. Robert shoved a hand into his pocket, jangled some coins. 'The problem, boys and girls, lies in the interpretation of the words "every" and "a". So today I'm going to demonstrate how we solve this problem using a fragment of English.' The audience raised their pens as he snatched at a piece of chalk and turned to the blackboard to write:

The proper treatment of quantification in a fragment of English

'Let's take a simple sentence like "Every man talks". Now the usual translation in logic would be

$$\forall x[S(x) \rightarrow (T(x)]$$

'But this is clearly unsatisfactory.' The class regarded his formula in cowed silence. A girl seated in front of Jay turned to her classmate and shrugged with a nervous grin, pointing to a large question mark with a bubble dot on her open notebook.

'So this is the solution I'm going to propose,' continued Robert.

$$\lambda Q[\lambda P \forall x[Q(x) \rightarrow (P(x)]](M)(T)$$

Jay watched the students' bobbing heads, mouthing as they transcribed, diligently counting the brackets.

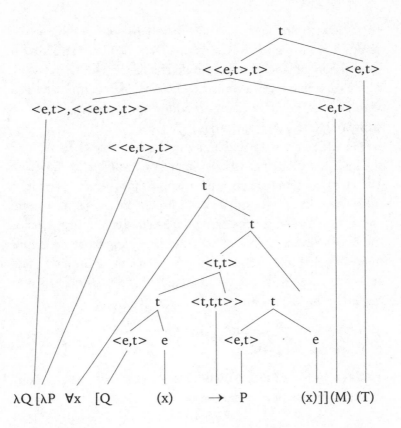

The chalk broke on the board and clattered to the floor at Robert's feet. The girl in front of Jay shook her head. Robert tapped a finger on the lectern and Jay could sense his brother's waning enthusiasm. His gaze travelled over the audience in barely concealed frustration. 'My God, this is even worse than I thought. We are all wasting our time,' and he grabbed his jacket and strode from the theatre.

Now, almost thirty years later, Jay could acknowledge that although Robert had been spectacularly misguided in his efforts to try and persuade Jay to abandon psychoanalysis, he had accurately predicted where the public love affair with introspection would lead. Despite the lack of hard evidence demonstrating its benefits, the masses had been seduced into believing that the talking cure was the key to a better life. Clients flocked to therapists when they could have gone for a jog, read a book, phoned a friend or taken refuge in the confessional where the priest's hands fiddled under the folds of his soutane as he battled against a purgatory of deprivation, inhaling the sweet scent of face powder and cheap perfume, reminders of all he had sacrificed in the craven service of the Lord: the touch of another skin; the bleak house; the lonely sperm. Of course, Jay reflected, priests have the power of absolution and what a consolation that must be. Playing God: now there's a career choice. Like the SS 'Schreibtischtäter', the desk murderers, pens poised over a list of names.

But God, of course, demanded a sacrifice in return for eternal salvation: prayer, selflessness, a life spent turning the other cheek. An analyst simply demanded the gift of speech, of memory as a panacea against the void.

Even after all this time, it still bothered Jay that Robert had completely misunderstood the thrust of psychoanalysis. What he saw were the headlines, the pseudo-science, the quackery, he was always so impatient with inexactness. You could hear it in his choice of music, his preference for Bach, all mathematical structure and precision. 'You can feel your brain expanding when you play a three-part invention,' he used to say, running a trilling finger over the top octaves of the over-strung piano that crowded the living-room corner at North Beverly Drive.

But perhaps, given time, Robert might have come to understand that the brothers were in fact united by a fascination with the mysteries of language, that Jay too was grappling with meaning and truth. He liked to imagine the kind of conversation they could have had if Robert had lived, sitting on studio chairs in the backyard, a sharp evening wind rippling the alder, the little cones clinging onto the branches long after the leaves had fallen.

'The patient loses their own language,' Jay would explain, 'and then I give them a better one.' He would describe for his brother how clients streamed through his door with their emptiness, their non-sense, dragged down and submerged by the weight of their own semantics, like cold reeds coiled tightly around their ankles. It was a grip that could only be released by a new interpretation, where the meaning of a word is altered and the context redefined. For language shapes and defines our experience, Jay saw the evidence daily: 'Mother', he would say to a client and this single word could be enough to trigger a life story, a whole spectrum of individual resonance and response. *This* was the real business of therapy, he thought, as he watched the struggles played out in his safe space, it was a great battle to adjust the semantics, trying not to get bruised, beaten and defeated by a simple word.

Of course, Robert might have dismissed this with a restless wave of his hand as the night gathered in and the alder's lichen glowed silver in the moonlight. Then Jay might lean forward in his chair to explain that the clinical practice of psychoanalysis is based on the premise that the telling of a story is useful, that the act of telling is a therapy, that the patient is healed by the soothing repetition of a ghosted narrative that is forever evolving. 'Analyst and patient collude to create a therapeutic fiction – the recovered, reinvented past,' he would say. 'It is the collaboration that produces the meaning, a provisional truth, a working title, the continually unfolding story of why they have arrived in the safe space.'

'So what's the difference between a case history and a novel?' Robert would ask and Jay might even have managed to ignore his brother's disdain and outline his grand plan to integrate science and art, to take his case histories – the fusion of fact and fiction, the collective struggles for meaning that were played out daily on his couch – and transform them into works of literature. In retrospect, however, he wasn't sure if he would ever have trusted Robert with the electric burden of this intimacy, knowing as he did how systematically his brother would annihilate any idea that could be logically persuaded of its own defeat. And how afterwards, when he saw the damage done by his carelessness, he would lock Jay in a conciliatory embrace as if the envelope of his affection could compensate for the trampling rampage through his younger brother's dreams. But these were like the lost conversations that his clients have with the dead and the abandoned, words cast over barren seas.

'So the patient tells you a story. And how is that going to help him?'

'"The act of remembering is to be planning a future."'

'Who said that?'

'Lacan,' Jay would reply in nervous and accurate anticipation of Robert's howling laughter.

• SEVEN •

'Jay Hamilton, I presume,' said a voice above his head.

Dana Flynn was instantly recognisable from the publicity shot on the back of *The Enigma*, although Jay noticed as he stood up to greet her that an overexposure had succeeded in editing out the scattering of freckles along the ridge of her nose.

'You are *so* like Robert,' she said, her hand lingering in his while she inspected his face and it struck Jay as oddly impertinent that she was already on first name terms with his brother. 'Except you seem more—'

'Substantial,' he proposed. 'My brother was a good deal shorter. And of course there's the hairline.'

Despite a certain tiredness about the pale stretch of skin under her eyes, the overall impression was of a youthfulness that the camera had somehow substituted with serenity. Not an easy subject to photograph, he'd concluded when he examined her book, for although the author's stare met the lens head-on, there was a tension in her lips that smacked of a perceptible discomfort. Her sleek dark hair was swept professionally off her shoulder and there was the blurred suggestion of a café awning overhead. Perhaps it was the lighting that created a subtle duality of mood, the sense of a woman struggling to get acquainted with a recent transformation, the glint of a diamond in her right lobe, the dark V of her jumper plunging into the fold of her arms. He wondered if the stylist had pleaded for abandon, tried to persuade Dr Flynn to spread her slim arms in a wide-armed welcome to the reader, pout those voluptuous lips and expose her décolletage in all its glory.

She sat down, placing an overstuffed black satchel on the ground by her feet and launched unbidden into an energetic account of her research in a strong and confident voice, a lecturing frequency that was not without appeal. Unexpectedly slender, almost delicate in proportion, Dana Flynn wore a thin black-knit sweater whose cuffs were fringed with tiny grey beads that suggested a small concession to eveningwear. She crossed a leg and the contour of her kneecap was visible through the silky folds of her skirt – long and, he thought, vaguely unseasonal. Reaching down to the satchel she pulled out a clear plastic envelope with a large white sticker on the flap inscribed, ROBERT MERRITT HAMILTON: 1930–71. The file bulged with documents of different sizes and Jay realised with a jolt that this was already a project with depth and breadth, with tentacles that delved into the sealed passage of his past and he could feel the accumulated silence of the long years since he had spoken of his dead brother to anyone.

'I was particularly interested,' she was saying, 'in the scientists and philosophers who migrated from Europe to the US before World War Two. People like Rudolf Carnap, Otto Neurath, Kurt Gödel, Philip Frank. You're familiar with the Vienna Circle? The *Wiener Kreis?*' He nodded, smiling at this American insistence on advertising the most elementary linguistic competence.

'I guess Vienna must be an essential pilgrimage for a psychoanalyst? You see I did my research on you too,' she said turning to the waiter who stood patiently by her chair.

'Indeed,' Jay conceded and it was true, he recognised the desire to see where things started, a fascination with the relationship between event and place, as if the magic of invention might be contagious. *What can be said at all, can be said clearly*, the Vienna Circle had declared in their manifesto and Jay recalled the opulent romance of the city, imagined the café philosophers gathered under the glint of chandeliers, the delectable sugar mice in the windows, the pirouetting Lipizzaner, the mellifluous strain of an elegant waltz, Freud and his hysterical women in the days before it all turned sour, before the accelerating quickstep of jack boots silenced the strings and history's door slammed shut behind the lucky few who just managed to escape into the safe and eager arms of America.

'Many of the Vienna Circle ended up at the top universities,' she continued, settling back in her chair, 'and were very influential in shaping the future of philosophical thought in America. In the last few months I've been digging around in the archives at Berkeley and that was how I came across Robert. I have to admit that I'd never heard of your brother until I came across his correspondence with a Polish logician—'

'Alfred Tarski,' said Jay. 'Robert was his star pupil.'

In October 1956 Jay had stood on the eucalyptus hills above Berkeley while Robert waved a proprietorial arm across the view of his alma mater. A sun flash caught the face of his watch as he hunkered down and scribbled *pu* on a scrap of paper torn from the little Moleskine notebook that he always carried with him. 'Summer 1940, right here,' he said, thrusting the paper into Jay's eight-year-old palm. 'Seaborg, Kennedy and Wahl identified element 94: plutonium. The beginning of the bomb.' He reeled off a list of Berkeley's Nobel Laureates as they walked down towards the Campanile, through slow streams of returning students, past a dull green knot of olive trees. They stopped underneath the fall yellow of a gingko and Jay felt the folded paper glow warm and secret in his pocket. 'This is where you'll come when it's your turn,' said Robert, ruffling his shaved head. But when Jay returned as a Psychology major in

1966, Berkeley was a haze of tear gas and truncheons, a brash centre of dissent for bright-eyed students who were busy putting the campus on the protest map. It was, however, just a stepping stone to his real vocation; he wasn't interested in taking on Governor Reagan and the National Guard, he had no time for the distractions and irrelevancies of politics. Jay was simply filling in time, as the San Francisco School of Psychoanalysis wouldn't admit him at eighteen.

'Berkeley is overrated,' he had announced at the end of his freshman year and Robert immediately sprang to its defence, jabbing his finger at the wheel as they bumped along the Santa Monica freeway. Wind sucked humidity into the car and Jay slid down in the passenger seat, turning his head to a window view of passing traffic. But it was true, he reflected, Berkeley had been an enormous disappointment. White-coated psychology lecturers pointed to caged rodents scuttling about in the sawdust and told their students that knowledge is only gained empirically. It seemed to Jay that the entire discipline was blundering about in the mysteries of nature. The big universal questions that might be answered by observing lab rat responses became very, very small, buried under the dry crunch of statistical method, the sum of all the things we do not know. There was no science at all to the study of humanity, he concluded, the white coats were only there to make them all feel scientific. There was no blood and guts in a psych lab, no bubbling potions, nothing happening at all, except counting and collating, checking the standard deviation and analysing the results. They were drowning in the tedious rigour of quantitative method, trying to find a way to organise the chaos. It was the same old dream, just like Dana's dead heroes in their slavish devotion to observables.

Jay had managed to relieve the monotony of his studies by embarking on a course of structured reading, spinning outwards from the freshman curriculum in a cross-disciplinary trawl that merely confirmed his suspicions about the paucity of human understanding. And he kept himself busy making his own personal psychological discoveries. For example, one February morning, he opened Primo Levi's account of Auschwitz over breakfast and found that he could stare into a mass grave with his milk-dripping spoon hovering by the side of the page, crunching the half-soaked cornflakes as he studied the twisted corpses. He spent two side-tracked months studying Holocaust testimonials and was reassured to learn that he could read survivor accounts with the cold clear eye of observance, for he felt that this would definitely be a strength in his future line of business. He turned the pages, mulling over the compulsion to tell, as if the act of telling might prevent reoccurrence, like a charm to ward off evil. There are no words, they whispered, but the gas didn't kill a good story, the hasty massacre of camp survivors didn't eliminate the plot. In quiet spring dawns, when the campus grass was thick with dew, Jay would lift his head from the page and think about the juxtaposition of desensitisation and the need to bear witness. He thought about Levi's book and wondered if the act of writing had devalued the experiment, if the successful articulation of horror had a diminishing return, for if language can capture the vividness of evil, does it also dilute the event? If you can put a structure on the chaos and make sense of the senseless, might this have a softening effect? And where, he asked, was the line between understanding and acceptance? Does understanding imply forgiveness? In Hebrew, he discovered, there was no word for forgiveness. Atonement was altogether a different concept.

Years later Jay was reminded of this at a conference in Jerusalem when he took the opportunity to spend an afternoon at Yad Vashem and lingered for an hour in the candlelit tunnel, where the photos of dead children gazed out at him against an echoing taped recitation of 1.5 million names. Standing in the underground darkness, he smelt Naomi's perfume before he heard her sobbing. 'Get me out of here,' she shrieked so he led her up for air and they sat in the squat shade of a yew. Naomi had found her grandfather in the Hall of Names, after a painstaking search through the Pages of Testimony. She was here on a self-appointed mission for her dead father, who had lived out his whole life as the guilty child, swaddled in the bitter belief that his survival was somehow to blame. Jay patted Naomi's hand, her sniffs subsiding into his handkerchief. 'They died so that we could know their stories,' she said and although Jay wanted to point out the fallacy of this statement, he decided against it. She seemed keen to retire to the comfort of his room at the Hyatt in East Jerusalem and as they made the slow ascent in the Sabbath elevator, Jay considered her soft moustache under the unforgiving fluorescent and hoped that he wouldn't be too disappointed, for Naomi was undoubtedly very hirsute in that pale-skinned way that is typical of so many dark-haired women.

In April 1970, he attended his last lecture at Berkeley. High up in the back of the theatre the air smelled of stale laundry and the drooping heads below him struggled to stay awake. Jay ran a hand along Skinner's cracked spine and concluded that the language of science failed. The truth was that creative writers were more qualified to explain humanity than psychiatrists and philosophers. This was what Levi the chemist had eventually realised, that he would have to resort to fiction and poetry to communicate the horror of Auschwitz. The psychologists and psychoanalysts who had staked out their territorial claim knew no more than the great novelists. On his last day at Berkeley, Jay packed up all his textbooks and left them in three boxes on the sidewalk. As he sat there waiting for his ride he decided to permanently dispense with the business of reading. He would find his stories and write the books he wanted to read. And he would bear his brother's scorn.

'Did Robert ever mention,' Dana's voice returned to him, 'that Tarski was on a visit to Harvard the day Hitler invaded Poland? He was persuaded to stay but he couldn't get his wife and children out until after the war. He lost his parents and his brother in the camps.'

'"The drowned and the saved",' Jay murmured but Dana didn't recognise the quote or chose to ignore it. 'I mean the irony of the symmetry,' he added. 'The clever get saved, the ordinary get gassed. Arbitrary selection.'

'Yes, I have wondered about how that must have felt.'

'So your book is about survivor guilt?' he asked. 'And America's shame? The great minds they rescued versus the ones they didn't save? You want to know about guilt? Or you want to apportion the blame?'

He was a little disappointed at her lack of originality. She had the air of a tomb raider who arrives after the spoils have been looted, picking over the remains, searching for something hidden or overlooked in the carnage. And diligence was no substitute for flair. 'This is a well-travelled road, of course,' he said.

'You're asking what I bring to the table?'

'A certain naivety, perhaps?' he said, unable to resist pressing the insult home. Dana took the slur, looking away to hide her annoyance. 'Please don't be offended. A different version of the same story can often be very enlightening. It depends on whether you believe the story-telling is of value in itself or whether you expect us to draw conclusions.' He noticed that her freckles had disappeared again, it was a trick of the light and not just the photographer's whim. 'But we digress. You were going to tell me about your interest in Robert?'

'He is fascinating,' she replied tersely.

'And of course he died unfairly young. Perhaps it is life's unfairness you're researching as well as guilt. Perhaps it has some personal resonance?'

'No, actually,' she snapped and Jay felt the thrill of striking rock. He guessed how she had been spending her days, wondering what it felt like to be Carnap or Tarski, to be Chosen when the others were condemned. What did they feel for all those left behind, the lesser mortals, the smaller brains? Was there a shadow of guilt on their shoulders as they yielded to America's embrace? He could see her rooting around in the library in whispered communion with some zealous archivist, Turing's curious phantom peering over her shoulder as she searched for the intrigue in strange and vibrant lives, trying to keep her mind off whatever it was that she was avoiding – real life or some approximate version that meant she often preferred the dead to the living. He imagined her drifting off in the arms of these corpses and the romance of their diaspora, hunched over the roll call of intellectuals who fled when reason left the country and abandoned it to a moral vacuum, a fertile yielding ground for submission and complicity. The thinkers were gone, the books burnt, Vienna was an empty dance hall, even the horses had headed for the hills. He thought of the ghosts who nudged at her biographer's elbow, all that spectral shuffling for the prime slot, how patiently Dana listened to their stories, how she ranked them into a ruthless pecking order as they struggled against the tyranny of her priorities. Gödel, who chose not to eat in the end, slowly starving himself to death in his Princeton chair forty-five years after evading the ovens; Schlick, shot in the chest on the University steps by a disgruntled student; Levi, who hurled himself down the stairs to smash his screaming skull on the marble floor, and all the others who died with their unfinished equations and formulae in their hands: Carnap, Frank, even Einstein, their reckless optimism that the brilliance will keep on shining, leaving their mark in the hands of a clock, the tick of a bomb.

Dana inclined her head as if listening to a distant call. The conversation had taken a sharper turn than expected and she was, he suspected, considering whether to engage in sidetracking debate. She reached for her glass, a fine silver chain sliding forward on her wrist. He would have to cajole her back.

'I read your Turing,' said Jay, balancing his elbows on the arms of his chair. 'It was a very well-researched work.' She nodded, accepting the compliment with a polite smile. 'I can imagine it must have been very difficult to break free after so many years with one man. And of course, the completion of a book is also a loss. A bereavement even. This takes time to assimilate and work its way out.'

'When I finished with Turing,' she admitted, 'it felt like I had exhumed and re-buried him. Sometimes it felt like a violation, more than prurience.'

'Preying on the inarticulate, the vulnerable dead?'

'I worried about dignity, the ethics of it all.'

'I have often wondered if biographers fall in love with their subjects.'

'Or analysts with their patients,' Dana replied. It was a triumphant point score and he saw that she was taking him on, it made her feel thrillingly brave to confront his paternalistic superiority, his underhand attempts to disrobe her soul.

'Actually I saw Tarski once,' he said. 'In 1963, it must have been, Robert dragged me along to a Charter Day lecture at Berkeley where Tarski was being honoured for his contribution to mathematical logic. I was only fifteen but I do remember his speech. He said the creative work of maths was not much different to the creative work of art, which is not at all the boring thing that people might think. He said—'

'That you can build a machine which will produce all possible truths in a given domain,' she interrupted. 'But unfortunately it is possible for some statements to be true and not true at the same time.'

Jay considered her crowd-pleasing smile, saw a little girl in plaits and pinafore elbowing her way to the front of the class. 'Tarski was talking about antimonies,' she said. 'Contradictory statements that can be given a precise definition within a formal or mathematical language.'

'Yes, I had grasped that much.'

'Oh I'm sorry,' she smiled. 'I know I have this awful habit of—'

'Finishing other people's sentences,' he said as she swept back her hair so the pale skin of her angled neck was visible all the way from the jaw line to the ridged dip by her collarbone where the light pooled in dark shadow. Jay could imagine his hand tracing the curve of her shoulder, how the light thread of her jumper would slide easily away to reveal the coquettishness that might be buried under the weight of her library years. Dana Flynn, he decided, would require a multi-layered seduction and plenty of assurance that the partnering intellect would be up to the fuck. She was wary of too much politeness and didn't see the thrill in a level playing field. She had no particular affinity for younger men, the sex never compensated for the horror of waking up to find that there never was a conversation to peter out.

'Dana,' said Jay, leaning forward in his chair as the waiter appeared by his side, 'that's a very bulky file. If we're going to carry on talking, we must eat. Would you like to have dinner with me?'

There was a hushed time delay and it seemed to Jay that the

waiter tensed empathically as he hovered on the brink of rejection. Dana looked across at Jay and then down at her hands, she was probing their intimacy in the way that women circumnavigate the shiny hard edges of the male, searching for the soft underbelly, some evidence that they are worth the emotional risk.

'Let's go,' she said, and the waiter beamed his relief. Jay waved him away with a note.

'You know,' she said, reaching for her satchel, 'it's been difficult in the past, interviewing people who have lost relatives in tragic circumstances. There is always the sense of voyeurism. And with Robert, there is an overwhelming poignancy.'

'Unfinished work. What might have been. And so you are anxious now. You are worried about picking over a family tragedy for me.'

She nodded, wrapping her coat around her body.

'You're forgetting that storytelling is very often therapeutic,' he said, 'that the teller is in any case acting out their grief every day in many ways. But I mean it most sincerely when I tell you I'm very happy that Robert is getting some attention. I've always felt he deserved more. So you must ask me whatever it is you want to know.'

She looked up at him with a frank stare, lips parted as if she was about to speak and then she hesitated, shifted her gaze over his shoulder, looking beyond him into some private view.

'It is thirty years since Robert was murdered,' said Jay, 'and I have thought about him every day since. You mustn't worry about me. I have come to terms with my loss.'

• EIGHT •

'Do you ever miss America?' asked Dana as they stepped out into the night, crossed Wilton Place and turned left onto Knightsbridge. Jay glanced across the street, strangely overwhelmed by the scale of her question and an urgent impulse to invent a longing for a some home-grown trivia, to admit that in sleep he still roamed the childhood deltas of the San Joaquin Valley, the waterways' promise of coastline re-imagined now in his dreams as some Californian Eden, bathed in the soft focus of an emigrant nostalgia.

'No,' he said, moving on westwards, for anything he could mention would be cancelled out by an over-representation of the things he despised: the impractibility of giant redwoods, the deep-harboured ugliness of Stockton, its lowlands decay. When he had finally left California, the stifling weight of climate and event slid from his shoulders and it felt like he could breathe for the very first time.

Dana stopped to grimace at Harvey Nichols' window where a pair of life-size angels sat on silver swings above fishbowl clouds, swirls of stars fluttering to rest in their hair. 'I always hated Christmas displays, even when I was little,' she said, and Jay was reminded of how casually women fling out invitations to the closed world of their childhood, the private memorabilia they scatter about like litter into the lives of those they wish to admire them, forgetting that it is the here and now that seduces and not the slack open mouth of the sleeping child they once were, a dreamy perfection in the virgin skin. But he did not respond, careful not to look as if he might be leaping into interpretation and analysis.

A sudden gust blew open her coat and it brushed against his knuckles like the smooth pelt of some fleeing animal. He had noticed before how the cold can push us towards a stranger and his hand slipped through her arm in a gesture of solidarity against the chill, a certain old-fashioned charm that is never lost on a woman. They hurried across Sloane Street, the movement had shifted the mood and a walk through the night bustle felt like a mutual adventure. They were companions on a journey that could lead anywhere on this rain-slicked street, the night was alive with possibilities, the nocturnal charm of a traffic light, the shocking glow of brilliant red suspended above their heads. Dana was telling him now how she had learnt to like Los Angeles, which so many East Coasters never do, a little anecdote about some freeway crisis, a wrong turn on I–10 where she ran adrift in the sinister daytime quiet of Watts. Women have to try so much harder to be witty, thought Jay, steering them gently to one side to avoid an elegant threesome whose long-legged stride was clearing a path through the oncoming pedestrians.

A short trip had persuaded Dana to stay on for six weeks in the leafy security of Westwood, a five-minute walk to the Charles E. Young Special Collections library at UCLA where she had first come across Robert. Jay imagined her shuttling between the Reading Room, the North campus café and a dark wood banquette at Jerry's deli on Weyburn where she ended her nights paralysed by a giant laminated menu of breads – pumpernickel, sourdough, rye, chala, baguette, bagels, Kaiser – slashing a red pen through the day's notes under the overhead blur of muted ice hockey. She had also, she said, developed an unexpected interest in jogging which started one October morning when a lap round the perimeter slopes of the campus prompted her to run a three-mile circuit and she seemed to have difficulty stopping, so she expanded her territory westwards to the coast. He could picture her in amongst the flooding community of joggers who streamed up from the pier along the cliff top promenade at Santa Monica in the early evening, past the sleeping humps of homeless buried under mounds of plastic bags, past out-of-season tourists who sat in the lotus position in the brown-grassed shade of clumpy palm trees, turning the pages of their guidebooks. Dana kept on running, because something seemed to happen after exactly nineteen minutes, a rhythmic pull of her body that sucked her consciousness inwards so that she stopped noticing anything, just the pounding in her ears and the punishing jerk of joints slapping against the tarmac. He saw her standing sideways in the mirror, looking at her shrinking nakedness. She was getting faster, lighter, more insubstantial. In sleep her legs twitched beneath the restless sheet and he wondered if she had thought of running as a metaphor, about the depths that were eluding her. Jay had the distinct sense she might even be dreaming about Robert, but that he vanished on awakening, leaving her bleary and bereft in the pre-dawn.

'Yuck,' said Dana, coming to a halt outside the crammed opulence of Harrods' windows where a lone reindeer negotiated his mechanical revolutions through a glittering landscape of snow. The tremulous 'Silent Night' of a boy soprano escaped from a speaker hidden under the awning above their heads. A portly Santa sat on his sleigh, his whiskered lips frozen in a scarlet leer, his bulging frame leaning over a fleet of tethered huskies whose paws were frozen above ground in an impossible leap. Jay watched the whirling flakes settle on their silvery fur and remembered Christmas Eve 1954 and the dull grey coat of a mongrel bitch that Robert had found tucked under the wheel of his parked car on Acacia and Center. 'Look at this Jay,' he'd cried, carrying her into the house wrapped in his tan jacket and together they fashioned a manger of blanket underneath the Christmas tree. Jay crouched over her trembling form counting her ribs with a tentative finger while the bitch's faint growl subsided into an agonised refusal of a bowl of milk. His mother rested a hand on Robert's shoulder. 'I can't take her back to college, Mom,' and he looked over at Jay. 'You'll have to be my Pet Man, look after her for me,' and so he entrusted to his kid brother the burden of a responsibility that a six-year-old certainly needed, something to love and care for, something to nurture and cherish. 'I'll call her Lassie,' said Jay, combing his fingers through the matted clumps. All night long he lay on the floor beside her, exploring a new sensation of heartache that seemed to radiate beneath his pyjamas while the little grey bitch jerked and quivered in a fitful sleep. He drifted off, dreaming of a future where Lassie skittered after a ball on the sidewalk along Woodward, where his mother sat smiling down from the red kitchen stool as he taught Lassie how to beg on her hind legs. He slept long and deep until a ghastly rattle shattered the dawn and Jay awoke to find the dog curled in a cold crescent of death.

His scream brought them into the living room. 'I guess her heart gave out,' said Robert, lifting the frail corpse. Jay stood in the middle of the room, his chest pounding with rage at his brother for thrusting into his life something that could be ripped so cruelly from him, the intolerable pain of loving and losing and he fled to the bathroom to insulate his dignity from any sympathy. Lying balled on the floor with his cheek pressed against the linoleum, he thought of the lost future where Robert would come home for weekends and marvel at Lassie's tricks. His mother rapped on the door, her wheedling tone quickly escalating to unapologetic threat. 'You open that door right now, Jay Hamilton, otherwise... ' Robert appealed to his rational side. 'She would have died soon anyway Jay and you can always get another pet. It would have been much worse if you'd had her for years.' But Jay needed the bathroom to contain his distress, his skin was raw, he felt as if his chest had been wrenched open and exposed to an icy reality, a head-battering fury that ended with a sideways whack on the edge of the iron bath. He lost consciousness for a moment but came round to hear the gush of the kitchen tap and his brother's humming in the bedroom next door, the wall so thin Jay could have punched right through it. When Robert's car backed away for chapel he sat on the floor blinking at the tears and a little blood that trickled from the cut above his eye where the corner had struck the bath, rocking back and forth as if the reassuring motion could put some safe distance between him and the dead dog and a heartbreak that couldn't be borne.

'So why is this not an enchanting scene?' said Dana, hauling him back to the Christmas present where the soprano lingered on an extended final note.

'Perhaps,' Jay replied, 'because alongside the real memory of our childhoods, there is a parallel image which is a corrective version of the real thing. An idealised Christmas. As if to say: this is what we should really have had, this is what Christmas should really have been like. But the reality always fell short and *this*,' he gestured at the window, 'therefore appears like a desperate parodying of our fantasies.'

'So what would an analyst suggest?'

'That for you, reality has been disappointing.'

'Then he'd be wrong.'

'I guess that's what happens when you ask a psychoanalyst a simple question,' he smiled.

In younger years or different circumstances, or maybe with another woman, Jay might have taken her in his arms right there but he could not be sure of Dana's response and awkwardness appalled him as much as unwarranted rejection. 'We are almost there,' he said, lightly touching her elbow. But she pulled forward, setting a brisk pace and Jay knew he had unsettled her with his card-trick analysis.

'You know I visited your old house in Stockton,' she said without breaking her stride or even turning her head and the sudden impertinent mention of Jay's hometown felt like a towel ripped from his body.

'Not the California everyone dreams of,' he said, struggling to shake off a ludicrous sense of personal violation.

'I guess it must have been a pretty bleak place to live,' she nodded into her collar, as if this thought had just occurred to her, although she could not have failed to notice the air of irretrievable decline that hung over the single-storey sprawl of squat brick houses in this hope town that was once a stopping post en route to Sacramento. Streams of would-be miners had passed through on their way to the gold country only to wind up sleeping on the bare earth, lapping at infected water until their dreams expired in the black mines and they returned months later, collapsed exhausted in Stockton. The town sagged under the weight of so much disappointment and the miners reinvented themselves as stevedores along the sixty miles of deep-water channel, where freighters ferried cargoes of agricultural produce to San Francisco and millions of tons of iron ore from Utah and Nevada began their long ocean passage all the way to Japan.

To inspire a nobler civic life, was the grand inscription above the columns of Stockton City Hall, but this didn't fool Jay as he sat in fourth grade, watching the listless flutter of the Stars and Stripes through the classroom window. 'Captain Charles M.

Weber,' said Miss Purdy tapping her ruler on the black-and-white photo of a podgy slit-lipped man with a waxed beard and indignant eyes. 'In 1850, he named our town after Commodore Robert Field Stockton whom he met during the Mexican war.' The children blinked and waited for the punchline, a story that would flesh out the man, some evidence of heroism perhaps, that the naming of their town was significant or at least evocative. But Miss Purdy had nothing to add, for the story ended at the beginning. Commodore Stockton didn't die in glorious battle or even gain notoriety, in fact he never even came to visit. Jay felt the chill of an inauspicious beginning, his hometown was a metaphor for failure, the odds were stacked against him in these badlands of disappointment. As if to underscore his suspicions, Miss Purdy concluded her lesson with a summary of the town's historical landmarks, which were nothing worth talking about, a handful of aspirational Victorian buildings – the courthouse cupola and the State Hospital for the Insane, built on a hundred-acre site donated free of charge by Captain Weber, so desperate had he become to secure some recognition for Stockton. For Jay, scratching his initials into the softwood of his school desk, there was no former glory and nothing to learn except the fastest route out of there.

The years slipped away, it was 1955 again and Jay was staring through the screen door on Woodward at one of the local buzz-cut boys with short crisp sleeves and scrubbed fingernails who appeared occasionally on the front stoop and asked polite permission from his mother for Jay to come and play. He trailed the boy out onto the street although he knew that this one, like all the other neighbourhood kids, had nothing to show, for Jay out-ran, out-shot, out-smarted all of them, they had nothing to give him, all they could offer was their mediocre friendship, their thrifty apple-pie moms and horn-rimmed dads. He preferred the thrill of his own company, going solo on a thorough exploration of his environment, pushing further and further afield on his bike, searching for something to feel, somewhere out there in the San Joaquin basin, a bone-dry valley that had been transformed by an ambitious system of aqueducts in the 1940s so that what was once a vast hopeless plain became the biggest fruit and vegetable farm in the world. The whisper of work spread out across the state and beyond, Greyhounds bussed in cheap labour in straw hats who filled huge sacks with onions, carrots, apples and pears for 20 cents a time, mopped their sweat-soaked handkerchiefs under the splintering heat of the midday sun, dragged their weary feet towards the dust-belching roar of the returning bus and slumped into a dead sleep, all their hopes and dreams bound by the Sierra Nevada and the white surf of the Pacific.

On late spring afternoons Jay used to cycle down to the waterways where slow dredgers ploughed straight cuts through the tired old riverbanks for huge vessels that couldn't handle the bends. He stopped to stare across the water at the Stephens Brothers Shipyards where they were building minesweepers for the Korean War, and then pedalled on past Deadreach, Fern, Tule Islands to the Delta farm lands, where he crouched in a crop of sour-smelling milo and watched a close-range ocean freighter cut a majestic line through the field channel. To see such giant vessels so far inland was uplifting and he was reassured to know there were many escapes: eastwards to the majestic peaks of Yosemite; westwards, to the Bay sprawl of San Francisco and southwards on the I-5 where long-distance trucks cut an efficient four hundred mile route to Los Angeles.

In the summer of 1965 Jay stumbled on a regeneration project that aimed to revitalise downtown Stockton and spent a whole afternoon watching a band of shirtless workers paint geometric shapes onto the intersections of San Joaquin and

Main Street. Two men stood underneath the Bank of Stockton clock looking on in amazement as a beak-like curve of blue and red and white materialised on the road. 'Some kinda bird,' said one to the other. 'An eagle maybe?' Jay returned at midnight when the town was bereft of traffic to inspect the muralled surface under the streetlights. Early next morning the workmen appeared on the corner of El Dorado where clusters of locals gathered to admire this brave attempt to achieve the impossible: to beautify Stockton, like dressing a mutant in a party frock, as if to advertise its shortcomings. There they stood, the residents of his hometown, surrounded by promise, by the sound of other hearts beating, a beacon of ugliness in a landscape of beauty: the Midwest transplanted into California's backyard.

• NINE •

Brasserie St Quentin was discreetly upscale, a local establishment for quiet Knightsbridge money where the emphasis was on good food and excellent service. The décor was vaguely art nouveau with etched mirroring and dark wood. Long red leather banquettes ran along the outer walls and elaborate chandeliers cast an authentic Parisian gloom over the tables.

Jay helped Dana with her coat, his hand slipping inside the silk lining to linger in its dying warmth, like the body heat of an inert animal. The maitresse d' led them to a corner table at the rear, murmuring something about Gaston, the chef for more than fifteen years, who had a particular affection for his American patrons and whose fishing adventures were recorded in a photo display on the stairs that led down to the washrooms. Jay's favourite was a black-and-white shot entitled, *Fort Lauderdale, Juillet 1980*, where Gaston stood grinning over a slumped marlin, his arm around a halter-necked blonde in cropped white shorts who held a nervous glass of champagne, one delicate sandal raised above ground to avoid the spreading pool of blood at her feet.

They passed a round table in the centre of the restaurant where a group of middle-aged men were vying for the attentions of a slim brunette in a strapless black dress who was young enough to be their daughter. The men scraped back their chairs, clutching their napkins at crotch level when she stood up, adjusted her chiffon wrap and sauntered off to the bathroom, leaving a trail of admiration in her wake. Jay watched them sit down, flushed and jostling for position, they were eating red meat tonight and hang the cholesterol, the years were slipping away, they were feeling wonderfully rejuvenated; they might order cognac and to hell with the consequences for they were twenty-five again and may even have a Cuban, they were in lust and invulnerable, they simply wanted to touch the soft melt of her throat, to hear her breathe, to see the backless strapless dress slip magically to the floor. Men, he reminded himself, don't appreciate how fortunate they are that women consistently fail to get their act together.

He ordered the St Emilion. 'Robert's favourite,' he confided to Dana who had already secreted her notebook to the side of her plate and was ready to turn this dinner into a working session. From the satchel propped on the chair beside her, she withdrew a large blue file with neon-coloured page markers stuck to the corners and passed Jay a photocopied line drawing of a church. It was an invitation to a recital at the First Presbyterian on El Dorado and Vine on 19 July 1956, where, 'Robert Hamilton, Minister of Music, will be playing three choral preludes including "Wachet Auf", Bach's Preludium und Fuge in A moll... ' and Jay recalled how his mother had clasped her hands to her aproned breast while he obediently read the *Stockton Tribune* aloud. 'Organist Robert Hamilton guided us up and down the ladders, in and out of narrow passages, through three storeys of organ. Everywhere were pipes, nearly 4,000 of them, for the First Presbyterian Church has commissioned one of the biggest organs in the San Francisco Bay area. Square wooden pipes that a man could climb into, little metal ones no larger than a pencil. Its sixty-five ranks can imitate each section of a full orchestra. It boasts a total of 3,621 pipes and is built from six different kinds of wood – yew, oak, ebony, pear tree – ' Jay had stopped, but his mother gestured impatiently, she was drinking in the detail and nothing was superfluous. 'It comprises a great organ (3.5' wind) and a swell organ (5' wind), a choir organ (4' wind) a solo organ (12+20' wind), pedal organ (5' wind), a pedal organ, seven swell pistons, seven choir pistons, seven solo antiphonal pistons, seven pedal pistons, seven coupler pistons, seven master pistons, eight general pistons. Air supply is furnished by blowers of 5 and 10 horsepower.'

Robert had come down from Berkeley a week early, summoned by a letter from Miss Edith Dicker who had funded his musical education since childhood. A benefactress with an excess of enthusiasm for Handel that culminated in her $11,000 donation of the organ, she had inherited her fortune from her father, one of the rare successes that flourished in Stockton's otherwise bleak historical landscape. Mr Edward Dicker had pitched up from Colorado in dogged pursuit of gold but was saved by the pitfalls that befell most of the desperadoes when a combination of innate cunning and latent vision kept him out of the mines for long enough to realise that the future lay elsewhere. By the 1950s he presided over a modest empire of music halls that stretched from Stockton to Bakersfield, though this was small consolation for the loss of his beloved Amelia who produced a daughter but died delivering the placenta, a tragedy for which Miss Edith Dicker begged forgiveness every day of her life.

After a rehearsal at the church on the eve of his performance, Robert had called round to Miss Dicker's house, leaving Jay to wait in the afternoon shade of the stoop, licking a sticky tumbler of lemonade. A sulking cat stared him down from the wicker chair until he snagged its paw underneath the creaking rocker and it fled mewling into the shelter of a topiaried hedge. Behind the window, Miss Dicker sat in a Chesterfield while Robert delivered an impromptu piano recital, skimming through a medley selection at her breathless request. A wasp sauntered into Jay's tumbler in the ponderous heat. He upended the glass, watched it overcome by a drowsy surfeit of sugar and he understood perfectly, as the insect gave up its struggle, that this was the kind of experiment boys needed to do – it was the route to invention and discovery, an examination of cause and effect. Even Miss Dicker's God had done it, creating the seven-day wonder of the Earth and then sending the floods to destroy His handiwork.

When Robert came back out to the porch he'd forgotten that Jay was there at all, so lost had he been in the warmth of Miss Dicker's admiration, standing in the doorway while she urged him to abandon his academic career for the worthy alternative of a permanent musical directorship at the First Presbyterian. It was an ambition she pursued until her death three years later, when, after a lifetime of squandering her father's music hall money on the church, she left a will which startled the community by insisting on a cremation and named Robert as the second beneficiary (after the First Presbyterian), with the condition that he give up his studies at Berkeley and dedicate himself to the state-wide musical future of the church. But Robert dismissed the offer, along with the request that he personally scatter her ashes over the San Joaquin River, so that Jay – by then aged eleven – and his mother, were charged with this responsibility and dutifully carried the urn in a blanket all the way along Fremont down to the deep water port, where he tipped the ashes into the water with a gentle splash. His mother held her hat against the wind and blessed herself in a hasty attempt to dignify the proceedings, while Jay looked down from the quayside into the rippled concentric and reflected on transience, how unreliable and alone we are in life even as in death.

A week after the recital Jay had fallen ill and was burning a fever when he heard the click of his mother's heels along the kerb in the after-school hush. Passing an indifferent hand over his damp forehead, she led him to the box room where he lay babbling in the shade and he remembered a moment of sudden sobering, when he turned his head to where she sat on the edge of the mattress, looking not at him, but at the photo of Robert's graduation on the dressing table, the exaggerated protrusion of his ears beneath the mortar board, the thin-lipped crease of his smile. She sighed, trailing a loose hand along the faded blue coverlet and Jay understood instantly and forever, that he was nothing more than an unfortunate accident and in this *precise* moment, he solved the mystery of what was wrong between them, why his mother often seemed startled that he was there at all, why he seemed invisible, why she felt no impulse to hug and touch him the way she did Robert, why her concentration drifted off in the middle of his enthusiasms.

Fortunately, survival is instinctive at eight years old, so Jay didn't waste time ruminating but learned quickly not to be a nuisance, for the distance between maternal indifference and neglect was indeed small. From then on, he took care not to be a burden, to be responsible and helpful, because he understood the precarious nature of his position, especially when the recently widowed Mr Donald Franklin began stopping by in 1958, diverting his mother's attention with flowers and cookies. Jay could sense the enormous risk of a man in the house to whom he would be just someone else's brat, so he was ruthlessly attentive to his mother's needs and never, ever the source of worry or complaint, none of which was particularly challenging for a solitary and capable youngster. Eventually, Mr Franklin stopped calling and Jay believed he even sensed a certain relief in his mother's demeanour. He grew up acclimatised to a great deal of independence, so busy was she between writing letters to Robert (first at Berkeley and then later at

UCLA), working in the supplies store on Wheeler and polishing the pews at the First Presbyterian, where Jay suspected she sometimes shook her head at her own stupidity and asked the Lord how, at the age of thirty-seven, when she knew she was married to a good-for-nothing wastrel, she could have gone and gotten pregnant again. But she stood by her son and Jay admired her grim determination, her staying power; it was an early lesson in how women will stick around and do their duty, submit to the tyranny of children and the thankless demands of domestic obligation.

By the time he was a teenager the preoccupation with his disjointed family had waned and Jay had become focused and purposeful. It had all started to fall into place one lunchtime in summer 1961, when he pedalled to a halt as a truck veered round a downtown corner and unsettled its load, spraying crates of tomato high and far, spattering the parked cars and the sidewalk with a trail of crimson splodge. A passing child clapped his hands and Jay, at thirteen-and-a-half, found that the ever-increasing circles of his exploration had finally delivered him to his destiny. The air was heavy with the sweet stink of crushed fruit on the corner of Center and Weber where winos sat in crumpled suits on the stoop of the Rescue Mission, scratching underneath the caked sweatbands of their battered hats and sucking on cigarette butts as they mumbled through stories at the Door of Hope, spitting out slivers of memory not yet dissolved by furtive brown-bagged sips, before slipping into a dribbling doze broken only when the soup-bearing ladies of the church prodded them into a reluctant wakefulness. For two whole summer months, Jay sat astride his cycle soaking up the store of their fragments and incoherence: tales of mangrove swamps and rust belt winters, the piss-soaked floors of countless correctional facilities, the gut-crushing thud of a truncheon, the loose rattle of smashed teeth in a broken jaw.

And as he listened to their accounts he saw the trail of connections lost along the way, the mothers, brothers, sisters, wives
and children whose names had been forgotten, obliterated by
the liquor or ground into the dust as the thread of their lives
unravelled. Time itself unspooled around street corners as the
storytellers stumbled through a repertoire of emotion that
swept them along on alternate waves of laughter and tears,
finally subsiding into the silent contemplation of a familiar
misery, punctuated by the memory of fleeting respites in the
soft arms of transient women. A nodding stillness fell heavy
and airless on the stoop of the Mission. The audience shifted on
crates or shuffled by the doorpost, grunting and chiding,
seduced by the broken rhythm of other lives, locked in the grip
of the stories that petered out into the tattered wreck of the
present.

Jay noticed that the quiet ones sometimes surprised
themselves by drifting into speech, as if they had just
uncovered a voice long forgotten. Like Luther, with a
permanently sealed eye and a palsied trembling in his left hand,
his grey-black skin cracked like the hide of a prehistoric animal.
It wasn't clear if Luther realised he was actually speaking when
one day he cut into a lull on the stoop and took them all to a
field in Michigan thirty-two years earlier, where he was lying
flat on his back in a yellow plain of maize that stretched out as
far as you could see, watching the cloud of cigarette smoke
hover and drift against the dazzling blue of the sky. He'd been
charged with looking out for his little sister Maisie, who was
playing with a stick in the dirt track that cut through the vast
corn belt. Two-and-a-half years old in a pink and white dress
and a ribbon in her braided hair, a little vision of loveliness
tracing patterns in the dust. Luther could hear Maisie's sing-
song as he lay there daydreaming of Delecta, a girl with amber
eyes and a come-on kind of smile, he could picture her sucking

on a piece of candy across the slow rumbling bustle on Lafayette, leaning against the shop window on the corner outside Johnson's place, like she was waiting for a ride or something, she's only twelve or thirteen, but Delecta's already got everything in the right place. She takes a step forwards, looking like she's going to cross the road when a pickup trundles past and Luther stubs out his cigarette and swallows hard, heart thumping, she's so close he can smell her hair oil and the next thing there's an almighty crash and tyre screech. Luther opens his eyes, hears a man's wail like a cat screaming in the dead of night and he's on his feet, crashing through the corn that slashes at his face, the fifty yards feels like miles, but it's too late. Little Maisie is lying there bent in broken-backed ugliness like a discarded doll, her dress pushed up over her tummy and the driver is staggering around in the dust, shrieking oh-god-oh-god-oh-god-oh-god. He's Johnny Fletcher, sixteen years old, making deliveries in his daddy's truck, he swears he didn't see Maisie, she just shot out in front of him like a little pink rabbit, but Luther whacks him to the ground, he is yelling at him to stop his wailing, he puts his hand over the boy's mouth, his eyes are rolling and he's pushing and scratching. Luther jumps up and kicks Johnny Fletcher hard in the stomach, stamps on his lolling head again and again and again and then he picks up a rock and would have smashed it into the boy's crushed face, but as he raises his arm Luther hears the distant rumble of a vehicle, looks up to see an approaching dust cloud. He stumbles over to Maisie, reaches out to close her dead eyes so she won't see Johnny Fletcher's bloody face, he pulls down her dress, covers her up and starts running.

They caught him before nightfall, it wasn't difficult with the haphazard trail he had left cutting across roads and sneaking through backyards in the neighbouring town and after they'd cracked Luther's rib, they slung him in the cell. Later, much later, they let his daddy come in to rattle the cold bars and spit in his good-for-nothing face, yelling it was a good thing his son was locked up or he'd rip him apart with his own bare hands.

He might as well have, for Luther raged and fought his way through seven years for attempted homicide in the County Correctional facility and then a couple of years on the outside where he drifted through backroom boxing rings all the way east to New York State, until a robbery gone wrong landed him in Sing Sing and a windowless cell that was three foot wide. Talking was not permitted and the stink from the buckets was so bad he could hardly breathe, so he just hollered at the walls until the guards came and worked him over. And each time Luther passed out he hoped it would be the last, that death would deliver him, but they always left him within an inch of his life so Luther could remain tormented by the shame and the memory of Maisie laying there like a road kill.

The Mission men nodded in the midday silence. Luther's head sagged heavy on his chest. Down below the stoop, Jay ran a slow finger across the baking chrome of his sunburnt handlebars, waiting for the continuance, for some sign that Luther might take up the thread. 'Oh Lordy,' sighed a man in the doorpost and Miss Ellison appeared on the threshold, her fingers pressed tight in bony prayer. 'The way of the transgressor is hard,' she intoned and Luther shook himself, rose from his crate and shuffled off with a furious limp. Miss Ellison blessed herself with a shiny pocket crucifix and raised her frown out across Weber into the horizon, beyond the world of the lost and hopeless that sat beneath her on the stoop.

Jay carried on listening to the stories into the fall, through the dry winter and late into spring nights after school, oblivious to the occasional taunts and offers the men flung his way. He maintained a stubborn silence and eventually they stopped noticing him at all and he faded into the background, the sidewalk clutter, he could arrive and disappear without comment. He never asked a question, for he learnt that if you listened long enough, you heard everything you needed to know. Even on the cusp of adolescence, he was already unusually attentive, he could hear how all the Mission tales merged and shifted in the telling, filtered through the unreliable membrane of memory. He saw how the men absorbed each others' pasts, so that they could no longer distinguish between beginnings and endings, between truth and falsehood, ownership and possession; it was a great dissolution of privacy as they raided each other's lives. He saw that the driver was the compulsion to tell, a desire to be anaesthetised by the narrative drone. They were trying to put a structure on their miserable chaos and there was something happening in the repetitive transactions between teller and listener, some kind of delicious comfort in this communion of souls, an absolution perhaps, or something universal that he did not yet comprehend. The Mission men furnished Jay with a permanent vision of failure, of those who floundered in the face of adversity, the groping power of the disenfranchised who have nothing to offer but their stories. They gave him a sense of the mean margin between winners and losers, the crushed backbone of the American Dream, the mumbling Hispanics, the negroes with their nicotine palms and the ones who disappeared without warning, shuffling off into the night to repeat their histories or maybe towards the mirage of a future in which they could transcend mistakes.

One parched afternoon in the spring of '62, a green Cadillac screeched to a halt in front of the Mission and a brown-suited man with oiled hair stepped out and raised a felt hat, stood with both arms spread wide before the crowd. 'Hey boys, 'member me?' he said with a broad grin. The stoop-sitters blinked in silence. 'Billy Jennings,' he prompted. 'Billy-no-good? Spent two years sitting on my ass on that there stoop?' One of the Mission men lifted a finger and pointed at the fender that shimmered in the heat. 'That there yourn, Billy?' and brown-suited Billy slapped the green bonnet. 'Yup, she's all mine. Bought and paid for,' and the Mission man cackled, 'Yooooooh Billy,' and the others crowed and slapped their knees and Billy said, 'Got meself a real job, a real girl too. Getting married in the fall,' and the audience was howling and whooping and pointing and waving and Billy spun round on an angry heel. 'Losers,' he spat into the dust and jumped back into his car, roared round the corner in a barrelling cloud of exhaust and was gone.

Later that summer Jay's hunt for stories led him up the steps of Stockton Library on Saturday mornings, slipping behind a shelf whenever he saw Miss Purdy chatting with the librarian, hiding from the seal of their approval, this teenage boy who was reading books instead of hanging around street corners. He embarked on a methodical search through the limited resources of the fiction collection, a voracious trawl through Melville, Hawthorne, Wharton, James and anything else he could find. It seemed that these writers were trying to inhabit souls. It was a vast endeavour of chronicling, a meticulous enumeration of characteristics and responses that might eventually equate to the essence of a man and Jay marvelled at all this bewildering intensity, but he knew he was on to something. At the end of the summer, he sat in a sunbleached corner of the library and concluded that there was only one story and an endless variation on the theme: it was all about the crippling struggle for love.

The following day as he stood at the foot of the Mission, he understood that, for him, the process of story-gathering was neither experiential nor empathic: he could unpick, he could see, but in the end, he still didn't feel. He had a good nose for plot and could dabble without ever breaking the surface. Unimpeded by an excess of emotion, Jay was free to skate on the surface of others' realities, peeling back the veneer with scalpel-like precision. He suspected even then that he could see more clearly than others, untroubled as he was by the hamstrings of emotion and so he gathered up all the stories he could find because he knew, in the way that we feel the first stirrings of a great idea, that one day he would be able to do something with them, although he wasn't yet sure what that thing would be.

'How are your grades?' asked Robert in the fall, flicking through Jay's high school math on the stoop while their mother rocked in quiet contemplation of her sewing. It was already apparent that Jay had inherited nothing of his brother's scientific talents and to make matters worse, his interests gravitated, apparently, in the wrong direction. Robert stood in his vest, both hands resting on the back of his mother's cane chair. The birdless air was thick with the humid promise of night. 'Why aren't you taking physics and chemistry?' he asked and Jay wondered if it was the rip in Robert's shirt that made his mother smile, or the pleasure of touching his still-warm clothes. 'A little less of this stuff would help,' said Robert, pointing to the Whitman cradled in Jay's lap.

'You should listen to your brother,' said his mother. 'He always came top of the class.' She bit down on her thread and offered up the shirt. 'Thanks, Mom,' said Robert, leaning down to kiss her cheek. Her hand slid up to pat the lingering side of his jaw and in that moment, Jay could see the outline sketch of a family in the hour before suppertime, the bread-winner returning home, ruffling his son's hair on the stoop, bending down to kiss his wife's face, a low sun burning a dull orange in the belly of the sky on any summer evening, anywhere in America, in 1962.

By the end of that year, Jay had constructed his personal destiny: he would be both story listener and story maker, it would be the perfect substitute for what he apparently failed to feel but what left others enthralled. He would capture landscapes of loss. He would collect other people's stories – his own seemed a paltry thing, very explainable, a natural progression of mundane events, so he would net other tales like butterflies, stretching the fossilised wings to get a better view of the variant strains of a species, little vignettes of humanity lined up in a display cabinet. This was Jay's homage to the human mystery that surrounded him, the best he could hope for and the most he could do, a sort of veneration, looking through the glass that separated him from others.

• TEN •

'Christ, I haven't seen that since the day,' Jay exclaimed, reaching across the table to grab a sheet of paper protruding from Dana's file. She raised a startled head as if she doubted the wisdom of this move, but he had already pulled the page towards him.

'The *Los Angeles Times*,' he murmured, running a finger along the photocopied banner. 'Monday, March 8, 1971.'

'I'm sorry,' said Dana. 'I didn't mean—' her voice almost a whisper as if volume could damage.

'"UCLA professor found strangled,"' he read the headline aloud. '"A UCLA professor was found strangled in his luxury West LA home, apparently by three men who then stole his car to escape, LAPD said. Robert Hamilton, 40, a professor of logic, was found on the bathroom floor of his $80,000 home by his brother James Hamilton. Mr Hamilton said he saw two men drive away in his brother's car. Police issued an apb for the men."'

At an adjoining table a cluster of dark suits were united in a subdued laughter. He looked up at Dana. Her face paled, as if the lights had dimmed. 'They got his age wrong by a year,' said Jay. 'And I never quite understood why in one small paragraph they chose to emphasise the "80,000 dollar home". But you know I searched the paper for what seemed like ages until I finally found it right here on page 8, in the metropolitan section. I sat for hours with the paper on my lap, read it cover to cover and over again. I can still remember every single little item. It was the day Captain Medina was charged with murder at My Lai and Nixon said: "I seriously doubt if we will ever have another war, Vietnam is probably the last one." There was something about Norman Mailer and *Harper's* – a row about an article on sexuality. And a thirty-one-year-old nun was implicated in some bizarre plot to murder Kissinger.' Dana smiled. He could see she was being indulgent now, she had already done her research, she didn't need him for any background colour.

'And of course the Manson trial was going on – there was a report from the previous day's court testimony from a psychiatrist who said Manson was like a father figure to the three girls involved in the killings,' he added. 'There seemed a hidden irony in everything, even the temperature.'

'I went to see it,' she said. 'Robert's house I mean, at 3840 North Beverly Drive.' Jay stretched a flat palm on the tablecloth. He would have liked to slap her impudent cheek. 'Of course it wasn't easy to find,' she continued, 'the address is kind of misleading seeing as North Beverly Drive becomes Coldwater Canyon. But I figured it out. It must have been a real sanctuary for him, way up there in the foothills.'

'The police transformed the house into a crime scene,' said Jay, and lifted his glass, letting the tepid wine flood his mouth. 'I remember the strangest things about that morning. Like for example, it was 43 degrees when they arrived just after 7 am.' He flexed his table hand. 'Memory is wonderfully selective. We cling to the peripherals in moments of stress, little slivers of reality that construct a defence against the trauma.'

Dana inclined closer, gripping her pen and he withdrew in his seat, overtaken by a dyspeptic unease. It was a base and relentless curiosity that propelled her on from the details of Robert's life to a morbid preoccupation with the circumstances of his death. Not yet, he thought, not yet, for he needed a moment, would like to stall her assault on his past, feeling vaguely unsettled by the black satchel that squatted on the chair beside her like a loyal dog.

'We are jumping ahead,' he said as the waiter arrived. Dana opened her mouth as if to protest but had the good grace to stop short, she had done time with anguished relatives who baulked at her unseemly romp through the buried treasures of their past. She laid down her pen, reconciling herself to an obedient patience, allowing him a brief respite from the avalanche of sensation that she held in her files.

'*Bon appetit*,' offered the waiter with a bow and Dana scrutinised her lifeless sole. 'I wanted to ask you about Robert's personal papers. If he left any diaries or letters?'

'Salacious details you mean?'

'I just wondered—'

'My mother handed over the contents of Robert's office to UCLA without consulting me,' said Jay. He remembered arriving at Dodd Hall a week after the murder to find a stack of grey card boxes in the corner of Robert's office, the desk drawers open and piles of documents arranged neatly on top. A woman with a long brown plait knelt on the floor. 'What—' said Jay and she looked up with a start. 'Can I help you?' she asked with a smile but he could not think what to say except to spread his bewildered hands. 'I'm his brother.' 'Oh,' she said, scrambling to her feet, 'I'm so sorry. I wasn't aware that the papers were to be checked before going to Special Collections.' Jay shook his head, turned away.

'So there was nothing of note at the house?' asked Dana.

'Most of the papers he left at home were academic. Pages and pages of formulae and notes. Robert was always scrupulous about discretion. In fact I'm not sure anyone he worked with even knew the truth about his double life.'

'Really? I would have thought—'

'Remember the political climate in the 1950s. The Cold War, the nuclear threat, McCarthy on the loose, the panic about ICBMs, Senator Wherry kicking up a storm about homosexuals in government positions – America wasn't just looking for reds under the beds, they were witch-hunting for sexual deviants. And there was Robert finishing up his PhD at Berkeley.' Jay looked up from the bloody side of his steak. 'Did you know that one of the first things Eisenhower did when he took office in 1953 was to rule that homosexuality was a reason to be kicked out of a government job? The fact is, the so-called "purge of the perverts" was a much bigger deal than the hunt for communists. So it wasn't like your Turing up at Cambridge where the environment was relatively tolerant of homosexuality.'

Dana ignored this snipe, making expert incisions in the side of her sole.

'The American Psychiatric Society officially listed homosexuality as an illness in 1952,' he continued. 'People often assume that psychiatrists are more liberal than the rest of the population but this has rarely been the case. In the 1940s, for example, the president of the APA publicly defended the concept of segregated psychiatric hospitals for blacks. And it took twenty years for homosexuality to be de-listed. In 1973 the APA finally accepted – by a small majority, mind you – that there was no evidence to support the definition of homosexuality as an illness. So they substituted it for the wonderfully creative term "sexual orientation disturbance".' He smiled, reaching for his glass. 'I remember a patient called Marvin, whose doctor decided he suffered from this newly invented disorder. This was San Francisco, mid-seventies and Marvin was an aspirational transvestite who used to dress his tomcat in pink booties and a diamanté collar every Sunday and parade the boards for the tourists on Pier 39. An exhibitionist who didn't mind getting the odd kicking.'

Dana laughed and twirled her glass in a manner that was almost flirtatious. He cut a small section of meat onto his fork. It is always satisfying to amuse a woman, he thought, biting into the pink flesh, and he was relieved to see that she ate heartily, unlike those women who proclaimed their hunger only to jab fastidiously at their plate. Jay had noticed a correlation between this lukewarm appetite for food and a lack of enthusiasm for oral sex, indeed for the whole carnal experience, as if these reluctant nibblers were incapable of abandoning themselves to any physical pleasure, so completely consumed were they by body dysmorphia.

'So what did Robert think about all this?' said Dana.

'Oh, he wouldn't have cared about the APA, he had no time for psychiatry and he didn't believe in pressure groups. He wasn't interested in carrying the torch for some political agenda. Robert had the arrogance of those who know that they are smarter than everyone else.'

'But he did write a letter once,' she said putting down her cutlery to rustle through her files. 'In fact I've got the copy somewhere. In 1964 Robert wrote to a Judge Woodmansee on behalf of an ex-student who was a transvestite and had been indicted on indecency charges. Here it is,' she announced, sliding an indexed page out from the lower half of the pile. 'Robert writes: "Josef Stavrosky is a former graduate student of the Philosophy Department. He has worn cosmetics during the whole period of our acquaintance at UCLA and we are convinced this is his only social deviation. He has agreed to relinquish cosmetics and is willing to consult a psychiatrist as soon as either a clinic will accept him or he can afford private consultation." The letter is signed by Robert and a colleague.'

'That was a rare departure,' Jay shrugged and waved away

the offered page.

'What about Vietnam? I mean, he did help to organise a number of student teach-ins at UCLA.'

'That was a more acceptable majority situation. Safety in numbers. An easy outlet for any anti-establishment tendencies. He wasn't totally immune to cultural influences.'

'I think he might have been more of an activist than you realise—'

'Dana, people who weren't around at the time can be forgiven for believing that every campus in the country was up in arms over Vietnam. But I can assure you that wasn't the case. Berkeley managed to establish itself as both a centre of excellence and dissent, but down at UCLA anti-war demos were very pocketed and confined mostly to the liberal arts area.' He slid the page back to her. 'Robert had very little time for politics and he was *never* a militant gay. He certainly never intended coming out. He had no time for the false camaraderie of the gay community.'

'You think not even if he had lived?'

'Robert just wanted to be able to fuck who he wanted and not get arrested,' he snapped. Dana's arm froze in recoil from her glass.

Jay pressed a soothing hand to his temple and allowed a brief silence to linger, dismayed by the force of his outburst. 'Please excuse me, Dana,' he said. 'It's a long time since I've spoken about Robert to anyone,' he added. 'And it's proving more difficult than I thought.'

She nodded, lowering her head to her sole. But Jay was momentarily derailed, he'd always prided himself on being vigilant and sensitive to his own reflexes, it was a reliable way of predicting when clients were becoming intolerable and a sign that he should act to terminate rather than dwell on its origin. This had been the case, for example, in the summer of 1996, when Jay had been alarmed to realise that he was becoming aroused during his sessions with Robin, whose elaborate tales of promiscuity were so prosaic in their delivery and so cinematic in their detail, that Jay found himself struggling to quell his erection while Robin sprawled on the couch regaling him with stories of a prolific seduction which seemed to involve most of the women in his Whitehall office, as well as random females he met in bus shelters and in the elevator of his apartment block. Despite his best efforts, Jay came to envy Robin's sexual fantasies, the lurid accounts of his sexual conquests and the soaring inventiveness of his imagination. After three months, he had become uncomfortable with his reflexive arousal and the fact that he looked forward with anticipation to each session. His collusion was merely encouraging Robin to stay locked in the safe confines of his imaginary castle and Jay concluded that it was high time for reality and fantasy to converge. In the end it came as an aggressively handled acceleration towards truth and, although he knew that the confrontation would be anything but trauma-free for the client, he needed movement which was why he decided on impulse to pierce their complicity with an abrupt intervention: 'Robin,' said Jay, 'I think it's time that we talked about the truth of what is really happening in your life.'

He had broken the spell. Robin had lost his faithful audience, and he was furious in his humiliation, white rings of compressed anger circled his thin lips as he rubbed a clenched fist against his trouser leg. 'You think I'm making it all up?'

'Aren't you?' goaded Jay. 'Isn't this all wish fulfilment?'

'I'll show you,' muttered Robin and stormed out into Edwardes Square trailing the banner of his shredded dignity behind him. Resolution came and, as Jay suspected, Robin found a way to deflect his anger. It turned out that he was very fortunate to have selected a woman who wouldn't blow the whistle and go to the authorities, who was sensible enough to realise that it would be her word against his and therefore impossible to prove anything under the circumstances. After all, as Robin pointed out, she had spent the evening drinking with him in the Slug and Lettuce and then let him pay for everything, even the cab to her place, so he could hardly be blamed for ignoring her last-minute change of heart, and it certainly wasn't his fault that he couldn't sustain an erection and grew so angry at his own humiliation that he was forced to use a hairbrush to penetrate her. 'Anyway,' said Robin leaning back in Jay's couch, 'technically speaking it wasn't rape. And it's not like I was some stranger in a dark alley,' and 'NO,' he definitely hadn't developed a taste for it, he just wanted to crawl back into his fantasy life, he was never getting involved with real world women again.

'I wondered if you ever discussed his sexuality with Robert?' Dana asked.

Jay lowered his head to the plate, cut a tepid triangle of flesh. 'We argued once,' he said, surprising himself with this spontaneous admission that he was now forced to embellish. 'I remember exactly where it was, we were walking down from Dodd Hall to Westwood Plaza, I was staying for the weekend, it would have been 1970 I guess, an exceptionally warm spring. There were students all over the grass, some outdoor tutorials on the lawn outside Royce. Robert had a bad bruise around his right eye. I told him I was concerned for his safety.'

He could feel Robert's clammy hand on his shoulder and hear the mocking whisper, 'Aren't you grateful to have a fag at close quarters to study? Didn't your hero, the great Freud himself, say that there was much to learn from the study of our deviants?'

'How did he respond?'

'Oh, he shrugged it off. Robert was very stubborn. But he was also expedient. He wasn't going to leave personal diaries lying around and I'm not sure he thought his liaisons worth writing about.'

'So no letters, nothing?' she said, quietly giving up on her sole.

'Dana, do you have any idea what it was really like to be out there? To be gay in the 1950s and '60s, stalking the night with the queer bashers and the vice cops hiding in the bushes? The LAPD used to have a field day. You could get arrested for just holding hands with another guy. If you were convicted, you were registered as a sex offender. Believe me, you were not going to leave a roadmap of your encounters in your office.'

Jay placed his cutlery in a final perpendicular. He knew, of course, curiosity had nibbled away at his teenage heart during Robert's weekend visits to Stockton, until he was finally compelled to investigate his brother's midnight disappearances during homecomings that were becoming more sporadic as the lure of music lessened. Jay could hear the sound of a ball thudding against the baseboard, he used to sit on the stoop on the first Friday of the month, watching every car that crawled by in a wide sweep of the tight corner, his mother's shadow just inside the screen door, her manic humming fading in and out of the hallway as she changed a skirt or a blouse two or three times, primped her hair in the mirror, dabbed a crumpled tissue on her lips until the creases filled with an even slick of matt colour. 'Well, well,' she'd murmur as Jay passed the ball from hand to hand in a firm drop.

11.48 pm on 3 June 1963 and Jay could bear it no longer. He lay in bed fully clothed, waiting for the creak of Robert's foot on the floor as he crept along the corridor, pausing outside their mother's bedroom door, which she always kept ajar at a precise

30-degree angle. He listened for the soft latch click, the faint squeak of the screen door hinge, the rumble of Robert's car engine and then he leapt out of bed, ran tiptoed through the kitchen and out the back, trailed the Mustang on his bike through the crisp night, flying southwards on Pershing where a plump moon bulged in a velvet sky. It wasn't difficult to keep up, for Robert was a zealous kerbside crawler, always trundling along as if every trip was a scenic drive. Jay sailed along the deserted sidewalks, wondering where his brother could be headed in this town that had nowhere to go and then the Mustang indicated right, a slow blinking red and a series of turns that took them down towards the harbour, the air fresher now with the night smell of water. Robert drove a half-mile along Port Harbour Road where a line of clapboard shacks petered out into scrubland and warehousing. The dark silhouette of grain silos loomed against the sky. Everything here was of monstrous proportion. Light pricks from the north side of the channel flickered on the black water and the night was full of creaks and clunks and whirrs, the sleep sounds of industry.

The car stopped. Jay ducked behind a bush and lowered his bike to the ground. He crouched down, watched the car door open. Robert got out, stood still, white shirt glowing under the faint wash of a streetlight, head turning slowly sideways as if he was checking the air. He took a cigarette from his shirt pocket, the match flame spit-flashed in his glasses and he started to walk down the road. Jay followed on foot against the bushside until Robert stopped dead, his cigarette glow cutting a slow downwards sweep. He coughed. To his right, Jay saw the outline of two figures who seemed to glide across the road, like shadow actors slipping soundlessly onto a stage. Robert turned, rounded a quick left corner towards a windowless building, the shadows followed and Jay crept along, loping so close to the ground that he almost collided with a man who emerged suddenly from the sagebrush in front of him. Jay lunged sideways, scrabbled up the steep scrub slope on knees and scraped hands until he was level with the corrugated roof of a warehouse. He lay there holding his breath, but the man had disappeared. All around him was the rustling of night creatures in the undergrowth, barely audible against the clash of iron and steel clanging across the water.

Jay crawled through the needlegrass towards the building until he came to a ravine where the ground fell away in a sharp thirty-foot drop and there below, was Robert's white shirt kneeling on the ground, his head buried in the crotch of a slim shadow who stood impaled against the warehouse wall, arms splayed in crucifixion pose, his black face turned to the side, where, a few feet away, the other shadow stood smoking silently at the corner of the building under the weak illumination of a wall-mounted light bulb. Robert's head jerked backwards and he struggled to his feet, wiped a hand over his mouth as the second figure, taller and much more substantial than the first, crushed his cigarette with a swift heel and moved toward him in a smooth sidestep from the corner. He muttered something inaudible and Robert rummaged in his wallet as the shadow fumbled with his belt, one large hand pushing Robert's face against the warehouse wall, so that all Jay could see were his brother's trousers around his ankles as the shadow thrust into him. A low whistle cut through the air, the two figures melted into the night and Robert turned, panicked, clutched at his clothes and hobbled off stage.

The morning after he had followed his brother to Port Harbour Road, Jay sat in the kitchen while his mother beat up a Sunday treat of pancakes in her bathrobe. At 8:46 Robert emerged with a sheaf of scribbled papers, rubbing his tired eyes. Jay sneaked a glance as he sat down at the table, wondering how it could have taken until now for the unarticulated truth to present itself. A furtive examination from behind the cereal box revealed to his astonishment that Robert's secret was everywhere, you only had to look at the pout of his thin lips, the exaggerated arch of his eyebrow, a glass-eyed bulge that was magnified and bovine, the limp hand passing over his thinning film of hair, a weak-wristed awkwardness with the teapot, the fastidious dance of manicured fingers on the curve of the sugar bowl: all his brother's substance had vanished overnight, he was a sapped presence, forever altered.

' "Breakfast of Champions",' Jay whispered, reading the logo on the Wheaties box. Robert's mouth had just swallowed another man's cum. Robert's asshole had just gripped another man's dick.

'F – a – g,' he mouthed experimentally over his cereal, electrified by the impulse to shatter the breakfast stillness, the radio jingle, his mother's egg-cracking hum. But he was suddenly overtaken by the sharp well of an imminent tear and, blinking urgently, he ducked behind the cereal as a burst of gunfire exploded in his head. A muted staccato of truths ripped through the air and Jay, for the first time, confronted the humiliating depths of his charmlessness, how he had consistently failed to captivate his distracted mother and his gifted brother, how he would never step inside their magic circle of love, his unworthy face would always be pressed up against the window pane. And now, there was new evidence of his own inability to seduce, as well as a further betrayal in the careless splurge of Robert's affections on deep channel nigger boys, those anonymous shadows that could effortlessly turn his head and lure him away, while his own flesh and blood failed to engage. Their secret warm-blooded pulse throbbed through the kitchen, the house, his life, and Jay realised that what he had lost was the sum total of everything that he had never really had: his father, his mother, his brother, even the abandoned dog who expired the moment she was entrusted to his poisonous embrace. And he knew, with absolute certainty, that he had somehow failed forever in the great struggle for love, his fractured heart, its missing beat.

• ELEVEN •

'Maybe it's an unfair question,' said Dana, 'but I wondered if Robert had been a patient of yours, what would you have thought of him?'

'You want me to psychoanalyse my own brother?' My God, thought Jay, was there no end to her insolence? He was growing tired now of all this eagerness, or perhaps it was boredom, coupled with the St Emilion that seemed a little heavier than usual. Dana was blustering about with these questions, like a child in an attic kicking over boxes to see what might spill out.

'I'm curious. Can you separate the brother and the analyst?' Her brazen stare indicated that she was unapologetic, encouraged by the wine, or just naive enough to think that he might be prepared to oblige. She was looking for the kind of psycho-soundbite that had lately become so popular with biographers who think analysis is like personality profiling, another tool for the neat dissection of a life.

Three days after the murder, Jay had started clearing out the desk in the corner of the living room at 3840 North Beverly in an attempt to try and impose some order on his fractured world. There was a bald patch in the carpet where Robert's foot had worn down the brown weave during the hours he spent hunched over the desk. He would raise a hand in greeting without turning round and then immediately forget there was anyone in the room. Once Jay sat in the couch for five hours watching the white downy strip of neck bent in the loose shirt collar, listening to the studious sounds of genius – the irregular scratch of pencil like an animal scuttling across the page, the whispering crackle of paper, the occasional creak of a hardback, the clunk of a closing volume and then the silent consideration, where the concentrated atmosphere around Robert's motionless head seemed to vibrate and Jay would find his breathing quicken, as if he was struggling for air, but when he inhaled there was nothing, just a burning desperation accelerating into skull-splitting panic. And then the pencil moved again, Robert wrote, and Jay gasped, a future came back into view.

Jay was squatting on the floor sorting documents into a cardboard box when Detective Green stopped by. He tapped out a cigarette while he flicked through a loose-leaf folder on Robert's desk. 'You read this stuff?' he asked, jerking a head at a fragment of calculus.

'No,' said Jay. 'Robert was the mathematician.'

'Your brother took a lot of risks, know what I'm saying?' Green said from behind the yellow flicker of his Zippo. 'Ran with a bad crowd,' he exhaled. 'You keep well clear if you've got sense,' and Jay's protesting head shot up in amazement.

'Hey, I did time in Vice,' Green sighed, scraping a paper clip underneath his fingernail. 'The fags in Pershing Square?' he shook a disgusted head. 'You wouldn't believe the stuff that goes on in this town.'

'I guess it's an unfair question,' said Dana, twirling the stem of her glass.

'Analysis is internal and suggestive,' said Jay, as the waiter removed their plates. 'To paraphrase Wittgenstein, it provides us with explanations that many people are inclined to accept. So what would matter in analysis is what it would suggest to Robert.' He reached for the water, running his tongue over the roof of his mouth that was unaccountably dry.

'I wondered what you made of his promiscuity? His preference for anonymous black men?'

'Robert liked to feast with panthers.'

'Oscar Wilde,' she said with a smile, keen to demonstrate that she has recognised a reference.

'My brother had a surprisingly well-adapted appetite for risk which fits perfectly with the natural arrogance of the gifted. Cruising was both rebellious and safe. Robert could have sex in a late night park and none of his respectable friends would know.' He stared at her scribbling pen. 'And perhaps he found the concept of dominance thrilling, it was after all, a rare sensation for a man of his extraordinary talent. Perhaps it was especially exciting for someone like Robert to experience that dominance from the kind of man that he would never be.'

'So you would say that his homosexuality was a sort of power play?' she asked. Seized by the frisson of indelicacy in a sibling analysis, Dana had decided it was worth running the gauntlet of his disapproval. Jay squeezed his palm around the wine bottle, he would like to smash his glass on the table between them, but instead he ignored her textbook simplicity and poured them both some wine.

'Was Robert always only interested in men?' she asked and he startled both of them by laughing out loud.

'You want to know if his homosexuality was a sort of compensation or if he simply didn't like pussy?' She flushed and looked down at her fidgeting hands, grappled with the lid of her pen.

'I'm sorry to be so crude,' Jay continued with an indulgent smile. 'But you see, Dana, as a heterosexual – if I might be so bold as to presume your preferences – you view Robert's homosexuality as an aberration, a deviation from the norm.' He waved aside the beginnings of her protest. 'You are flying back to LA tomorrow, so I don't think we have time for political correctness, do you? The point I'm making is that you think sexual orientation is loaded with significance. You think it is defining. You think this is the stuff that biography is made of. And you want a ringside seat where the subject's pants are down.'

Dana opened her mouth but stopped short at his raised hand; she was where Jay wanted her. Let her pay some price for her source. 'Freud once wrote to a concerned mother that being homosexual was certainly no advantage, but it was nothing to worry about. It was not an illness, just a malfunction in the sexual development. So you are in good company, my dear. Of course, Freud's rather mild remarks had some unfortunate consequences – I'm thinking here of the psychiatrists who administered aversion therapy and ECT to gays in America in the 1940s and '50s. You see, Dana, the sinister side of understanding is the desire to correct. This idea – that homosexuality is a variation in sexual development that must be accounted for and explained – is what results in so much lengthy analysis. And, I should add, so much tedious detail in biography.'

Let her stew, he thought, watching Dana purse her lips. In her biography of Turing she had diligently paraded her bibliographic research into the environmental and cultural factors at work in sexuality, but Jay knew where she really wanted to go: down to the raw depths, to the places she could not go alone, she wanted to follow Robert just as Jay had followed him whenever he was home, watched him lavish attention on a host of nameless strangers all through 1963. Down Port Harbour Road or further afield, at dead ends where the harbour gave way to cropland, or in dirt tracks in the valley sink scrub that cut through what used to be the wetlands, Miss Purdey had sadly explained, until the irrigation programme dried out millions of acres across San Joaquin County, and the songbirds and the ducks, the shorebirds and peregrine falcons all disappeared. Even when Robert returned to UCLA after the weekend, Jay found that he carried on ghosting his brother's haunts and finding new ones. It was like searching for bugs under rocks, not difficult when you knew their habits. Once he'd stopped beneath the hull of a moored freighter at duskfall and stood astride his bike watching three men swap a bottle in the dust, flicking stones at a coconut that was balanced on a crate. One of the men turned his head and offered Jay a go, with a sideways wink at the others.

'Come on, boy, let's see what you're made of,' the man urged with a gap-toothed leer, his eyes locked on Jay's deliberation, his brown arms snaked with purple tattoos. Jay wheeled his bike a little closer. The man slugged on the bottle, slid a slow hand into his trouser pocket, a slab of tongue wetting his lips and Jay stopped, scanned a cautious eye from the leader to the coconut.

'Reckon he's jus' chicken,' said a voice behind him and Jay spun round to see a fourth man snuffspit on the ground ten feet away, a stained red bandana tied around his hairless skull. 'Reckon he's jus' a pretty boy,' he said, dangling a curl of rope that was twisted round his left wrist. Jay jumped hard on the pedals as the men rocked with laughter and took pot-shots at the spinning wheels of his bike, one stone hitting blade-sharp in his shoulder but he rode away as if his life depended on it and didn't stop once in all the eight miles home until he staggered breathless through the back door. 'Your dinner's in the oven,' his mother yawned from the couch and Jay bent over the steaming plate, his thumping heart subsiding while she opened a magazine onto a photo of Jackie Kennedy's face obscured by a black veil. She shook her head and turned the page, clucking her sympathetic lips.

Despite his best efforts, Jay still agonised over the detail of his brother's nocturnal transactions. It seemed vital to know the sexual specifics. Was Robert always the sucker or sometimes the suckee? Did a cock taste of piss? Did he always swallow? Did his asshole ever bleed? Did he kiss on the mouth? How many in one night? Did he drive home sore and sated? Did he long for more? Had he ever fucked a woman? But there was never a way of having the conversation and Jay struggled with the discomfort of being at his most puerile on those nights when he lay sleepless, peopling the night with a scripted melodrama of revulsion and hyperventilating rage, all saturated colour and vivid detail and freely available fucks. But he still braved a return every Saturday night, creeping out of the house after midnight to trail the shadows emerging from Robert's underworld, he watched them fucked and paid for and disappear, leaving the night animals to reclaim their territory. One February night he saw a tiny kit fox for the first time, its long legs making a timid emergence from some culvert den, its white belly, silvery winter coat and blacktopped tail just visible in the brilliant starlight. He saw plump little kangaroo rats scuttle into abandoned pipelines in the scrub, he saw skulking coyotes and once even, a mountain lion – a procession of endangered species congregating in the hard-won peace of the night.

All through the winter, he watched endless blow jobs, boys wiping their cum-streaked cheeks, men fucking in pairs, lone peepers who paid a few crumpled bills to choreograph a pantomime of tricks while they stood in the shadows biting down on their cigarettes. Once he even saw a writhing daisy chain of four men fucking, their bare asses ghostly in the moon-seared fog-night. He watched youth on age, black on white, white on white (but never black on black, he assumed it must happen elsewhere), and then one spring night from his incline hiding place, he watched a kneeling blond boy blow a fat grey-haired man in a tired suit, both of them oblivious to the low rumble of an approaching car freewheeling down the sloping dirt track, until the sudden flood of headlights captured the frozen figures of the communing couple. The car doors flung open and a pair of college kids jumped out, chased after the blond but were too drunk, laughing too hard to tackle the steep hill so they turned back to the fat man and chain-whipped him across his shoulders until he collapsed with a single bone-splintering scream into a foetal curl, trousers entangled around his fleshy knees. Jay watched his unresisting judder as their boots thwacked the small of the fat man's back, his belly, his head, until a sudden spray of blood spattered the trouser leg of the kicking boys and they stopped and staggered back to their car. They stood, swilling from beer bottles, gasping and swaying and then one of them took out his cock and pissed, giggling, on the head of the fat man who lay beaten and unconscious, while the other picked his wallet clean. They lingered uncertainly for a moment, as if there was something they might have forgotten, and then jumped back into the car and drove off in a wheel-spinning rev.

Jay waited in the sagebrush inhaling its sharp smell, watching black blood seep from the fat man's mouth. A fog wisp drifted over his smeared face. He considered the possibility that the man was dead, that he had witnessed a murder. But he stayed, braving the cold, wondering whose side he was on. He needed to see the end, to witness the consequence, to know who it was, exactly, that had it coming. Then the fat man stirred, resurrected himself with difficulty to a sitting position and leaned back against the warehouse wall. He fumbled in his pocket, found a crushed cigarette, held it unlit in his blood-soaked hands and sat immobile for so long that Jay thought he might have passed out again, when the sudden wail of his heartache shattered the still night and Jay looked down, horrified to realise that his own right hand had somehow slipped like a pickpocket inside the warmth of his trousers and was cradling his damp cock. He stumbled to his feet and ran fast and furious to his bike, pedalled at heart-bursting speed away from the flooding desire that had almost swallowed him unawares, racing along Center, along Vine, through the deserted streets, away from his flirtation with the outcast and delinquent, from the disintegrating line between voyeur and participant and the depravity that threatened to engulf him.

Back home, twitching in his terrified bed, Jay forced himself to confront his ambivalent response to Robert's promiscuity and this manworld, and he knew he was vacillating between hypnotic fascination and a ferocious disgust. He lay underneath the stifling blanket and probed right down to the core of his anxieties: the fear that his own curiosity might overwhelm his loathing and propel *him* towards these downtown couplings, that all this thirst for specifics might one day lead to someone else's cock in his own asshole.

In June 1964 Jay saw a group of boys in the schoolyard sniggering over a picture of gay men posing outside the Tool Box bar in San Francisco, torn from *Life* magazine's photo spread immortalising a 'sad and sordid world'. His private theatre was being turned into an art form, it was leaking into the public domain and Jay resolved to cease his nocturnal investigations, fearful that his adventures might be corrupting his consciousness. Like a searchlight bleaching out more wholesome fantasies, they had shifted his gaze to linger on classmates in the changing rooms, stolen glances at limb-swinging negroes on the street and so he took immediate corrective action. During his last two years at high school, Jay conducted a relentless predation on his female contemporaries with a controlled professionalism that was remarkable amongst his peers. It was a joyless and methodical exploration of girlish delights: the sudden squeals and giggles and squirming, the snake-silky hair, the damp pantyhose stifling his nose, the hidden folds of flesh that were alternately slimy and musky or else raw-dry to taste, the bizarre secretions and unexpected smells, their invisible comings. More than anything, Jay was astonished at all the cuddling they seemed to expect. He sat in the back row of Stockton Movie Theater with popcorn balanced on his lap while their scented heads pressed against his shoulder, these girls who demanded interminable hand-holding, impossible gestures of affection and thoughtfulness, the whole business of sex for them a completely different concept, their unquenchable thirst for caring, as if a man should have vast reserves of nurturing in him. They nestled and snuggled up to him like needy babies. It was all distinctly unsavoury and he understood nothing except that there was a vast potential for shame.

'You're right about Robert's archives,' Dana announced, patting her envelope file. 'There was no personal stuff in there from the early years. But that seemed to change in 1964.' She looked at Jay with a belligerent calibration, trying to assess what he might know. 'It's in the detail that seeps into the papers – a theatre programme, a postcard, letters – a growing casualness. As if he'd stopped caring as much about leaving a trail. I wondered if you'd noticed anything around that time?'

'You are forgetting I was just a kid. And of course I saw very little of Robert. He wasn't coming home as much then.'

'But you stayed with him in the spring vacation in 1964,' she insisted. 'He mentioned it in a scribbled response to someone's invitation. It was the year he moved into North Beverly Drive.

There's a mention of your name in a note signed "Ish".'

Jay smoothed his irritation with a palmed sidesweep of the tablecloth. He would have to be pre-emptive here; it was the only workable tactic. 'You mean Christopher Isherwood,' he said. 'He was a Regent's professor at UCLA around that time.'

Of course Jay had noticed the change. He remembered an April evening, how he'd known something was up when Robert had collected him from Union Station, distracted, excited and even smelling of booze at 6pm. They were 'going somewhere fun', he said, instead of back to North Beverly and Jay resisted but Robert ignored him. 'You'll like it, some different kind of people.' He veered off the freeway, twisting and turning through side streets until he pulled up untidily on a kerb somewhere in Santa Monica. Robert stood fiddling with his collar on the stoop when the door swung open and an older man with a flick of ashen hair over a tanned forehead said, 'Well, well, if isn't our little philosopher,' in an accent that seemed to come from the movies, looking not at Robert but at Jay. 'I am Christopher,' he said. 'And you must be Robert's baby brother.'

Robert beamed behind his oversize glasses, toting Jay like a gift for the host, pushing him forward into a crowded living room where someone stuck a tumbler of bourbon in his hand. Christopher laughed, drifted past, beckoning a playful finger at Jay.

'Are you a genius too?' slurred a voice in his ear and he pulled back, knocking into a side table and sent his glass clattering to the ground. 'Didn't mean to frighten the children,' said the man, leaning back against the door, licking his fleshy lips.

'Fuck you,' Jay growled, clenching his fists.

'Temper temper,' goaded the man and blew him a kiss. Jay lurched forward but found his arms pinned behind him. The man grinned. 'Where's your sense of humour?' Jay struggled free, found Robert in the kitchen chattering to a group.

'Let's split,' he whispered.

'What's wrong, past your bed time?' said the man with the fleshy lips and Jay could feel his face burn and his mouth go dry and Robert joined, flushed and excited, in the laughter of hyenas that reverberated through the house; he would fling his brother to the wolves just to make himself look interesting, offer him up as bait if that's what it took to impress his new friends.

'I think meeting Isherwood might have been a turning point for Robert,' said Dana eagerly. 'You see, up till then his notes are mostly full of maths and academic matters. But he started to attend Isherwood's talks and was even reading his novels, according to the library slips I found in the archives. I think he was hanging out with a whole new scene, something far more adventurous than what he would have been used to – parties, writers and artists, very bohemian. And of course there were a lot of interesting people on the gay scene in LA in the mid-sixties,' said Dana. 'Isherwood could have introduced Robert to David Hockney, John Rechy, Gore Vidal—'

'I'm sure the name dropping will make a wonderful sales pitch,' said Jay.

'No, no, that's not what I mean to suggest. It's just that you get the vague sense of liberation looking through Robert's papers from the time he met Isherwood.'

'Those people cared nothing for Robert. He was an amusing plaything, a geek, a groupie for a cast of self-absorbed mediocrities beached up in LA. But no doubt the references will help you sell your book.'

'So you think Robert's sexuality is irrelevant to his life story?'

'Please don't think me too patronising, Dana,' Jay replied, 'when I say that you yourself can read any amount of psychoanalytic musings on the relevance and meaning of homosexuality. You don't need me to outline them for you. So I will leave it to you, if you don't mind, to do the legwork, to go through the literature and pluck out what's useful. Or what might capture your reader's imagination. Isn't that what writers do when they stray outside the comfort zone of their experience?'

'So what's your view then?' she said with a sharpness that surprised him. This bold response to his face-slapping was impressive, like a snarling vixen who defends her corner from the baying hounds.

'I could suggest anything,' he said. 'Lack of fathering, no suitable male role models, over-identification with the mother-figure... I could say, as Freud did, that the infant is bisexual and that it is the influences in his early development that decide who will be the object of his sexual attentions and desires. I could even speculate that unsuccessful breast-feeding might have led to an oral obsession with sucking. I could say Robert had stalled in his development, stopped dead at the pre-pubertal stage, that he had never benefited from intimacy with his indifferent father, that his mother was stifling and dominant, that he was searching for his absent father in other men. In any man.' He shrugged and leaned back in his chair. 'Or I could conclude that Robert was entirely comfortable with his sexuality, his closetedness was just a sign of the times, a necessary precaution he took to preserve his reputation and his career. But what I *will* tell you, Dana, is that you are on the wrong track. Homosexuality didn't shape Robert. It is inappropriate in my view to view him through that prism. He might have spent time with a bunch of arty bohemians who sat around talking about sexual politics, but make no mistake about it, what was most relevant in Robert's life, what he loved, what consumed him *entirely*, was his passion for his work. He spent almost every waking hour at his desk with his papers. He was always working. He was obsessed.'

Dana opened her mouth and he waved aside her interjection. 'Have you ever known anyone like that? They are truly not of this world; they operate on a different plane. Ruthless with their time and their affections. They simply have no need of human distraction and the complication of relationships. They are on a mission, on a quest. That's all the meaning you need.'

Dana steeled her jaw with the look of a reprimanded child. 'What do you do to let off steam?' he asked with a gentle rap on the table. 'You run? You drink? You get laid? Maybe that's all there was to it. Robert worked fiercely hard all day and half the night and then, sometimes – I don't know how often, I wasn't living in LA – he would go out cruising and pick up a few tricks. Pershing Square, Griffith Park, wherever. He just acted on impulse and then it was over. Remember this was all pre-AIDS, pre-Stonewall even.'

The pen wilted in Dana's hand. She had the air of a crestfallen beachcomber at low tide, suddenly pale and overwhelmed in the small slump of her shoulders. Jay wondered if she was losing her grip on the evening, on Robert, on the whole project. Or perhaps she was just losing heart, the thread of her story elusive now, taunting her from behind a tree like a child who hides far too long till the seeker grows weary and gives up the search. She stroked the back of her right hand, a slow slide from knuckle to wrist and back again. Like the kind of comfort one might offer to the dying, as if such a gesture could provide consolation in the face of impending oblivion.

The waiter arrived to pour the last of the wine in the shifting silence that fell on the table. There was movement and bustle at the next table as the elegant brunette navigated a slow high impact return to her admirers after another extended absence. The men stumbled to their feet, one of them fussing with her chair, and for a moment she appeared startled, her hand strayed to her throat and there was a brief pause where Jay wondered if she might walk away, but she sat down and the table burst into animated chatter.

Dana tucked back a strand of hair and started flicking backwards through her evening's notes, like a Halloween child who runs home and dumps her bag on the table to check her trick-and-treating loot. The threaded beads around her cuff clinked against a small steel watch, a juxtaposition of ornament and function that struck him as distinctly unappealing. She reached for her glass of water and he saw the beginnings of a prim determination gathering about her lips. She had decided to cling on, she was not ready to capitulate, she was not easily deterred, her hand would be up in a minute with another answer for the teacher. She was still seeking what she had come for and why not, she was a researcher grubbing for useful versions of truth and Jay had something that she wanted. There was a certain robustness that he saw more infrequently these days, so used was he to spending time with the fragile and the lame.

'Did you ever think that Robert's promiscuity would get him killed?' she asked, low and fast.

Jay looked away over her shoulder, recalled a moment, kaleidoscopic, indescribably fleeting, staring up at the steep crest of Mulholland at dawn.

'It did occur to me. The thought crossed my mind.'

• TWELVE •

' "Gentlemen," ' said Jay, setting down his coffee, ' "it is a fact that every philosopher of eminence for the last two centuries has either been murdered, or at the least, has been very near it; insomuch that if a man calls himself a philosopher, and never had his life attempted, rest assured there is nothing in him." '

'I'm not familiar with the quote,' said Dana.

'Thomas de Quincey.'

A burst of laughter rose from a departing group who were shaking hands with the maitresse d'. Jay checked his watch. Although it was not yet eleven, the restaurant was thinning out.

'You want to hear about Murder Day,' he said and watched her hand slide across the tablecloth, a purposeful drift towards her pen, this insatiable appetite for detail and a beaverish conviction that she might one day make something useful of it. In the right hands, of course, Jay knew that it would all make a great story. But he did not believe that Dana was up to the task and he asked himself now, considering her alert composure, why he bothered to talk to her at all. Perhaps it was simply because, in thirty years, no one else had the vision to be curious, all they wanted was to glean what they could from Robert's model theoretic proofs, his extraordinary brain, desperately trying to unpick his brilliance.

'Sunday, March 7, 1971,' he began, considering the pricks of light reflected in the steel glint of his spoon. 'I called the LAPD just before 7 am. It took maybe five or six minutes for them to arrive.' An uncooperative windlessness hung in the early morning as he stood waiting on the drive. He had pulled on a pair of jeans and a shirt and then wondered if it seemed callous to have done something so pre-emptive as thinking to dress. A morass of black ants spilled out of an arid corner by his bare feet. There was no wailing siren, no flashing lights, just the slow deflating crunch of tyres as they parked both cars at the foot of the slope.

'I watch Detective Green and his boys haul out of their cars. They are not in a hurry. I say something, I don't remember what.'

Two uniforms disappeared round the back of the house while Detective Green emerged from the nearside car door. He paused for a moment and looked up into the trees, inspecting the hills from underneath the felt brim of his hat.

'The screen door to the back must have been open because the uniforms come back out through the front door. They call out to Green that the house is secure. I guess I'd assumed they would take my word for it, that there was no one inside.'

Green walked up the drive, stood on the threshold appearing to sniff the air and then turned back towards Jay, looked him over with a grey-eyed glance of cool appraisal. There was an investigative protocol to which Jay wasn't privy. No introductory preliminaries, no handshake, just a perfunctory confirmation of his identity.

'You hear your brother come home last night?' Green asked, as if in passing. A flat voice with all traces of accent ironed out. Jay shook his head. He had the vaguest memory of stirring to a sound in the night, but up there in the foothills there were often unexplained noises, sparsely populated as it was then, a dense topography of rustling raccoons and coyotes and bobcats, predators patrolling their nocturnal paradise.

'I think it was the car engine that woke me so early. I can't be sure. As soon as I opened my bedroom door I could feel the draught from the front door. They'd left it ajar. I ran down bare-chested as Robert's car pulled away, but I don't know if they saw me. I watched the car disappear down towards Coldwater Canyon. It was sometime after 6am Sunday morning and there was no one about.' He caught a glimpse of their fleeing outline, a confusion of limbs and clothing, a frantic fumbling in the front seat of Robert's Mustang, but all he could really see were the distinguishing characteristics of generic black. There were two, maybe three of them, it wasn't even possible to tell if Robert was in the car, but their hurry looked like the panic it clearly was. Jay understood immediately that he was witness to some crime and assumed a robbery, that Robert had finally got his comeuppance and been ripped off by some low-life rent boys.

'So you couldn't be sure exactly what you saw?' asked Dana.

'No.'

'Wasn't it still dark? I mean, March? In LA, in the early morning?'

'You want to know if I can be sure that I saw two or more black guys getting into Robert's car and driving off? You're wondering if I am a reliable witness or if I filled in the blanks?'

He watched Dana bite down on her lip, considering herself rebuked, this little girl playing detective who didn't quite have the stomach for his directness.

'It was only as the car disappeared round the bend that I realised I hadn't seen Robert. My first thought was that he must be still asleep in the house. That they'd stolen the keys while he slept.'

A sudden splinter of birdsong shattered the air and Jay turned on his naked heel in the drive. Behind him, the alders rustled and already it felt lighter, his eyes registering the creeping advance of dawn.

He didn't call out as he climbed the quiet stair to the landing. In the shadowed mouth of Robert's bedroom he could see the outline of the wardrobe, the end of the bed, a shoe on the floor, a heap of clothes bunched on the carpet. To his left, the bathroom door stood open wide, like an ominous invitation.

'The police made their way up the stairs, slowly, almost leisurely it seemed to me.'

It felt like stepping onto a film set where the actors were jaded and bored with the script, anxious to step into a new plot. Detective Green shouldered the doorjamb, staring down at the bathroom floor. Robert's head was facing towards them, his legs in an outward sprawl either side of the WC. Green hunkered over the body in the centre of the camera-snapping crime scene. A slow rivulet of sweat trickled down between Jay's shoulder blades. He swallowed hard, struggling to look anywhere but down to where Robert's purple face was leering up at him.

'His face was... engorged, suffused with blood. His skin was pricked with a starburst of blood vessels. The whites of his eyes were speckled with red spider veins, as if a creeping disease had infected his face.'

'I didn't mean to—' croaked Dana, in a vain attempt to stall this grim narrative, but Jay shook his head. She was still, poised on the brink of where her insistent curiosity had led her, right into the private chamber of someone else's horror. She lowered her lashes, had the good grace to appear humbled by what she had come looking for, this unseemly romp through his past, like a heedless child that tramples a flowerbed in her single-minded pursuit of a prize. She blinked as if stemming a tear, but it was too late now for her to affect a cheap remorse, Jay was made of tougher stuff and he would not stop until it was over.

' "The nose and mouth are oozing a very minimal amount of blood," ' he quoted. ' "The sclerae show multiple patchily punctuated areas of hematoma. The ears are congested. The entire face is congested." '

Even now, thirty years later, Jay could reproduce the autopsy report word for word, with all its misspellings and grammatical transgressions. The language contained an incredible understatement of how Robert's face had been, but a coroner, of course, would have seen it all before. On 10 March, 1971 Jay hesitated on the corner of Broadway and West Temple, looking up at the grey stone of the Hall of Justice, so familiar as a downtown landmark where, two years before, he'd stood watching a gaggle of long-haired girls chant support for Charles Manson who had been incarcerated on the fourteenth floor jail during his trial. Steeling himself underneath the arched entrance, he pushed through the revolving doors, hurried across the marbled hall and down the cool sweep of stairs to the basement, stopping by a drinking fountain to splash his face. A middle-aged woman sitting at a small desk administered the brisk bureaucracy of death with cheerful ease. She scanned Jay's written request, didn't blink at his relationship to the deceased and she didn't offer condolences. For her, it was business as usual, another day, another dreary death. He waited on a brown plastic chair, contemplating the tremor in his left hand. Men and women sauntered in and out of the Coroner's Department like any other office workers, there was no sign that the city's violent crime was taking any toll. Perhaps, at ten murders a week, the novelty was wearing thin.

The receptionist called out his name. Jay approached her desk and signed a receipt for a copy of file number 71-2755. Outside, the sidewalk was empty in the midday sun and he sat down on a stone ledge, steadying himself against the dizzying sound of traffic and the prospect of what might be revealed by the documents he held in his damp hand, the transcript of the events that had occurred in Crypt Number Three, the secrets of the dead prised from their stiff fingers.

The body is that of an adult male which appears to be slightly older than 40 years, weight of 155 pounds and height of 65 1/2 inches. The body has not been embalmed and it shows a marked rigor and livor mortis.

In the end, reading the report had proved to be a therapeutic experience. Jay sat shaded from the stark spring sun by a squat spray of palm, immersed in the bland language of observable fact, stripped bare of sensationalism, a syntax that wouldn't inflame, words that insulated from the passions they regarded. It was a reassuring, orderly reconstruction of the advancing footsteps of death. *The body is opened by a Y-shaped incision*, Dr Alexi Hererra announced on page 2. Jay imagined the gowned pathologist raising his gleaming scalpel over Robert's cadaver as he began his chronicle of indisputable fact, a methodical account of all that he could say he was certain: the weight of the brain, the heart, the state of the organs, the sum of collected data that revealed absolutely nothing about the man, or, indeed, the truth.

'What can be said at all, can be said clearly,' Jay quipped, but Dana met his smile with an apprehensive glance. He has, of course, unsettled her with his macabre quotes and she did not appreciate the irony, that her beloved Vienna Circle would have considered the autopsy an entirely appropriate form for a dead scientist. Dr Hererra produced a most diligent document, unsullied by emotion, untainted by intimate connection, neither cinematic nor dramatic. There was nothing about what it felt like to watch, nothing about the raw experience or what Jay had to endure when he beheld his brother naked on the bathroom floor. He'd been horrified by how lifeless Robert looked when, only minutes before, he had cradled his warmth in his arms, how unrelated he seemed to the brother he knew, bathed in the fluorescence of death. It was the first dead body he had ever seen.

'His face was cyanosed,' said Jay and sipped from his glass. Dana made a small inquiring movement of the head. 'The medical term for a face turning blue,' he explained with relish, savouring the term, its poetic precision but she simply nodded, didn't even write it down and this, he reflected, was precisely what lay at the heart of Dana's shortcomings as a writer. She was not bewitched by language, she didn't linger over words, their unfathomable secrets, she was not enthralled by linguistic propagation, by the miracle of inventiveness that can spawn such gems as 'cyanosed', she didn't savour the gift of a sentence, she did not delight in how a word defines the object and becomes forever inseparable from the concept. And *this*, of course, the very essence of humanity, was the universe that Robert had set out to conquer. He would reduce language to a quantifiable process, peel back the skin to reveal a luxuriant semantic abundance, pare it all down to dry matter in a series of logical clauses. He would conduct his own autopsy to excise its tumorous ambiguity, classify and grade the natural exuberance, demystify the miracle, bag it up and explain it away. It was a deflowering, this desire to harness the fundamental power of language and it was preposterous, Jay thought even now, Robert's claim that he could account for all this; it was tantamount to a rejection of language as irrational, illogical, inexplicable, impure. Perhaps it was a response born out of fear – a fear of the inexpressible, of all that cannot be explained.

'You know,' Jay mused, 'the irony was that the autopsy confirmed Robert was very healthy. A little overweight towards the end, but he never worried about running to fat, he was above concern with such trivia.'

In fact, it was Robert's surprising flabbiness that had so appalled Jay when he'd found him on the bathroom floor – the unembarrassed paunch, an unpleasant excess of flesh that had been so efficiently disguised by clothes, but was so striking in his nakedness.

'But he was very particular about his hands and nails,' he said, recalling the meticulous banality of the report: *The hands, fists and nails are unremarkable.* 'Like most musicians, they were always his best-maintained feature. Sometimes he'd come home from hours on the organ with his fingers aching from so much practice and my mother would massage his hands with a little oil. She taught him how to manicure with a metal file.'

When Jay was seven years old, Robert had ruined the surprise of collecting him from school by deciding on impulse that he would teach him to play the piano in the abandoned hush of the assembly hall. Jay sat with his legs dangling on the stool, staring down at the black-and-white expanse, struggling to decipher the flood of instructions, the unintelligible symmetry of a keyboard, its unreachable extremes. It was difficult for Robert to tolerate his little brother's clunking mental process, brimming as he was with an enthusiasm for moulding him in his own likeness with a handful of careless hours here and there, expecting him to deliver the goods in one session, like the half-hearted way an owner might train a dog. 'If you just concentrated, you could do much better than this,' he sighed after a few minutes, but Jay's breath was coming short and shallow as his clumsy fingers blundered about on the keys, his vision blurred by the threat of angry tears. 'Listen to this,' said Robert impatiently, shunting him to the edge of the stool and flexing his elbows to play, a masterful, effortless three-part invention that filled the empty hall with an extravagant spill of notes, every floorboard resonating with the glorious complexity. Jay placed a delicate finger on the underside of the piano to feel the vibration as Robert's transformational hands flew over the keys, his head bent in concentration, consumed by the magnificence of his own outpouring, the impact he had on the world, the sheer magic of his gift. He played on, the lesson forgotten, Jay's presence, in fact, forgotten, so that the reluctant pupil could slip down unnoticed from the stool and sneak out the door, running all the way along the perimeter fence to the bike shed, cutting through the gap onto the street where a warm breeze lapped against his cheeks. He rode blind, a frenzied pedalling that must surely one day yield some result, but was, for the moment at least, directionless, spinning, burning with random intent, his ears throbbing so hard that he thought his head would explode and his heart seize up for want of beating.

'The police took one look in the bathroom and they made up their minds,' Jay continued, watching Dana's pen glide across the page.

'Your brother usually bring his boys back here?' Green said as he knelt over Robert's body, his eyes travelling slowly around the room.

'How do you know about that?' asked Jay.

Green jerked a thumb at the jar of Vaseline on the washstand. 'You pick up a few things after twenty years on the job.'

He pointed to a twisted white skein of cloth underneath Robert's bruised neck. 'Recognise that? Or the tie?' he indicated the brown and purple striped ribbon that stuck out under Robert's shoulder.

'He was wearing it last night.'

'Show me where you were,' said Green, rising to his feet to follow him across the narrow landing into the second bedroom.

The contents of Jay's jeans pockets lay on the bedside table where he had dumped them the previous night. The keys to his rental in San Francisco, his student ID for the SFSP, some loose change. A round-trip bus ticket for Tuesday that he wouldn't now be taking.

'The body condition was described as viewable in the report, but even the undertakers couldn't disguise the face.'

In the days after he read the autopsy Jay had been obsessed with the physiological minutiae and had found himself poring over *Gray's Anatomy* in the library, examining the facts, like why each lung might weigh a different amount, what was meant by poorly concentrated bile in the spleen, how the body is reduced to the sum total of its components, how it all added up, with no missing parts, the incredible fragility of life.

He turned away, scanned the depleted restaurant, but nothing could distract from the relentless onslaught of remembrance. *The skull shows no evidence of any trauma. The only unusual feature is edema.* He could hear the wheeze of the saw above the sound of the subsiding chatter, smell the acrid burning stench of splintered bone as Dr Hererra hacked through Robert's skull and prised open the tabernacle of genius. *The brain is markedly congested and weighs 1530 grams, which is way above normal.*

Average brain weight, Jay subsequently discovered, was 1400 grams and it seemed extraordinary that exceptional ability could not be detected in its wet grey tangle. Had Dr Hererra guessed he was in the presence of a pristine intellect? As he watched the scales settle, did he calculate the cost of all that was now lost to the world?

The heart, Jay recalled, closing his eyes, *weighs 40 grams. The cardiac chambers are normally developed. The valves are smooth and pliable.* As it quivered on the cold steel dish, that vibrant dripping heart that had pumped a furious energy, could they read the signs of all those nights in Griffith Park, Robert's mouth impaled on a black dick, his fingers groping for some new experience? And could they read the imprint of his mother's love, skewered now by grief thirty miles up the road in her little duplex? Such a paltry thing to need, 340 grams of love.

On the last page of the coroner's report someone had scribbled:

Detective Green requested anal smear.

And then a final typewritten addendum: *There was no semen present.*

'We buried him at Oakwood Memorial. It was a closed casket.' Jay had stood by the graveside imagining Robert's corpse patched up with an artless needlework. He assumed they didn't need to take a great deal of care with the stitching on cadavers. 'My mother didn't look, she wanted to remember him the way he was.' As a child particularly, Jay suspected, or perhaps those times when Robert laid his head in her lap on the couch at 1152 Woodward and she soothed his brow in the evening calm. Jay lingered in the doorway, witnessing this quiet transaction of love beneath a 1956 calendar that had the same picture of the blind gaze of the Statue of Liberty on every page, a quiet confirmation of stasis. His mother smiled down at Robert's still head, his eyes closed, breathing deeply under the caress of her smooth-browed peace and the regular stroke of her palm as she streamlined the pressures of his greatness. And it seemed to Jay that all three of them could stay that way for hours until he finally drifted into sleep doubled up on the floor, imagining he too was swooning under the gentle pressure of his mother's hand.

'I'm wondering—' Dana hesitated. Jay waited. She has done this before, stirred up mud in a pond and learnt to tread carefully, to be wary of prodding a nerve with a forensic enthusiasm that might juggernaut over sentiment.

'D'you think,' she said, leaning closer to the table, 'that the police investigated the case properly?'

Jay ran a firm quick hand across the tablecloth in an effort to soothe his annoyance at the suggestion that she could somehow breeze in and spot something that everyone else has missed.

'The LAPD's antipathy for homosexuals was well-known, but what do you really expect a couple of detectives would think when they arrived at 3840 North Beverly Drive? Picture the scene through their eyes: a naked white guy lying strangled on his bathroom floor, no signs of forced entry, a known gay with a taste for cruising in the badlands of downtown and picking up black guys. What they thought when they stood in that bathroom was this: Robert knew the risks. He was careless. He took too many chances. The cops did as much as you could expect. They went downtown, hassled a few known degenerates round Hope Street, Pershing Square, all the usual hang-outs. They got all the verification they needed about Robert's habits. They found his car on Spring Street but there were no prints that they could match. It was a dead end.'

Afterwards in the kitchen, Detective Green scratched at his chest while he dictated his summary report to Lieutenant Rosenbock who wrote it all down sitting at the table. Jay sat staring at the chequered lino, fingers inside his pocket tapping his thigh. He was waiting to be told something, some explanation of what the cops believed had happened, although they of course knew no more about the incident than he. All through the morning he kept hearing the mournful loop of 'Wachet Auf', a most unusual occurrence, for he had never shared

Robert's affection for Bach. It was extraordinary, he mused, how trivial detail looms so large and vivid in memory, the stubborn adherence of commonplace in recall, like the clear articulation by his third grade teacher that she just adored apple sauce, or the cab driver in Houston who told him he'd once kissed a girl called Venus, the fleeting scent of wet grass or an unnameable flower, a particular shade of red. Jay could hear the crackle of the police radios that shattered the morning quiet of the house, the smack of peeling crime scene tape, the clicking camera shutters, the smell of cigarette smoke, the slow heavy footsteps of the night shift up and down the stairs, for they were all tired, the call had come in just as they were going off duty.

'Incident: Homi strangulation,' Green dictated, stirring his coffee. They were hours into overtime and he wanted to file the report as soon as possible. He leaned back and stretched his arms wide, his ass spilling over the side of the kitchen stool. 'Decedent is an instructor and Professor of Logic at UCLA and lives at 3840 North Beverly Drive in the vicinity of Mulholland Drive and Coldwater Canyon.'

Rosenback scratched away in his notebook. Green pulled a pack of cigarettes out of his shirtsleeve. 'Decedent's brother, Mr Jay Hamilton, was staying for the weekend and witnessed the below.' Green patted his pocket for a Zippo. 'Decedent arrived at 20:00 hours on Saturday evening when Mr Jay Hamilton was already there. Decedent said he was going for a ride downtown, as he sometimes does. Mr Jay Hamilton stated that he was going to bed and retired for the evening at around 22:00.' Green stood up, moved to the kitchen window and tipped his cigarette ash into the sink.

'There were a couple of quakes in the basin last night,' he said, addressing no one in particular. 'Felt the tremors downtown.' Jay followed his gaze out to the beginnings of a fair day; the thermometer on the deck had already inched up to 59 degrees.

'This morning sometime after 6 am,' Green continued, 'Mr Jay Hamilton heard a car start. He went out to the driveway and observed two or three male Negro occupants inside Decedent's vehicle. He did not observe Decedent.' Green swivelled towards Jay looking for confirmation. 'Mr Jay Hamilton then went upstairs to check on his brother's wellbeing and found Decedent lying on the bathroom floor. The LAPD was summoned by Mr Jay Hamilton and Decedent was pronounced dead on above date at time?' He looked over at Rosenback and cracked a large knuckle.

'07:25 hours.'

'Decedent was lying supine on the bathroom floor,' said Green, turning back to the table. 'Decedent was naked,' he added, lifting up the *LA Times* from the table in front of him to study a photo of Trudeau and his bride Margaret skiing on honeymoon. 'What about this,' he snorted, tapping the front page. 'Says here a Sacred Heart of Mary nun conspired to kidnap Henry Kissinger.'

Rosenback lifted his large square head and grinned, expertly flicking his pen between index and middle finger. Green folded the paper and let it fall back on the table, took a deep puckered drag from his cigarette.

'There was fecal matter on the bathtub and on Decedent,' he said. 'A small jar of petroleum jelly, or Vaseline, was noted to be lying on the bathroom washstand.'

Jay set his jaw against a sudden swell of outrage at the filth and grime that surrounded them. It was typical of Robert not to notice how slovenly it had all become: the kitchen with its scuffed lino torn at the edges, a multitude of old footprints browning the white squares, the table top encrusted with scraps of solidified food, the window pane where someone had elbowed a view through the irregular smears; but Robert, lying dead upstairs on the bathroom floor, would dismiss such trifling considerations, operating as he did on a much higher plane and now the squalor of his personal circumstances was revealed for all to see, the naked spill of his flesh sprinkled with his own shit.

'Let's hear it,' said Green, resting a hand on Rosenback's shoulder. The lieutenant bent his head over the report and opened his mouth.

'Detective Green?' A uniform interrupted from the threshold and Green raised a silencing hand while Rosenback duly read aloud what he had written.

'One more thing,' said Green. 'Mr Jay Hamilton stated that Decedent was a known homosexual.' Three pairs of eyes turned expectantly to Jay who straightened up in his stool.

'Yes,' he said, with schoolboy reluctance.

'And had a particular preference for male Negro companions?' Green prompted. The audience watched and waited. Jay nodded and looked away.

'Add all that in,' he said to Rosenback who sat with his mouth agape.

'Ready to remove the body, sir,' said the uniform.

Green assented with a sideways gesture of his head and said to the lieutenant, 'Note down that the house was not secured at 13:05 as police investigation was still in progress after the body was removed from the scene.'

Even in the methodical chaos of a murder investigation, a certain flatness filled the house. The detectives seemed more incurious than Jay had expected in the execution of duty, but that might have been because there were no signs of forced entry or struggle, no sign of beating or assault or rape, no robbery that they could see, except for the stolen car. Any money taken would have been all that was in Robert's wallet – forty bucks tops according to a cursory glance at his bank account. Slowly Jay had realised that this murder, for all its remarkable rarity in his day, was mundane for them. And there were no victims. No children, no wife, no lives destroyed but that of a man who was old enough and wise enough to have calculated the risks. As he stood behind Green watching the gurney's slow progression down the drive, he began to understand that this murder was of a type, an unsolvable type and that Robert, who had mattered so much in life, would find a democratic levelling in death. Jay had seen the toe tag before they zipped up the body bag.

After they finally left, he sat for a long time on the deck in the unseasonable warmth while birds rustled in the alders and a golden lizard picked its jerky trail along the planks before it vanished into the undergrowth. By mid-afternoon, the sky had cleared and Jay watched a private parade of memories unroll all around him, but all of it was happening somewhere outside his emotional range, as if the force of Robert's death had silenced his world, and he wondered if it was like having airplane ear, where everything is muted until it pops and you shout in the transition.

'Jay, I'm so sorry,' Dana said. He stared down at the pale crouch of her ringless hand that now covered his and was seized by a sudden longing to lift and stroke it along the side of his face, like a mother might trace the contours of her child.

'Yes,' he said, because he could not immediately think what else to say. His hand slid out from under hers, raised itself towards her cheek in a fleeting gesture that could be construed as encouraging and paternal and might even invite her to tilt very slightly into his touch if he hadn't let it fall back to the table.

'I sometimes feel a bit like a dog at a bone.' Dana admitted with a mawkish smile, an infuriating twitch of the mouth's extremities, as if a half-hearted apology might disguise her true investigative zeal.

'You need to be single-minded. To find your story.'

'To find the truth,' she corrected.

'But what is the truth in a life?' he replied. 'Even Napoleon admitted that history is nothing more than a fable agreed upon. Remind me how that famous little syllogism of Turing's goes?'

'Turing believes machines think,' she enunciated, reverentially as a prayer. 'Turing lies with men. Therefore machines do not think.'

• THIRTEEN •

Dana excused herself and made a slender retreat to the ladies. Jay had registered the reflex glances of other men when they arrived at the restaurant: Dana was keeping herself well, with the attentiveness of someone who is still available, although he had noticed her unmanicured hands, the kind of grooming detail that women like her neglect, like their arrogant disregard for a trim bikini line. But somewhere at the centre of all this self-possession would be the footprint of a man, for Jay had long ago concluded that the fatal design flaw in female psychopathology was their susceptibility to the male. Alive or dead, current or ex, real or imagined, there is always a man at the centrepiece of a woman's life. It is the ruling object, the magnetic north and the killer blow that sucks them dry: the lump in the couch, the bundle in the crib, the architect of a fractured self-image.

Rose was a recent case history in point. She had come to Jay complaining of loss of appetite and insomnia after her house was burgled while she was away for the weekend. She felt violated by the thought of a stranger standing in her bedroom, touching her pillow, rifling through her possessions. She confessed to Jay, eyes averted and appalled, that she imagined the burglar fingering through her underwear drawer and now she couldn't sleep for wondering what he had looked like, how he smelt, so she lay awake at night waiting for his return. His presence had invaded the house, she longed to know the colour of his hair and eyes, his name, the sound of his voice and she felt that if he did not come back she would surely lose her sanity. Jay suggested that her fear was based on her own desire to have been present when the burglar was there – that it was, in fact, a rape fantasy. The intruder had rejected her by coming at a time when he knew she wasn't there, it was a confirmation of her unattractiveness.

Rose admitted that it was seven years and three months since her fiancé had broken off their engagement. She had retaliated by rendering herself invisible as punishment for her own inadequacy and smeared a dedicated landscape of misery all over her days. 'What shall I do?' she sobbed. 'I can't bear it anymore.' Nor, it seemed, could Jay, who had originally thought Rose might be a candidate for his short story collection, but had since revised his opinion and therefore decided to dispense with their therapeutic alliance by giving her some sound advice. 'I'm going to be very frank with you, Rose,' he said as she stared at him through her jagged fringe. 'I am going to tell you how to take charge of your life.' She nodded, in concentrated anticipation. 'You need to get a makeover, a complete overhaul. And,' he added with an encouraging smile, 'you need to get laid.'

The waiter returned with the paperwork. The restaurant was virtually empty and Jay realised that he had missed the finale of the temptress and her consorts, so distracted was he by memory and recall. He checked his watch, he would be home by midnight to prowl around the dark confines of his study wondering how to proceed with Cora's story.

'It feels like we've had so little time to talk,' said Dana, sliding into the banquette. She had retouched her lipstick and run a brush through her curls and in the flickering light, Jay noted a suggestion of pink along the cheekbone, a sliver of tongue wet her lower lip, and he wondered if, when her head hit the pillow tonight, she might well ask herself whether or not she should have slept with him. He imagined the questions that would nag her restless sleep: Would sex with a psychoanalyst be like fucking a gynaecologist? Would she be just another clitoris past its best? Would he be able to tell if she was faking it? Would he be able to read her sexual history in the taste of her wetness and would she feel, when his fingers slid inside her, like she was strapped in a consultant's chair, her stirruped legs quivering about his head? Or might Jay be the consummate lover, the kind who could turn to her in an elevator and between the ground and third floor bring her to the brink of a desperate yearning? Would he anticipate her transient fantasies with a sudden fuck in the pre-dawn? Would the imprint of all past lovers be obliterated (he estimated low double digits) and would he close the departing door and leave her aching for more?

Jay doubted that Dana makes the first physical move. He wondered how she liked it.

'Maybe Jay, you might have some time tomorrow morning before I leave?' she asked. Now, at the end of the evening, as the restaurant shed its last diners out into a light sleet, she was worried that she had been hasty. Their imminent separation cast an urgent pool of light over what hadn't been won and the prize became all the more alluring in parting. Jay was the closest Dana would ever come to her subject, she could feel a good source slipping out of her reach. But he was done with her pestering, her earnest questions and he wished now to be alone, the whole business has sapped him of energy. She waited for his answer, leaning expectantly across the table and she seemed to Jay to occupy an extraordinary amount of space, as if she had somehow grown more substantial over dinner. It was tiredness, he thought, an extraordinary fatigue that had enveloped him.

'I'm afraid I have a client appointment first thing in the morning,' he said, standing up, although it struck him now with certainty that Cora Miller would not show up for her 8 am appointment. In fact, he thought as he lifted Dana's satchel, he did not now believe that Cora had gone to her doctor but would have somehow managed to make it home to sit all night hunched and hyperventilating in her living room, staring at the floor. A street light bisected the darkness; the ansaphone sound of Larry's voice confirming he's on the red-eye Friday and looking forward to seeing her. 'Miss you honey,' he would yawn before ringing off but Cora would no longer hear, a fierce roaring in her ears that drowned out everything but the senseless muttering of her own distress calls.

'Let's get you a ride,' said Jay, his offer sounding like a curt dismissal as they stepped out into a wet slap of wind. Dana shivered and turned up her collar and Jay had the sense that Robert had fled, his binding presence dissolved in the midnight rain. A clutch of unavailable cabs rumbled westwards in a hiss of spray. He stepped forwards onto the kerb, a light mist beading his face as he scanned the eastbound traffic across the street. Dana stood behind him under the awning, her arms cross-wrapped tightly around her body to fend off the cold, and he was reminded of Cora sinking down inside her coat this afternoon. He recalled her fifth session where she had presented him with a detailed and colourful account of a second dream. Cora was playing on giant grey boulders in a yellow sea and had swum out to a distant island where she found a colony of giraffes. She pleaded with a mother giraffe to borrow a baby, which she tucked to her breast secured by string and swam through the yellow sea back to the mainland. 'The next thing I knew is I was in some sort of military operation in Asia, holed up in a villa with all this elaborate technology and surveillance devices. I was there to rescue some mountain children, but we were losing the battle, the terrorists were multiplying so I decided to cut my losses and sneak out of the house. But I forgot that it was school-going time. Down the mountainside were snakes of children being led to class by armed and masked men. They were like hundreds of dots of colour getting closer and closer, singing that song kids sing in Club Med, "Oh la-la, le mini club est là". I lay on my side behind a broadleaf bush outside the house. The men shouted instructions and the children stopped right in front of my hiding place, they were picking at each other, looking round and I thought *please please* don't see me and then a boy of about six slowly raised his finger and pointed at the bush, and I knew it was my eyes that had given me away. The men dragged me out and the leader held up a garrotting wire and I woke up screaming.'

A sheet of rain struck Jay's cheek, he heard the sudden wail of a police siren and at that precise moment, he realised with an exquisite force that he had found his story. Of course, he smiled at the blue light speeding past, it was there all along, the seed had lain in quiet germination all through these last weeks and was now ready to burst into bloom. He could feel the plot building, light breaking behind closed lids, he could see the outer limits, his fingers barely touching the keyboard, for Cora's story would write itself. He could almost hear her communing with him, illuminated in the corner of his room like the artist's muse.

A lighted cab bore down upon them. Dana lingered in the open door, but Jay was impatient to be gone now, maintaining a steady distance like driving two chevrons in front. 'I wish you the best of luck with your book,' he said shaking her hand with a bright finality, he has already been more than generous with his time and would like to hurry her along. There was another woman waiting for him, he could already see the lowlight of his purring screen. He closed the door firmly on the evening. Dana waved through the streaked window, turning her head to keep him in her departing view but Jay had already started walking quickly westwards to Edwardes Square, gripped by an unexpected and definite anticipation.

PART TWO

The end is where we start from

T. S. Eliot

FOURTEEN

At 8.47 am, Jay stood in his first floor study considering the emergence of a still dull day framed in the window. At the northern boundary of Edwardes Square the slate roofs of tall villas cut into the dirty skyline. Grey sodden grass was just visible through the garden railings and on the street below, a parking attendant smoothed a clamping notice to the windscreen of a car in the residents' parking bay and stood back rubbing her hands under a lacklustre drizzle.

Jay checked his watch again: Cora was now forty-eight minutes late for her appointment. The possibility that she might never come back had reasserted itself at exactly 3.35 am while he was putting the finishing touches to her story. He had stepped out of a cab just after midnight and sprinted up the stairs, closing his thoughts on the evening with Dana. As he wrote, he could feel Cora's strength ebbing away and he remembered a dying fox he had found the previous year on the eastern side of the square, how he'd felt its heartbeat slow under a moonlit sky, blood trickling through its bared teeth as the fur cooled on the roadside, how the body seemed unmarked until his prodding shoe revealed the shattered skull.

Cora's case was now predictable within a narrow range of possible outcomes. There was still an outside chance that she would show up late to contaminate his story, but Jay didn't really believe this would happen. In fact, he was convinced that his client had reached the limits of her endurance and that yesterday's sudden flight confirmed she might be on the verge of any desperate act. Larry would be home in less than forty-eight hours, a fact of which Cora would now only be dimly aware. He could find anything when he turned the key in the door. Perhaps, Jay mused, watching the parking attendant disappear round the corner, reality will meet fiction in a slow melting waltz; perhaps Cora will follow the precise trajectory that he had outlined in her story, where all perspective evaporates, where past overwhelms present and devours the future.

Jay smiled, a broad full stretch of the lips. Even after all these years, it was still reassuring to be correct in a client diagnosis and prognosis, it was like the satisfying exercise of a skill, the steady defeating serve. Although he knew it could often be far more enlightening to be proved wrong. Popper's objection to psychoanalysis had been that it was not predictive, that the scale of its grand ambition as a theory to account for human behaviour was in fact its Achilles heel, so he relegated it to the status of a pre-science, reluctantly conceding that it might generate some interesting observations, but that it would not be a science until its theories were falsifiable. Robert, of course, could not even manage this grudging generosity. 'Allow me to introduce my younger brother to your unconscious,' he'd joked to a colleague on the stairs at Dodd Hall, his face flushed after the climb to his third floor office. An emaciated senior lecturer with a coffee stain on his shirt offered Jay a damp hand and an unmistakable sneer while Robert's high-pitched giggle reverberated in the airless stairwell. Jay gripped the metal banister as if to wrench it from the concrete steps and hurl it through the casement windows, but the philosophers were already huddled over some mathematical scribble that the lecturer had pulled from his pocket. Jay composed himself and looked out the window to the edge of the quadrant, beyond the half-moon fountain and the low stone balustrade into a blank haze that consumed the afternoon over west LA.

Earlier that morning, as they bounced along Sepulveda, Jay had announced to his brother that he'd claimed Wittgenstein as his hero. 'He wasn't smart enough,' said Robert, 'he didn't believe in general theory.' He ran a finger inside his grimy collar, swerving as he switched lanes. A cab overtook them on the nearside, horn blaring. Jay turned to the window but Robert had already launched into a detailed account of the philosopher's shortcomings without waiting for further elucidation. The car rattled over the spurs, up ahead was a line of stationary traffic at the Wilshire exit. Jay lowered the window, let the freeway roar drown out his brother's voice. It was his final term at Berkeley and he had decided to align himself with Wittgenstein precisely because he was concerned with all the stuff that *didn't* make sense. Here was a philosopher who understood that the really important mysteries were the non-facts, the non-verifiables, like art or God or beauty. Unlike the Vienna Circle who struggled to impose a structure on a chaotic world, to make it less frightening, dividing it up into the meaningful and the nonsensical, pretending that vast tracts did not exist. They railed against language, horrified by its sprawling disarray, and scuttled off to formulate artificial versions like Esperanto, elaborate mutations that were stripped of torturous nuance and unaccountable ambiguity.

But Wittgenstein – like Freud – was fascinated by the unsayable, the subtext that emerges underneath the articulated. He was also, in Jay's opinion, the first person of consequence to appreciate the cultural significance of psychoanalysis, although his curiosity was repeatedly mistaken for endorsement. However, as Jay had explained in his first book:

Wittgenstein's position on Freud was absolutely clear: psychoanalysis was based on myth. It was not scientific. Its power lay
in the fact that it provided explanations which people were
prepared to accept. He was therefore the first to identify the
fundamental and enduring appeal of psychoanalysis and the
first to predict the magnitude of its cultural impact.

Jay believed that what had so intrigued Wittgenstein was
the realisation that Freud had stumbled upon a different way of
speaking, a means of communicating the inexpressible that is
the secret gift of the artist. When they begged him to attend a
meeting, he stood up and read Tagore aloud while the Vienna
Circle worshipped nervously at his feet, misinterpreting his
position. They had misread the code in the last line of
Tractatus: 'What we cannot speak of we must pass over in
silence', thinking that this was an echo of their manifesto
instead of realising this was a signpost to the schism. They
built an island of rationality as a defence against the threatening human mystery erupting all around them and even as
they fled across the Atlantic, they vowed that philosophy would
be the handmaiden of science.

Jay looked again at the northern approach to the square but
there was no sign of Cora. A man in a dark wool coat stopped in
the middle of the road and stared at the clamping notice on the
windscreen. He stepped back, swivelling his head and moved to
the kerbside checking for markings. The parking attendant
appeared out of nowhere and paused by the car. The man
straightened up and snatched at the ticket. She pointed to the
residents' parking notice nailed to the railings and he moved
closer, studied it. He turned round, speaking, but she had
already disappeared from view.

Jay moved from the window back to his desk and ran a

congratulatory hand across the manuscript where Cora lay safely embalmed on the page. In the end, he had known exactly what to do and had not faltered in the precise arrangement of her story into the most exquisite composition. At 4,837 words it was the perfect centrepiece for his collection.

CORA – FRAGMENT OF AN ANALYSIS OF
A CASE OF CHILDLESSNESS
J. Merritt

Jay was immensely pleased at his choice of title, intended as an ironic homage to Freud, a sly sideswipe at his infamous case history. He reached up to the bookcase above his desk and pulled out volume sixteen of *The Standard Edition of the Psychological Works of Sigmund Freud* and flicked the pages until he found 'Dora: An Analysis of a Case of Hysteria'. Although the similarities between J. Merritt's story and Freud's Dora were largely superficial, they guaranteed an excited response from the critics who seized upon such minutiae to advertise their own erudition. Both cases had been abruptly terminated after three months and two dreams. Both patients had provided the inspiration for their analyst's *pièce de resistance* and both had fled when the lid was forced open on their repression.

Freud had dithered about the publication of Dora's case for a full four years. You could almost hear the man squirm as he wrote, his nervous prefatory remarks contained a litany of warnings for the uninitiated, a parade of disclaimers excusing his invasion of privacy, as he tried to assert the moral rights of exposing an eighteen-year-old girl spread-eagled to the world. The delay was usually attributed to stage fright at his unauthorised disclosure and mistrust of the public attitude to the sexually explicit nature of the case. But Jay knew better: Freud was tormented by the suspicion that he had created a monumental work of fiction that had no scientific basis whatsoever. Dora's case had little to do with her and everything to do with his own unresolved phantasies. Jay turned the yellowing pages, imagined Dora lying on the couch, her pale fingertips exploring her beloved jewel case while Freud sat all aquiver, chewing on his feverish cigar as he watched her steady hand stroke up and down in her lap. She sighed and he thrust his lurid interpretations upon her – a grotesque miscalculation, for Dora fled, horrified, leaving him to stare at the empty couch. And because she had the temerity to reject him, he turned his avenging pen upon his cruel muse, offered Dora up as a living demonstration of his science, shoe-horned into a theory that was already written. It was all in the interests of science, Freud insisted, clutching his trembling pen, walled in his room, tormented by the lingering trace of her scent.

Jay snapped the book shut and returned it to the shelf. He was dismissive of the revisionist commentators who suggested that Dora was a casualty of analysis. Like most patients, she knew the solution to her own misery but simply failed to trust her instinct. In all his years of practice, Jay had been both astounded by his clients' insight and dismayed by their lack of courage. Early on in his career, he realised that he would always find it difficult to wholeheartedly embrace the therapeutic imperative to help. It was an impossible Hippocratic position. Yesterday when he watched Cora stumble in the pelting rain, he had remembered the plaintive cry of a classmate from all those years ago: 'How can you let a patient go in such pain?'

It was 1970 at the San Francisco School of Psychoanalysis and the voice of Angeline, who had a penchant for getting mired in hypotheticals, like the ethics of the fifty-minute hour and the sanctity of its boundaries. 'Say if a patient is on the verge of losing it completely?' she exclaimed to the class, waving her bangled hands. 'Say if a patient is unsafe, say if they are a danger to themselves?'

Metzling surveyed the group, flexed a sandalled foot where a yellow rind of skin bulged over an ingrown toenail.

'Let them go,' said Jay. 'It is the transaction.'

'Well, I know there's just no way I could do that,' said Angeline, tossing a blaze of loose curls.

Jay followed her down the front steps after class and they stood looking out over the commanding sweep of Sutter Street. 'Tuck your bleeding heart away,' he said as she stepped out into the warm drizzle. 'And ask yourself, for whom does your heart bleed? Yourself or the patient?' He reached out and squeezed her shoulder with a spontaneous condescension. He could hear the distant rumble of a cable car. A sparkle of silver droplets netted on her frizzy hair and she raised the tip of her tiny nose, contemplating his hand with a private smile that Jay completely failed to de-code.

The cloud cleared, she covered his hand with an unspoken invitation and they leaned into the breathless gradient, up into the damp afternoon, through Lower Haights towards Buena Vista Park. It was the tail end of the summer of love and Jay was expecting joss stick sex, candle grease congealed along the windowsills, so he was taken by surprise when Angeline kneeled before him in the dense shade of the Monterey pines and unbuttoned his fly to find his willing cock which she sucked efficiently. Jay understood that she wanted something more, so he gathered up her voluminous hair and yanked it so hard that the skin of her temples webbed. He jammed her head against his groin and ejaculated deep down in her throat. Afterwards, he let her slump to the scented forest floor gasping for air, where she stroked his punishing hand.

Angeline was silent but apparently enthusiastic, because she led him homewards along Ashbury, stopping briefly to admire the Dead House. He followed her up a side street stair into the cramped disarray of a small room whose centrepiece was a mattress screened by a muslin curtain that diffused the sunlight even as it hit the window. She slipped her shirt off and lifted his palm to her breast, a slight swelling with no more substance than his own. He could feel the soft beat of heart on breastbone as she pressed into his touch. Pulling back, she wriggled out of her jeans and knelt on the mattress, bent double and gracelessly offered up her thin white ass. But Jay was aggrieved to find events so orchestrated, to find himself so objectified – this was unfamiliar territory and he felt that the outcome might be falling short of everyone's expectations. She swung her face sideways as he fumbled with her wetness and it seemed to Jay that she was mocking him with her determined submission, so he grabbed a bottle of massage oil and poured it over her pale cheeks as if smoothing her slithery compliance could calm the fury rising within him. His hands slid over the greased bone of her hips, the narrow dimensions of a small child that he could have picked up and hurled across the room. Jay's sudden penetration took Angeline unawares and when he thrust even deeper into her asshole, she cried out in pain. His left hand twisted a fistful of her hair and he bent a sharp elbow across the back of her neck, he was pinning her to the pillow and swallowing hard on a lurch of nausea, consumed by a simultaneous coming and a revulsion at the thought of her shit on his cock.

He wrenched free and kneeled back on the mattress while she lay bunched on her side. 'There's blood,' she murmured, her finger tracing red spots on the grubby sheet. He stood up, jeans pooled at his ankles. 'You need to get in touch with your anger, Jay,' she said propping her head on a folded arm. He stared down at her bed-bound smirk and realised with a jolt that Angeline was suffused with a pink-cheeked vindication, a gloating pride, for she had bared his ugly soul and Jay had revelled in the liberating joy of cruelty. She had released the beast lurking within him – it was a carefully planned assault, this was her party trick for men who needed teaching a lesson about their true nature.

'You're a textbook case,' she said and it was all Jay could do to keep his shaking hands away from her neck. But he had the sense to back away, to hoist his trousers and flee, it was a moment of revelation he would never forget, as well as his first and last experiment with anal sex, and the shrill memory of that afternoon would never leave him.

Jay reached across the desk for Cora's casebook, turned to a new blank page and wrote:

10th session
Cora did not attend

He had not sheltered her from the truth but the question now was whether or not she would survive it. It seemed entirely appropriate that the completion of his story might coincide with Cora's permanent disappearance from his safe space. Jay had no further requirement for her presence and it would be naturally fortuitous not to have to endure the tedious process of weaning her off. He had always felt that terminations are sentimentalised in his business and that analysts romanticise the privilege of invading another's life. Destiny, he reflected, putting down his pen, is where we place our dreams when we have decided to abdicate responsibility, when we choose instead to delegate our welfare to others.

On his last day at the San Francisco School of Psychoanalysis, Metzling shook Jay's hand and pressed a folded page into his palm. Jay read the handwritten quote as he walked along Sutter for the last time.

Whoever has eyes to see and ears to hear will be persuaded that mortals can hide no secret. He whose lips are silent speaks with his fingertips; betrayal threatens from every pore. That's why the task of making conscious the most hidden business of the soul can certainly be resolved.

He smiled into the sudden mist chill and dropped the crumpled paper in the gutter.

FIFTEEN

The intercom cut through the silence. Jay stepped into the landing and glared down at the front door. The buzzer blared again. Exasperated, he hurried down the stairs. It seemed he had miscalculated and would have to answer, for Cora could remain on the step indefinitely, jabbing at the bell. He would invite her into the hallway, arrange another session and dispose of her, he thought as he turned the latch.

'Thank you for last night,' said Dana, nudging a bouquet of lilies towards him. 'I'm just on my way to the airport. I hope I haven't called at a bad time.'

'Not at all,' he said, with a smile of relief.

'You sure?'

'My 8 am appointment has turned out to be a no show.'

Dana smelled of outdoors and the vague trace of some androgynous scent. A long thin crimson scarf was coiled tightly around her neck, highlighting the translucence of her skin. She dropped her travel bag in the hallway and Jay directed her straight ahead, down three steps into the breakfast room, an excavated semi-basement with a maple floor and a blaze of pinprick spotlights glinting off an oversized stainless steel hob. Dana accepted his offer of coffee, her eyes roving around the room, and he wondered if in fact she had come with some unfinished business.

'I didn't realise this was where you lived,' she said. 'I mean, I thought it was a clinic or something. Is this where you see all your patients?'

'I find it more conducive here. The suggestion of home is very powerful to a client, whether they realise it or not. They are entering the analyst's space. It's a big opening statement, a gesture of trust.'

'Is it safe?'

'For the analyst or the client?'

Pink thumbprints of cold glow were fading into her pale skin and the overwhelming impression was of appetite, a radiant vividness as if the room could barely contain her. He filled the half sink and placed the lilies in the water, holding his breath against the stinking perfume.

'So do you get a lot of very disturbed people?'

'I have treated unmedicated psychotics, if that's what you mean. But I've never been interested in the extremities of personality disorder.'

'I thought that sort of work would be fascinating.'

'There are analysts who argue that psychotherapy is useful for psychosis, but there's no consistent evidence to support this view. It's based on the fallacious premise that understanding what drives an individual to commit an evil act is both possible and useful.' He turned to the countertop and slashed the coffee carton with the flat blade of a knife.

'Take the Manson murders, for example. It wasn't far from where Robert lived, you know, La Cienaga Boulevard, in Benedict Canyon. I remember well how a psychologist stood up in court and tried to explain why a young woman could stab another pregnant woman to death, oblivious to the eight-month-old foetus beating inside her.' He turned back to face her, leaning against the counter and folding his arms. 'Caligula, Mengele, Manson, Bundy, Columbine – these are horrors that linger in the public imagination. But they are not especially informative. They tell us nothing we can't guess at.'

Dana raised her chin. So finely and precisely angled, he thought. The whites of her eyes oddly clear as a child's. 'In 1924,' he continued, 'Freud was invited to Chicago to advise on Leopold and Loeb, the notorious murderers. He declined on the grounds of ill health, but I think he had identified even then that there are certain conditions that are untreatable. He knew there was nothing of real interest or value to find. So much talk and time wasted trying to understand the fine print of human behaviour, our deepest fears and longings. But we still seek out the aberrations, the serial killers, the child murderers, we still crave the monster in our midst to make us feel better. The moral high ground is a wonderfully inviting vantage point, don't you think?'

'Are you saying there is nothing that can be done?'

'On the contrary, Dana. That is exactly what medication is for – the most expedient, maybe the *only* way to manage dangerous cases. We learn nothing from a study of true insanity, at least nothing very useful. We simply need to be able to identify and medicate, to prevent. In today's world, drugs are the new prison. Psychiatrists remain, as they have always been, our jailers, the buffer zone between polite society and those who tear their hair out in the asylum. They maintain our dialogue with that section of the community whom we would prefer to incarcerate or eliminate. The great social benefit of medication is that we can keep dormant what we are too squeamish to kill. And of course it's cheaper to drug people than to lock them up – it also makes us feel civilised and liberal.'

Dana tugged at her scarf and began to slowly unwind the long coils of knitted silk until two uneven lengths dangled like scarlet rope from her neck.

'Of course, we're talking here about a tiny percentage of the population,' Jay added, placing two small china mugs on the table. 'Apparently the urgent issue of the day is the alarming deterioration in the mental health of the masses.'

'You don't agree?'

'Insanity was once rather engagingly defined as not being able to find anyone who could put up with you. It was Wittgenstein who suggested that madness should not be treated as an illness at all. He asked why it shouldn't be seen as a sudden change of character.' Indeed, Jay reflected, turning back to the counter, his most intuitive clients whose capacity for rational thought hadn't been completely submerged by their neuroses, eventually stumbled upon this realisation themselves. For years they would lie buried under the weight of their own pathology, transfixed by the frigid stalactites of memory, until one day they followed a tiny flicker of light and stumbled out of their cave into the sun, finally seeing that their madness, their psychological turbulence was simply rooted in a certain way of viewing themselves.

'We insist that everyone should be in harmony with our expectations,' he continued. 'Anything that we cannot stand, we expect to be eliminated. The moody teenager is put on Prozac, a child that is too exuberant and exhausts its parents with an excess of energy is diagnosed with Attention Deficit Disorder and prescribed Ritalin. We medicate as our intolerance grows.'

'So you don't believe in drug therapy?'

'Strictly speaking the question is not how to get cured, but how to live. That was how Conrad so aptly described it a hundred years ago. The real problem, Dana, is our faltering endurance, our loss of stamina. It is as if the human race is losing muscle tone. We expect not to have to suffer distress. *This* is what is interesting – our growing intolerance of the pain involved in the actual business of living.'

'You mean we're becoming soft?'

'Let me give you an example,' he said, pouring coffee into

Dana's mug as she lowered herself into a chair. 'A woman, let's call her Lisa, comes to my practice. Lisa is upset, anxious, she can't concentrate, she is underperforming at work. For no apparent reason, she thinks. Until, slowly over the following weeks, we uncover her story – for there is always a story – of a terminal breakdown in Lisa's relationship with her mother, whom she cut out of her life many years ago. Now the mother has died, depriving Lisa of what she has been waiting for all her life: the chance of a grand reconciliation. This is what has been keeping my client going, despite her denials. She is distraught with guilt, mourning the lost opportunity to correct the mothering experience that has left her wanting all her life. "I can't bear the pain," she says to me. "I can't eat, I can't sleep. I think I'm losing it." Lisa wants me to make the pain go away, she doesn't want to face up to the consequences of a decision made years ago in anger to which she stubbornly adhered. She does not want to be the hard-hearted daughter who refused to visit her mother on her deathbed; she does not want to see herself as the person she has become. So, I tell Lisa that the only resolution is to come to terms with her past, to accept the guilt. To grow up. Her real fear is that she has lost her mother forever. I tell her she can create a positive maternal image, repair her internal mother if you like. But Lisa doesn't have the stomach for this, it will take too long, she wants the quick fix that Prozac will give. And I am not interested in talking to the drug.'

Dana leaned her chin into the folded angle of her wrist, she was still and captive, framed in his open palms. These were the moments Jay remembered, the weight and impact of each word. 'The real crisis is our dwindling appetite for life,' he said reaching for his coffee. 'We are fleeing from our own humanity.'

Dana stroked the rim of her mug. He read her studied silence as a signal that she wished to return to her true agenda, that he had only briefly managed to elbow in front of Robert's ghost, that he would always be disadvantaged by the third person at the table.

'I have something you might like to see,' he said, pushing back from the table to open a cabinet door below the counter. 'I took it out last night with the intention of bringing it along to our meeting.' He placed a red box file down on the table in front of her. 'Open it,' he urged and she leaned forwards, ran a caressing finger along the edge of the file with the careful touch of a scholar.

Once, in the shuttered shadow of his mother's bedroom during the hour before she came home, Jay had lifted the flimsy wooden lid of her jewellery box and dipped his curious fingers into the soft interior. A solitary pearl rolled and knocked against a clip-on earring – tarnished gilt with a dull grass-coloured stone embedded in the centre. He undid a jiggling length of necklace, swung the multicoloured beads in the air. Groping for treasure in the lush velvet compartments, he found the smooth oval of a locket with a verdigrised chain that tickled his palm. The two halves were held together by a thread of eroded gold but he prised open the worn catch with the delicate touch of a spy, only to reveal the infuriating trace of excised memory, a smudge of greyish glue that had hardened where once a face had been. Buried underneath all of this finery, he eventually reached the inner core: guarded by the removable shelf in the concealed heart of the box was the secret of the Hamilton family, the hidden force that bound these random human elements together recorded in a folded marriage licence dated 23 July 1928. 'Doris McKay and Frederic Hamilton', the ink scrawl proclaimed. Underneath, he found the birth certificates for Robert Merritt Hamilton and James Hamilton.

Jay held his breath in the cricket-scream heat of the afternoon and cradled the mystery of family in his hands, wondering exactly what would be destroyed if he took a match and burnt the evidence, if it would be like voodoo and the whole structure might all fall apart, collapse and die.

After his mother's death Jay pared down all the paperwork to a tidy sheaf of legal documents and photos. He kept the marriage and birth certificates, prevented from throwing them away by a vague suspicion that it might one day be necessary to prove his family had ever existed. Jay used to wonder if the genetic configuration that had produced a prodigy like Robert might have had its roots in some distant ancestral brilliance, but he was now, in so far as he was aware, the sole surviving Hamilton and there would be no one left to shuffle their dutiful feet to his graveside. His mother's death had marked the end of any opportunity to easily add to his paltry knowledge of his heritage as he knew nothing except her maiden name and birth date.

'Just like my aunt June,' his mother had muttered once with unmistakable ferocity as they walked to church, clucking her lips at a young woman who bent down to check her reflection in a car window and Jay was stunned at the realisation that his mother had a beginning, an origin, that there might be others.

'Where?' he asked.

'Colorado,' she snapped, striding up the steps and he understood the subject was permanently closed and that although the accident of family history is an unavoidable affliction, it is a completely survivable misfortune.

A year after Robert's murder Jay had stood outside 3840 North Beverly Drive and decided on a thorough reorganisation of his past. There really was no space to accommodate family mementoes in his life and so he packed the documents into this box file and loaded everything else – his mother's and brother's clothes, furniture and all their other possessions – onto a waste truck and had them driven away for disposal. 'A year is an eternity in real estate, Mr Hamilton,' said the broker who had assessed the house and assured Jay that buyers in Beverly Hills were relatively crime insensitive, even after the Manson murders. Within a week he had produced a far-sighted couple who believed that 3840's homicide association was incidental when it came to the location advantage and the long-term possibility of price appreciation, and were therefore only too happy to overlook a murder in the bathroom.

'Christmas 1958. It's the only one of us all together,' said Jay with an embarrassed rush that startled him like a spray of cold water.

'It's a little out of focus,' said Dana, peering into the black-and-white patch of shaved lawn where Jay, with a zealously cropped haircut, wearing short trousers and a short-sleeved shirt obediently buttoned to the neck, gripped the handlebars of a large-wheeled bike and squared up to the camera with a guarded expression. Robert grinned broadly at the lens, his eyes squinting into the sun. His shirt was open at the neck so that the line of his vest was just visible. A thin covering of dark hair lay slack against his skull; thick-framed glasses dominated the white face, his chin and upper lips shadowed by an imperfect shave that had left its trace in what looked like a nick underneath his nose. 'The looks are from your mother's side,' she said, tilting the photo under the light, taking in the pale oval faces, the dark hair, the narrow-shouldered brittleness, although Jay, at ten years old, was already looking like the next generation: broader, heavier and better-equipped, a presence that would prove more enduring.

His mother stood in between her sons but not equidistant,

her full-skirted dress spattered with a chaotic floral pattern. She had just smoothed Robert's shorn sideburns and flecked a dust speck from his collar with the grooming possession of a wife. She was looking not at the camera but sideways, in proud contemplation of her eldest son. Her arm had slipped through Robert's, one hand resting on his shirtsleeve. She couldn't be near him without touching, as if his escape from her uterine clutch had been premature. Jay stood like an uninvited guest in the space she had created on her other side, like an extra in the frame on his big-wheeled bike.

When he finally took his last backward glance at Stockton, he remembered how he'd searched for a route out of there ever since he was a child, a westward dash that would follow the waterway to the ocean, his only romantic indulgence. Unreproachful, his mother had done her time and didn't abandon him until the appropriate juncture, which she deemed to be the day after he graduated from high school on 23 June 1966. Cuffed and collared in a new cocoa blouse, she gave him $93 and a shoulder pat, her gloved hand tucking a curl under her white pillbox as she boarded a silver Greyhound for LA. Jay followed her progress down to the middle of the bus where she settled in a window seat behind glass that was smeared with a heavy interstate dust. She sat there waving a radiant goodbye, even blew Jay an extravagant kiss, so delighted was she to be leaving after all that interminable waiting, finally unshackled from the nail-biting tedium of counting the months till it seemed acceptable to make the move. When the bus pulled away in a cloud of exhaust, Jay waited for a quiet rage to wash over him, for he knew his mother didn't really care if she never set eyes on her youngest son again. Instead, he felt cleansed of the humiliation of being born at all, relieved that she no longer felt compelled to stay put against her will.

As the bus receded into the lightening horizon, Jay

understood that he was the recipient of an inadequate mothering and must simply repair that fault like he would change a bike tyre. Over the years, he had generously shared this valuable insight with his clients, convincing at least some of them that a lack of motherlove need not in fact be an impediment at all. But it was becoming increasingly difficult to get clients to embrace this position for lately the industry of therapy has raised the bar and overcomplicated the issue. Having a mother is not the simple business it was once thought to be: any rationing of love and affection, the slightest childhood trauma and his clients expect to teeter on the brink of a possible disintegration, a gaping festering loss that they will schlep around with them for the rest of their lives.

Rental prices kept his mother on the northern periphery of LA and she settled in Van Nuys, thirty square miles of farmland in the San Fernando Valley that was exploding into suburbia in the mid-sixties. A Spanish-style duplex near the railroad tracks just above Saticoy and Woodman and half an hour's drive from Robert. With dutiful regularity she wrote to Jay every Monday, telling him how the move had been a seamless transition, how Robert took her every month to Nate 'n' Al's deli on North Beverly Drive for hand-pressed potato cakes. 'A long way from Stockton', she exclaimed, and Jay could see her installed in one of the Naughahyde booths, where waitresses in pink pinstripes showered her with attention. In the afternoon, Robert ferried her the scenic route home through Beverly Hills, past Shirley Temple's house on Sunset, down a line of jacarandas on Palm Drive where Marilyn lived with DiMaggio, before finally beginning the slow ascent up through Coldwater Canyon. Robert sat in the backyard under the alder reading a mathematical journal and tucking into some pastries his mother had secreted in her handbag, he was busy with *Universal Grammar* and a grand vision that completely distracted. She sipped tea, tugged at clusters of needlegrass that poked through cracks in the rocks, watching over her son as the afternoon sun sank down behind the bush-covered foothills and the sky unrolled its grey shade over the invisible city.

When she died, Jay had been astonished to find a drawerful of photos in her apartment, so much pictorial evidence of outings with Robert – little day trips where she posed outside the homes of the stars, or leaned against the bumper of his Mustang, or looked through a penny telescope on the Santa Monica pier. There was an entire set taken on that evening in September '68 when Jay had made up a rare threesome for a visit to the Anheuser Busch Gardens in Van Nuys. The air reeked of warm beer and doughnuts and the park rang with the shriek of tropical birds that squawked and dive-bombed all around them. He was shocked to see his mother so carefree on a red bumper car, clutching her headscarf and laughing like a girl while Robert wrenched at the steering wheel. From a small curved footbridge Jay monitored their covered gondola ride along the waterways, past gushing fountains and waterfalls spilling out over the rocks, over to the brewery where you could look in and see the Budweiser being brewed. That same night his mother discovered an extraordinary affection for the parrots that landed easily on her wrist to peck at the seeds in her cupped palm.

Three months later Jay arrived at Van Nuys on Christmas Day to find a veiled domed cage on the table. 'It will live for fifty years,' Robert announced with a flourish, whipping off the cover to reveal a large African grey who shuffled its black claws along a wooden perch, shallow eyes like dials, lifeless and unblinking.

'Oh, he's just wonderful,' his mother cried and the parrot cocked his blunt head to one side as if he recognised her voice. 'What will I call him?'

'He's already got a name,' Robert pointed to a small ceramic disk at the top of the cage.

'Peter,' said Jay, stepping closer. The bird flapped hysterically, feathers whirling to the floor.

'He doesn't like you,' said his mother. 'He knows you don't like him.' Peter nodded, twitched a long grey tail with a crimson splash at the vent.

'African greys sometimes pluck out their feathers when they're bored,' warned Robert reading aloud from a leaflet. Peter settled on his perch, squeezing a contemptuous dropping while he fixed a malevolent eye on Jay.

'You need to get safe toys for his cage, Mom,' Robert tapped the instructions. 'Parrots can be strangled by some of the ropes they like to swing on.'

Peter never demonstrated any interest in coherent speech but he thrived in Van Nuys and became a regular mention in her letters to Jay, which had, by the late '60s, become more infrequent. And although he didn't live to be fifty, he did outlast Robert by a few months, during which time he seemed a rare and blessed comfort to their mother. But late in 1971, Southern California was ravaged by Exotic Newcastle Disease, a fatal virus that travelled on shoes and clothing and millions of demented birds succumbed to tremors and anorexia before thudding to the ground, a green discharge leaking from their dead eyes. It was like the visitation of a great plague, you could drive along the valley and see rotting carcasses on the freeway. Jay's mother stopped leaving Peter's cage out on the balcony where he was visible to passers-by, she even tried to keep him quiet by draping a sheet over him, but he was having none of it and squawked his noisy protest, a blood curdling and unmistakably avian shriek that eventually brought the Department of Agriculture to her front door.

'I'm sorry ma'am, African greys are carriers,' said the

official, showing her their compulsory permits. 'It's a statewide euthanasia programme. The only way to protect the fowl, the foodstuffs,' and he took out a tank of carbon monoxide, a plastic bag and a rubber hose. 'Twelve million birds,' he sighed, 'sixty-five million dollars,' and stuffed Peter into the bag and gassed him while her fist stifled a scream.

Dana reached into the box file for the second black-and-white photo.

'If you look at the back,' said Jay, 'you'll see it was taken in February 1971, a month before he died. I never found out who took it or why it was developed in large format.'

Robert's three-quarter profile was looking off-camera with a lingering smile of recognition, his brow furrowed in amusement. His lips parted to reveal two large symmetrical teeth, he had just been or was about to speak, it had the look of a witty remark delivered to someone standing to the side. Clearly in transit, he stood in an open doorway, an exit of some sorts, the slim striped tie, the narrow jacket lapels, the thinness of his upper lip mitigated by the fullness of his smile – Robert had his mother's unfortunate labial arrangement which she tried to conceal with a lipsticked cupid's bow.

'Funny the little things you remember,' said Jay, 'For example, the fact that the autopsy report didn't say that Robert always wore glasses. "The eyes are brown,"' he quoted, '"the pupils are round and equal measuring 0.4 cm in diameter."'

'Pupil measurement can be an indicator of trauma to the head,' Dana said, without looking up. 'Some blow that might not have left any visible sign,' and Jay was reminded of how assiduously she researched and how hard she worked at over-compensating. A fervent believer in Einstein's little quip about genius and perspiration, she reached out for what was beyond her grasp, like a child mesmerised by the red flame, inching closer until, with a soundless air rush, she was consumed by fire.

'I think he's saying something. What a pity we don't know who took it,' she said, as if the photo was a clue, as if Robert could be looking into the off-camera face of his murderer. 'He looks relaxed, happy. How sad,' she sighed, as if hers was a personal distress and Jay felt the press of irritation, how dare she claim a posthumous intimacy while flexing her biographer's claws to dismember the dead.

'His skin was exceptionally pale,' said Jay, caressing his own stubble-less jaw. 'Library white.' It was a soft indoor pastiness, with bands of pigmentation marking his wrist, hands, face and neck, some unavoidable exposure to the elements. The lighting arrangement in the picture flattered Robert with an overexposure and bleached out the fleshy folds that had begun to advance over the rim of his collar, whitening what would undoubtedly have been a less than pristine shirt, greyed from overuse. He had always been sloppy about bathing, there were occasions when Jay had to mouth-breathe against his body odour in the baking car. But Robert shrugged off his complaints, as if time squandered on such inessentials was wasted, as if genius cannot be expected to wash. Jay looked away from the photo and his brother's grinning face and thought how we are supposed, in the end, to forgive the dead their lapses in personal hygiene.

'So the official cause of death was asphyxia?'

'Due to strangulation by ligature,' said Jay, carrying the coffee cups over to the sink. 'There was nothing in the autopsy to mark him out as particularly unusual. The physical characteristics fitted the profile of strangulation.'

The Medical Examiner at the scene had explained that the pressure of the ligature around Robert's neck constricted the trachea, occluding the jugular vein and the carotid artery. Breathing became impossible and Robert could have drifted into unconsciousness within three minutes. It would have taken maybe ten for him to die. The corpse didn't yield anything fruitful. All that Dr Herrera found out at the post mortem was less than useless in the investigation.

'There was a mark on his leg,' said Dana.

'How did you know that?' said Jay, swinging around to face her at the table.

'"The lower extremities are unremarkable,"' she began to quote nervously, '"except for an abrasion on the right anterior femoral area which could correspond to a rug or a corduroy type of pattern somewhat related to this type of shape."'

Her right hand moved up to stroke her shoulder; he could see a light down of hair below her earlobe, a throbbing pulse at her temple. 'I'm sorry,' she said, 'I meant to tell you last night but—' she pursed her lips, straightened up in her chair. 'I did actually see the autopsy a few weeks ago. When I went to visit the LAPD.'

Jay turned away from the table, banging his knee against the handle of a floor-level cupboard, suddenly light-headed. He looked down at a patch of spilled coffee grains on the counter and swept them aside into the sink. The steel bowl seemed to glare up at him.

'They just read out a little from the report,' she said from behind him. 'I mean I just – I wanted to find out about the procedure for the reopening of old cases. I don't know if you've read about the Cold Case Unit that's been set up recently in LA?'

Jay shook his head, set his mouth to a tight horizontal in an effort to steady the squeeze of his heart. Pushing the cafetière to one side he picked up the knife and turned around to face her, blinking his quiet disbelief at her seated form.

'There are more than six thousand unsolved homicides in LA going back to the 1960s,' she said, her voice quick and earnest. 'And there's lots of pressure for a clear up, it's become a real political issue. The Cold Case Unit is mostly driven by technology. You know, processing old crime scene evidence, fingerprints, DNA, that kind of thing. It's a slow business. But if they get a match, the case can be re-investigated.'

Jay put the knife back on the counter and sat down at the table. 'My dear,' he said, 'do you know of a reason why anyone would want to reopen Robert's case?'

'Well,' she spread her hands flat in front of her and then, taking a deep breath, announced with thinly disguised anticipation, 'I found something interesting in the archives at UCLA.'

She reached into the file and pulled out two stapled pages marked with a red tag. Jay recognised the neat slope of his brother's handwriting, the oversized capital letters and moved to take the photocopy but Dana held firm. 'It's a letter Robert wrote when he was just twenty-three, but never sent,' she said. 'It's addressed to a coast guard base at Tongue Point, Oregon,' she added and began to read aloud in a clear and practised voice.

' "April 19 1953.

Dear Bob, Thanks for your Christmas card. It was the swishiest I received. I ought to explain why it's taken until now for me to reply.

I've had, you know, a little excitement. I was beaten and robbed by a hitchhiker. Not only was I clobbered profession-ally (the man – a negro – had been, he said, a boxer), he beat my head against the ground and strangled me unconscious.

What an interesting experience, so rare in these tame

days. I kept thinking; too bad I shall not live to relate it, but then I've passed my prime. When I awoke it was with the impression of having dreamt a real thriller-killer. Then I opened my eyes and found myself lying in what might imaginatively have been called a pool of blood. The man had taken my wristwatch, ring, automobile & what is more crucial a briefcase containing my organ shoes.

They caught him in Bakersfield with all the loot except, damn it, my organ shoes and he is now residing in Alameda County Jail. And Bob, you should hear the lurid story he told the police! Imagine a person of my eminent respectability being so maligned. I'm looking forward to the trial, it will give me an opportunity to vindicate indignantly my horror. I so love being indignant. It is I suppose wicked of me to take such pleasure in the prospect, since the poor fellow is confronted with five years to life of penal servitude. According to his story, he thought he'd killed me. The scare should be sufficient punishment. Besides, I really ought to be grateful to the man for introducing me to the hitherto untasted pleasures of hospital life.

I presented for a time a highly grotesque appearance. Half my head was shaved, my eye was filled with a blood clot, and linen thread protruded from me in unexpected places around the lip and chin. The doctor who sewed me up was a woman and an excellent seamstress. While I was in hospital interns would parade by in throngs admiring her artistry.

They tell me I shall bear no scars. Shall I be completely without trophies? Have I gone thru this for nothing? Robert." '

'May I?' said Jay, reaching for the letter although what he really wanted to do was ransack the contents of the blue folder that lay open on the table. He felt the prickle of Dana's stare as he scanned without reading, wondering what other posthumous secrets she might have uncovered. A curious thumping struck up in his heart, his breath was coming in shallow snatches and a damp chill settled on his fingertips. He thought of Robert coming round, choking and spluttering by the side of the road. Imagine, if he had died then, when Jay was only five years old, he'd be a barely existent memory, an outline much like their father was, and Jay felt a sudden pang that it didn't happen this way – he would have been spared having to *deal* with so much.

'I never heard Robert talk about being a key witness in a trial.'

'That's because there never was any trial,' said Dana with a triumphant smile. 'The guy who tried to strangle him – Timothy Virgil Wright – pleaded guilty to robbery and attempted homicide and was sentenced to eleven years in Alameda County. He was released in 1962.'

Jay thought of Timothy Virgil Wright, imagined his disbelief when this puny little white boy with big glasses had offered him a lift, he should have known then it was funny, but Robert would have engaged him in chat and then, when they'd stopped to relieve themselves on that long straight road, the boy was down on his knees beside him, muttering filthy suggestions, his bony hand brushing his thigh so T. V. Wright had to defend his manhood and honour, but he couldn't stop lashing out even though he knew he was putting the boy within an inch of his life. Even when he heard the splinter of skin-covered bone he just kept on hitting until the boy slumped in the roadside dust and a gut-wrenching fear prickled over T. V. Wright and he grabbed at the wristwatch – the first of many mistakes – knowing even then that he was never getting away with this, the wallet engraved RMH and a brown leather satchel that looked like it might have something useful, but there was only a pair of soft-soled slippers. He jumped into Robert's car, petty thief turned avenging killer in a heartbeat and drove off to Bakersfield where his trembling knees made him veer into the centre of the road and he tried to dump the car practically in full view of the sheriff's office, drawing all kinds of unwanted attention to himself, so the cops were there in no time at all and T. V. Wright was confessing before they even asked him a civil question, before they even found the boy ten miles back. It might look better, they said in between blows, if T. V. would talk. And so, because the truth was all he had, he told them how the boy had tried to touch him, how he'd panicked and left him for dead, but they just shook their disbelieving heads. 'What would a nice college boy see in a big negro mothafucka like you?' they jeered and T. V. Wright knew there was no sensible answer to that question. 'What do you expect with that kind of filth?' the court-appointed lawyer would have said the next day. So T. V. took his advice and confessed to robbery and attempted homicide which meant there was no need for a trial, no need for the boy to testify in court, just a cursory sentencing in front of the judge, and T. V. did nine or ten years in Alameda County Jail, he forgot exactly how long, he was so busy breaking rocks and getting in fights, years folding into one another but when he got out he could still remember the name of the boy who put him away.

'The police never mentioned anything about this when Robert was murdered,' said Jay, passing the pages back to Dana.

'They wouldn't have known about it unless they had a reason to go back and look through manual records. T. V. Wright pleaded guilty so Robert didn't have to go to court. Open and shut case.'

'So what happened to him?'

'T. V. was released in 1962 but he did time later for a string of other convictions, although that was his first and was by far the longest stretch. He died in 1983, of natural causes. No family.'

She tapped the letter and leaned forward to Jay, eyes bright with anticipation. 'In March 1971, T. V. Wright was living in downtown LA,' she delivered her proud punchline.

'A coincidence.'

'Possibly. But you've got to admit it's an interesting one.'

Jay stood up and retreated to the sink, leaving Dana at the table. He busied himself with a coffee refill, glanced at her side profile, saw her lips tighten in irritation; she was of course somewhat deflated that her little informational scoop didn't get the reaction she expected. This strategy of revealing secrets was a regular feature with Jay's clients. After weeks of withholding, they were invariably disappointed at the anti-climatic effect when they finally played their trump card.

'So let me get this right, Dana,' he said. 'You went to the LAPD to try and get the case reopened because you think Robert was killed as an act of revenge? You think that T. V. Wright hunted down and murdered the man who put him away in 1953?'

'The police still have the physical evidence collected from the scene. At the very least I'd like to get that checked against T. V. Wright's fingerprints. I met with a Detective Rodriguez who has been very helpful. It's a question of prioritising cases—'

'But T. V. Wright is dead, so all that would really be achieved is closing a cold case, not putting a killer away.'

'That doesn't actually have to matter to the CCU. A case closed is still a statistical victory from their point of view.'

'You expected the police to listen to a biographer's hunch?'

'I thought it was worth a shot.'

Jay could imagine how Dana would have turned a few passing heads at the LAPD as she sat at Rodriguez's desk, trying to convince him of the urgency of her cause, wearing him down with her tenacity. The detective would have listened with an air of lugubrious patience that he has developed since being moved from Live to Cold, would rustle up some paperwork, let her see the post mortem. Jay remembered the photocopied motto tacked to the wall of Detective Green's office: *To err is human. To forgive is against department policy.*

'I wonder if Turing's shadow falls heavily on Robert?' said Jay, folding his arms as he leaned back. 'One dead gay scientist leads to another? It may even become a specialty of yours, Dana. In Turing's case, you rejected the suicide verdict. Although you shied away from saying so explicitly in your book, I suspect you believe that he was murdered. That MI6 injected the apple with cyanide?'

'I simply highlighted the absence of conclusive evidence.'

'Perhaps in your enthusiasm for Robert's case, you are ignoring the fact that some people deliberately choose the high-risk option. They may not calculate the risks, or risk itself may have been the object of the game. Now what could that mean?'

She returned his question with a defiant stare.

'It might mean,' said Jay, 'that they crave the excitement of the sexual outlaw, but the physical experience doesn't match up to the intellectual. Their carnal adventures never produce the same fireworks, so they up the stakes, searching for a thrill that never comes close. But we wouldn't understand that. People like you and I are a different species, lesser mortals dazzled by their glare.' He moved closer, resting his palms on the table in front of her. 'Sometimes we look for conspiracy theories when we are unwilling or unable to accept the truth. When it is too painful. We rail against the truth when we think it's unfair. A little childish don't you think?' Her mouth stretched into a grim smile. 'You were angry that Turing died young and brilliant. You believed he was betrayed in the end by those who courted him. And now you're angry about Robert, so you want to make his murder more than it is. You want a better story.'

Dana was shaking her head. Jay straightened up and folded his arms. 'Perhaps it's really a work of fiction that you want to write and not a biography. You think the explanation that Robert was killed by a couple of tricks that he picked up cruising is sad and sordid. Even worse, you think it's mundane. You would prefer a more glamorous conspiracy theory.'

Jay rested his eyes on the blank wall behind her head. 'Tell me, Dana. Have you given any thought to my feelings about a reopening of the case after thirty years? Have you any idea how distressing that would be?'

'I thought Robert's brother would want justice to be served. I know this is a shock but—' She stopped mid-sentence, sighed and bent her head. And for a moment they both remained still and motionless in the kitchen, so still he could hear her breathe.

'Jay,' she said, looking up. 'The LAPD did take my biographer's hunch seriously. Last night after I got back to the hotel I checked my email. That's why I stopped by here on my way to the airport. Detective Rodriguez wrote to let me know that the Cold Case Unit has decided to officially reopen the investigation into Robert's murder.'

• SIXTEEN •

A sharp buzz cut through the kitchen and they both turned their heads towards the wall. Jay walked over and pressed the intercom.

'Mr Jay Hamilton?' boomed a male voice.

'Yes?'

'Metropolitan Police. Could I have a word?'

Jay stood mute listening to the crackle. 'Of course, I'll be right up.'

Dana contemplated her hands, trying not to show any curiosity about the unannounced visitor.

'Excuse me a moment,' he managed and in the few seconds it took him to cover the short distance between the kitchen and the front door, Jay monitored his pulse-quickening response to this intrusion. Pausing on the matwell with a wariness that put all his instincts on high alert, he took a deep breath and reached for the latch, knowing already what to expect.

'Good morning,' he said, in a voice that immediately struck him as too loud.

'Detective Morrison,' announced a tall heavy-set man in his late thirties. He withdrew a large palm from inside a short raincoat and flashed an ID which he immediately returned to his breast pocket. Jay nodded, unable to find a voice in his constricted throat. It was an anxiety response, of course, an allergic reaction to the presence of policemen, the legacy of having lived through a murder investigation, of watching a life

179

picked clean.

Jay let his hand fall and stepped aside as the detective brushed his coated bulk past him, reminding himself that these house calls are never accompanied by gentle preliminaries lest they prejudice the ensuing proceedings, as if the police might unwittingly shake hands with a criminal. A dark tie skirted the opened top button of the detective's shirt. He had the air of a man who has slipped out of a regular sporting habit. Morrison moved down the hallway and stopped at the door to the living room.

'No, please, go straight ahead,' said Jay for although this path would lead him into an unavoidable encounter with Dana, it was preferable to a violation of the safe space. Jay would simply have to expedite the issue.

Morrison stood just inside the threshold to the kitchen, blocking Jay's view of Dana, his head skimming the low voltage spotlights. The room seemed suddenly cramped as if he had managed to lower the ceiling by several inches.

'Sorry to interrupt,' he said, without sincerity.

'Dr Dana Flynn,' Jay introduced from behind the detective. 'I am assisting her with some research.'

'Maybe I should give you a moment,' she said, rising from the table. 'I'll just wait in the living room.'

'No!' Jay exclaimed. Dana stopped. Morrison turned to Jay.

'I mean it's my consulting room—'

'Is there someone in there at the moment?' asked the detective, intrigued by this outburst.

'No, no. It's just – it wouldn't be – appropriate,' said Jay. Morrison regarded him with an exaggerated arch of his eyebrows.

'Maybe I should leave,' said Dana.

'No, not at all, why don't you wait upstairs in the study? I'm sure this won't take long,' Jay turned a prompting smile to

Morrison who was apparently unable or unwilling to offer an opinion on this subject.

'It concerns Cora Miller,' said the Detective, deciding to hurry the proceedings along, and Jay had the distinct impression that he had deliberately volunteered this information while Dana was within earshot.

Morrison rested his large hands on the back of the chair that she had just vacated in a gesture that struck Jay as offensively territorial. The detective glanced down at the open box file and the photo of Robert and looked up at Jay as if checking the likeness.

'My brother,' said Jay, approaching the table. 'He's dead,' and Morrison nodded, as if to say that is exactly what he had expected.

'Are you a doctor, Mr Hamilton?'

'No, I'm a psychoanalyst. Cora has been a client of mine for almost three months. She missed her 8 am session this morning,' he said, knowing that Morrison will already be in possession of this information, that some appointments book or diary will have led him here. 'I've been here all morning but she hasn't called.'

'When was the last time you saw her?'

'Yesterday afternoon. For her 4.30 session.'

'Why was she seeing you?'

'Why does anyone see a therapist?' Jay said, but his glibness was rewarded with a neutral stare from the detective. 'There were things she needed to work through.'

'Specifically?'

'There are issues of confidentiality here.'

Morrison straightened up and fixed him with an intent gaze. 'Mr Hamilton. Yesterday, at approximately 6 pm, Cora called round to visit her godson Christopher who is ten months old. While Christopher's mother was upstairs, Cora disappeared with the baby. Neither of them have been seen or heard from since.'

Jay took a blind step forwards and for a moment the scene, the kitchen, Morrison and everything that had happened took on the quality of a dream. He lowered himself slowly into a chair, placing both hands palm down on the table. Biting down hard on the inside of his cheek, he blinked, waved a hand in front of his face as if batting away some flying insect. It was an illusion, of course, this apparent collision of fiction and reality, the impression that his imagination might have shaped the actual course of event.

'So, Mr Hamilton, I am investigating the abduction of a child,' said the detective, sitting down with heavy permanency in the chair opposite him. 'And I think you'll agree, that under these circumstances, you may want to tell me everything you know.'

'Of course, of course,' said Jay, nodding his head. 'Well, there is rarely one simple reason as to why a person comes to therapy, but Cora was struggling to come to terms with her childlessness. She had become increasingly preoccupied these last few sessions. She was anxious. Agitated. Upset.'

'And yesterday?'

'She was very... distressed.'

'Is Cora on any medication?'

'Not that I know of. She was originally referred to me by Dr Ralph Laekin. He practises in Abingdon Villas. You should check with him, I'll give you the number.' Jay gathered from the detective's disinterest in this information that he had already pursued this line of inquiry and he felt a charge of anger at Laekin for not calling him in advance.

'So what, in your opinion, is happening here?'

'First of all, I have no idea where Cora is. This – *abduction* – is not something she ever discussed as a possibility. Never,' he repeated with emphasis. 'I would say that she is likely to take good care of Christopher. I can only speculate, but her instinct will not be to harm him. She will feel guilty, appalled by what she has done.'

'And?'

'I would expect her to return the child.'

'To give herself up?'

'To return the child.'

The detective stood up abruptly, shifting his bulk off the chair with a surprising grace. 'I'd like to see your consulting room now,' he said and Jay swallowed his indignation at this peremptory request. Did this oaf imagine that he had Cora stashed away in his front room? But Morrison wasn't waiting for his assent, he was already making his way into the hall. As Jay reached for the key above the doorframe, he could feel the detective's eyes leech into the nape of his neck. He pulled aside and Morrison stepped inside ahead of him, head bent out of habit rather than necessity.

Jay stood on the threshold, tracking the detective's gaze around the room, feeling as if he had been absent for a long time and had come back to find everything slipped into disrepair. There was a palpable sense of vacancy, a dry stale smell of enclosed air that he had not noticed before, as if the space had languished unused. A film of fine white dust had settled on the lower frame of the Picasso. The desiccated corpse of an upended fly lay on the narrow windowsill. His clients' feet had worn uneven patches in the carpet by the couch and the velvet cushions were shiny and bald. The white walls were streaked and yellowing and in the far corner was the unmistakable stain of mildew. Jay was reminded of an abandoned theatre, some local rep where lame productions of ambitious dramas are attempted by enthusiastic amateurs and, for a moment, he could see it all through the detective's reductive lens: it was the dressing room of an impostor, with all its sad props and the trappings of disguise, and Jay was some peepshow pervert whose grubby hand twitched in his crotch while feeble-minded clients paid him to watch them undress.

Morrison made a clicking noise with his lips as if to declare his distaste at the chicanery that was practised in this space, as if Jay was some muttering crone who foostered about with herbal scraps and potions, bamboozling empty-headed idiots with his hocus-pocus. Jay bent his head, wiping his palms on the side of his trouser leg, the deflated costume of a clown.

'As a matter of interest, Mr Hamilton, how do you treat people?'

'By providing a safe space where they can come to talk.' But he could hear how the empty clang of this explanation must reverberate in Morrison's sceptical ears, a disbelief that anyone would dare to provide such an ephemeral service that masqueraded as something useful when there is no prescription pad, no scientific method, just like those carpetbaggers in the movies, who roll into town and peddle their three-cent bottles of vile-tasting elixirs from the back of a cart. The truth slid like an icicle down Jay's back. He was nothing more than a charlatan who swindled gullible fools out of their stories with a bouquet of false promises, promising a poultice for the soul, when all he really had to offer was a couch in his living room where clients can vent their hysteria or hatch their criminal plans.

Morrison shook his heavy head. There was an unspoken accusation that this was a most unsavoury arrangement and there was also a suggestion of guilt and blame, that Jay might even have failed in his duty of care, that rather than indulging Cora's rantings, he should have found a better way to manage her distress. The stink of negligence hung in the air, for this crisis might have been averted if she had been placed in the hands of a competent professional, someone with verifiable medical skills, someone like a psychiatrist, or maybe even Laekin, who could have recognised the gravity of the situation and taken affirmative action, put Cora on a drug regime. It was the age-old debate about science and quackery and Jay flinched at the memory of Robert's slur flung out across the lecture theatre, the cheap joke about Freud, the stinging letter warning him off his chosen career path, Robert urging him to do something more constructive, more worthy, more scientific; something more like Robert. Jay could see it all reflected in Morrison's contemptuous regard: the suspicion that analysts are good for absolutely nothing and should be kept well away from any serious matters.

'Cora believes her infertility is the punishment for an abortion she had when she was nineteen,' said Jay, in an attempt to convince the detective that he could see the dangers hidden in Cora's depths. 'Her desperation for a child has made her unhealthily attached to her godson. To Christopher. She believes they have a special relationship. So, in her desire to have a child—'

'She abducted one,' interrupted Morrison and Jay realised that his effort to try and demonstrate his insight had simply inflamed the situation and proven his culpability, reducing him in the detective's eyes to a loose cannon: Jay knew everything and he did nothing, he didn't take pre-emptive action, didn't warn, didn't do anything useful or heroic or manly, he simply sat in his armchair and waited for the axe to fall.

'There are always a number of possible outcomes in therapy,' he muttered. 'No one can predict these things.'

'So tell me, Mr Hamilton, when *would* an analyst intervene?'

'It is very difficult to know what the right moment is,' Jay admitted. Morrison considered him sternly, rolling backwards on his heels, preparing to depart now that he had satisfied himself that Jay was incapable of providing constructive assistance in this urgent matter. He would leave him to reflect on his fraudulence, satisfied that he had made his point. Jay followed him back out to the hall and took the offered card.

'Going away?' the detective asked, eyeing the travel bag on the floor.

'Actually it's mine,' said Dana's voice above them and at that moment Jay remembered how she had been marooned upstairs in the study with her biographer's snooping nose. How her prying eyes must have widened when she saw his manuscript invitingly positioned on his desk – the lure of the title page would have been too much to resist, of course, especially since she'd heard Morrison use Cora's name. She would have reached out a cautious hand, lifted the first page, with half an ear to the landing trying to hear the conversation in the kitchen.

'I'm flying back to LA this evening,' she said, hurrying down the stairs, 'But I really should get going now,' she cast a quick glance in Jay's direction.

'Oh, surely you can stay a little longer,' he said, stepping forward to the bottom of the stair, for he could not let her leave with all the wrong impressions. But Dana slipped neatly past him, studiously avoiding eye contact, talking in a rapid bright chatter about being wait-listed for an earlier flight and getting stuck in motorway traffic, as if this incessant stream could disguise the fact that she had most definitely read Cora's story and was now confused but alert enough to pursue an instinct that urged her to leave this uncomfortable situation with the large detective who was now gallantly helping her with her coat.

'My satchel,' she bleated and Morrison looked over at Jay who stalled, resistant, but was forced to retreat to the kitchen and retrieve her bag. Dana thanked him and slipped it over her shoulder. She had aligned herself firmly on the capable side of law and order and was being discreetly removed from his custody.

'Let me at least call you a cab,' he said, in a final bid to keep her but she insisted that she would pick one up on the street, she had plenty of time and anyway she hated sitting around waiting. Morrison nodded in approval, endorsing her decision.

'Perhaps I could drive you to the airport,' Jay offered recklessly and she stared at the floor as if this was the most improper of suggestions. He suspected that the detective was enjoying watching him squirm on what he believed was the hook of a failed seduction.

'If you don't mind, Mr Hamilton,' said Morrison, 'I think it would be wise if you could stay here for the next couple of hours. On the off-chance that our party contacts you.'

'Yes, of course. I'm sorry,' said Jay, apologising for being so insensitive as to forget that a baby had been abducted, that little Christopher's life hung in the balance.

'Well, goodbye, Jay. And thanks again for all your help,' Dana's hand slid out of his grip. They crossed the road, Morrison wheeling her cabin bag behind him while Jay watched from his step as they disappeared round the corner of Edwardes Square.

• SEVENTEEN •

'Baby Christopher latest,' yelled a newsstand seller outside the tube station and Jay swivelled round, for a moment expecting the passers-by to turn towards him and demand an explanation, or at the very least an admission of guilt. He hurried across Wright's Lane, heading west along Kensington High Street, through the disjointed stream of Christmas shoppers until he stopped dead, right in front of Cora's face. Suspended in the late afternoon gloom, in the centre of a window display, was a large flat screen, flanked on either side by a column of three smaller screens, all of them linked by twisted ropes of silver tinsel. He guessed the photo was maybe two or three years old, for Cora appeared slightly fuller about the face, healthier and more vivid on screen than in the flesh and sporting a staged smile that she seemed to have embraced with excessive zeal. Her hair was a glossy chestnut, her cheeks rosy, her eyes bright with future promise: this was not a picture of a woman who would run off with her best friend's baby.

As Jay stood transfixed by the display, some invisible remote control erased her photo and replaced it with a young man and woman wearing red-and-white Santa hats beside an over-decorated Christmas tree. The girl put her hands to her cheeks in a gesture of exaggerated amazement as the camera panned back to reveal a bewildered reindeer standing behind her in the studio, two gold baubles dangling from its antler. The reindeer took a step forwards, lowering its head. The girl jumped and threw her arms around the male presenter's neck who raised his clenched fists in mock fighting pose. A large screen behind them zoomed into a close-up of a snowy landscape and a shot of the huddled and now be-furred presenters taking off on a dog sled driven by a red-coated and rather morose Santa. The sled bumped and whooshed in huge dollops of snow and vanished into a blue horizon.

The scene shifted to an ashen-faced man in his thirties, red-rimmed eyes averted from the intrusive glare of the camera. At the bottom of the screen a scrolling banner read

17:01 BREAKING NEWS: CORA MILLER'S HUSBAND PLEADS FOR BABY CHRISTOPHER'S SAFE RETURN

Larry Miller sat between a uniformed Detective Inspector and a middle-aged woman who had the sympathetic gravitas of a psychologist. He stared down at his pale hands splayed on the baize-covered table, clearly appalled by this public scrutiny. Unshaven, wearing a dark suit jacket and an unbuttoned collar with no tie, Larry had no doubt been bundled off the plane at Heathrow into a makeshift newsroom so that this bulletin could be beamed out while there was still a chance that Cora's trail was fresh. Jay guessed that the police were aiming for saturation publicity, inspired perhaps by the success of the Amber Alert in the US, which suggested that a media blitz in the first thirty-six hours after a child abduction is critical for a successful outcome. After that time, the trail goes cold, memory dulls and you're far more likely to wind up with a corpse on your hands.

The Detective Inspector leaned forward in direct address to the camera but Jay kept his eyes focused on Larry's bowed head, imagined him slumped in some interview room before the news conference being gently but firmly pressed for information about Cora, any little detail that might be helpful in this search, any little habit, anything at all. But Larry wouldn't have been able to think of anything unusual, possibly because he's been so much in New York working on some incredibly complex transaction that leaves him too exhausted to be observant on the weekends when he's at home, but still apparently alert enough to have arranged a regular 'Wild at Heart' delivery to his wife's office. Cora had told Jay about the weekly bouquet of white roses she received every Thursday and the card that said 'See you tomorrow, all my love'. Once the shop had made a mistake or perhaps some assistant had thought the ordered message too predictably bland and put in xxx after Larry's name, something he would never think to do, although he *was* thoughtful, if not always spontaneously and he never complained about long hours or the tedium of shuttling back and forth on the red-eye. Jay suspected that Larry's transatlantic spell was a well-timed opportunity to absent himself from over-exposure to Cora's interior space, although she did insist that he had always been magnanimous about her gynaecological shortcomings, repeatedly assuring her that he would happily countenance a childless future, especially as it was all happening in his career right now, albeit slightly late out of the box.

Larry was replaced by a shot of a South Kensington villa that Jay recognised as Pelham Crescent. A female reporter with severely cropped hair gestured at the white house behind her and the scene switched to a home video of a smiling toddler with large blue eyes and curly blond hair who stood clinging to the arm of a couch. He started unsteadily towards the camera dressed in a Winnie the Pooh T-shirt, clutching a teddy bear with his left hand, looking up with a red-cheeked enquiry. The lens panned frantically backwards as Christopher wobbled closer and flopped down on his nappied bottom, flapping his hands in delight.

Larry's face reappeared in close up and Jay lip-read the

words: *Please Cora come home.* Larry will have been advised to appeal directly to her – to talk to her calmly and reassuringly, to focus on repeating her name, to emphasise the personal. *I just want you to come home.* To hook a direct line to her conscience which would be shattered and fragmented, her reserves close to depletion as she sputtered towards disaster. *Christopher needs his mummy.* But Jay knew Cora wouldn't be listening, by now she would be tuned in exclusively to the internal narrative of nonsense that swirled around her head with all the clanking dissonance of a Stockhausen piece.

The woman psychologist patted Larry's shoulder and his face came back into view, the contortions of grief had drained all colour from his skin. *Please, Cora. Bring Christopher home. I— I— I—* but his head flopped down, he could not bring himself to complete the sentence which might have been the reassuring declaration of love he had been instructed to deliver, three little words that have tripped so easily from his lips for years now, but he couldn't do it, he couldn't say it, for Cora had, in one movement, become a person he didn't know, a monster of hidden passion and resolve that was apparently his wife.

He raised his head and looked past the camera with a bewildered squint. Jay nodded at the screen, this was a familiar moment that he has witnessed so many times, for Larry was staring now into a past that he no longer recognised. The fact was, he hadn't been watching Cora at all, but rather the outline of what he'd expected she would be when she first appeared in front of him one Saturday lunchtime in the crowded Oyster Bar at Grand Central, a faint acidity of Chardonnay on her English lips. He remembered how she'd been introduced by some woman friend of an ex whose name escaped him now and how afterwards, he couldn't stop thinking about her and it wasn't long till he had her, after a quick divorce from one of those disposable first marriages that don't really count. Perhaps the seeds of this tragedy were sown even then, for Larry hadn't really been listening and Cora hadn't really volunteered much about herself, she treated the past as if it was an irrelevance, as if there was not necessarily a causal relationship between one moment and the next and, in fact, Larry had thought it refreshing that she seemed intent on living exclusively in the here-and-now, when the previous women in his life were always time-travelling in reverse. He knew that Cora had been feigning sleep on the nights when he was home but he never saw the point in dwelling on stuff that his wife chose to remain silent about and anyway Larry fell asleep as soon as his head hit the pillow.

Larry shook his head slowly, his jaw slack, lips parted. He was, Jay could see, transfixed by the realisation that he had completely failed to detect the subtle emphasis in Cora's life, it always had the feel of something remote that was happening far away in another person's world and now his inattention to her silent broodiness was screaming in his ear, making him look foolish and insensitive. Didn't he know well enough that it's always a mistake to rely on what people tell you, to just *assume*? Yes, Larry would admit now that there has always been the sense of something lurking beneath the surface, and yes, he had certainly failed to accord sufficient urgency to Cora's need for a baby but how could he have foreseen that this thwarted desire could transform her into an abductress, like a snake in the fruit basket? Nothing prepares you for the discovery of this ice hole, the strange and barren landscape that subverts your days. Larry's fingers scrabbled at the table. The psychologist patted his hand but he didn't even register her touch, for he was clawing at some desperate fantasy where Cora would appear on their doorstep, hand over the baby and they would flee to some private sanatorium in Switzerland like the characters in a Fitzgerald novel. A bleak sob escaped his lips. Surely she wouldn't, surely she couldn't, harm the baby?

'*Le pauvre,*' muttered a woman's voice, tipping Jay out of reverie and into a sideways glance away from the screen to a luxurious fur collar that completely obscured the lower half of a woman's face. 'How could she steal that little *bébé?*' she demanded, turning a pair of green eyes to Jay and immediately refocusing on the specifics of their encounter. Straightening her shoulders, she smiled and reappraised the situation, patted her dark chignon with a gloved hand as if checking whether the distressing footage had disturbed the arrangement. 'That woman must *never* be forgiven,' she pronounced and Jay was struck by the accuracy of her verdict – it was true that indefinite psychiatric incarceration would be the most merciful punishment Cora could expect. The woman considered his ineffectual response and tilted her head upwards and to the left, offsetting her profile to its best advantage. 'It is a tragedy,' she sighed, with a theatrical softening of the 'g' to advertise her Frenchness, in case Jay had missed this crucial detail. 'These things, they bring people together,' she fluttered a glove.

Once, Jay recalled, he had met a woman just like this in Waterstone's and allowed her conversational gambits to chart a relatively straightforward route to bed after the brief interval of drinks and dinner. She had left her book bag behind in his hallway, a copy of *How to Transform Your Life in Seven Days*, but had never returned to claim it, as he had known she wouldn't after his unceremonious dismissal of her at midnight. Lately, he has begun to find it tiresome, the investment of time in seductions that had invariably yielded so little in return. There was, Jay thought, staring at the window, very little left to do.

'We must all unite in hope,' the Frenchwoman added, but she was flagging now in the absence of a response. She cast a quick glance at the street and disappeared into the moving crowd.

Cora's photo seemed to have faded and aged even in the few

minutes since last viewing, as if the print was evaporating. Seven screens replayed the press conference, although Jay imagined that Larry was at home by now on the advice of the police, waiting for Cora to return or call, cradling a heavy glass of whisky, something perhaps he doesn't normally drink but he'd sip it obediently at the insistence of his friends, because all the rules have changed, his life has been laid bare, his marriage, his photo collection, and he is numbed to any further exposure, clinging to the memory of better times but unable to escape the madness that leers back at him from Cora's televised face. How does your wife go crazy right under your nose? And what does that make you? Where were the boundaries of blame and guilt in the small circle of their intimate life? It seemed for a moment as if Larry knew nothing at all about Cora except her dress size.

Jay could see him beached in the couch, fending off the stalking guilt. What could I have done differently, Larry will ask his bleak hands and his best friend, for he will need to have some fellow American on the premises at a time like this, someone called Andy or Chuck or Bob who will say things like, 'Hey, don't go there. There was nothing you could have done. Come on, Larry, you've got to keep it together now, man.' Someone to comfort him in this new alien life that has claimed him, someone who will quash his floundering self-recriminations with a sturdy rebuttal, someone whose wife will make coffee and sandwiches in the kitchen, in a background attempt to introduce some reassuring domesticity to the proceedings and frown warningly at the whisky bottle, summoning her husband into the hall to whisper, 'He needs to stay sober. You know, in case the police—' she gestures for the right word to cover a host of possibilities that Andy/Chuck/Bob will dismiss with, 'Jesus, what the hell difference is that gonna make now?' But they both jump at the sound of the doorbell and watch the detective stride past them into the hall. Back in the couch,

Larry's head lolls, Cora has catapulted him into chaos, with one fell stroke he has lost everything and he wonders if there is a worst, or if that already happened when his wife exploded into a media sensation on the screens above the trading floor at the bank where he works and all over the world, gaining him international notoriety.

He will never again think of her with ease. He will never lose the suspicion that she faked everything and that he somehow failed to spot the fatal flaw that allowed her to do something so terrible. Larry is already in flight and wants to erase the memory, to be shipped home by his accommodating employer, to downshift into something more anonymous, lower key – the Midwest or maybe Denver, somewhere forgettable where he can start over.

Jay pulled back from the shop window and continued along Kensington High Street, turning a sharp left into the sanctuary of Abingdon Road. He stopped outside the police station on Earls Court Road where a hastily assembled poster of Cora and Christopher was housed in a wall-mounted glass box by the entrance. The print had the washed-out impermanence of a colour photocopy and already looked as if it had been there for some time. Hurrying along the bricked boundary of the station, his footsteps echoed on the tarmac as if they were announcing his presence to the empty lane, they were keeping step with his contracting heart. But Jay could not slow his pace, his legs accelerated as he rounded the corner to Edwardes Square with the jerky motion of a speed walker on the home run and he fell upon his front door like a finish line.

He heard the ringing phone and stood panting in the hallway, listening to Laekin's message.

'Dreadful business with Cora Miller. I – eh – imagine the

police have been round by now, Jay.' He sighed. 'I didn't know she had taken my advice and was seeing you. Must be very distressing. Anything I can do, well you know. So, we'll – um – be in touch. And of course – eh – naturally hope for the best.'

Consequences. Jay could feel the air thicken, like the hour before a storm and he climbed the stair, loosening his collar, stopping at the top, short of breath and leaden as if at high altitude. A slant of streetlight shone through the French windows, illuminating his manuscript in a yellow glow. There on his desk lay Cora's story, a full and accurate account of today's headline news.

This morning, after he closed the door on Dana and Detective Morrison, Jay had sprinted up to the study, taking the steps three at a time, to watch the departing couple heading north towards Kensington High Street under a light drizzle. He stared at their receding figures, as if by concentrating he could eavesdrop on their conversation. Dana would have mentioned Cora's name at the first opportunity, reminding Morrison that she had heard it from his lips as she left the kitchen. The detective would have volunteered the public information that he was investigating Cora Miller in connection with the abduction of a baby. When Dana stopped dead on the pavement, her mouth popping open as if she'd hit an air pocket, Morrison would bend a solicitous head and ask if she was all right and she would compose herself and mutter 'Oh yes, yes, thank you, how awful,' not knowing what else to say, for anything she did say might sound ridiculous.

The detective had the kind of reassuring presence that invited the disclosure of silly fears, but Dana knew better than to say the first thing that came into her head. And what could she actually tell him, except that she had seen what she believed was a case history on Jay's desk about a woman called Cora and, driven by the base curiosity of a biographer who spends her life riffling through other peoples' possessions, she had to confess that she had sneaked a read, she couldn't resist the title. In the case history, the woman called Cora had abducted a baby and the weird thing was that stylistically it read more like a work of fiction than a case history, but then so did Freud in her opinion, she had to admit she wasn't really qualified to judge...

But Dana had not spoken, had obviously decided to hold her peace and let Morrison hail her a taxi on the High Street, deposit her bag in the back and shake her hand, ignoring an angry car horn behind the stalled cab. Jay suspected she had lost her nerve in the rush and the confusion and the stink of exhaust, but all the way to the airport it would gnaw at her as she pondered the convergence of reality and fiction, thinking there must be something she had missed, for how could Jay have known? How could he have predicted? She must have got it wrong.

Jay stepped up to the glass, his reflection swallowed by the dark well of the garden square below him. The house was alive with the whispered fragments that haunted his safe space, rolling out from under the door up the stairs, filling the night with their fictions. He stood in the extinguished light, watching a lone vixen slide out through the railings and cut a sly northwards dash to a night banquet in Holland Park. A large Mercedes nosed around the corner and began an ambitious attempt to manoeuvre itself into an undersized parking space. A man stepped out of the passenger side and hurried to the front gesturing impatiently at the driver. The car inched forwards and the man shouted, smacking the bonnet and flinging his hands into the air. The driver's door opened and a tall woman in a fur-trimmed hat emerged. She glared at the man over the roof of the idling car and then turned on her high heel and walked away. The man shook his head and walked round to the driver's door. The car lurched forwards and followed the woman down the street.

Jay moved back to the desk and patted his manuscript. Gently, as if it was incendiary. There was nothing left to do now but wait. He was powerless to impact Dana, a call on her mobile would only compound the issue and might even tip her over the edge, she was out of range and he needed to operate within controllable constraints. In twelve hours' time she will be standing by a baggage carousel at LAX with a planeload of sullen passengers and she would still be thinking about Cora. She'll take a cab straight to her rental on Tiverton and Le Conte, log on to her PC and check the international news, study the footage of Larry's appeal. She will decide to go for a run, telling herself it's all explainable but Cora's story will snake through her day. Buried in the basement archives at Special Collections, Dana will press her fingertips into the polished wood desk but her misgivings will simply fuel her interest in Robert and she will continue to mine his papers for every last clue.

He looked at his watch. Just about now Dana would be queueing at the departure gates in Terminal 4 with the bowed head of a long-distance traveller. He imagined her looking over the shoulder of the woman in front at the cover of the *Evening Standard* where Christopher's and Cora's photos take up half the page. The queue shuffles forwards. Dana takes out her mobile. She hesitates, tapping her fingers on the warm curve of the phone, thinking you don't call detectives on an abduction case on a whim. She looks back at the photo, Christopher smiles up at her and the phone grows hot and slippery in her hand. 'No,' she says aloud, and steps out of the line. She calls Directory Enquiries and asks for Morrison's number.

Just in case.

You never know.

Jay rolled a slim pen across his desk, over and back. Cora could not go on much longer. It has been twenty-six hours, the nets were closing in. He reached for his keyboard and logged on to AOL news.

HUNT FOR BABY CHRISTOPHER CONTINUES. 11-MONTH-OLD BABY CHRISTOPHER WAS ABDUCTED FROM HIS CHELSEA HOME YESTERDAY EVENING BY A FAMILY FRIEND WHO HAS BEEN NAMED AS CORA MILLER, AGED 37. SHE IS DESCRIBED AS 5 FOOT 4 SLIM BUILD BROWN HAIR AND GREY EYES. POLICE ARE CONCERNED FOR BOTH OF THEIR SAFETY AND ARE ASKING THE PUBLIC TO BE VIGILANT AND REPORT ANY SIGHTING

Jay was convinced she was outdoors, along by the river perhaps, or in the dark open spaces of a park, clutching Christopher to her breast. He might be asleep, not yet missing his mummy too much or the world that is trying to find him. Cora would be having moments of exhilarated light-headedness. Christopher may start to cry, a long forlorn wail that will not stop. Cora will need to find a way to make it stop.

Jay turned the pages of his manuscript, thinking about the Cora in his story who acted on impulse, who drove through the night in an unforgiving straight line right out of her own past only for it to meet her full circle. It will come full circle in real time as well; Jay sees no reason to expect a different ending. Cora will understand that her best friend, Christopher's sobbing mother, is itching to wrap her hands around Cora's throat. This was not something you can forgive. There was nothing Jay could do other than wait. And hope that reality and fiction have not met. Hope for a different ending.

When Dana tells Morrison, which could be very soon now, the detective will lift his large head and immediately follow his line of enquiry back to Edwardes Square. Naturally, he will want to read the story, so Jay will have to endure the humiliation of watching while he reads. If Jay lied and said there was no file to show him, it could be traced by a simple search of his cyber trash, for a story is like a person, even after they've been eliminated you can never be sure you have erased all traces of the experience. He reached for the mouse and scrolled down the File option, remembering a client, an IT specialist called Kevin who used to spend entire sessions talking in coded language about the intricacies of his job, his real issues screened by the firewall of his expertise. Kevin got his kicks from tapping into his colleagues' emails, stalking their cyber lives to give his own a little colour. 'People think they can get rid of files. They think they can create and destroy at will, hah. No way. It's like a black box,' he sneered, describing in laborious detail how the purged file leaves a sprinkling of incriminating data on the hard disk that gradually decays over time through overwriting, but never completely disappears. 'The only way you can be sure is to take a hammer and smash the disk to bits. And even then a forensic expert could piece the fragments of those together.'

No, thought Jay, it would be madness to delete the file.

Morrison will not enjoy Jay's story at all. He will ask more impertinent questions about his practice. He will want to know exactly how Jay could possibly have predicted the outcome in Cora's case. From her story, it will be but a short step to the revelation that Jay's clients serve a dual purpose as unwitting muses for his literary career. Morrison will consider this type of activity distinctly objectionable. He will make incredulous remarks about educated guesses. The word 'unethical' will roll heavily across the carpet. Morrison will want to take it somewhere. He will explore Jay's failure to take pre-emptive action. He will consider it a failure to save. He will invite Jay down to the station. Although Jay is convinced that there is no legal culpability in what he has done, he knows that all of this will somehow make its way into the public domain. The BPS will naturally be appalled at this prurient use of client material, the abuse of the therapeutic space, the papers will buzz about the ethics of psychoanalysis and the whole issue of regulation will become vibrant again with consumer warnings. His name will disappear, his book quietly removed from the teaching syllabus. His analytic reputation, so hard won, will collapse.

Cora's story can never now be published. J. Merritt will be outed and publicly disgraced, vilified as a writer who doesn't have the imagination to think up his own stories but must prey on others' misery. His agent and publisher will terminate their business arrangement in their embarrassed rush to disassociate themselves from such a tawdry alliance. His novels will be considered pathetic. Former clients who recognise their fragmented appearance in his novels may even try to take legal action. His magnificent construction, his beautiful artwork was crumbling before his eyes. A life's work interrupted.

The phone rang. Jay's hand moved across the desk and lifted the receiver, heard the background sound of movement and bustle.

'How did you know?' Dana's voice was tense and small.

'I wish you hadn't left so abruptly, I wanted to explain.'

'Cora Miller is a patient of yours, isn't she?'

'Yes,' he admitted, closing his eyes, reminding himself it was important to keep a placatory tone.

'Your story – how did you know this was going to happen? Did Cora tell you what she was going to do?'

'Of course not.'

'Then how did you know?'

'I didn't. It is simply a coincidence.'

'I don't believe you. It's too – unlikely.'

A blur of airport noise flooded the earpiece.

'Sometimes, Dana, reality meets fiction in the most surprising ways.'

'But you must have known the risks. You must have known this woman was unstable.'

'The story you read is simply one version of a life, one moment chosen out of a range of possible moments, one truth in a possible world. There is no such thing as a guaranteed result.' A stream of tannoy announcements invaded the connection, there was a clicking sound and Jay could not be sure if he had lost her. 'Dana?'

'I've seen your books here at the airport,' she said in a flat determined voice. 'I know who J. Merritt is.'

'Clever girl.'

'What are you going to do? You don't even sound like you care.'

'There is nothing I can do. Cora's story is still playing itself out as we speak.' He looked at the mute TV screen in the corner of his study. 'We have not reached an ending yet.'

'In the story, Cora—'

'The story is a work of fiction.'

'Did you tell Morrison?'

'Do you really think the detective is interested in the speculations of a novelist?'

'I want him to know,' she snapped.

'Then why haven't you called him and not me? Might I suggest it's because you know that the story is irrelevant? The fictional ending cannot affect the real outcome. You are grappling with the illusion that I can impact upon the course of future events. This is not the case, Dana. You have simply read a story.'

'I don't like what you do,' she said, her voice very close to the receiver. 'You are using your clients as cannon fodder.'

'I am simply following in a grand literary tradition of writers who have always raided their personal experiences. Freud used his patients for his own ends. We are all each other's experiments in an encounter. As a biographer, Dana, you should understand that better than most. You exhumed my brother without compunction. You engineered the reopening of Robert's murder, resurrected a family tragedy. And for what? Because it makes a good story.'

'That's different.'

'Ah, but you are ringing me up instead of the detective because you know this is true.'

'It's not the same,' her voice fading, losing conviction.

'You must make your own decision about what to do, Dana. I have registered your disapproval and I understand your concern. But if you think rationally, you will see that there is no real difference between you and me. As writers we feed on other people's lives to further our careers. Everything is fair game. That is the human condition. So, this is your ethical dilemma, not mine.'

'I'm going now.'

'Have a pleasant flight, my dear. Let us hope that reality will be kinder than fiction. Goodbye, Dana,' and the line went dead.

• EIGHTEEN •

The rain beat out a steady rhythm against the glass. Down below him on the street, the vixen had returned and was skirting along the garden railings, stopping by the wheel of a parked car to begin a delicate inspection of a scrap of paper.

Jay wondered how long it would take for the LAPD to call. He assumed there must be some protocol that required the next of kin to be informed when a cold case was reopened, but even if there wasn't, Detective Rodriguez would want to speak to Jay in his capacity as the only witness to the events that occurred at 3840 North Beverly Drive on 7 March, 1971. Dana would in any case have given him Jay's London phone number and will probably soon find a way to voice her reservations about his literary analytic career.

He imagined that the Cold Case Unit would require a different kind of detective work entirely and Jay wondered if Rodriguez was the analytical type, the kind who is undeterred by the passage of time between the crime and the investigation, but rather motivated by the chance to clean up history. Perhaps he relished the challenge of bodies long since decomposed, relatives who have become inured to grief. Maybe he liked long odds. Maybe he was done with handling fresh corpses and was intrigued by the letter that Dana had found in the archives – T. V. Wright lying in his bunk in Alameda County Jail dreaming of the day when he would get out and track down the boy who put him there, how he would lure him to his death by posing as a downtown trick. Maybe Rodriguez had been on the force long enough to know that stranger things have happened than a slow-burn revenge.

Dana would have a wonderful story, the professor and the thief. Perhaps herself and Rodriguez would appear on *Larry King Live*, an unlikely double act, the biographer-and-cop team who solved a thirty-year-old murder mystery with a killer combination of painstaking research and supreme detective work.

Robert's records would be yellowing now, the long dry foolscap frayed at the edges. Rodriguez would study the autopsy carefully, the language of death would be second nature to him. In certain cases, as the Medical Examiner had explained to Jay and Detective Green at the scene, strangulation causes sudden death: when the sheer pressure of the ligature or the killer's hands crush the vertebrae that protect the spinal arteries and cut off the blood supply to the brain. This triggers the lethal Vagal reflex and the heart immediately stops beating. The victim will exhibit minimal physical signs of injury – perhaps some bruising around the neck – and the face will be pale, with no engorgement.

But that's not how it was for Robert.

The Medical Examiner had told Detective Green what Jay already knew – that Robert had taken much longer to die. He pointed to the face speckled with petechiae, blood vessels burst in the skin and eyes. This meant that Robert had struggled for two or three minutes before lapsing into unconsciousness, which is what he was when Jay had found him. It would, the examiner confirmed, have taken up to ten minutes for Robert to actually die. He might even have lasted longer.

To this day, Jay could not work out why he had woken at 06:02 on Sunday, 7 March 1971, only that he had found himself staring out the window just in time to see some movement around Robert's Mustang. He ran downstairs, through the open door, down the drive of 3840 North Beverly, where he saw two or three black men speed off in the car. Jay stood watching as they disappeared.

He ran back into the house, up the stairs, but when his foot touched the landing, Jay froze. He had the distinct sensation that he was on the brink of a transforming event, although *how* he knew this was indescribable; it was something in the quality of stillness, something he didn't recall articulating, but he remembered the conviction that his life was about to be irrevocably changed.

The bathroom door creaked open onto its ugly display. He looked down at Robert's supine body, his contorted face, the lurid purple, the red raw neck, the naked spill of flesh, the jar of Vaseline on the washstand, flecks of dark brown on its slimy contents, the unmistakable stink of shit and he gagged on a virtual retch, slamming a fist into the doorjamb. 'How could you?' he screamed, crouching over Robert's bruised face. 'You stupid—' he yelled through a rage of tears, pummelling the naked expanse of chest, the waste, the futility, the careless inevitable outcome of promiscuity, the ease with which it can all end, for end it looked to be. 'How could you let this happen?' And just then, a hideous twitching began, Robert was making small sudden jerks, like a sleeper racked by nightmares, it was as if the perpetrators could still reach their victim, as if invisible fingers were twisting the tie around his neck. Jay understood this was some sort of muscular reflex, that the dampening in the hue of Robert's skin meant he had found a clever escape route on the threshold of extinction and was clawing his way towards some remarkable recovery, he was trying to outwit death with the same grim determination that he had pursued the illicit thrills which left him half-strangled on the floor. Jay groped for his brother's limp wrist and felt a slow but steady pulse that took him back to Christmas 1954 and the faint thud of the mongrel's heart through her juddering ribs as she sleep-whimpered in the darkness. He could hear Robert's voice saying, 'Promise me you'll take good care of her,' he could feel the delicious touch of his brother's hand on his six-year-old head as he snuggled down on the living-room floor and dreamt of all the brotherly moments they would share, with the dog leaping through the long grass. But dawn had come and Jay's vision of a fraternal future was quickly unravelled by the loosening thread of Robert's affection as he slipped further and further out of reach, lured away by numbers and strangers, both equally incomprehensible, until there was no space left to accommodate the nudge of a kid brother. And it came to Jay as he held his brother's wrist, that Robert had wrecked everything: he had driven away the father, he had stolen the store of available motherlove, leaving an impossible abyss for Jay to fill, and now, sprawled naked on the bathroom floor, he teetered between life and a death brought on by the squalid expenditure of desire.

'Your own fucking fault,' Jay shouted and he pulled at the tie that was wrapped around his brother's neck with a gasp of recognition, for it was a Christmas present from their mother. Robert's arms twitched, his throat gurgled and Jay sensed a flutter of the eyelashes, he felt a straining in his fingers and looked down to see his own hands pulling on the murderous tie. 'Let go, let go,' he pleaded, blinded now by his own tears, or perhaps the memory flash of the dead dog, but the striped tie bit into the flesh of his palms, he stared down at his clenched fists as they tightened the twisted noose around Robert's neck and it was all unstoppable, inevitable, the logical next step for both of them. Jay's was an unreleasable grip and Robert's face was turning a ludicrous violet hue, the moment passing where an actioned response might save him. For Jay was choking his brother to death, he could feel it in his burning hands and he thought of the earlier moment, the little dog and the weight of consequence and loss, but he could not let go and in a sunburst revelation he understood that he had never reconciled himself to anything, that everything that ever had happened had been nothing more than the most bitter consolation, it had *never ever ever* for a second been all right. Jay had been screaming for this moment all his life.

And then it was done. Jay was spent, chin slumped against his chest. His stiff knees ached, pressed into the cold bathroom floor. He was drained and exhausted, but his hands throbbed with a new-found peace, for he was released and so too, was Robert. Jay fumbled for a pulse, but it was gone. He looked into his brother's bulging eyes.

This is where love will get you.

In the deep and curious calm that followed, there was time for Jay to think, kneeling on the floor, time to reflect on the semantics of death, as life fled and the cadaver arrived. Survival, not death, was really the mystery, underrated and under-explored – the instinct to cling on gasping, to do your time. He was stunned by the intimacy of strangulation, it had none of the distance of a gunshot or a stab wound, none of the impersonality of a weapon, it was such a passionate way to kill, and such a feminine way to die; it was the way men murder women, the perfect way to slay a lover, when a slow agonising death seems appropriate; it was an act of real engagement, intensely personal, how you kill when love meets hate, when you are so consumed by your victim that your body must become the weapon, you must crush the slender windpipe, feel the hot thrash of flesh before the body goes slack in your arms. And then, in the quiet aftermath, a few moments peace for killer and victim to reflect on how they could both have avoided this outcome, time to consider their shortcomings and flaws, an opportunity for pure remorse while the victim drifts into unconsciousness and a final expiring embrace.

Jay could see clearly now how little there was that separated hate from love.

Very quickly, he believed it was likely that he could evade all responsibility. To begin with, the whole business had been kick-started by unknown assailants, so Jay had simply completed a job left undone. If he had called 911 as soon as he had found his brother on the floor and assisted as he was coming round, it was possible that Robert might have lived. But he could just as easily have died in the initial attack. The outcome was unpredictable. One could only speculate on who was the real murderer. Jay knew, however, that any further delay in reporting this crime would not help his case so he stood up and turned his back on this tableau of death, hurried downstairs and picked up the phone. There was no question in his mind that what he faced here was an obstacle in the administration of justice that needed to be circumvented. And that was exactly what he did.

He could smell his own sleep-stained skin as he stood waiting on the drive. Pebbles and sharp, crushed twigs pricked his bare feet. A scatter of pine cones hit the ground in front of him, as if flung by hiding children. He jerked his head at a furtive rustling in the needlegrass, but the road was still and empty in the creeping dawn. Up there in the dense foothills, a host of nameless creatures trembled in the undergrowth terror.

Behind him, at the top of the drive, the front door gaped open on all that he had fled and he bent double to ease his scorched lungs. A coyote screech split the air and his eyelids burst open onto a moment drenched in monochrome, a dry suspension of breathing, the surge of adrenaline that had forced him down the stairs and it seemed, in memory, as if he had taken flight all the way along Mulholland up into the cool starless sky.

Everything Jay told Detective Green was true. He simply omitted to say that he had found Robert close to death and had finished him off. His estimates of what the police investigation would yield turned out to be accurate: Jay's fingerprints were entirely explainable by the act of untying the tie in an attempt to resuscitate his brother, his lack of alibi paled against the evidence of other (unidentified) prints on the body and the ligature, the stolen car (found the next day on Spring Street). The sexual implications of the scene dovetailed perfectly with Robert's sleazy habits. And so it was. There was never any suggestion other than that Robert had brought this tragedy upon himself, which of course he had. If he hadn't gone cruising and brought home a couple of tricks, he would never have been attacked in his own home and Jay would never have found him lying unconscious on the bathroom floor and himself in a situation where his lifetime had converged on a single instant with such extraordinary consequence. Jay could tell himself that his involvement was small, a last-minute contribution.

'I have to go see my mother. To tell her,' Jay said to Green as they watched the gurney slide through the waiting doors of the coroner's van.

'That's a tough one,' Green conceded, inspecting the sky with a thoughtful frown. 'You might wanna clean up the details. Y'know what I'm saying,' he added, grinding his cigarette into the ground. He patted Jay on the shoulder, more of a backslap really, but in this parting gesture, the Detective confided his personal verdict, a little reassurance that the LAPD was satisfied that there was an explanation for everything that had transpired here. It was a release for Jay, it was the best outcome and he was intrigued that murder had never presented itself as a conscious wish before. The real mystery was that more people were not killed by those who loved them.

So now, after so many years, what did Jay really have to fear from a reopening of Robert's case? What was there that could alert Detective Rodriguez's suspicions? Was all the evidence preserved, did fingerprints decay? Could forensic testing somehow reveal that Jay had gripped the tie with a murderous force that was consistent with the *tightening*, not the loosening? He did not seriously believe there was a way that he could be incriminated. Any case against him would be circumstantial and Jay did not see how Rodriguez could find a thing. And what purpose would be served by truth, he would like to ask, other than the law, justice, balancing of scales, the administration of a legal morality? To prove murder they would have to establish motive and there was no evidence for a rage that only found its articulation in death.

Or was there?

Something he had forgotten? Something overlooked but survivable, some crucial evidence buried and bagged and removed from the scene. Something he did not recall? Something that would not escape the tentacles of rigorous scientific method?

Sometimes Jay was no longer sure what the truth was, after all this time. Perhaps he had imagined it all.

But having survived one investigation, he would not care to be re-examined, especially in the light of his joint career and the coincidence of Cora's story already written that appears to predict events. He would not welcome the scrutiny, for in communication there is always risk. There are so many theories that collapse under the weight of closer inspection. All these years he had been happily reconciled with his own past but there was no release now from the uncertainty that will dog each second, from the possibility that one day he will answer the door and a clean-cut invasion will yield its damning results. Taking evasive action would simply create suspicion and Jay was not about to make a fool of himself by trying to escape. Now, he must endure a purgatory of waiting and then take the consequences that are offered him without objection. He has spent a lifetime listening to the turgid chronicle of stories with the same twist. How astonishing, he thought, watching the vixen disappear through the railings, that it never before occurred to him to end it all, that his life has been a vigorous and persistent search that has simply confirmed the absence of something essential.

At 4 pm on 7 March 1971, Jay got in the car and headed for Van Nuys, sped along the I-170 with the burden of his news, which Green had said would probably be reported in the following morning's *LA Times*. In a triumph of timing, he caught his mother alone and her voice through the intercom was loud and irritable at the unexpected call. He ignored the elevator and sprinted up the three flights. The door to her apartment stood ajar but she was already shuffling away, hadn't even bothered to stay on the threshold to greet him.

'You never said you were coming,' she grumbled, settling with some difficulty into the armchair and he watched, a little chagrined at how much the arthritis had slowed her down in recent months. He felt cheated not to have found her at the top of her game. 'Why didn't Robert come with you?' she asked looking irritably towards the door. Peter squawked and flung himself against the wall of his cage. Jay sat down beside the bookcase. In the shrine on her coffee table, his brother was already looking posthumous.

'I have bad news,' said Jay, looking behind her at the parrot's unblinking gape. Her mouth wavered on the cusp of a querulous complaint. 'Some very bad news,' he said, moving over to hunker down in front of her chair. Peter head-butted a silver mirror, shuffled along his perch, pecking at the empty air. Jay reached up a hand to where his mother's arm rested on the wing, but decided against actually touching. She considered him from behind her glasses, reluctant and impatient.

'You sick?' she said, with obvious distaste, fingering a button on her cardigan and he realised that her conception of bad news did not extend to the unthinkable.

'It's Robert,' he said.

When he told her, slowly and with emphasis, the veined whites of her eyes executed a bovine roll, she slumped backwards and for a moment he thought her heart had failed but she shrieked and lashed out, catching him with a blow on the side of the cheek, delivered with a force enough to bruise. The parrot shrieked and crashed about, battering his wings at the walls of the cage. His mother grabbed Jay's lapel and he wondered if he dared pin her flapping arms to her sides. 'It's the truth, Mom. The police have been there all morning. Robert's been strangled.'

The moment he told her had been so rich in its anticipation and so utterly barren in its delivery. His mother's grief was anti-climatic. It was private and utterly inaccessible in its visibility. For if Jay could not fathom love, he could not experience the agony of loss. He could not feel her pain, only bear witness to a torment that served to reveal the void within him, the barren hole where his own humanity must have withered before it had a chance to blossom, assassinated at birth. He turned away from her wretched sobbing and moved to the safer confines of the kitchen where he called her doctor, finding the number pencilled in an address book in the lobby. An hour later she was dry, drugged and husk-like, a metamorphosis that would never leave her in the few months she had left. It was as if the juice had been squeezed out of an orange and the flesh left there to shrivel. She sat in the armchair and stared at the rim of her teacup. She had no intention of surviving this.

'Robert was homosexual, Mom,' said Jay when the doctor had gone. 'He liked going with Negroes.'

Her face wobbled under the assault of so much detail but she would not dignify him with a response.

'Robert went out last night about ten. First thing this morning I saw a couple of them jump into his car. I found him on the bathroom floor. He was strangled with his tie. The one you gave him for Christmas. The police think it was the guys he picked up.'

Her eyes regarded him with such consummate disgust that Jay could not return her gaze. 'It was horrible,' he surprised himself by saying in a small whining voice.

'You didn't hear anything in the night.'

'No.'

'Nothing you could have done?' In the unspoken exchange she managed to communicate her personal suspicion that Jay had somehow failed to save his brother and at that moment he longed to confess the whole truth, so that his mother would understand that responsibility was really hers, it was all her fault for never loving him, that she had driven him to seize such an opportunity.

'You can call Betty, she'll sit with me. Then you go,' she said, closing her eyes as if the very sight of him revolted her.

His mother had decided on death. It would be somehow arranged. She willed it to happen and so it did, just a few months later in an overheated hospital room in Van Nuys. She managed to engineer a substantial malignancy on her breast that had already taken up secondary positions in her liver and intestine, it was the third act in the family drama and she would be the next character to clear the stage. Jay came down every weekend from San Francisco, undeterred by her indifference, his turn now to do the torturous journey, to accolades from her nurses and friends. It was a privilege to watch her die. The pain in the end was substantial and they were feeding her morphine as she drifted in and out of consciousness. 'She'll be in considerable discomfort,' the physician said, explaining the drug, but Jay would have preferred her death throes not to be alleviated and it took all his self-control not to hold a pillow over her mouth. It had been a delicious experience, hearing the confirmation that the cancer was terminal, with a short-term end in sight, but a triumph that clattered emptily when he contemplated the impossibility of making her suffer more. It was astonishing how she'd managed to wriggle out of her own circumstance. She lay in a stupor of anticipation that transcended any physical distress, lost not in the pain of her decaying body but in the agony of bereavement and therefore propelled by an urgency to get this dying business over with so that she could join Robert in some celestial reunion. She couldn't wait to get out of this world.

Week after stubborn week Jay offered soup to her lips, watching for the smallest indication that his mother might discover some belated affection for her sole surviving son. But she seemed impervious to his presence, he could sit in the chair for hours while she stared at Robert propped in a silver frame on her bedside table. She couldn't take her eyes off him, the dead son who could French-pleat her hair, who could play exquisite Handel, she was always touching the things he touched, greedily gulping in his air, so that she often forgot the incidental fact of Jay's existence, was startled when he spoke, as if he'd slashed through the umbilical cord that bound her to her firstborn. Jay felt the fierce heat of a love that would never be his, he knew the only alternative would be the negotiated love of the adult, all calculated compromise and reluctant trade-off, such a humiliating second-best. He had missed the opportunity of exclusive motherlove and was forever consigned to a life of correction, of making do, of gritting his teeth and learning to love his own inner child, inventing a fiction of self-worth that his own mother had never managed to discover. His entire life would be a protest against the scabrous mutant that he knew himself to be, concealed by the undergrowth of normality, camouflaged by his talent for observation and mimesis.

For there really was a critical age for learning how to love. It was like language, which linguists have lately discovered will not develop spontaneously or correctly if the child is not exposed to speech before the onset of puberty. Something to do with the lateralisation of the brain. Robert had once told him the story of Jeanie, a girl in Chicago who had been kept tethered by her demented parents in a backyard hovel, so that, at an estimated age of eleven, it was already too late: Jeanie could learn to speak but the free gift of automatic linguistic expertise had been denied her by a childhood spent in a pigsty. And so it is with the unloved child, there is a cut-off point where what you have never learnt becomes an emotion that you can only imitate, you are forever denied the human experience.

His mother dozed in the hospital bed, her breath snagging on some unwelcome half-dream and Jay wondered: who was she, this woman who bucked the biological trend? How did it happen? Did it creep up on her when his hungry infant cry shattered the humid dawn, did it slowly come into view as daylight sneaked under the curtain, illuminating the bundle in the crib that wouldn't cease its fretful protest, the gap where love should have been, apparently all used up by Robert? Perhaps there isn't always an unlimited supply. Of course, duty of care is a fine substitute, an admirable and noble alternative. But it is the most heinous of crimes, the failure to love. A crucial detail forgotten in the rush of event, in the press of living, a scarf dropped, a flower untended that grows but never blooms. Jay the choreographer, the voyeur, would be forever lying in the sagebrush, watching the business of life played out beneath him.

He recalled an afternoon from long ago, his earliest conscious memory, when his mother stood in the kitchen with a bowl clasped to her hip, making cupcakes for Robert's weekend visit. Jay spun a clattering top on the kitchen floor while she hummed, beating the mixture in uniform strokes, the colour warming her pale cheeks. Looking up from his toy, he was mesmerised by her beauty, by this vision of maternal splendour and he stepped closer to smell her vanilla-scented hair. A needlepoint desire crept over his skin right out into his fingertips as he reached out a shy hand to her apron, he craved the blissful touch of that flour-speckled palm that could smooth his brow, his heart, his entire life. She looked down when he pawed at her elbow, startled at the appearance of this three-year-old who nudged her with his mute demand and in that moment, Jay believed his mother could have changed the course of their history simply by gathering him into her arms and claiming him for her own. But reluctance stole like darkness across her face. 'Get away now, shoo,' she snapped, stepping quickly back. 'I'm baking for Robert,' and he shrank away, withdrew like a loathsome beast to the furthest outreaches of his cave. Now, fifty years later, this moment returned to him in memory as his mother's last chance.

Jay shivered involuntarily, running a hand up and down his bloodless arm. My God, he thought, staring into the black gardens, he had been so utterly predictable in the end, acting out his childhood jealousy and rage against his mother. For of course his hands had really been around her neck, not Robert's.

A few days before she died, Jay's mother had dispatched him to her Van Nuys duplex to get the pillbox and the gloves that she had worn when she boarded the Greyhound at Stockton back in 1966. Death would spare her the indignity of extended old age with the son she despised, she would rejoin Robert in the heaven that she had always believed would be her birthright. So dying was a relief, a welcoming smile upon her lips and she wanted the gloves and the hat for this final journey. In the final thirty-six hours she was breathing through a tube; a soft-soled drift of nurses whisked through her doors to check her vital signs and offer a comforting word to Jay. As she got closer to the end he wished he could slow the process down, or at least get them to stop the pain relief so that he could deliver a crushing blow to her consciousness, that she might experience her own death. He stood resting his hands on the stiff-backed chair, watching her chest labour under the sheet, until a nurse slid a practised hand over her face and shut her eyes for the last time. His mother had finally left, taking everything with her, all the tidy details of her existence, closing the lid on a family that seemed now like such a nebulous concept. Jay patted her fingers as they lay cooling on the green bedspread. He had never dared touch her when she was alive.

• NINETEEN •

On the street below, a car engine screeched in the chilled dense winter. Jay was suddenly exhausted, overwhelmed by memory and event. He looked at the manuscript on his desk, glowing in the darkness with deadly promise. 'I have written my best book,' he whispered with a compensatory stretch of his wan lips. 'My work here is done.' A police siren wailed in the distance and he turned his head to check the screen.

Cora was still out there, they had not found her yet.

He sank back into his armchair, head cradled in its high winged embrace and closed his eyes. It is true that the appetite becomes somewhat dulled for a life spent waiting for the sound of a ringing phone.

In psychoanalysis, he reminded himself, there are only victims. If one was to apply the Hippocratic oath to Jay's profession, or even to hold it axiomatic that all life is worth saving, he had undoubtedly been remiss in the line of duty. But what is an acceptable rate of attrition? Deaths in his care – at least those which he had counted – included Robert and perhaps five or six others towards whom his contribution could be considered significant. Those times, for instance, when he had simply grown weary of his clients' sullen resistance and agreed that suicide was the only comfort left in their tormented world. He has been guilty of a failure to save, to grab the wheel and steer away from the rocks, to avert the disaster looming on a clear horizon. Like Cora just yesterday, in flight from an irrefutable truth that he knew would surely destroy her.

'Sometimes,' he told clients, 'what frightens us most is that which is nameless.' Jay understood the importance of nomenclature, how essential it was to be able to classify things. It is a process of demystification that creates the illusion of control. Clients seized on the cheap comfort he could offer with a professional diagnosis, their bright reassurance when he concluded, for example, 'You have obsessive compulsive disorder.' It was apparently a relief to know that their condition was so well understood that it had an acronym. And they were often learned, worthy words, like 'Anorexia nervosa', such a wonderful term that called to mind a sharp and delicate flower. Or 'Bulimia', weighty and solid, thrives in shade.

He remembered Susan, his bird-girl patient in December 1983 and the inspiration for his first novel, how he had been fascinated by the changing landscape of her face as she grew rapidly thinner. The hysterical luminosity in her eyes was exaggerated by the gradual emergence of her cheekbones and a certain strictness about the chin. She was winter pale, almost translucent, her evangelical skin glowing with mysticism as she approached the delirium of her anorexic vision. A fierce and rampant energy was burning her up. Susan dreamt of herself as a swan in flight, her snow-white wings cutting a straight and powerful arc against a blue sky. She was flying towards her incineration.

'I feel so pure,' she murmured and the expression on her face was the closest he had ever seen to what would be described as beatific. 'Metacarsal,' she whispered adoringly, stroking the spine of her mid-finger, for her anatomy was now all on proud display. 'Phalanges,' she continued, tracing a line out to the tip. She was hospitalised by this point, refusing food, and Jay had broken his own protocol by agreeing to see a client outside his safe space. A stricken gaggle of family hovered on the fringes and the consultant psychiatrist looked up in annoyance at the mention of an analyst, until he recognised Jay's name and his sneering derision was replaced by a conspiratorial welcome.

'Christ, I hate anorexics,' he confided as they stood in the corridor looking out the window onto the car park and the multi-coloured shimmer of August rooftops. 'They are so fucking committed.' Jay thought of a painting he had once seen of a Bride of Christ, a fresh-faced novitiate in her mantilla'd anticipation, prostrating herself at the bishop's feet so she might be penetrated by the mysteries of God. 'We're losing her, you know,' the psychiatrist said. 'I've had a parade of them recently.'

Some months earlier, after Susan had spent an entire session flicking through an insolent copy of *Vogue*, Jay decided to place a full-length mirror in front of the couch so that each time she came, she could dwell on the lake of her absorption and he could watch her eyes caress the approving jut of her collarbone.

'You are returning your body to its prepubescent state,' he said. 'I presume your periods have stopped?' He invited Susan to take off her top and they sat in quiet contemplation of the bony torso of a frail overgrown child. The sagged pockets of her bra accommodated the ghost outline of a vanished womanliness. She was slipping further and further back into a deadly recreation of the age of innocence.

'Anorexia-induced hypertrichosis,' said Jay, as she examined her puny arm. 'One of the unexplained side effects of your condition.' She looked up, puzzled. 'Your entire body is covered in down.' He leaned forward and pointed to the carpet of unpigmented hairs that provided a fuzzy halo to the white skin of her forearm. 'You are turning into a monkey.'

'I don't see it,' she glared at him.

'Soon you will have a beard,' he added, resettling in his chair. Susan turned her unseeing eyes back to the mirror.

She persisted in her fierce attempt to win his admiration for her achievement, she liked to wear her tightest latex top to accentuate her skeletal torso. He saw that she was full of glory; it was a sort of transcendesence, like the woman who lovingly straps a belt of explosives around her chest and steps into a sunlit square, bathed in the radiant vision of martyrdom. The onlookers gasp in horror and blunder about in a panicked meddling. But this was choice. The misery was all for the audience. Susan was in love with withholding. She would celebrate her specialness by refusing all sustenance so that she could remain in a permanent state of agonising desire. Jay didn't hold with the feminists' explanation of anorexia as gender fear, denial of womanhood, starvation as destruction. It was all about control.

The ward was a parade of mental health professionals feeding on the curious manifestations of their patients. They gathered in clustered conference around the water cooler as if they were in the hushed presence of the saintly, believing they could detect a kind of heroism in the distorted thought patterns of slow and deliberate starvation. Jay laughed out loud when he overheard a psychotherapist whisper that it was a humbling experience to work with eating disorders, that it brought you so close to the fundamental question of life and death.

In early September, he sat by Susan's bedside marvelling at a web of blue veins sketched underneath the waxen surface of her skin. She lay asleep, or feigning sleep, earplugged to Stevie Nicks, the companion she had adopted as a bedfellow in the last stages of malnutrition.

'Why not kill yourself quickly?' he asked when her mother went for tea.

'Do you think you should be saying that to someone in my condition?' she said, tremulous but aroused.

'I'm just curious to know why you chose a slow death rather than, say, sleeping pills?'

Susan chewed a grey lip, picked at her bitten nails, so soft now they sometimes fell off without her noticing. Her sister had collared him in the elevator the previous day, asked him if they should explore the idea of shock tactics. Pictures of Auschwitz victims, that sort of thing.

'I think it's because you want us all to watch your grand finale. The romance of dying in front of an audience.'

The bitten lip trembled and Susan's huge eyes filled with tears.

'You think it's like *Swan Lake*?' he said. 'But the swan, like Juliet and Cleopatra and all your other heroines, they were beautiful in death. You will die ugly. A malnourished corpse.' He patted her bones. 'Is that romantic? Is that glamorous?'

A febrile silence enveloped the bedside.

'I assume you've given some consideration to the funeral arrangements. You wouldn't want the occasion to be ruined by lack of planning.' A complicit grin spread across her receding gums. 'Actually,' she said. 'I've made a list.'

The image of her grieving mother at the funeral excited her, it was almost sexual, the idea of weeping relatives. She knew the songs they would sing, of course, for she had orchestrated the entire event. They would finally know they hadn't loved her enough, hadn't appreciated her impossible uniqueness while she was alive and so she would give them something unforgettable by offering up the enforced spectacle of her death. Her family floundered for an explanation that could accommodate this behaviour: Was it a joint she had when she was sixteen? Was it drugs, Mr Hamilton, do you think? Was it bullying at school? Was it her younger brother being born when she was only thirteen months old? What did we do to deserve this?

Jay returned one last time to the hospital where Susan's mother dozed in her vigil armchair. She woke with a gasp, shifted into a continuous rocking motion, clutching the drooping rosary beads and resumed her incantation in the half gloom. Susan's hand was green in the subdued light, her eyelids flickering in a cadaverous sleep. A white cotton nightgown revealed the razor edge of her clavicle and her head seemed to have shrunk so that even her short hair looked like an over-sized wig.

She weighed thirty-eight kilos when she died. The gravediggers tugged in disbelief as they hoisted the ropes under her adult coffin. In the early years, Jay used to attend funerals of dead clients, a sort of after-sales service, a deferential nod to the relatives of the lost souls, but he found they clung too fast to him – the parents and the siblings and friends, all scrabbling to erase the burden of responsibility, trying to bury the grief and anger in the choking wet earth. He stood slightly aside under a malignant yew and imagined Susan dragging her emaciated form through the wood of the suicides, her family howling with pain from the fringes. Then he turned on his heel and walked away.

The phone rang with a shrill urgency that reverberated through the house. Jay opened his eyes on the darkness and slid his arm along the wing of the chair, struggling to keep hold of the dream trace before it slipped into hidden recesses, like a silver-side fish plunging to the murky depths. His fingertips massaged the crackling ridges at the base of his neck. The screen glow behind him reflected his faint outline in the French windows. A face in black water, eaten away by shadow, almost formless. This is how he has always seen himself, of course – half-made.

The phone rang off and he swivelled his chair slowly round to his laptop where the news scroll read:

22:52 BABY CHRISTOPHER FOUND SAFE AND WELL IN THE CAR PARK OF A LONDON HOSPITAL

Now it was just a question of waiting for Cora to be found and this wouldn't take long. Jay knew exactly where she was.

His head sank back into the armchair and he drifted into a half-dream where he was just south of Calgary, 800 miles from his destination, looking down from 36,000 feet at a mono-chrome landscape of snowy peaks, broken only by a ribbon of frozen river that stretched away into the desolate peaks of the Clearwater Mountains. The white range was choked with trees and through the patchy cloud he could see a long straight road connecting a sparse habitation with a distant somewhere. A perfect triplet of S-bends gorged on hundreds of miles of bankside, eventually disappearing into the velvet black ice of an oxbow lake. Spokane's flattened grid lay frozen below him, the straight confident lines of the interstate smoothing the whimsical twist of the Purcell River. The town melted away into a level snow plain and a heavenly purity of sky with the faintest suggestion of crescent moon fading into the graduated blue.

A woman in the seat behind him muttered, 'Think how beautiful it must be in springtime.' Stray cloud wisps hung on the horizon like so many smoke fires and beyond, Canada fell away into unbroken snow.

A car engine roared and screeched to a sudden halt on the street outside and Jay shuddered, opening his eyes to a strobe of blue light in the window. A door slammed and the intercom buzzed. Jay nodded gravely as the world sprang into life on his case. He struggled on the edge of his waking dream, but he

didn't move, closed his eyes again and let the pulsing light play
behind his lids.

It was one hour and thirty-two minutes to San Francisco
with a 15 mile-an-hour tail wind and another life. He felt the
chill of an empty homecoming, a remembered scattering of
connections long since lost. Perhaps he would rent a car and
drive clear to the ocean, walk out into the air and a time before
all that, a moment barely remembered where Robert had driven
his mother and himself to the Big Sur. Jay was four or five,
young enough to be confused by the fuzzy family boundaries
between much-older brother and absent father. He knelt alone
with bucket and spade as a giant sun sank into the orange sea
and the shadows of his mother and Robert on the sand glowed
immobile, his head in her lap, both of them staring out on a
blissful burnt horizon.

The dream shimmered and re-formed, swooping down to
the fourth grade classroom where Jay sits tracing the wooden
grooves of his desktop with a pencil. Miss Purdy reads aloud
into the hush, a solitary tear rolls down the shiny curve of her
cheek, the little girls in pigtails are sobbing too at the fate of the
brave little swallow who grew to love the Happy Prince and
could not abandon him when winter came. Jay looks up from
the desk, awestruck by the powerful tentacles of love. Think to
have inspired that, to have known oneself to be the object of an
irrational and glorious desire, the source and the instrument of
love, a thing of beauty. The dream clouds and crumbles, leaving
a foul taste in the pit of his mouth. It has been so profoundly
disappointing to be an observer of the human experiment, to
see so clearly and to be so unmoved. Beating out a shout that
echoes unanswered and forever in a dark cave, a yearning for
pain, the chance to feel, for a life to be driven by passions so
fully regarded. That Jay once longed for all of this was perhaps
the measure of his humanity. The only mystery, the Happy

Prince and the leaden heart that would never melt.

The buzzer screamed on the fringes of his consciousness but Jay sank back into remembrance and dream. He did not believe you could mourn the unknown. Time passed, the drift backwards was too pressing, he felt a swift air current fraught with danger and he needed to land this flight. When he thought of Robert it was increasingly in the younger years, although he knew this was a futile effort to retreat to a time of innocence that proved impossible to recall without a sense of violation. There was a persistent hammering in the background that seemed to reach deep down inside his ear and he struggled at the edge of waking but was catapulted from the classroom to a vision of Larry, sprawled on the couch in his crumpled suit, much as Cora did last night. A lifetime ago. Larry's mouth lies agape in an open drool and he twitches, making little mewling distress calls and Jay takes refuge in Larry's black-and-white graveside fantasy, where a herd of umbrella'd mourners stand behind him on the drenched grass; his hands are clasped in front while the rain streams over his face. The image wobbles uncertainly and Larry stirs on the couch, perhaps something private would be more appropriate, like a quick cremation, although he cannot for the life of him think where to scatter the ashes. Never mind, never mind, a cab arrives, he can hear the engine, its open trunk swallows his suitcases and he slides into the back seat of a relocation and a new life which will not include the distressing memory of an abducting wife. We can wipe out selectively and reinvent. Larry will propel himself forwards and take shelter in a new fiction.

Jay's head lolled deep in the armchair's embrace, willing himself back into his own dream where he begins the descent to San Francisco. In the porthole window the view gives way to a slow creep of colour, matt brown and dark green on the mountain ridges that form a loose protective arc around the northside of the city. The inland waterways are a pale grey, the snow-less plains a dull brown with the lightest scattering of grass. And everywhere the approaching footprint of habitation. He flies over a soft burst of low hills, dried mud slopes like scooped-out moulds, and into the first glimpse of the Bay area, where hidden communities nestle shyly in the dips. A geography that cannot decide if it should be land or water, procrastinating over its identity. He sees the first car since leaving there twenty years ago, cutting a slow trail along a hilltop road. It seems he is going back to school, some crucial class that he missed on Sutter Street. Metzling is waiting, stroking a long white beard that lends him a wizardly gravitas. The group is assembled in a silent seated circle, there is Angeline with a mane of grey curls, rimless glasses balanced on a crumpled nose, beckoning a bangled hand. The class lifts their solemn faces towards him. They want to know what Jay has to say.

The white surf crashes all along the shore as he flies along the south side of the Golden Gate. The wing dips and an aerial ugliness fills his window as they veer over freeways thick with traffic and a dense grey housing grid behind an angular harbour. He watches the plane's shadow, a faint moving blob keeping pace on the flat shallow sea where the water just skims the seabed. A last skywards lurch over the protective cradle of the mountain range, over sectioned brown sea fields, currents rippling like oil slicks across the surface. It all feels like an extravaganza, a circus show and not a landing, like a stripper who bares all and kills the suspense. The wheels lower, juddering over a shore-side golf course and an orderly marina where a dark grove of trees dip into the water. A startled cluster of waders huddle in the shallows like a gaggle of nervous children. Jay's throat is cabin dry, his ankles bitten by the cruel heels of shoes that were a perfect fit just hours ago.

The wing flaps spring up, a rushed sway announces the landing, the heavy thud of footsteps on his stairs and Jay momentarily loses concentration, flips open his eyes and the gaping emptiness of his life leaves him gasping for air.

• APPENDIX •

CORA

Fragment of an analysis of a case of childlessness*

J. Merritt

December 1999

* unpublished

Cora Miller had an affair.

She got found out, was dragged from her bed in the early hours of a hot August night and spilled the beans. Or rather they were slapped out of her.

Her husband was not a dangerous man, not at all given to violent outbursts. He'd got through college without ever getting in a fight but that was what had made it worse: what she had done, how she had wounded him, how the mitigating circumstance wasn't mitigating in the face of his howling pain.

Cora knew she was lucky to be alive, fingertips exploring her burnt cheek while her husband puked up in the ensuite. Overcome by what he had heard, what he had done. She stared at her cheating reflection in the full-length mirror, her bare browned legs poking out from underneath an outsize T-shirt, and then she fled downstairs, grabbed the car keys and disappeared.

But she didn't take the baby.

Months later, even when it was clear that Cora wasn't coming back, that was pretty much all anyone ever said. Her husband said *I can't believe she didn't take the baby*. Her mum said, *I do NOT believe she didn't take that baby*, who was asleep at the time in the cot in the next room, his nappy ballooning in a wet sag. And years later the baby himself, who grew up to be an unemployed teacher prone to binge drinking and infrequent showering, would say *I cannot fucking believe she didn't take me with her.*

So what was going through Cora's mind that night? She had a cut lip. This was what she noticed as she sped through darkness, flicking her tongue over the salt dryness. Not crying now, just fleeing from what was inside, checking the rear-view mirror for some invisible pursuer. It wasn't until she screeched to a halt in an unlit lay-by to pull on jeans and trainers that she saw the empty car seat with a little teddy dangling from one arm and she remembered she had forgotten the baby. She staggered out of the car into the watery glow of the headlights, heard a rustling sound in the crusted litter heaped by the roadside and looked down at the flutter of a small blackbird perched on a broken bottle, a worm wriggling in its orange beak. Impossible, she squeezed her eyes, for she knew that birds are not nocturnal hunters and when she looked again it had vanished. Odd, all the same, how trivia can intrude on a critical moment.

Cora drove on. Because once you start running the problem can be how to stop and the tank was full, it was an effortless automatic drive and she was only a few hundred yards from a slip road to a motorway that went fifty miles south in an irregular line to the coast. There are no hold-ups at 2 am.

Of course there was never going to be any satisfactory way of explaining all this to the Growing-Up Baby, except to say that his mother had just left, which worked fine in the early years when he was young enough to believe this was normal mother behaviour, but took on a whole new meaning when he hit double digits. Years later Cora's husband realised that he should have told his son his mother was dead, then the Grown-Up Baby wouldn't have had the excuse of maternal rejection that he said blighted his entire life, sapped him of ambition and rendered him unable to form lasting relationships with girls. He didn't think his beer-soaked impotence was a factor, or his lapses in personal hygiene, but even if they *had* been, that was his mother's fault too, for destroying his sense of self-worth, although he couldn't remember a single thing about her because he was only ten months old on that August night when his world stopped turning, which was how he was inclined to think of it, as he nursed a bewildered bitterness over his brooding beer.

But at least Cora's husband had a happy ending, he got a lot of casseroles and mothering, more than he ever believed existed and they did actually help to lessen the blow of desertion and heal his wounded pride. He sorted a complicated timetable around his mum and a nanny to look after the baby while he went out to work, honed his story down to a romantic saga of self-sacrifice. Everyone was very impressed with his coping skills, like he was a hero for not abandoning the child as well. But men always get a medal for sticking with a messy domestic situation. For that one time they don't behave like cunts.

And it turned out that there was plenty of upside. He was a walking babe magnet down the weekend playground, what with his story and the baby who had a small scar on his cheek from where he had fallen off a swing when his father was reading the newspaper, but it was that very accident that introduced Cora's husband to a recent divorcee in the sandpit, who knew all about abandonment and could tell him not to bother with stitches (head wounds always look worse than they are), and nine months later they moved in together and had two kids in rapid succession: boys who didn't grow up impotent and took a keen interest in personal hygiene.

In Cora's husband's version of the story, he doesn't actually give her a slap. In fact when he thinks about it now (which is not often and usually for some reason when he's stuck in home-flow traffic in fading summer evenings), he finds himself rewinding further, to an earlier point in the story: to the morning he and Cora were getting married and he stood on the steps of Chelsea Town Hall with his best man (in an agony of not smoking, but it seemed wrong not to wait until after the ceremony). He saw the white ribboned limo pull up and watched Cora get out and, even though he knew she was a vision of loveliness in that short sea-blue dress, her straight brown knees bending athletically as she smiled her way up towards him, even at that very moment, he still managed to wonder if this, in fact, was their high point, if it would be downhill all the way from here. He shifted one leg, loosening his dick inside his suit.

Later, maybe two years later, he was squatting down on the third green to fish a ball out of the hole and he said to his best man, who was also his best friend, *Sometimes I wonder if that's it, you know*. The best man grinned, he was a whole year and two children wiser, *Wait till you start the school fees, mate*.

That night they stayed up drinking shots while Cora flickered through REM sleep in her pregnant sea of pillows, dreaming she was building sandcastles on a Long Island beach. Downstairs, her husband and the best man leaned two full heads of hair back into their armchairs and listened to 'Thunder Road'.

They were thirty-one and just getting comfortable with cliché.

But let's return to that August night and Cora gripping the steering wheel, blinking into the darkness. She had seen *Thelma and Louise* and was occasionally given to headscarf fantasies about open-topped cars and girlish death pacts and if she'd had another sinner in the car she might have done a similar thing. (Women make such expert victims. They've had thousands of years to perfect the skill.) It was panic that had made her leave without the baby, but it was guilt that would keep her away, something Cora realised even as she cut through the night: this would be her punishment. There were easier options, of course: she could throw herself off a bridge, slash her wrists in the toilets of a service station, smash the car into a brick wall, but none of these seemed appropriate and so, as she stared out of the windscreen and dawn stole over the South Coast, Cora resolved to choose the slow burn inferno of all maternal purgatories: Giving Up My Baby.

Tell me, why would a person do such a terrible thing? she asked at our first meeting. This was almost nine years after that August night and Cora sat on the edge of the Corbusier, picking at her cuticles. *I need to understand how this could happen*, she said, a single tear rolling down her cheek.

For three decades now clients have beaten a path to my door: the twitching obsessives, the over-compensating mother-haters, the compulsive hand-washers, the tearful comfort-eaters, the tranquilised depressed – they bring me the gift of their pasts, like returning cats dropping dead trophies at their owners' feet. And I can assure you that if listening to people's couch-ridden misery teaches you anything, it is that you will never find the true beginning to the story of a life, no matter how far back you go. Nothing can be satisfactorily explained. No one is ever cured of their own life.

Of course, my colleagues would not agree. They would encourage you to mine the past at £60 an hour for the clues that lie embedded in your childhood, they would have you believe there is some scientific method in this retreat into fantasy and dream, excavating fragments of personal history which you piece together to fashion a whole. I tell you now that it is the scam of the century – we are a profession of liars and cheats descended from the greatest illusionist of them all, for even after years of stuttering through the half-remembered fictions of your life, you will still be no closer to the truth you sought: how it began; who you are.

Cora progressed from the Corbusier to the couch but she was not satisfied with me, she wanted her past transposed into an extravagant storyboard with the reassurance of plot. Like you, the reader, who demands a story, a reason to turn the page, she wanted an ending so that there could be a beginning. I could have told her that such a scrabble for coherence is like baying to false gods in the moonlight, clinging fast to the belief that there is a meaning lurking in all this human disarray. But the customer is always right and an analyst grows weary of endless variations on the same theme, so, eventually, I complied. I gave Cora the explanation she wanted and an idea of how she might develop her plot. And although she left before we were finished, I think you'll agree that she understood exactly what kind of ending her story would require.

Cora was predisposed to guilt. It jangled in her like the coins she stole from the classroom money box for starving children in Biafra when she was seven years old, the spoils hidden in the belly of her pyjama dog and discovered by her mother while she was changing the sheets. Her father's stern silence was deafening when he lifted her skirt and spanked her bottom but her sobbing didn't stop her mother's flamboyant production of the stolen goods when she marched her daughter into the headmistress's office. Cora confessed her crime, was named and shamed in front of the class on the first Friday of the month (Catholics, you see, they know how to do these things), and this public humiliation laid a trail of shame that snaked through her life, clung to her clothes like a rancid smell, you could see its trace in the little things she did and it was, she told me, the collection box theft that she was remembering as her car sliced through that August night. It didn't matter that her rational brain said, *Fucking hell, Cora, if that's your biggest crime, stealing money from a collection box when you were in third class, Jesus. Get over it.*

Now the robbing was crowded out by her new big crime – infidelity and there wasn't room in her seeping conscience for two sins. She'd had years of intimacy with the hellfire of guilt and even though there was a context to the betrayal (husband had a post-natal fling the previous year), Cora knew that didn't absolve her, for there had been a moment six months before when all of this could have been avoided, that moment when she'd plucked at a speared olive and a voice said, *I thought only people in James Bond movies drank martini,* and Cora smiled up at the Other who was standing there, suddenly looking like Sean Connery's fucking double, and she wondered why she'd never noticed this before, was it because they had grown so used to the professionalism of each other's collegiate presence after seven years of career-sharing office space with a thousand other drones, the corporate album of highs and lows? There was nothing new in what he'd said or what she'd said, it was just the way that the smoked glass behind the bar reflected the possibility of a break in the monotonous glamour of their predictable young lives and marked the end of the unsung, unphotographed story of good working relationships that don't always end in tears, that often end in dinner parties every quarter and playmate provision for the kids.

You see the danger. The shark in the dark waters. Why some men feel compelled to lock their women away in a pre-emptive strike, why others cover their women up in a black shroud and say they're just following Allah's instructions.

By the time her husband found out, the affair was over but

that didn't matter to Cora. How she thought: just because we're not still gassing Jews doesn't mean the Holocaust is over. Which might give you some kind of insight into her firefly thought patterns. She knew that things don't just end because there's nothing actually happening, when the screen goes blank, the lights go up and everybody's rushing for the exit. Nothing ends, even when you die.

A couple of weeks before she disappeared, Cora walked into a bookshop to kill an hour and picked up a self-help manual where a therapist was quoted on infidelity: *the screwing you get is not worth the screwing you get*. The book leapt from her hands back onto the shelf and she hurried off to the parenting section to find something reinforcing, reminding herself that there were other things going on in the world that were important. Like the massacres in the Congo or genetically modified crops and why nobody seemed to care, but she couldn't get the book out of her head, she was back in the guilt loop again and she ran from the shop and hailed a passing cab, leaned her head back as they rolled along Park Lane, stared at the hotel facades. *No, it's never over. It will always be there in the space between us.* The lie, the betrayal wedged in between Cora and her husband on the couch as they share a late glass of wine, listening to the baby snuffling through the monitor. Guilt was the hidden text in what she did, the choreographer of her days.

So let's fast-forward now, seven years from that August night where we find Cora in Greenwich, Connecticut with her new husband Larry, a broker at Merrill Lynch who met her shortly after his first wife traded down to a local real estate broker who did a brisk trade in upmarket clapboards. Listen to the hush at the dinner table while Cora shares her true life-story with her new best friends, a story that has somehow (she's not sure exactly how she did this) morphed into a candlelit tearjerker about being kicked out in the middle of the night and a torturous custody battle. The women shake their yawning heads as their midnight tyres crunch home over the frozen snow and Cora drifts into sleep, almost remembering exactly which outfit she wore to the carefully orchestrated legal proceedings of her fantasy past.

Sometimes, standing by the mirror on late afternoons, she runs a hand over her slim-hipped profile and wonders if she has in fact given birth at all, or if that too was part of someone else's life.

Larry B. Olsen, her new husband, is not at all partial to pasts, he prefers to deal with things that he can see and touch. He is at best incurious about Cora's first marriage, preferring to imagine her on emotional life-support until she met him. Estrangement doesn't faze him in the slightest since his own child (a slight six-year-old boy from an early mistake-marriage) lives in California now and Larry finds the emotional pain of severance a whole lot more bearable than the alimony.

Fast-forward another year to the dry spring night when everything is set to change: Larry bursts through the front door with a bottle of Bollinger and a wild grin and tells Cora that he has taken a promotion in the London office – not an obvious move at all – 'But hey, honey, I'm thirty-nine and this is a once in a lifetime chance,' and she knows resistance would be futile and finding a third husband would only be harder at thirty-six-and-a-half, despite the slim hips, so she consoles herself by believing it might be just for a couple of years.

The trouble starts already in the holding pattern over Heathrow when Cora calculates that The Baby would be nearly nine by now. She looks out into dense cloud and wonders if he ever looks at photos of her, although she's pretty certain he doesn't have any, from the tone of her first husband's last letter six years ago where he wrote that his second wife is the mother Cora had never been and that he would fight her tooth and nail if she EVER EVER tried to come crawling back begging for custody. Or even access. *You are the most selfish person I have ever known*, he said, and Cora was actually relieved that someone had finally confirmed this ugly truth. But as the cab inches towards the Chiswick roundabout in the afternoon rush hour, she is pitched forward, doubled up by a desperate ache in the pit of her stomach that radiates out across her whole body and Larry tells the cab to pull over, but when Cora staggers out onto a garage forecourt she realises the ache is an overwhelming desire to hold her little boy in her arms, to hold him forever and ever and ever, to never let him go. For seven years she's been absolutely fine, thrived on her self-imposed punishment but it turns out now that all she wants is to have a baby, her heart is crying out for it, she absolutely *must* have a baby, it is life or death, and nothing will ever be the same again.

Nine months, three specialists, three D&Cs and three laparoscopies later, Cora is struggling to ignore the breaking news that there is a problem with her tubes, a problem with her hormones in the dark brown phial of blood, a problem, in fact, with her entire reproductive system. But she carries on using ovulation sticks every day, just in case medical science is wrong (you never know, she'd read an article once about a girl who swore she'd conceived two years after pretty much everyone on Harley Street had confirmed her infertility), and Cora isn't going to let some doctor have the last say, she's too busy to even eat in between her acupuncture and massage and tai chi and thinking-yourself-pregnant classes, as well as the IVF cycles that Larry notices are all beginning to add up, although he's quietly confident about a generous bonus at year end.

'Just remember, honey, it's fine by me if we don't have any,' he says by her bedside, because Mr Farrakheem told him, while

Cora slept off the anaesthetic, that it's important she comes round to the overwhelming likelihood of a negative outcome.

Three days later they have their final consultation. A Mont Blanc sits fatly on Farrakheem's desk, gold cap glinting. Cora counts two or three distinct offspring sealed inside the silver photo frames.

'I am ha-fraid,' Mr Farrakheem raises his head from her file, eyes like polished marbles. Larry pats her hand. She would like to sink her teeth into his comforting flesh.

'Heuw see here,' says Mr Farrakheem, tapping the little box that squats beside his desk. Frozen on the screen is the wedge-shaped blur of Cora's redundant ovaries.

She sits, a bright blinking smile fixed on her lips while Mr Farrakheem outlines the boundless extent of her reproductive failure. She bolsters herself sideways against the chair, feels the tenderness in the top of her thigh, a watery purple bruising from the daily hormone injections that she administers with an autogun sitting on the edge of the bath.

'So you would advise—' prompts Larry. He leans forward, pursing his lips at the grey screen. Cora thinks of his ties colour-filed in the wardrobe.

'There hees noh-point. Hany-more,' says Farrakheem, patting the closed file. 'So very sorry, Meesus Olsen.'

'Miller,' she says with a sharpness that jabs Larry's ear.

Mr Farrakheem nods his head at a gracious incline. 'Mee-ler,' he soothes as if humouring a petulant child. Cora would like to rip his tongue from his mouth but a carriage clock on the mantelpiece indicates she is out of time.

She rises but does not take the hand that Farrakheem offers, she lets Larry guide her elbow across the plush expanse of carpet, looks up at the dizzy height of ceiling, and gasps at the flutter of a black wing in the corner. The receptionist spins round but Larry nudges Cora forward, down the sweeping stairs, past the waiting-room where the door gapes open on a limbo of women perched on stiff-backed chairs and a photo montage of all the chubby-cheeked babies who owe their existence to Mr Farrakheem's wizardry.

They emerge into a sunless noon. Larry puts his arm around her shoulders and presses her close on the corner of Devonshire and Harley Street, startled by the slightness of her frame (how slender she's grown all of a sudden, he thinks, how disposable). He leaves a curt message at the office and decides on consolation lunch at San Lorenzo where he suggests a skiing trip in the New Year and tries not to be put off by the fact that Cora doesn't seem to even notice that he is talking, but is staring somewhere beyond his shoulder into the oblique view of rainy Beauchamp Place.

And it is shortly after this that the blackbird business starts up. What begins as a throwaway remark from Cora quickly blossoms into the conviction that the birds are predatory, (they have live worms wriggling in their beaks) and they have, according to her, found a way into their Battersea house (the attic? the Velux windows? the back door?). They appear on the bedroom sill in the early morning and their tremulous song can, she insists, be heard all over the house, although whenever Larry, or the cleaning lady or any one of their diminishing circle of new-found friends between the Commons call round to visit, the birds are nowhere to be seen. Of course people understand it is a phobia, but that doesn't mean it isn't extremely tiresome and after all there is only so much you say to a woman who is more interested in surveilling her house for birds than having a chat.

By December, however, things seem to have stabilised. Cora is unusually inert at home, spending a good hour over a cup of tea in bed in the morning according to the cleaner, but Larry takes this as a good sign after her months of restlessness – it is a change in pattern – maybe it's the medication finally kicking in. Gradually her inertia gives way to walks on Wandsworth Common, which everyone agrees is a healthy sign. She takes the same route every day, across the narrow railway bridge that stinks of fox piss, cutting along the eastern border of the stagnant lake, past the little playground where she always stops, even when there is no one there, and that's how she sees a little toddler bash its forehead on a swing.

Cora's heart goes out to him (– or her – you can't always be sure in the winter at that age, and *It* is wearing a woolly hat) and the Spanish nanny seems so stressed, with another infant bawling in the pram, that Cora opens the gate, offers to help, amuses the little boy – for *It* was a He – makes him smile by pulling faces and singing a bright song that she has dredged up from her own maternal pre-history. Juanita rubs her gloveless hands and laughs at his tearful recovery, turning back to the infant, struggling with the Tupperware container inside the baby bag underneath the Silver Swan (so impractical but Alicia insists on it, although she's back at work now and of course not the one who is hiking it round the Common in mid-winter). By the time the bottle is inserted into the baby's screeching lips and Juanita turns round, her toddler charge has vanished and with him the friendly woman.

Cora has swept him up into her arms, he was irresistible with his big brown eyes all glittery with tears, so like (she told herself) what the Old Baby, the Original Baby had been (golden curls, strawberry cheeks) and of course she knows EXACTLY what he wants, what he wants is a big teddy with a green bow like the one she's seen in the window of 'Daisy & Tom' on the King's Road so she packs him into the back of the SUV, thinking how ironic that she never drove one in all the years in Connecticut. She's a little concerned that she doesn't have a child seat but it isn't far to drive at high spinning speed, away from the Spanish nanny and her trembling disbelief, marooned in the playground for a full minute before she even remembers her mobile phone but she can't operate the speed dial and her English, which is elementary at the best of times, has vanished, and she needs the assistance of a dog walker who arrives on the scene and can quickly and practically help her call the police.

Well, you could write the rest of the script now for there are usually only two likely outcomes in this kind of case. We don't need to dwell on Larry's shock when he takes the call on the trading floor at Merrill Lynch or indeed his whisky vigil at home, waiting for Cora to end this madness and come home. He listens to the police alerts that reveal her identity by the following morning using the portrait photo he gave them (her favourite suit already looking a little loose around the waistband), his speechless new friends who share an uncomfortable drink before sloping off with the redundant promise of their support through the forty-eight hour hell which finally ends with the pale faces of Detective Matthews and WPC Fletching in his living room, telling Larry that the toddler has been left in the A&E Department at the Chelsea and Westminster hospital and he is absolutely fine, nothing wrong with him whatsoever and that Cora has also been found, although – eh – not with the baby. And even though they are speaking very slowly, it takes a while for Larry to understand that when the Detective says 'hanging from a tree in Hyde Park', this means that Cora is actually dead and has been since the early hours, found at dawn by a traumatised jogger.

'So you see, Larry,' says WPC Fletching, patting his arm, 'your wife didn't mean the baby any harm in the end.'

In memory of Kate Jones who died on 1 February 2008

• ACKNOWLEDGEMENTS •

The Semantics of Murder was inspired by the life and work of Richard Montague and supported with assistance from the Arts and Humanities Research Council and the James & Sylvia Thayer Fellowship at the University of California at Los Angeles.

The text includes extracts from unpublished archived material at UCLA and also from the Los Angeles Department of Coroner official records relating to the murder of Richard Montague.

I am especially grateful to Cindy Newsome and staff at the Special Collections Library at UCLA, the LA Coroner's Office, the Detective in charge of the Montague case at the LAPD Cold Case Unit and to Jeanette and Rob Appleby for their hospitality during my time in LA.

The transformational tree in Chapter 6 is based on a version included in *Introduction to Montague Semantics* by David Dowty and Stanley Peters (Holland: Reidel, 1981). I have also borrowed a line from Anthony Cronin's *The Reductionist Poem*.

I am indebted to Professor Jens Allwood at the University of Göteborg for first introducing me to Montague Semantics, to Patricia Duncker for her unflagging enthusiasm during my time at the University of East Anglia where much of this book was written and to the Corporation of Yaddo where final editing was completed.

Finally, special thanks to Oscar for some very important advice on the title.

Goodbye,
Sweetwater

HENRY DUMAS

Goodbye, Sweetwater

NEW & SELECTED STORIES

Edited and with an Introduction
by Eugene B. Redmond

THUNDER'S MOUTH PRESS
NEW YORK

Copyright © 1988 by Loretta Dumas
and Eugene B. Redmond
All rights reserved
Published in the United States by
THUNDER'S MOUTH PRESS,
93-99 Greene Street, New York, N.Y. 10012
Design by Loretta Li
Grateful acknowledgement is made to the
New York State Council on the Arts and
the National Endowment for the Arts
for financial assistance with
the publication of this work.
Portions of this book were previously
published in Ark of Bones, Rope of Wind,
and Jonoah and the Green Stone.
Second Printing August 1988
Library of Congress Cataloging-in-Publication Data
Dumas, Henry, 1934–1968.
Goodbye, sweetwater : new & selected stories / by Henry Dumas.
p.   cm.
ISBN 0-938410-59-8 : $19.95.
ISBN 0-938410-58-X (pbk.) $10.95
I. Title.
PS3554.U43G6 1987
813'.54—dc19   87-29039
CIP
Distributed by
CONSORTIUM BOOK SALES
213 E. 4th Street
St. Paul, Minnesota 55101
612-221-9035
Manufactured in the United States of America

Acknowledgements

PEOPLE'S COMMITMENT to the art and memory of Henry Dumas has assumed various forms, from praise-song gatherings to read his work aloud, to stage adaptations of his writings, to serious scholarly explorations, to the persistent laborings over his ideas and language in classrooms across the nation. Among many persons who have participated in this vital support system over the past two decades are: Edward Crosby, Donald Henderson, Hale Chatfield, John S. Rendleman, Ronald Tibbs, Sons/Ancestors Players, Toni Morrison, Jayne Cortez, Quincy Troupe, Rosalind Goddard, Clyde Taylor, Tommy Ellis, Oliver Jackson, Maya Angelou, George A. Jones/Ahaji Umbudi, Vernon T. Hornback, T. Michael Gates, Keith Aytch, Raymond Patterson, Imamu Amiri Baraka, Marie Brown, Jay Wright, Walter Lowenfels, William Halsey, Anthony Sloan, Avery Brooks, Hoyt Fuller, Val Grey Ward, Sterling Plumpp, H. Mark Williams, Joseph Harrison, Larry Neal, Sherman Fowler and members of the Eugene B. Redmond Writers Club (of East St. Louis) who have been the most recent sounding board for the amazing genius of Henry Dumas. And, finally, there has been the ever-present support, input and faith of the brave Loretta Dumas.

—E.B.R.

Contents

Introduction

The Ancient and Recent Voices Within Henry Dumas

T HAT HENRY DUMAS felt and thought deeply about his people—and the global flock—is evident in the abundance of sensitivity, love and insight embedded in *Goodbye, Sweetwater*, a magnetic collection of tales and visions. Dumas's territory—read laboratory—was wherever the imagination could roam free. Within such a limitless sphere of folk and fantasy Dumas projected his powerful fictional universe, an Afro-centered mirror-world that included fascinating fables and frame states for which he has become—one can't say "famous"—idolized and emulated by a growing diasporan tribe of storytellers, critics, multiculturalists, Africanists, folklorists, mystics, students of the occult, linguists, songifiers, ethnomusicologists, and poets. In my introduction to *Ark of Bones* I noted that, "already he is being compared to . . . Jean Toomer and Kahlil Gibran."

For some time following his violent death—which occurred deep in a Harlem subway on the night of May 23, 1968, at the hands of a New York City Transit policeman—factual components of Dumas's own life merged with those of his fictional characters, producing a bizarre grapevine of tales ominously immersed in government conspiracies and witch hunts. Indeed, many who knew about Dumas's constructs for ideosound, designed to wage "spiritual" combat against Big Brother, found easy connections or parallels between his death and what was perceived as the counterrevolutionary mission of an oppressive and trigger-happy "system." The fact that this young Black male, then not quite thirty-four years old, was shot by a white policeman, under what still remain unclarified circumstances, was all the more reason why many in the Movement waxed "suspicious." The precedents were all there, had been there—in fact and fiction: from the FBI's covert Cointelpro operations to the CIA–engineered murder of an Afro-American writer in John A. Williams's *The Man Who Cried I Am*, a best-selling novel of the late 1960s. Given Black people's history of "healthy paranoia," as some scholars put it, and in view of that tension-pregnant and anxiety-armed era, one needed very little imagination or coaxing to conclude that Dumas's awesome abilities as a seer-sorcerer had been deemed dangerous enough to destroy.

Dumas himself was ever mindful of this "threat"—so widely believed that it is discussed as "fact" among Black activists, writers and intellectuals. The broader theme of Black male vulnerability, which one hears and reads about everywhere these days, is one of the vital thread-messages in Dumas's fictional quilt. We see it over and over and over as in "The Waking Dream" (from *Jonoah and the Green Stone*) where elder Mrs. Haley, mother-admonisher, accosts young Jonoah regarding his role and responsibilities: "We aint got many men these days. They kills em off as fast as we birth em. What you gonna do, young man? . . . What you gonna do, young man?"

But what of Henry Dumas? Friends and colleagues testify that his electric personality, intellectual energy and creativity drove him at an almost dizzying speed. And yet, ironically, he seemed to have time for those close to him. His widow, Loretta Dumas, recalled that his artistic intensity was so all-consuming that he appeared to be wide-awake even when he was asleep. Another observed that being Black prompted Dumas to "live the way he lived, to become so wide and wise, and certainly it 'helped' him to die the way he died." Hale Chatfield, author of that statement and coeditor of the Southern Illinois University editions of *Ark of Bones* and *Poetry for My People*, also said of Dumas:

He was complex, intricate, variable, wise to innumerable ways of life, eclectic in his interests, and at ease in almost any com-

pany. Or at least he had acquired the appearance of these quali-
ties, so that any of us who were his friends had to feel ultimately that at best we knew only facets of the entire man, had
access, at best, only to those elements of his being that were
available to us as individuals somehow more specialized, more
restricted, in our perspectives. Nobody I know fails to feel or
hesitates to affirm that Henry Dumas exceeded him in the
breadth of his experience of human situations.

Jay Wright was also well acquainted with the many-sided
Henry Dumas. A gifted poet and thinker, Wright contributed
the introduction to *Poetry for My People* and its republished Random House edition, *Play Ebony Play Ivory*. His description of
Dumas is a picture of order-centered hurriedness, of a disciplined
and calculated rush:

> Henry Dumas lived very rapidly, and very slowly. We could
> never seem to keep up with him, or catch him, or hold him
> when we did. It wasn't that Dumas avoided any of us. There
> was simply so very much to do. He had so many friends . . .
> During the time he was an on-again off-again student at Rutgers
> University, he spent a great deal of time trying to organize in-
> formal readings, or starting or promoting small publications, or
> persuading one or another of his friends to go to a gospel con-
> cert. It was very hard to figure out just when he had time to
> write. But he did write, and quite a bit. Whenever he appeared,
> he had stacks of new poems, pages of a novel, articles, prose po-
> ems, sketches for a play. To conclude that he lived in an absurd
> swiftness would be a mistake. For Dumas had heavy roots, in
> his people, in the land. . . .

Although he later speaks about Dumas's poetry, Wright's
observations nevertheless provide brilliant insights into the
broader cosmos of Henry Dumas, writer, and the Afro-American creative mind in general:

> Dumas asserts that the language you speak is a way of defining
> yourself within a group. The language of the Black community,

as with any group, takes its form, its imagery, its vocabulary, because Black people want them that way. Language can protect, exclude, express value, as well as assert identity. That is why Dumas's language is the way it is. In the rhythm of it, is the act, the unique manner of perception of a Black man.

In 1964, Dumas staked out the arena in which he would construct his religious-folkloric-literary frames of references. In a letter to George Hudson, he exclaimed that:

> I was born in the south (rural Arkansas) and come quite definitely from the rural elements. . . . My interest in Gospel music coincides with my interest in folk poetry, and the folk expression. There is a wealth of good things to be developed in our heritage. The Gospel tradition is among a few.

In a biographical note accompanying his contribution to *Black Fire*, the late-1960s anthology edited by LeRoi Jones (Imamu Amiri Baraka) and Larry Neal, Dumas admitted: "I am very much concerned about what is happening to my people and what we are doing with our precious tradition." The statement echoes his earlier call for "full–time, devoted scholarship" designed to establish a proper perspective on the Black heritage and simultaneously to create appropriate vehicles for utilizing traditional folk forms in the service of serious literary expression. His research, which represented a major undertaking, had hardly been completed at the time of his premature death. But Dumas had come far enough along that one could easily touch and enjoy with him his wonderful and multi-storied world. For as Jay Wright reminds us, "Dumas is there. The rhythm is the perception. The language is participation in the act."

According to Jay Wright, who brings righteous vision to the greatness of Dumas's craft:

> Dumas found this rhythm of perception most readily, as others have, in music. And he brooded a lot about musical structure.

The blues and gospel music, particularly, were his life breath. Dumas haunted gospel concerts, photographing, when he could, the singers and the action. For him, the songs and the style of the singers linked him to the land, pinpointed that sense of dispossession that he felt, living in the alien, crass and prejudiced cities, where too many people ignored what he was as a Black man, and too few cared enough to learn or honor him because of it. His singers [and poets-storytellers] have the wisdom of African priests. The music is more than gospel; it is mythic gesture and indicative of a social structure.

Henry Dumas was born into the racially segregated but culturally pluralistic world of Sweet Home, Arkansas, on July 20, 1934. At the impressionable age of ten he was taken to the even more segregated world of Harlem in New York City. There, in the Upsouth, he attended public schools, completing Commerce High School in 1953, and enrolling at City College that same year. Ever the searcher, the adventurer, the inquirer, Dumas broke off his college studies to join the Air Force. He was stationed at Lackland Air Force Base in San Antonio, Texas, and later spent one year in the Arabian Peninsula, this latter experience helping to generate his interest in Arabic language, mythology and culture. Selections from *Jonoah* and the awesome story, "Goodbye, Sweetwater," seem to recall some of the experiences he may have had in the south.

On September 24, 1955, midway through his four years of military service, Dumas married Loretta Ponton. The year following his 1957 discharge, Dumas's first son, David, was born. Enrolling at Rutgers University around this same time, Dumas began a full-time pursuit of courses in etymology and sociology before discovering his natural habitat in English. Two years were apparently all he was able to devote to a full-time college program, having to work, as it were, assume responsibilities of father and husband, write, organize on the little-magazine circuit, and involve himself in America's great sociological practicum—

the civil rights movement. A part-time student at Rutgers over the next seven years, Dumas finally quit the university in 1965 without finishing his degree. His second son, Michael, was born in 1962; and homebound responsibilities, coupled with a widening interest/involvement in the civil rights movement, detoured Dumas from his most passionately pursued subject—religion. He juggled his role as a part-time student and husband-father with his job as an operator of printing machines at IBM from 1963 to 1964. In this vortex of student, writer, wage earner, organizer, activist, father and husband, Dumas still managed to find the time and means to cart clothing, food and supplies to inhabitants of tent cities in Mississippi and Tennessee. From *Ark of Bones* through *Jonoah* through *Rope of Wind* through *Goodbye, Sweetwater*, there exists an oxymoronic constellation of hope and drudgery, pride and dispossession, advancement and setback, Black strength and resilience against omnipresent racism and degradation. It's all there in some phase or form—from racial volcanoes, covered by pretty wavy cotton fields, to Paul Laurence Dunbar's human mask that "grins and lies."

In my introduction to *Rope of Wind,* I engaged in a debate with certain critics and aestheticians, especially some who had suggested that a particular ideology—say Black nationalism—was the highest state of Afro-American fiction. My response was:

When one considers that mothers, fathers, and children make up a community, however, one must search beyond ideology, contemporaneity, or hysteria. All of these foregoing elements are, of course, a natural part of Black writing, but a reader must be given a full "gulp" in order to savor the entire work of the "cook." Hence, Dumas's preacher in "The Map of Harlem" tells his audience that "the soul of the black man is an unexplored region."

Hence we enter, with Dumas, "the world of . . . surrealism, supernaturalism, gothicism, madness, nightmarism, child-men [girl-women], astrology, death, magic, witchcraft, and science fiction." I personally like the word comfortable when I'm thinking or talking about Dumas's work. Comfortable in the sense that he is not filtering his words and thoughts through some mechanical censor. He is not playing to the tube or the microphone. His is not a Top 40 prime-time rap. Instead he gives us interior songs, stories from the viscera. Therefore, the hippest way to "bop" with Dumas is to let yourself go "down-home"—to those down-home blues, with funky fictional arias, with low-down fables duffing through infinity. And, yes, this earth language and rhythmized way of seeing reach across the spectrum of these stories.

But while Dumas's fictions may appear to be "new" in the literary sense of that term, they are ancient in origins, archetypes, meanings and structures. This item was particularly arresting in the 1960s when a proliferation of "media"–conscious artists occurred. For, as Baraka saw and felt:

> Dumas's span shows a feeling (again!) for *all of our selves* or *all* of our self—the large black majestic one. A truly *new* writer (in the sense that the nationalistic consciousness all of us need is here) as a *true art form* not twenty "Hate Whitey's" & a benediction of sweaty artificial flame, but actual black art real, man, and stunning.

Such, too, were the exuberant echoes in Clyde Taylor's searching and unselfish ode to Dumas in "Henry Dumas: Legacy of a Long-Breath Singer," which appeared in the September 1975 issue of *Black World* (*Negro Digest*), where Dumas's fiction and poetry had been published in the 1960s. Earlier pithy reports on Dumas's vision and technical virtuosity were confirmed by Taylor who reminded us that:

> Dumas aspired to the oldest, most honored version of the poet, that of poet-prophet to his people, to incarnate their cultural

identity, values and mythic visions, but further to codify and even reshape those myths into modalities of a more soulful existence. . . . The miracle of Dumas's work, worth the name genius, is that he had already successfully integrated the formidable demands of this role when the new concept of Black writing was just emerging.

Dumas's ambitious and successful undertakings as a 1960s Black writer, according to Taylor, included avoiding the pitfalls of transient hipness, or microphone mentality, and reintegrating Black literature into natural processes—or nature. This observation could not have been truer coming from Dumas himself. Taylor elaborated with his own brilliant Dumas-construct:

> As a language, hip is the expression of the modern city. Dumas's voice and vision absorb that part of hipness that preserves an African ontology. But his freedom from the jive and flash superficiality of full-blown urban hipness is exceptional in recent black poetry [black writing]. His eye is always on the line of the diaspora, from Africa, across the ocean, the deep rural South and on into the Northern cities. And he weights and scales his perceptions so that the older strata of culture and experience are always the heavier. *His* South, like Toomer's, is dense African. His North is African still, following the presence of Black folks. The city as background to his people is rendered in a fantastical, opaque, sketchy way, insanely electric and as absurd as his own subterranean death.

In his earth lore, his cultural reclamations and his creative far-reach, Dumas is reminiscent of James Baldwin, Ernest Gaines, Alice Walker, Toni Morrison, Ralph Ellison, Sherley Anne Williams and Lance Jeffers. However, there is a mellowed-down "freshness" in Dumas, that one looks hard to find in Black or, for that matter, any current writing. Thus he is both ancient and contemporary.

I first met Dumas in 1967, when he came to Southern Illinois University's Experiment in Higher Education, where I taught, to take a position as teacher-counselor and director of language workshops. EHE was part of an interdisciplinary and experiential consortium that included Katherine Dunham's Performing Arts Training Center. The two institutions frequently presented concerts or performances during which Dumas joined other literary artists in choral readings. Such collaborative rituals usually featured drum, dance and woodwind ensembles.

During the ten months or so that he lived in East St. Louis, Dumas's life continued to be hurried and productive. He vigorously overhauled old things and wrote new ones. He loved to visit the Celebrity Room, a local hangout for activists, poets, dancers, intellectuals and street denizens. The bar featured jazz, great conversation, poetry readings, fashion shows and other cultural events. It was there that Dumas first read his great poem, "Our King Is Dead," an inspiring but frightening elegy to Martin Luther King, Jr. Dumas also spent countless hours walking, driving and talking in East St. Louis and he was especially fond of Naomi's, a soul food restaurant, which he frequented with Sherman Fowler, Joseph Harrison and myself. I took him to the South End and to Rush City, sections of East St. Louis in which I spent my childhood, and he exclaimed about how "southern," "real," and "basic" the people and the land were. That was Henry Dumas: eternally observant, thoughtful, peripatetic. The EHE-PATC-Community fulcrum inspired Dumas and he wrote, in the way that Jay Wright recollects from the earlier 1960s, with a passion and a fury. Whenever we had been away from Dumas for a few days, he never failed, upon his reappearance, to favor us with a reading of fresh work or to give us photocopies of new creations, usually signed and often dedicated to one of us.

Much ideological and intellectual thrashing and winnowing occurred within the healthy crucible of the long days and nights of 1967–68. Intellectual ferment, electricity and raw energy

poured into lectures, horns, drums, debates, dances, performances, concerts, Frantz Fanon staff sessions, curriculum development, the Movement, Black Arts, theories of literature, the notion of the African Continuum, Pan-Africanism. In the midst of
it all, Dumas wrote, lectured, lived, shared.

During those electric and trying years of arts and activism, I
doubled as an editor of the *East St. Louis Monitor*, a weekly
newspaper owned by the late Clyde C. Jordan. Henry Dumas
became a familiar figure around the *Monitor* offices and when
news of his death was received, the staff of the paper expressed
grief and shock. The *Monitor* published a loving obituary and
my editorial, entitled simply "Henry Dumas Poet: 1934–
1968." I drew some loose parallels between Dumas's and Dr.
King's death—noting that in "Our King Is Dead," Dumas had
ironically and prophetically cried: "I am ready to die." In that
same poem, he admonished Blacks for allowing too many of
their "kings to be sent to the volcano," even as he himself was
headed for that very same fate. The editorial, which appeared in
the June 6, 1968, edition of the *Monitor*, spoke of Dumas's "instinctive communication with the spirit and soul of blackness, his
remarkable insight into, and understanding of, the sources of
Afro-American poeticism, his undying love for humanity and his
insatiable quest for truth."

Such were the lives and times of Henry Dumas, who
picked up his gauntlet, carried it with grace, funk, speed, seed
and honor, and then passed it on to us. And what a grandilo-
quent baton! Dumas always, always insisted that we *listen*, a request he often followed with the communal exhortation, "Man,
let's just *tell* it!"

EUGENE B. REDMOND
July 2, 1987
East St. Louis, Illinois

ARK OF BONES

Ark of Bones

HEADEYE, he was followin me. I knowed he was followin me. But I just kept goin, like I wasn't payin him no mind. Headeye, he never fish much, but I guess he knowed the river good as anybody. But he ain't know where the fishin was good. Thas why I knowed he was followin me. So I figured I better fake him out. I ain't want nobody with a mojo bone followin me. Thas why I was goin along downriver stead of up, where I knowed fishin was good. Headeye, he hard to fool. Like I said, he knowed the river good. One time I rode across to New Providence with him and his old man. His old man was drunk. Headeye, he took the raft on across. Me and him. His old man stayed in New Providence, but me and Headeye come back. Thas when I knowed how good of a river-rat he was.

Headeye, he o.k., cept when he get some kinda notion in that big head of his. Then he act crazy. Tryin to show off his age. He older'n me, but he little for his age. Some people say readin too many books will stunt your growth. Well, on Headeye, everything is stunted cept his eyes and his head. When he get some crazy notion runnin through his head, then you can't get rid of him till you know what's on his mind. I knowed somethin was eatin on him, just like I knowed it was *him* followin *me*.

I kept close to the path less he think I was tryin to lose him. About a mile from my house I stopped and peed in the bushes, and then I got a chance to see how Headeye was movin along.

Headeye, he droop when he walk. They called him Head-

3

eye cause his eyes looked bigger'n his head when you looked
at him sideways. Headeye bout the ugliest guy I ever run upon.
But he was good-natured. Some people called him Eagle-Eye.
He bout the smartest nigger in that raggedy school, too. But
most time we called him Headeye. He was always findin
things and bringin 'em to school, or to the cotton patch. One
time he found a mojo bone and all the kids cept me went round
talkin bout him puttin a curse on his old man. I ain't say nothin.
It wont none of my business. But Headeye, he ain't got no devil
in him. I found that out.

So, I'm kickin off the clay from my toes, but mostly I'm
thinkin about how to find out what's on his mind. He's got
this notion in his head about me hoggin the luck. So I'm fakin
him out, lettin him droop behind me.

Pretty soon I break off the path and head for the river. I
could tell I was far enough. The river was gettin ready to
bend.

I come up on a snake twistin toward the water. I was
gettin ready to bust that snake's head when a fox run across
my path. Before I could turn my head back, a flock of birds
hit the air pretty near scarin me half to death. When I got on
down to the bank, I see somebody's cow lopin on the levee
way down the river. Then to really upshell me, here come
Headeye droopin long like he had ten tons of cotton on his
back.

"Headeye, what you followin me for?" I was mad.

"Ain't nobody thinkin bout you," he said, still comin.

"What you followin long behind me for?"

"Ain't nobody followin you."

"The hell you ain't."

"I ain't followin you."

"Somebody's followin me, and I like to know who he is."

"Maybe somebody's followin me."

"What you mean?"

"Just what you think."

Headeye, he was gettin smart on me. I give him one of my looks, meanin that he'd better watch his smartness round me, cause I'd have him down eatin dirt in a minute. But he act like he got a crazy notion.

"You come this far ahead me, you must be got a call from the spirit."

"What spirit?" I come to wonder if Headeye ain't got to workin his mojo too much.

"Come on."

"Wait." I grabbed his sleeve.

He took out a little sack and started pullin out something.

"You fishin or not?" I ask him.

"Yeah, but not for the same thing. You see this bone?" Headeye, he took out that mojo. I stepped back. I wasn't scared of no ole bone, but everybody'd been talkin bout Headeye and him gettin sanctified. But he never went to church. Only his mama went. His old man only went when he sober, and that be about once or twice a year.

So I look at that bone. "What kinda voodoo you work with that mojo?"

"This is a keybone to the culud man. Ain't but one in the whole world."

"And *you* got it?" I act like I ain't believe him. But I was testin him. I never rush upon a thing I don't know.

"We got it."

"We got?"

"It belongs to the people of God."

I ain't feel like the people of God, but I just let him talk on.

"Remember when Ezekiel was in the valley of dry bones?"

I reckoned I did.

". . . And the hand of the Lord was upon me, and carried me out in the spirit to the valley of dry bones.

"And he said unto me, 'Son of man, can these bones live?' and I said unto him, 'Lord, thou knowest.'

"And he said unto me, 'Go and bind them together. Prophesy that I shall come and put flesh upon them from generations and from generations.'

"And the Lord said unto me, 'Son of man, these bones are the whole house of thy brothers, scattered to the islands. Behold, I shall bind up the bones and you shall prophesy the name.'"

Headeye, he stopped. I ain't say nothin. I never seen him so full of the spirit before. I held my tongue. I ain't know what to make of his notion.

He walked on pass me and loped on down to the river bank. This here old place was called Deadman's Landin because they found a dead man there one time. His body was so rotted and ate up by fish and craw dads that they couldn't tell whether he was white or black. Just a dead man.

Headeye went over to them long planks and logs leanin off in the water and begin to push them around like he was makin somethin.

"You was followin me." I was mad again.

Headeye acted like he was iggin me. He put his hands up to his eyes and looked far out over the water. I could barely make out the other side of the river. It was real wide right along there and take coupla hours by boat to cross it. Most I ever did was fish and swim. Headeye, he act like he iggin me. I began to bait my hook and go down the bank to where he was. I was mad enough to pop him side the head, but I shoulda been glad. I just wanted him to own up to the truth. I walked along the bank. That damn river was risin. It was lappin up over the planks of the landin and climbin up the bank.

Then the funniest thing happened. Headeye, he stopped movin and shovin on those planks and looks up at me. His pole is layin back under a willow tree like he wan't goin to fish none. A lot of birds were still flyin over and I saw a bunch of wild hogs rovin along the levee. All of a sudden Headeye, he say:

"I ain't mean no harm what I said about you workin with the devil. I take it back."

It almost knocked me over. Me and Headeye was arguin a while back bout how many niggers there is in the Bible. Headeye, he know all about it, but I ain't give on to what I know. I looked sideways at him. I figured he was tryin to make up for followin me. But there was somethin funny goin on so I held my peace. I said 'huh-huh,' and I just kept on lookin at him.

Then he points out over the water and up in the sky wavin his hand all round like he was twirlin a lasso.

"You see them signs?"

I couldn't help but say 'yeah.'

"The Ark is comin."

"What Ark?"

"You'll see."

"Noah's Ark?"

"Just wait. You'll see."

And he went back to fixin up that landin. I come to see what he was doin pretty soon. And I had a notion to go down and pitch in. But I knowed Headeye. Sometimes he gets a notion in his big head and he act crazy behind it. Like the time in church when he told Rev. Jenkins that he heard people moanin out on the river. I remember that. Cause papa went with the men. Headeye, his old man was with them out in that boat. They thought it was somebody took sick and couldn't row ashore. But Headeye, he kept tellin them it was a lot of people, like a multitude.

Anyway, they ain't find nothin and Headeye, his daddy hauled off and smacked him side the head. I felt sorry for him and didn't laugh as much as the other kids did, though sometimes Headeye's notions get me mad too.

Then I come to see that maybe he wasn't followin me. The way he was actin I knowed he wasn't scared to be there at Deadman's Landin. I threw my line out and made like I was fishin, but I wasn't, cause I was steady watchin Headeye.

By and by the clouds started to get thick as clabber milk. A wind come up. And even though the little waves slappin the sides of the bank made the water jump around and dance, I could still tell that the river was risin. I looked at Headeye. He was wanderin off along the bank, wadin out in the shallows and leanin over like he was lookin for somethin.

I comest to think about what he said, that valley of bones. I comest to get some kinda crazy notion myself. There was a lot of signs, but they weren't nothin too special. If you're sharp-eyed you always seein somethin along the Mississippi.

I messed around and caught a couple of fish. Headeye, he was wadin out deeper in the Sippi, bout hip-deep now, standin still like he was listenin for somethin. I left my pole under a big rock to hold it down and went over to where he was.

"This ain't the place," I say to him.

Headeye, he ain't say nothin. I could hear the water come to talk a little. Only river people know how to talk to the river when it's mad. I watched the light on the waves way upstream where the ole Sippi bend, and I could tell that she was movin faster. Risin. The shakin was fast and the wind had picked up. It was whippin up the canebrake and twirlin the

willows and the swamp oak that drink themselves full along
the bank.

I said it again, thinkin maybe Headeye would ask me
where was the real place. But he ain't even listen.

"You come out here to fish or fool?" I asked him. But he
waved his hand back at me to be quiet. I knew then that
Headeye had some crazy notion in his big head and that was it.
He'd be talkin about it for the next two weeks.

"Hey!" I hollered at him. "Eyehead, can't you see the
river's on the rise? Let's shag outa here."

He ain't pay me no mind. I picked up a coupla sticks and
chunked them out near the place where he was standin just to
make sure he ain't fall asleep right out there in the water. I ain't
never knowed Headeye to fall asleep at a place, but bein as he
is so damn crazy, I couldn't take the chance.

Just about that time I hear a funny noise. Headeye, he
hear it too, cause he motioned to me to be still. He waded
back to the bank and ran down to the broken down planks at
Deadman's Landin. I followed him. A couple drops of rain
smacked me in the face, and the wind, she was whippin up a
sermon.

I heard a kind of moanin, like a lot of people. I figured it
must be in the wind. Headeye, he is jumpin around like a perch
with a hook in the gill. Then he find himself. He come to just
stand alongside the planks. He is in the water about knee deep.
The sound is steady not gettin any louder now, and not gettin
any lower. The wind, she steady whippin up a sermon. By this
time, it done got kinda dark, and me, well, I done got kinda
scared.

Headeye, he's all right though. Pretty soon he call me.

"Fish-hound?"

"Yeah?"

"You better come on down here."

"What for? Man, can't you see it gettin ready to rise?"

He ain't say nothin. I can't see too much now cause the clouds done swole up so big and mighty that everything's gettin dark.

Then I sees it. I'm gettin ready to chunk another stick out at him, when I see this big thing movin in the far off, movin slow, down river, naw, it was up river. Naw, it was just movin and standin still at the same time. The damnest thing I ever seed. It just about a damn boat, the biggest boat in the whole world. I looked up and what I took for clouds was sails. The wind was whippin up a sermon on them.

It was way out in the river, almost not touchin the water, just rockin there, rockin and waitin.

Headeye, I don't see him.

Then I look and I see a rowboat comin. Headeye, he done waded out about shoulder deep and he is wavin to me. I ain't know what to do. I guess he bout know that I was gettin ready to run, because he holler out. "Come on, Fish! Hurry! I wait for you."

I figured maybe we was dead or somethin and was gonna get the Glory Boat over the river and make it on into heaven. But I ain't say it out aloud. I was so scared I didn't know what I was doin. First thing I know I was side by side with Head-eye, and a funny-lookin rowboat was drawin alongside of us. Two men, about as black as anybody black wants to be, was steady strokin with paddles. The rain had reached us and I could hear that moanin like a church full of people pourin out their hearts to Jesus in heaven.

All the time I was tryin not to let on how scared I was. Headeye, he ain't payin no mind to nothin cept that boat. Pretty soon it comest to rain hard. The two big black jokers rowin the boat ain't say nothin to us, and everytime I look at Headeye, he poppin his eyes out tryin to get a look at somethin far off. I couldn't see that far, so I had to look at what was close up. The muscles in those jokers' arms was movin back an forth every time they swung them oars around. It was a funny ride in that rowboat, because it didn't seem like we was in the water much. I took a chance and stuck my hand over to see, and when I did that they stopped rowin the boat and when I looked up we was drawin longside this here ark, and I tell you it was the biggest ark in the world.

I asked Headeye if it was Noah's Ark, and he tell me he didn't know either. Then I was scared.

They was tyin that rowboat to the side where some heavy ropes hung over. A long row of steps were cut in the side near where we got out, and the moanin sound was real loud now, and if it wasn't for the wind and rain beatin and whippin us up the steps, I'd swear the sound was comin from someplace inside the ark.

When Headeye got to the top of the steps I was still makin my way up. The two jokers were gone. On each step was a number, and I couldn't help lookin at them numbers. I don't know what number was on the first step, but by the time I took notice I was on 1608, and they went on like that right on up to a number that made me pay attention: 1944. That was when I was born. When I got up to Headeye, he was standin on a number, 1977, and so I ain't pay the number any more mind.

If that ark was Noah's, then he left all the animals on shore because I ain't see none. I kept lookin around. All I could see was doors and cabins. While we was standin there takin in things, half scared to death, an old man come walkin toward us. He's dressed in skins and his hair is grey and very woolly. I figured he ain't never had a haircut all his life. But I didn't say nothin. He walks over to Headeye and that poor boy's eyes bout to pop out.

Well, I'm standin there and this old man is talkin to
Headeye. With the wind blowin and the moanin, I couldn't
make out what they was sayin. I got the feelin he didn't
want me to hear either, because he was leanin in on Headeye. If that old fellow was Noah, then he wasn't like the
Noah I'd seen in my Sunday School picture cards. Naw, sir.
This old guy was wearin skins and sandals and he was black
as Headeye and me, and he had thick features like us, too.
On them pictures Noah was always white with a long beard
hangin off his belly.

I looked around to see some more people, maybe Shem,
Ham and Japheh, or wives and the rest who was suppose to
be on the ark, but I ain't see nobody. Nothin but all them
doors and cabins. The ark is steady rockin like it is floatin
on air. Pretty soon Headeye come over to me. The old man
was goin through one of the cabin doors. Before he closed
the door he turns around and points at me and Headeye.
Headeye, he don't see this, but I did. Talkin about scared. I
almost ran and jumped off that boat. If it had been a regular
boat, like somethin I could stomp my feet on, then I guess I
just woulda done it. But I held still.

"Fish-hound, you ready?" Headeye say to me.

"Yeah, I'm ready to get ashore." I meant it, too.

"Come on. You got this far. You scared?"

"Yeah, I'm scared. What kinda boat is this?"

"The Ark. I told you once."

I could tell now that the roarin was not all the wind and
voices. Some of it was engines. I could hear that chug-chug
like a paddle wheel whippin up the stern.

"When we gettin off here? You think I'm crazy like
you?" I asked him. I was mad. "You know what that old man
did behind your back?"

"Fish-hound, this is a soulboat."

I figured by now I best play long with Headeye. He got a notion goin and there ain't nothin mess his head up more than a notion. I stopped tryin to fake him out. I figured then maybe we both was crazy. I ain't feel crazy, but I damn sure couldn't make heads or tails of the situation. So I let it ride. When you hook a fish, the best thing to do is just let him get a good hold, let him swallow it. Specially a catfish. You don't go jerkin him up as soon as you get a nibble. With a catfish you let him go. I figured I'd better let things go. Pretty soon, I figured I'd catch up with somethin. And I did.

Well, me and Headeye were kinda arguin, not loud, since you had to keep your voice down on a place like that ark out of respect. It was like that. Headeye, he tells me that when the cabin doors open we were suppose to go down the stairs. He said anybody on this boat could consider hisself *called*.

"Called to do what?" I asked him. I had to ask him, cause the only kinda callin I knew about was when somebody *hollered* at you or when the Lord *called* somebody to preach. I figured it out. Maybe the Lord had called him, but I knew dog well He wasn't *callin* me. I hardly ever went to church and when I did go it was only to play with the gals. I knowed I wasn't fit to whip up no flock of people with holiness. So when I asked him, called for what, I ain't have in my mind nothin I could be called for.

"You'll see," he said, and the next thing I know we was goin down steps into the belly of that ark. The moanin jumped up into my ears loud and I could smell somethin funny, like the burnin of sweet wood. The churnin of a paddle wheel filled up my ears and when Headeye stopped at the foot of the steps, I stopped too. What I saw I'll never forget as long as I live.

Bones. I saw bones. They were stacked all the way to

the top of the ship. I looked around. The under side of the
whole ark was nothin but a great bonehouse. I looked and
saw crews of black men handlin in them bones. There was
crew of two or three under every cabin around that ark.
Why, there must have been a million cabins. They were
doin it very carefully, like they were holdin onto babies or
somethin precious. Standin like a captain was the old man
we had seen top deck. He was holdin a long piece of leather
up to a fire that was burnin near the edge of an opening
which showed outward to the water. He was readin that
piece of leather.

On the other side of the fire, just at the edge of the ark,
a crew of men was windin up a rope. They were chantin
every time they pulled. I couldn't understand what they was
sayin. It was a foreign talk, and I never learned any kind of
foreign talk. In front of us was a fence so as to keep anybody
comin down the steps from bargin right in. We just stood
there. The old man knew we was there, but he was busy
readin. Then he rolls up this long scroll and starts to walk
in a crooked path through the bones laid out on the floor. It
was like he was walkin frontwards, backwards, sidewards
and every which a way. He was bein careful not to step on
them bones. Headeye, he looked like he knew what was
goin on, but when I see all this I just about popped my eyes
out.

Just about the time I figure I done put things together,
somethin happens. I bout come to figure them bones were
the bones of dead animals and all the men wearin skin
clothes, well, they was the skins of them animals, but just
about time I think I got it figured out, one of the men haulin
that rope up from the water starts to holler. They all stop
and let him moan on and on.

I could make out a bit of what he was sayin, but like I said, I never was good at foreign talk.

> Aba aba, al ham dilaba
> aba aba, mtu brotha
> aba aba, al ham dilaba
> aba aba, bretha brotha
> aba aba, djuka brotha
> aba, aba, al ham dilaba

Then he stopped. The others begin to chant in the back of him, real low, and the old man, he stop where he was, unroll that scroll and read it, and then he holler out: "Nineteen hundred and twenty-three!" Then he close up the scroll and continue his comin towards me and Headeye. On his way he had to stop and do the same thing about four times. All along the side of the ark them great black men were haulin up bones from that river. It was the craziest thing I ever saw. I knowed then it wasn't no animal bones. I took a look at them and they was all laid out in different ways, all making some kind of body and there was big bones and little bones, parts of bones, chips, tid-bits, skulls, fingers and everything. I shut my mouth then. I knowed I was onto somethin. I had fished out somethin.

I comest to think about a sermon I heard about Ezekiel in the valley of dry bones. The old man was lookin at me now. He look like he was sizin me up.

Then he reach out and open the fence. Headeye, he walks through and the old man closes it. I keeps still. You best to let things run their course in a situation like this.

"Son, you are in the house of generations. Every African who lives in America has a part of his soul in this ark. God has called you, and I shall anoint you."

He raised the scroll over Headeye's head and began to squeeze like he was tryin to draw the wetness out. He closed his eyes and talked very low.

"Do you have your shield?"

Headeye, he then brings out this funny cloth I see him with, and puts it over his head and it flops all the way over his shoulder like a hood.

"Repeat after me," he said. I figured that old man must be some kind of minister because he was ordaining Headeye right there before my eyes. Everythin he say, Headeye, he sayin behind him.

> Aba, I consecrate my bones.
> Take my soul up and plant it again.
> Your will shall be my hand.
> When I strike you strike.
> My eyes shall see only thee.
> I shall set my brother free.
> Aba, this bone is thy seal.

I'm steady watchin. The priest is holdin a scroll over his head and I see some oil fallin from it. It's black oil and it soaks into Headeye's shield and the shield turns dark green. Headeye ain't movin. Then the priest pulls it off.

"Do you have your witness?"

Headeye, he is tremblin. "Yes, my brother, Fish-hound."

The priest points at me then like he did before.

"With the eyes of your brother Fish-hound, so be it?" He was askin me. I nodded my head. Then he turns and walks away just like he come.

Headeye, he goes over to one of the fires, walkin through the bones like he been doin it all his life, and he holds the shield in till it catch fire. It don't burn with a flame, but with a smoke. He puts it down on a place which looks like an altar or somethin, and he sits in front of the smoke cross-legged, and I can hear him moanin. When the shield it all burnt up, Headeye takes out that little piece of mojo bone and rakes the ashes inside. Then he zig-walks over to me, opens up that fence and goes up the steps. I have to follow, and he ain't say nothin to me. He ain't have to then.

It was several days later that I see him again. We got back that night late, and everybody wanted to know where we was. People from town said the white folks had lynched a nigger and threw him in the river. I wasn't doin no talkin till I see Headeye. Thas why he picked me for his witness. I keep my word.

Then that evenin, whilst I'm in the house with my ragged sisters and brothers and my old papa, here come Headeye. He had a funny look in his eye. I knowed some notion was whippin his head. He must've been runnin. He was out of breath.

"Fish-hound, broh, you know what?"

"Yeah," I said. Headeye, he know he could count on me to do my part, so I ain't mind showin him that I like to keep my feet on the ground. You can't never tell what you get yourself into by messin with mojo bones.

"I'm leavin." Headeye, he come up and stand on the porch. We got a no-count rabbit dog, named Heyboy, and when Headeye come up on the porch Heyboy, he jump up and come sniffin at him.

"Git," I say to Heyboy, and he jump away like somebody kick him. We hadn't seen that dog in about a week. No tellin what kind of devilment he been into.

Headeye, he ain't say nothin. The dog, he stand up on the edge of the porch with his two front feet lookin at Head-

eye like he was goin to get piece bread chunked out at him. I
watch all this and I see who been takin care that no-count
dog.

"A dog ain't worth a mouth of bad wine if he can't
hunt," I tell Headeye, but he is steppin off the porch.

"Broh, I come to tell you I'm leavin."

"We all be leavin if the Sippi keep risin," I say.

"Naw," he say.

Then he walk off. I come down off that porch.

"Man, you need another witness?" I had to say somethin.

Headeye, he droop when he walk. He turned around,
but he ain't droopin.

"I'm goin, but someday I be back. You is my witness."

We shook hands and Headeye, he was gone, movin fast
with that no-count dog runnin long side him.

He stopped once and waved. I got a notion when he did
that. But I been keepin it to myself.

People been askin me where'd he go. But I only tell em
a little somethin I learned in church. And I tell em bout
Ezekiel in the valley of dry bones.

Sometimes they say, "Boy, you gone crazy?" and then
sometimes they'd say, "Boy, you gonna be a preacher yet,"
or then they'd look at me and nod their heads as if they
knew what I was talkin bout.

I never told em about the Ark and them bones. It would
make no sense. They think me crazy then for sure. Probably
say I was gettin to be as crazy as Headeye, and then they'd
turn around and ask me again:

"Boy, where you say Headeye went?"

Echo Tree

Two boys on a hill. Evening.

"Right there! That's the place!"

"How can you tell?"

"*Shhhh.* Be careful. Don't step where the roots is, not yet . . . I know, cause we always come here together."

"These hills all look the same. How can you tell from last year?"

"You gonna get in trouble talkin like that. Don't you know that spirits talk, 'n they takes you places?"

"I don't believe about . . ."

"Careful what you say. Better to say nothin than talk too loud."

"Did you and Leo always come this far?"

"That's right. Me 'n him."

The wind fans up a shape in the dust: around and around and over the hill. Out of the cavity of an uprooted tree, it blows up fingers that ride the wind off the hill down the valley and up toward the sun, a red tongue rolling down a blue-black throat. And the ear of the mountains listens. . . .

"Did Leo used to want to come up to New York?"

"He ain't thinkin bout you whilst you way up yonder."

"How come you say that? What's wrong with up there?"

"Leo's grandpa, *your'n too*, well he say up in the city messes you up."

"Aw, he's old."

"Makes no difference. He know. That's how come Leo know too."

"Leo is dead."

"So, I bet he never teach *you* bout this here echo tree."

"He was my brother."

"Makes no difference. He my friend more'n your brother."

"What're you talking about?"

". . . 'n he taught me how to call . . ."

"What you bring me up here for?"

". . . how to use callin words for spirit-talk . . ."

"What?"

". . . *Swish-ka abas wish-ka. Saa saa aba saa saa.*"

"What's that?"

"Be quiet. I'm gettin ready . . ."

The wind comes. Goes. Comes again. Across the sky, clouds gather in a ritual of color, where the blue-black, like muscles, seems to minister to the sides of the sun.

"Leo never talked that stuff."

"And he's dead now anyway, laughing at us."

"He *did* talk. He ain't all dead either. You get in trouble talkin like that."

"Why so?"

"Peep over there. See them little biddy trees? Well, if you want to know somethin then I tell you. One of them is another echo tree."

"Another?"

"Right there is where the first one died. And we dug it up and built a fire, and the smoke sailed out, *see?* Just like the dust."

"How can a tree grow all the way up here to us?"

"Cause it's the echo tree! Don't you know nothin?"

"If you don't believe in the echo tree and believe what it hears from the spirits and tells you in your ear, then you're in trouble."

"What trouble?"

"*Real* trouble! If you curse the echo tree, you turns into a bino."

"A what?"

"Can't say that word but oncet. You better start listenin."

"To what?"

"Quick! Let me look at you!" (He runs and examines the other boy's face.) "Aw, it's too late, too late. You's already beginnin to turn . . ."

"What?"

"Hurry! Hurry, boy, and stand in the echo place. Where the tree is . . . Hurry up! You're turnin white . . .!"

"I . . . what?"

"*Shhhhhhhh*. Hold still. You be safe for a while there. Now I gotta tell you how to get outa trouble."

"Nothin's worse than a bino, nothin. A bino is anything or anybody that curse the echo tree and whichever spirit is restin there."

"I didn't curse."

"You got to be careful, I'm warnin you."

"But I didn't curse."

"You cursin right now . . . If you don't believe in the echo, if you don't believe what it say, 'n if you laughs, if you pee, or spits on the tree, it's all the same as cursin. Then you's finished."

"How come?"

"*Shhhhhhhh* . . . cause the spirit leave out your body, you pukes, you rolls on the ground, you turns stone white all over, your eyes, your hair. Even your blood, 'n it come out your skin, white like water."

"But I . . ."

"Bino! Then you's a bino."

"Albino?"

"Naw. That's different. If you let yourself to taint all the way till you's a bino, then you don't eat, you don't sleep, you can't feel nothin, you can't talk or nothin. You be like a dead dog with a belly full 'o maggots, and you thinks you livin . . ."

"I didn't really curse."

"Makes no difference."

"I . . ."

"*Shhhhhhh*. See the sun yonder?"

"Umh-humh."

"Well, he's gatherin in all the words talked in the daylight. Next, them catcher-clouds churns 'em up into echoes. When the time is right, the echo tree will talk. Be still, cause when the butt end of the sun sit down on them mountains, then . . . *be still!* Then we can talk to Leo in the . . ."

"Leo is dead."

"*Hush, man!* Can't you see it's almost time? Iffen I'se you, I ain't want to be no bino."

Shadows begin to fade into a tinted haze.

Red Oklahoma clay darkens.

Green stretches of Arkansas pine finger their way into the land.

White blotches of clouds edge into open sky, fading into oblivion.

Orange filaments stream from the sun.

And blue-red-blue, green-blue, white-blue—all ink the sky.

Shadows become fingers of wind in the night.

Shadows take on shapes. They come to breathe.

And the blue-blue prevails across the heavens, and the weight of the mood is as black as night. . . .

". . . *Swish-ka aba swish-ka.* Quick! Say the openin words!"

"Er . . . *swish* . . ."

"Stop! *Saa saa aba saa saa!*"

"What're we saying?"

"Be still. I had to seal them off. You started too slow 'n you cursed."

Silence.

"Shhhhhhhh. Now I have to make the call. Watch the sun yonder."

(He stands behind the other boy and dances a strange dance. He stops, but continues with his arms, and jerks his body toward the valley and the sky.)

"Laeeeeeeeooooooo!"

The sound pierces the wind. It rides down into the valley, rolls up Laelaelaeeeooo! toward the sun. It resounds like notes of thunder made by children instead of gods. It comes back LaeLae-eee-ooo!

"What is . . .?"

"Shhhhhhh. He's still talkin."

There is silence . . . the silence of an empty lung about to breathe in. Again the sounds vibrate and answer from the boy's throat. Again they travel and return as though wet, as though spoken. . . .

"I'm going."

"Shhhhhhhh."

Echoes come. Again and again and again.

"Is it talking to me too?"

"You're the tree. Be still and listen."

"I feel funny. I better go."

"*Saa saa lae-ya saa saa.*" (And the echoes trail off. . . .)

"Do you think you really talked to somebody?"

"Hush. We gotta be quiet from now on till we gets home."

"Huh? Did you?"

Silence.

"Aw, you didn't talk to nobody but yourself!"

"I warned you oncet. Iffen you curse again, not even me and Leo put together, 'n your grandpa too, can save you from taintin."

"What am I doing?"

"Talkin too loud like you don't believe in nothin."

"I'm not doing anything."

"Don't move! You standin in the echo tree taintin it. Spirits be after you for good. Iffen you move now your soul leave your body."

"I don't believe you."

Silence.

"Then iffen, after I tells you what Leo said about you, and you still don't believe, you'll be a bino fore we gets down the hill."

(He points to the sun. He does a dance. He sings the magic words.)

"Step out of the tree!" (The other boy runs out of the cavity.) "Now you's safe for a while. I had to open for you to come out, and then seal 'em back before they reached out after you."

"I hear something."

Silence.

"Talkin spirit-talk, you gotta open everything and seal it too."

"What's that?"

"That's them spirits in the echo tree down there, 'n Leo is there with them."

"What is he saying?"

"He say you his brother, but iffen you don't get that hard city water out your gut, you liable to taint yourself."

"Taint?"

"Taintin is when you just feels tired, you don't want to do nothin, you can't laugh, and your breathin gets slow. You's on the way to bein a bino."

"Were you really talking?"

"With the spirits and Leo."

"Shucks, that kind of talk sounds like those tongue-speaking people who get on their knees in the dark in that sanctified church at home, a block around the corner."

"That's right."

"Leo teach you that stuff?"

"You just gotta know how to talk to the spirits. They teach you everything."

"How does it go again?"

"Can't tell you now whilst you laughin."

"I'm not laughing."

"Makes no difference. You is inside."

"Leo was my brother."

"You never stayed down here with us. You always lived up there."

"I don't care about it anyway . . . *Swisher Baba!*"

"Now! Oh now! Now you *is* in trouble."

"Shucks."

"You is marked for cursin whilst standin right in the echo tree. All of them heard you. Leo too. Ain't nothin you can do except . . . Ohhhh, boy, you is dead. You're worse than a bino now. Deep deep trouble."

"Nothing is happening to me."

"Just wait a few minutes."

Silence.

"Are you going to tell me about this echo tree?

Silence.

"You won't tell me much. If I'm really in trouble . . ."

"I been splainin it all to you, but you got so much city taint in your blood, you be a bino fore you go back."

"I'm not scared."

"Oh no?"

"No."

"You'd better be."

The wind, the wind. All of a sudden it sweeps across the top of the hill like an invisible hand swirling off into the darkening sky. Whispers echo from the valley throat, and all motion becomes sound, words, forces.

"I hear something."

"*Shhhhhhhh.* Spirits done broke through. They comin."

"Where?"

"Here."

"I . . . don't."

"*Swish-ka aba swish-ka.* Let the seals bust open!"

A moanful resonance, a bluish sound, a wail off the lips of a wet night, sweeps over them . . . Shhwsssssss!

"I'm not cursing anymore! What is that?"

Shhhwsssss! The small valley seems to heave, and the sounds come from the earth and the red tip of its tongue. And then a harmonic churning swells up and up! and as the ink-clouds press in on the sun, a motion in the sky, a flash of lightning, a sudden shift of the cloud, churns up, and a speck of sunlight spits out to the Shhwssss! of the spirited air, and the ears of the boys hear and the sounds are voices—remade, impregnated—screaming out to the world. . . .

Wide-mouthed, one boy cannot speak now. He stands near the spot of the tree. He seems ready to run.

"Iffen you run, a spirit'll trip you up. Then you falls

down and down, like you do when you dreams, and you never hit bottom till you is a bino, a foreverbino."

"Where is my brother? Leee!"

"Spirit got you now."

"Leeeeee!"

"*Swish-ka aba*, take the tainter,

"*Swish-ka aba*, count to three,

"*Swish-ka aba*, take the hainter,

"*Saash-ka Lae*, don't take me."

"Stop! Don't say it! I'm not cursing anymore!"

Silence.

"Please . . ."

"One . . ."

"Please . . ."

"Two . . ."

"I want to hear it too, please."

"Then seal 'em out. Seal 'em out!"

"I . . . er."

"Two 'n half."

"*Saaaa . . .*"

"*Saa saa aba saa saa.*"

"*Saa saa aba saa saa.*"

Two shapes on a hill. The sun has fallen down.

Two forms running the slope. And in the wind it is whispered to the ear of the hearer . . . The sun will rise tomorrow.

A Boll of Roses

A CHILLY wind reached under Layton Fields' collar and batted it against his neck. He snapped the collar up, stepped quickly in front of Floyd and picked up a rock. Aiming with one hand at the red horizon where the sun had fallen he hurled, "Umphh! How you know they comin tomorrow?" he asked Floyd.

"If they comin at all, they got to come tomorrow, cause sheriff say he gonna run all them out of town, them girls too."

"Can't run one of the colored ones out, cause she born down bout two miles from Greenville."

"If a white man run you outa his town and you a nigger, then you go, born there or not."

"They ain't comin then?"

"They got to come, if they comin at all."

"They can come and talk to me. I ain't scared of a few questions."

"They ain't got to do nothin. You ever see any poll takin people come and mess around with us niggers in a cotton patch before?"

"Ah, I know why you want them to come. Cause tomorrow the last day that professor be in Greenville. He leavin and takin all them students with him."

[*Editors' Note:* The author left behind a large number of literary pieces to various degrees unfinished. This story is one such piece, but one which seemed complete enough to justify its inclusion in this collection. Throughout the following text we have inserted daggers at points where the manuscript makes it clear that Dumas intended to elaborate further, or to insert additional elements.]

"Well, they might skip us."

"They might if they got any sense," said Floyd. He was a lean, tall boy, bent and humorless. He hunched as he walked.

When Layton heard that, he leaped forward and picked up another rock and hurled it toward the dark line that reached out from the land to the red haze. He was black, with quick, pulsing eyes. His nose, round and large, gathered directly in the center of his face and his constantly moving mouth was full and even. He was not as tall as Floyd, but more intense.

"Hey man, how much you say you pick today?" he asked.

"I told you once, man. Ain't you got no memory?"

"Yeah, but you say when you weighed up, them two girls was there askin questions?"

"Man, you crazy! That girl ain't thinkin about no cotton pickin nigger like you!"

"All right, Floyd Moss, watch who you messin with. I just asked you a simple question."

Floyd sucked his tongue and shook his head in controlled pity. He toned his voice as if a third person were listening, talking in a sing-song rhythm of semi-taunt.

"Yeah, this guy thinks so much of hisself, he think the United States government in love with him."

"How you get the government in with what they doin?"

"I bet the government sent that college professor down here with them girls and that uppity nigger to spy on what colored folks are really doin."

"Shucks," said Layton. "You the one crazy. I was listenin to them the other day, just before the truck took off and

I could hear them from the road. That girl, all three of them were civil rights workers down in Louisiana last summer. They takin outa school now to help the professor get done with what he doin."

"Well, they best skip our field tomorrow, cause when they come to me I ain't answerin no questions about nothin."

"Well, I'll take your place, Floyd Moss. You ain't good for nothin no way but pickin cotton."

"Hell, they don't pay you anythang to ask you all that damn stuff, do they?"

"You know more bout it than me. I tell you they wouldn't have to pay me. That pretty Miss Stiles, she don't have to do anythang but look at me and . . ."

"You crazy, man. They ain't got no business astin questions without givin out some pay for it. That's law."

"What kinda questions they ask?"

"All kinds, but they tryin to find out if we gonna register and vote. My old papa he ain't vote, and he said niggers never vote in Haxfall County."

"Damn," said Layton, hitting his hand in his fist. "That little brown girl bout the prettiest thang I ever seen in a cotton field."

"Yeah, but you mess with that white gal and I know them crackers hear about it as fast as thunder follow lightnin. They come after you like a hound on rabbit tail."

"Man, ain't nobody thinkin about that white girl. But I tell you somethin, man. I think I'm gonna make it back to the field tomorrow, just to get her to ast me questions."

"Yeah. Your head messed up, nigger. I can see that."

Layton slapped his fist again. They were moving up a hill along the dirt road. Large granite rocks, gaping out of

the ground like teeth, faded into the shadows. The two boys
felt the wind pushing at their faces, and after a brief silence,
both instinctively picked up [their] pace.*

Layton Fields hadn't planned on going to the fields tomorrow, but all week there had been a lot of talk about the
civil rights kids down there taking a poll. They actually
picked cotton with the people. Layton had hoped that they
would make the rounds to his field, but so far they hadn't
made it. Now that tomorrow was their last day, he would
have to miss school again. Besides he could use the three dollars. "Hot shank!" And he hit his fist, thinking about the
girl.

When they reached the point where the road leveled
off, Layton threw one last rock. He threw it over the house
which sat some distance back off the road.

"Loose trigger, Layton Fields, you a crazy nigger. You
be done busted a window out your own house."

"I ain't chunkin at my house, fool."

"What you chunkin for? Look like to me, you save that
arm. Hard as I pick today, you don't see me runnin around
in the dirt pickin up rocks and chunkin in the sky at nothin,
do you?"

"How much cotton you pick today?"

"Told you once. Ninety-five."

"I beat you then. You work all day, pick ninety-five. I
work from noon and pick sixty."

"How come you work from noon? You come all the way
down in the field for nothin. That ain't no money—sixty."

"I got paid. Ha, ha! Don't worry bout that. Hap Kelly,
he ask me help him unload that boll weevil killer. Then he

* Ms. reads: "both instinctively picked up his pace." [Eds.]

ask me help him fix that cotton pickin machine. He say he
pay me for hundred pounds if I pick fifty."

"So what you want me to do bout it?"

"Thought if you wanted a chance at some easy
money..."

"Hell, I don't see nothin easy bout that. If some of that
bug juice get on me, it eat a hole in me same as it do a damn
boll weevil. Man, you must think I'm crazy. You sure want to
see that ole skinny girl a lot."

"She ain't skinny, man. I like to just talk with her
once."

"Shucks, what a old cottonmouth scoun like you gonna
say to a rich chick like that? I bet she one of the richest niggers in the United States."

"Ah man, shut up. She'll talk to me."

"Bout what? Bout what?"

Layton turned and faced the other boy as they approached an unkempt rose hedge. The thorny branches, dipping and blowing in the wind, leaned and flopped over a
rotting fence-prop. The sky was still red, but evening had
pushed away, and the fading of the shadows ushered in the
night. From Layton Fields' house came the deep rhythmic
pulse of gospel music. Two front windows, lit up on either
side of the door, appeared like eyes.

Floyd laughed. "Bout what? Bout cotton and how
much you pick and if you gonna vote when you get old
enough, and do your mother and father vote?"

"She talk to me. Don't worry," he said, going around
the rose hedge. He fell forward as if he were going to fall,
caught himself on his left arm, spun around and sat down on
the step of the porch.

Floyd looked at him from beyond the bush. Neither

said anything. Floyd slowly came around the hedge and up the rock path where the remnants of an unkempt flower garden lay brown and dark.

"So you see me with Florence. Don't get mad."

Layton clenched his fist.

"Hell," said Floyd, "that black gal like you, but you just ig her. You mess with that city chick, 'n she gonna cut you down like a hoeblade cut a weed. She ain't studyin bout no young nigger like you, got mud all over his shoes and cotton in his mouth."

Layton stood up, stepped off, as Floyd approached the step. Layton headed around the house. One of the rose bushes struck his neck. "Ow!" He slung his hand at it as if striking at a mosquito. He went around the side of the house. "Yeah, you'll see, Mr. Floyd Moss. She talk to me."

He wanted to get away. He didn't care if Floyd followed him in the house or not. He had to get away from him. It was dark now on the east side of the house. He could hear his mother working to the sound of radio music. His grandfather was still up the Lane with the Ryans. They were getting ready to kill hogs, and his grandfather was an old hand at that. Layton struck his fist. Lord, he had to go to the cotton patch tomorrow. She was the prettiest dark brown thang he ever seen from New York. And she talked so nice and pretty. He had never heard a voice sound so pretty. He had heard pretty singing, but never had he been conscious of the sound of the human voice. Not like that. She must be what angels sounded like.

He went around to the back of the house. Floyd was hollering at him. He didn't holler back. Floyd hollered several times. "You comin tomorrow? Hey! Layton Fields! You pickin tomorrow? Hey? Cotton or rocks?"

He went into the house. The screen door slammed *whack!*

"That you, Layton?" His mother's voice, mixing with the sound of the wind and hushed chill of the evening, followed the slamming of the door.

Layton stomped his feet free of dirt before he went into the kitchen. He replied with some vague, and reluctant, monosyllable that barely he could hear. He knew he would have to plan what he was going to say to Rosemarie Stiles. What was he going to do to get her to talk to him? After all, nobody had interviewed him yet. The gospel sound of the Five Blind Boys suddenly came up. He went through the kitchen door, feeling bits of dried mud crumple beneath his feet.

His mother was building a fire in the wood stove. She was a stout woman, brown-skinned, heavy boned, but with a delicately chiseled face. Her eyes swept over Layton as he stomped through the kitchen. The dull lamp seemed to waver in its brightness as the wind and the night approached and struck the old house. Shadows in the room hid in corners. Mrs. Fields reached behind the stove and brought out the last stick of wood. With one sure motion she fed it to the leaping tongue of flame from the large iron stove.

"Who that hollerin like a crazy man?"

"Floyd Moss," he said.

"Boy, I need some wood to cook yawl som'teat." She never stopped her motions. A rolled-up, wet newspaper lay on the window sill. A few flies buzzed near it. The smell of fish hit Layton as he passed by. He knew his mother would want something done. He was planning to go down to the Blue Goose Inn. He shoulda never come home. If he'd had some clothes, he'd been down to the Blue Goose before dark.

If Rosemarie ever dropped in . . . and he knew she might, because Floyd had said that twice the civil rights people had stopped in. But Layton knew that it would be dangerous if that white girl ever came into the Blue Goose. But if Rosemarie came, nobody would pay it any mind, except him . . . He thought again . . . Knowing those crazy niggers down there, he knew they might try to mess with her. The thought made Layton clench.

"Boy, didn't you hear me talkin to you?"

He lit the lamp in his room. "Yes mam, I get it. But don't fix nothin for me. I'm eatin . . . in town."

"Better save them few pennies you make out there. I need some money now for groceries. What you talkin bout eatin out? Eatin out where?"

He knew she wouldn't understand.

"You better stay away from that place. All you do is waste your money."

Layton pulled out a suit his brother used to wear before he left home. It was an old-style suit, faded, torn, and unpressed. He tried not to listen to his mother. He shook the suit. Dust leaped from it like smoke. He threw the suit on the bed.

Another gospel song filled the house from the living room. His mother broke into a chorus.

"Didn't papa* cut some wood?" Layton asked. He knew where the old man was, but he wanted her to know that somebody else could keep the place supplied with wood as well as he could. His grandfather was doing nothing all day. Why couldn't he take time out from messing with other folks' hogs and horses and cut more wood than a couple of sticks now and then?

---

* "Grandpa"? [Eds.]

"Eatin or not, you better get me some wood."

Layton marched out of the house. He didn't mind getting wood for her, but he was tired. At least he was sorry he ever came straight home. Maybe he should've stopped in town and put a down payment on one of those silk vests that he saw some guys wearing. Maybe he could get himself a shirt, an English collar, French cuffs, and all. . . . Then she would know him . . . she talk to him then. . . .

He went out the front door. The sun had gone, but a faint red glow sifted upwards as if the hills were squeezing out the last bit of color. Layton paused for a second on the porch. He looked up the lane to see if his grandfather was hobbling along. A rooster crowed. Layton hurried to the woodpile in the back of the house. Suddenly he became conscious of the dying and the falling of things. He could hear in his head an echo and he could see where the echo was going without even taking his eyes off the axe and the echo was soft and pretty like a human voice and it flew like a bird flies across the sky, slow and fast but never too fast, and up and down in the wind and all he knew suddenly is that he felt real good and nobody could tell him different.

He raised the double edged axe and brought it down on an old oak log. The log had been taking a whacking since the beginning of the week. He struck the log, splitting it in one stroke with a grunt. Every time he heard his voice, something came alive and took him further and further away, and made him grasp at some notion, some vague connection of what to say to her. He wanted to laugh but he had to show Floyd and them ugly gals that he wasn't gonna pick cotton all his life. He didn't care what Floyd Moss said about Florence. That silly country gal couldn't do nothing for him except one thing. He picked up the wood and hurried to the house, kicking open the screen door and dumping the wood down in the kitchen wood box behind the stove. The screen door slammed behind him.

> Somethin's got a hold on me
> Yeah, yeah, yeah, yeah
> Somethin's got a hold on me
> Lord, I know somethin's got a hold on me.

Mrs. Fields had turned the radio up louder. Layton watched her sprinkle corn meal over six long gutted carp that lay on the table in a large platter. Hot grease boiled and popped in a black skillet on the stove in a rhythm all its own. Mrs. Fields, wearing an apron made from flour sacks, hummed and her voice held as much fire and conviction as the singers. Listening to her, Layton suddenly winced. He liked gospel but he didn't know how to like it when he was feeling good thinking about her. He felt ashamed. But something irritated him.

"Mama, you got to play that thing so loud?" He pretended his head hurt, knocking it a few times with the palm of his hand. "I can hear that thing all over the Lane."

Hardly before he had finished, his mother turned and faced him.

"Boy, what's ailin you?"

Layton knew that he had made a mistake. He felt a funny feeling rise inside him. He turned and was going out of the kitchen. It was the feeling he got, when, walking along the levee, he would come up on a bush or a pile of dirt and something would tell him 'look before you step,' but he wouldn't look, maybe just because he was in a hurry, but mostly because he was plain foolish, and every time he didn't look there would be a snake or a lizard there. Then he knew he had made a mistake, but it was too late because his foot was stepping there at that moment.

"Layton Fields, don't you hear me talkin to you?"

"Yes mam, I hear." He grabbed at the suit, flung its dusty shape back across the bed, and then sensing some wild terror running loose in the room and outside the house, he leaped off the bed toward the kitchen.

"Mama, I got to get some money."

She stood there, the dim light of the kitchen not hiding the troubled ridge that had marred her finely chiseled face. The sound of the Five Blind Boys rose again. . . .

I come to The Garden alone

"I gon quit and get me a job . . ."

His mother turned away, placing a mealed fish in the skillet as if she had not heard him. It was a familiar gesture and Layton, coming to the doorway, knew again that he had made the wrong step. But he did not care. Nobody knew how he felt about Rosemarie. He would quit school. He would pick no more cotton. He would get a job in Greenville or even go to Memphis, and he would make some money, some real money, not no three or four dollars a day picking cotton. . . . That wasn't no money. He felt ashamed of staying out of school just to pick cotton. Not that he liked school, but to go to the cotton field. . . . He gathered himself to approach his mother.

The sound of the singing surged in the house. With the rhythm of the music going, he knew that he didn't have to follow up what he said. He could just let it ride, let what she had said ride, and put on a sweater and his good shoes and make it out of the house before his grandfather came in to eat. . . . He could do that and just go up to the Blue Goose, mess around outside there a while, and come back before it was too late.

He wouldn't go to school tomorrow either, and then

maybe Monday he would start in and go the whole week. But it was Friday tomorrow. Only one day left in school.

He dug in a cardboard box stuffed with musty old clothes and pulled out a ragged green sweater. "Mama, I got to get me some money." The smell of fish rose to his nostrils. He wanted to get out of the house.

"Money ain't worth losin your soul over." She moved now with a hesitancy in her muscles. She knew the boy was troubled, and that he had been wanting money. But she also knew that he didn't know the value of an education. She wanted him to stay in school and someday go to college. And here he was thinking about quitting high school. She put the last fish in the hot grease.

"But Mama, I can't make no money pickin cotton, and Grandpa don't make none . . . I got to get somethin for you." He felt himself lying. He wasn't good at lying to her.

"I know you gettin so you want things, Layton, but fore your papa died I got down on my knees. Lord, I did. And I prayed that He see me through so my youngest finish school. My oldest got away from here without finishin, but I see that I want my youngest to finish. You be round here tonight and talk with them voter people."

"Aw, I'm gon finish school, but I first gots to get some money. We the poorest niggers . . . ."

"Don't use that word in this house!" She faced Layton. He slipped the sweater over his head and noticed for the first time, the terrible strain in his mother's voice. Somehow, he wanted to reach and touch her. She was right about a lot of things, but he couldn't give in on this one thing. He knew how he felt. That was all. He was going by how he felt. Her dark brown face, pulled and drawn, seemed to plead with him.

"I don't want to hear no more of this talk, Layton. The

Lord promise me what He was gon do with my youngest. I ain't worryin . . . Money or no money, you gon finish. I ain't never seen Him failed yet . . . And if God can't fail, then He ain't gon let one of His children fail . . ."

With that she went to fixing plates on the table.

Layton turned to go, but he heard footsteps on the front porch, and the grunting and groaning of his grandfather. The old man knocked through the front* with his cane and then grunted about in the front. Layton thought about going out the back, but something had got a hold of him. He went back into his room, kicked the tiny stove with his foot, looked at his school book in the corner, looked at the dusty suit sprawled on the bed like a broken body. . . .

For a second, the terror that had raced about the room and outside in the yard came upon him in a sudden heave of hatred for his mother and his grandfather, for Floyd Moss, for the whiteman who had all the niggers picking cotton, for the world, for the whole world, for everybody, except. . . .

He went out the front, paying no attention to his grandfather who had fallen wearily in his rocking chair and was puffing and blowing to catch his breath.

He frowned at Layton and Layton passed on through the door, closing it and looking at the darkness spitting out its stars. He walked outside around the house until a chill drove into him.

He wasn't chilly. He wasn't cold. He saw a star. He saw the moon, far over there, getting ready to jump there in the sky and take over from that head-whoopin sun. He looked at the faint profile of the bushes and the trees, bending, bowing, swaying, back and forth, dancing, a whole field of cotton in the night waiting for the morning, waiting for the morning. . . .

* "front door"? [Eds.]

After supper he talked to his grandfather.† He wanted to
get over to the Blue Goose Inn, but he would wait and go
tomorrow. Friday night was better anyway. Something held
him to the house. He didn't know if it were fear, or what.

He got out his good shoes and began to clean them. He
hadn't worn them in months, not since the big baptism back
in July at Blue Goose Lake. He looked at the shoes. They
were cheap, worn, and had been polished once or twice. That
was one thing he'd have to do. Polish his shoes. Everybody in
the city wore clean shoes. He knew that. Anytime you went
anywhere outside of the damn country, people wore decent
things. They never had mud on them. He could hear his
grandfather now, complaining about the weather not being
right for killing hogs. His mother was standing next to the
radio now, where she had propped the ironing board. Layton
could see her face, and there was something about the way she
had told him he was her youngest. . . . Somethin about it. . . .
Maybe he wouldn't go out to the Blue Goose. Maybe he'd
stay home and think about what he was going to say to Rosemarie Stiles. . . .

Would she want to talk to an old cotton pickin nigger,
like him, unless he had some clothes? Deep down he feared
Floyd might be right. That girl was from the city, and she
wouldn't pay him no mind. But he had to talk with her.
After all, wasn't she supposed to interview all the people?
He would find out exactly what questions she was asking and
then he would find out all the answers, and when she came to
him, he would be the smartest. He might even tell her that he
would be down at the Blue Goose and if she wanted to hear
more answers, then she could come down there. But she
couldn't bring that white girl. He didn't want to be a part of
them getting lynched or run out of town. He knew what he
would do. With the $9 he had saved he would buy him a

vest, a pair of dress shoes, a pair of gaberdine slacks, a silk white shirt, like he saw the guys wearin at the Blue Goose, a slim tie, a cuff-linked shirt, French style, and everything else. Nobody could tell him from the rest of the cats that had gone to the city and come back sharp. He knew what he would do. There wasn't nothing stopping him.

Layton took the great box of rags, dumped them out on his bed and began to ramble through them.

Before he came out of the room he heard the visitors' voices, at once strained and alien. And one of them he knew was not the voice of a colored person.* He was seated on the floor, with piles of old clothes barricading him in. He had made three piles, taking items from the big heap on the bed with deliberate care.

". . . Mrs. Fields has offered any help she can give to get started . . ."

Layton knew that voice. It was Mrs. Hooper. Sometimes she picked cotton, but she had gotten old now and didn't go to the fields. The highway people gave her some money for making her move. Only now and then would she do any picking. Layton came and stood in the doorway. Only the young girl, Sheila Bauden, glanced his way when he appeared.

They had come to his house. He looked toward the door, then back to the old woman he knew so well. Mrs. Hooper was explaining the whole thing to his mother. The young white girl, relaxed and not at all nervous, listened and seemed to nod as Mrs. Hooper explained the project. Layton looked out the window. He could see no one else.

"It ain't just us who got youngsters who want to see this thang through, but everybody is behind it. At first I was like some of the rest. I didn't want to get into nothin I thought

* Ms. indicates the author considered omitting this sentence. [Eds.]

didn't mount to nothin. But this is gonna work. Like Rev. Tucker say, 'I know God got a hand in this thang.' We gonna set up the best school in the county."

"I said I would hep. Then I hep," said Mrs. Fields. "But somebody have to show me what to do."

The white girl began to explain something. Layton watched her. He tried to detect a patronizing attitude. He shivered at the thought that somebody from town knew she was out here in the woods in a poor nigger's house. What would they do? Layton fought the urge to leave the house. He wanted to ask them when the professor was going to leave. He wondered if the rest of the group were down the road, if they were interviewing, if Rosemarie Stiles were with them. Maybe they would come to the house when they finished down there.

He stepped back into the room and continued to sort the old clothes.

He could hear them talking. His mother was going to take part in a drive in which many kids, pre-school kids, were given some training. . . .

He listened to them. He had never heard Mrs. Hooper excited over anything done with or by whitefolks, but something had got a hold on her now. Layton looked at the young white girl Sheila. She was blondish, with greenish eyes, and wearing a light brown coat which covered her slacks.

They talked for half an hour. Layton's grandfather even nodded approvals and twice he rose up and grunted "Amen." He, too, caught the enthusiasm of Mrs. Hooper.

Mrs. Hooper took out some papers and passed them to Layton's mother.

Layton came out and stood near the door. The white girl, holding a stack of forms and papers under her arm, smiled, he thought. Her face was tiny and sharp. What she smiling at me for? But then, when he went past her he realized that he hadn't even caught her eye, and that what he thought was a smile was just a twist of her head. He wanted to ask them what they wanted out there. Suddenly he stood in the center of the room.

He paused to swallow. All eyes turned on him. He couldn't say what he wanted. His mouth worked rapidly now as he swallowed air. He was suspended in the room, held up by the quiet gaze of their eyes. He could feel them letting him down easy, but still he struggled. He had to get things out by himself. He knew how he felt.

He felt a sudden quivering inside. They told him he would be a part of a group of young people to meet at the church Sunday evening. The girl Sheila took his mother in the lamp light and showed her how to get people to fill out forms. But he went outside and stood on the porch. He thought he heard people down the road.

Layton felt himself breaking inside. "Yall gon be goin to the cotton field again?"

They had all stood up to go. Sheila turned to Layton. Layton didn't know how he had said what he said. He found his lips saying things that he didn't know he was going to say. Then, when he found that he had said it, he felt ashamed.

"Yes," she said. "But just tomorrow."

"How come yall never come to Hap Kelly's field?"

"Tomorrow we hope to visit all the fields we missed."

"You know somethin? Is that other girl, is she gonna come tomorrow?"

"Who?"

"You know, that girl always be with you?"

"Rosemarie? Well, I think so."

Where she at now? Layton thought he said that but when he saw Mrs. Hooper nodding at his mother and saying good night, he knew it had been only air.

He stepped out into the night. Mrs. Hooper and Sheila B. left, walking out into the yard and past the flowers, the moon, and out into the road. Down the road the moon had taken up a spot as if to watch and shine on that spot. He wanted to follow them. But he knew what Mr. Hooper would say. They got into Mrs. Hooper's car, and the lights came on, and the car went on down the lane.

Layton Fields! Go with them! Fool! He walked out to the edge of the garden. The headlights turned like search-lights pivoting through the night. They struck him. He jerked his hand instinctively and let it relax into a wave. Lifting his arm, he felt a sudden urge to run after the car, but instead he fell away from the light and watched the car disappear down the lane. The moon held itself in the distance like a piece of ice, and he squinted at it, wondering if the sun* were as strong as the sun. Which one could burn up the world? Which one could cool it off?

He clenched his fist. He walked a piece down the road trying to follow the disappearing tail lights. But he knew they weren't going to the Blue Goose. . . . But maybe they would in this moonlight and stop in to ask a few questions. He could see the one-wing blue bird flying nowhere in the broken neon light and he could hear the loud shouts of beer-voiced field hands dancing because you had to shake the dust and the cotton off your back at night, after the sun under the moon. . . . You could smell the beer and frying fish on the road—

It was the wind which told Layton to return. He had

---

* "moon"? [Eds.]

slowed his pace, feeling the chill bite into his sweater and the moon shining on something else instead of him. He stumbled once on a rock. What was he doing out in the night?

He tore himself away from the urge to fly down the road. . . . And he wandered back toward the shack, whistling with gospel music. His mother's animated voice touched a great weight gathering up in his chest. He didn't know. The whole night swallowed him up.

He heard an owl once during the night and after the fire in the stove was built up, and the house settled, as it seemed, back into the earth, he found himself sprawled across the bed, covered and buried in the rags, like some ancient mummy or dead man. The smell of the rags angered him and he went to sleep, thinking about the smell of cotton.

He dreamed of a great streamlined train, a red streak, shaped like an arrow, zooming through the cotton patch, not following any kind of tracks but weaving and twisting in and out of the rows. It was like a giant red, black, orange, and green stinging worm. He himself was dressed in a fine silk suit, and all the world was bowing to him. He was a king, the king of something, but he didn't have any shoes on and he had to keep his beautiful robes down and spread out to cover his bare feet. Suddenly the train sounded. Light flashed from it and the wind whistled from the horn. Layton jerked, grunted. Then sitting bolt upright, his hand slapping his neck where he thought a worm was stinging him, he leaped out of bed. The sun was gathering up itself out the window. A faint line of dust rose from the rags when he leaped up. He hadn't changed clothes all night.

He could hear his mother humming in the kitchen. She was up early. The sound of her voice was like the waving of a fan over a fire which had smoldered all night, and then in the morning, when a piece of good, dry wood was lain on, it

would catch and rise up. Layton knew she wanted him to go
to school today. He walked out of the room, through where
his grandfather sat, tying his shoes and spitting tobacco juice
in a can beside his cot. He spoke softly to his grandfather,
but the old man's eyes hung on him suspiciously. Layton
opened the front door and the sun leaped in on the old man's
cot.

"Better mind out and stay out that cotton field, boy. You
got people come way down here to get poor colored folks to
help themselves. And you a young man. Ain't many young
people left that's go out an pick cotton all day."

Layton heard himself saying "Yes sir," but he was off the
porch, into the sun, passing the garden, when the smell of cotton . . . then the rose garden, and then wet dew . . . the bowing of the dew laden bushes . . . and he hoped it would be his
last day. He knew that they would come and he knew what
he would say to her. He reached and pulled a rose stem, and it
stuck him, and he thought of the worm dream, and off
snapped the rose and he put it into his chest pocket.

He didn't care about eating breakfast. He wasn't hungry.
Leaving the shack in the morning, especially this morning,
made him feel as if he were leaving it for the last time. Never
again would he live there. He would get a job, take his mother
out, take the old man out, buy them a house, and he wouldn't
never never work for the whiteman again. He ran along the
road now, not looking back. If he heard her voice calling
him, even if he heard the sound of the radio, he didn't know
what he would do. But he would keep going.

He could see the road now. He ran a little faster. About
this time the truck would be pulling along. It might already
have gone on without him. They knew that sometimes he
didn't go to the fields. Maybe Hap Kelly thought today that
he wasn't going.

He wondered if old Floyd had come this way. The truck might have picked him up down by the Blue Goose. There was always a large crowd that waited there in the mornings, and then the truck would pick them up. But in the night it wouldn't go directly there, but would drop them off about a half mile away, along the Bottomsuck, and then go on to drop off the rest. But sometimes that whiteman wouldn't even drive the folks home. Layton recalled the time when he told all the pickers they'd have to walk home, or ride the best way they could, but he would make it up to them on the next day. And the people went along with that whiteman but that whiteman didn't do anything but the same thing the next day. Instead of making it up, he lied again and claimed that Negroes were trying to mess over him. He said the cotton was too wet to pick, and that he was paying less for it today than on dry days. There were seven or eight who quit pickin for him that very day. Hap Kelly was mean when he wanted to be, and that was most of the time.

Before Layton reached the road he heard the truck. He ran, but he could see that at the curve they wouldn't see him from the truck, and they would keep going.

He made a last effort to reach the bend before the truck passed the lane, but when he reached it he saw a cloud of dust. The truck had passed.

Layton ran out on the road. What did he look like running after a cotton truck? He threw up his hand, almost stopping, but seeing that the people on the back were hollering for the truck to stop and the truck was slowing, he ran on. . . . He leaped up on the truck, and it lumbered back onto the road, grinding gears, and made the wide turn that took it into the delta flats. Layton stood for a while, looking over the cab of the truck. Old Lady Rusmaker pulled on his coat and coughed.

"Sit down, boy. You be standin all day. No use to do it on
the truck."

They made room for him. The same people. Floyd was
sitting near the front. Dust and the smell of weeds and cotton
stalks filled Layton's nostrils. He sat down, squeezing himself
in between Mrs. Jackson with her walking stick and the cab
of the truck.

He looked at the people. Didn't they get tired of picking
cotton and riding the truck? They were the same people. He
knew that he would have to leave. He would get him a job.
No more cotton. He would get him a job.

He looked at the faces. At the end of the truck was old
man Jesse. He had picked cotton all his life. He had been a
tenant farmer once, but now he picked with whoever was
doing the hiring. Old man Jesse was stubborn, but Layton
liked the way he sang. When old man Jesse sang, the whole
field raised up a bit. Somehow the burden of the sack was
lifted. Next to him was Sister Leah. She was a short black
woman, with bad eyes. Years of cotton picking seemed to
have even put a bend in her face. It drooped, even when she
smiled, which was seldom.

The truck reached the downgrade. Everybody leaned
forward a bit.

Two of the Parker children, both sitting next to Sister
Leah, began coughing. They were two boys, no more than
eleven years old. Layton looked at them. If there was anybody
should be in school, it was them.

The truck rumbled on. Layton tried to look back
through the dust. He knew that sometimes a car followed the
cotton pickers into the field. He knew that the interviewers
rode with the truck sometimes, and sometimes they came in
a car. He had seen them. He was going to ask Gladys Fisher,
who was sitting with a silly grin on her face across from him,

ask her if they were going to come to the field. But he held back. He better not say anything to her or Florence. Them two would be picking at him all day. He couldn't stand no ugly girls, but they all time found something to nag him about.

He looked at Floyd, squeezed in between Mrs. Hattie Jones and Omelia Diggs. Layton wanted to laugh but he knew Mrs. Jackson next to him would detect it. She wouldn't hesitate to strike your feet with her cane. Layton never knew how she managed. She had been picking cotton since they invented cotton. He leaned out to try to catch Floyd's eye, and when he did, he saw Floyd laughing at him. Floyd was pointing at him and laughing. He drew back. What the hell you laughing at, nigger? He felt everybody looking at him. He felt a sharp prick in his chest. The rose was sticking out of his pocket. As he stuffed it back, he could hear them all snickering.

"Ain't nobody studyin yawl," he said, but his voice was drowned by the rumbling of the truck. He coughed, as if to challenge them. Even the Parker kids were laughing at him, but not because they knew what was going on. They were laughing because they saw the older kids laughing, and even *at* the older kids.

Layton could see that Floyd was really trapped in between the two fat women and they were slapping him back and forth as if he were a piece of dough ready to be rolled out and flattened for biscuits.

Layton wanted to laugh but Old Lady Rusmaker across from him was shaking her head watching everybody. She didn't like young people. Once in church she caught him and Floyd messing around, and sent them out of the church. Both of them got a whipping. He never forgot that and even though he spoke politely to her, said "yes mam" and "no mam," and all the right things, he never liked her. He rubbed his feet together. The truck picked up speed on a sandy stretch toward the levee.

"Boy, what your mama gonna do with them whitefolks and Mrs. Hooper?" asked Mrs. Jackson. She propped the cane up and leaned on it with one arm.

"I don't know."

"Heard they come out to your house last night."

"Yes mam."

"What your grandpa think?" Mrs. Jackson was always like that. She asked questions and got into people's business. Layton didn't mind telling her what he thought was going on because he knew it had to be good, since Mrs. Hooper was in it.

"He think it be good."

"You gettin mighty big yourself, now. You gwine get with them people, and let them send you back to school?"

"Yes mam."

"I picked cotton all my life, chopped, planted, cleared land, and I ain't got nothin to show for it. You younguns oughta get out of this field and get with them rights people. They got the Lord on their side."

Old Lady Rusmaker, sitting across from Layton, leaned her body over to hear. "What's that, Clara?"

Mrs. Jackson pointed the end of the cane at Layton's shoe. She jabbed it and held it on the toe.

"I say," she yelled, "these younguns gwine have to get out of the field and work with those gov'ment people. Colored folks' time is comin now. I just tellin this here boy to get with them people."

"Ain't it the truf," nodded Old Lady Rusmaker.

Layton was glad when the old women got into a conversation.

The truck rumbled slowly over a rutted road, and stopped in front of a dilapidated cotton gin—one of the old shacks that was now used to house a tractor and cotton pickers. Everybody got off.

The chill in the air was gone now. The sun had found its way up through the dust and dew. Layton leaped off the truck and looked around. The fields were empty. Their truck was the first. He wondered where the two big trucks were with the rest of Hap Kelly's pickers. He knew a lot of people on that truck* too. He had to get out and choose a good row so he could be on the outside and when she would come along then he would be in a good spot. The cotton sacks were hauled off the truck. Another whiteman came out of the barn. He walked over to Hap Kelly and they talked briefly. He knew the other man, a narrow red-faced white man, named Fane, whose skin was so weathered that it looked like brown leather. To look at him you would think he was an Indian or a Negro, but then you would see the wrinkles and the shape of his nose, the blueness of his eyes and his matty hair. Layton pulled up a handful of grass and stood near them.

"There's that shale strip yonder and I want it picked clean first. It don't matter none after that who gets to the pecan trees. Yonder pass them trees is all from now till next week."

The man named Fane kept nodding his head and smoking on a cigarette. Layton didn't hear him say a word. It was all Hap Kelly. And Hap Kelly was keepin his eyes on Florence Meadows. Floyd had his sack and came over to Layton. Layton picked up a rock and threw it into the trees. The two white men moved off to the barn. The pickers gathered up their sacks and waited under a great live oak by the road.

* "those trucks"? [Eds.]

"There he is," laughed Floyd, pointing at Layton. "There he is. Layton the Claytoe."

"Aw shut up. Didn't you see how that whiteman messin with Florence?"

"Yeah, I see. That gal old enough to take care herself. Funny you ain't say nothin about it till now." He laughed again at Layton.

Layton kicked some dirt toward Floyd. "Get away from me, fool, talkin that mess."

"Yeah, we all know what you got, boy. That city gal got your head messed up."

"Ain't nobody thinkin . . ."

"Or it must be that white gal. They tell me she and Mrs. Hooper come all over the Lane last night."

Layton didn't say anything. The rose in his chest pocket pricked him again. He wanted to take it and throw it at Floyd. What right had that overall-wearing nigger to make fun of him? What right had he even to see that flower? Layton wished he had kept his feelings to himself. He walked off. "Man, don't mess with me. I told you yesterday, I tell you today, if you mess with me . . ."

"You what?" He felt some dirt hitting him in the back. He turned. It was Floyd. He was standing beside the two girls, Florence and Gladys, and they were all watching him, laughing. The Parker kids even joined in.

"All right, yawl," Layton heard the whiteman's voice. The truck started up. "This here field is new." Fane pointed.

The day's work began. People listened briefly to Fane. Mrs. Jackson, as if she anticipated everything the man was saying, limped across the road, followed by old man Jesse, mumbling to himself. Fane kept talking as if he didn't see them.

Layton moved to the outer edge of the circle. When the

meeting broke Layton drug his sack across the road, clutching his stomach and wishing he had brought something for lunch. He would have to buy some lunch or beg. And he would not beg, and he could not buy. He was saving all his money for his clothes.

Approaching the cotton he hit an outside row. It was lower and the cotton was scrawny. There was something in the soil at that particular row which stunted the growth of the cotton. Layton swung his sack around, letting it drag comfortably from his right side. The first few bolls were tight and the cotton fought his fingers. He knew he was on a bad row.

For a long time he held his head down. When he finally looked up, everybody was ahead of him, except Mrs. Jackson, and she was about even. He had picked a clean row, but he was moving slow. Over the field he saw none of the inter-viewers.

When he was sure no one was looking, Layton took the crumbled flower from his pocket. He felt like slamming it down in the dirt and stomping on it. He squatted and ex-amined the flower. He ought to spit on it. He ought to be in school. He knew what he was going to do. He was going to get a job. Hell, here he was. Maybe Floyd was right. So what if she did come today. She wouldn't look at him. He clenched the flower. Sweat began to rise out of his body. He ought to spit on it. He didn't have any clothes yet. Hell, he hadn't even went to town to look for any. What would she say to a dirty nigger in the cotton patch? He looked at the flower. Suddenly he had to stand up quickly. He felt himself giving way to a sudden urge to cry.

He put it back and went on picking.

Across the field he could make out Floyd. He had got himself a row next to Florence and they were laughing. He knew he didn't want to be next to them. He had gotten one next to Mrs. Jackson. Only trouble with her was that she was going to bother him about first one thing and then another. Picking *alongside* her was just the same as picking *for* her. The first time he ever got beside her he figured the best thing to do with her was to tell her to go and rest in the shade less she have a sun stroke, and he would take care of her sack and his too. It would be easier to do that than to have to put up with her noisiness and peskiness. Layton looked up ahead. Old man Jesse was just ahead of her. The next row over was the Parkers. They were ahead. One of the Parker boys would soon act as the water-boy. Between the two of them they could pick over a hundred pounds of cotton, and when the sack got too heavy for them Mrs. Parker would put all of the cotton in hers and the boys would go right on. They were a team. And nobody could outpick a team.

Sweat gleamed on his left arm. The morning had gone. The crew was working fast. They finished a couple of rows, going up, turning around, starting back, dragging their sacks. Old man Jesse had begun a slow hum that grew stronger and louder as he bent under the weight of the sack. Layton was in a row next to Gladys now, and Floyd was next to her. Mrs. Parker was next and then Old Lady Rusmaker. Over the fields cotton stretched beneath rises in the land as far as Layton could see. He wondered if people planted anything else in the world besides cotton. He swung at flies buzzing around him.

Suddenly he lifted his head. Way across the field he saw dust spreading out over the black edge of a car moving along just above the tops of the cotton. It wasn't going toward the field on the other side of the pecan trees. It was coming toward them. Like a wind striking the tops of cotton, an urgency swept over the pickers. They knew that the car was headed their way. Layton picked faster. Twice the rose worked itself out and fell on the ground. It was noontime. They had come. He picked faster, squinting his eyes at the movement of the dust.

The car stopped under the grove of pecan trees. Layton could make out several figures getting out. A truck pulled in behind the car. It was loaded with pickers. They were going to pick the other field.

"Boy, what you think you doin?" It was Mrs. Jackson. She had been watching him. Layton bent over, laid the sack down. "Yes mam," he said, and stepped over the next row and headed toward the trees.

"Boy, where you goin?" He kept going, saying, "Yes mam. Yes mam."

That's what he had to say: Yes mam, yes mam. . . . Hell, what did old people have to come to the cotton patch for? Mrs. Jackson was crippled and she was always sitting up on somebody's truck, going to pick three dollars worth of cotton. She had helped her children all the way through school. Some of them sent her money. He couldn't figure what made her come back to the fields. If he had people sending him money, he would never come to a cotton field.

He saw Rosemarie Stiles now. People were crowded around her and the white girl, Sheila. The white man, driving the car, was talking to the pickers. He was the professor. Somebody had said he was working for the government. There was a young colored guy with the group. Layton approached from behind, coming into the shade of the grove on the field side. For all they knew, he might have been on that truck.

Layton brushed himself off, his pants, and shirt, trying to send the dust away.

He got in among the crowd. He could see her now again.
She was laughing. Those niggers had her laughing. What
could she be laughing at? Layton moved in. He asked the
driver if they had any water. The man pointed to a tank on
the back of the truck. He leaped over the tail gate. Rosemarie
Stiles had her back to the truck. When Layton jumped
up, Sheila, having seen him crossing the field, looked up at
him.

Layton tried to remember everything in the world to say,
but his throat was dry and filled with dust. He found a paper
cup, filled it, and leaned against the high truck rails. Sheila
looked at him again. He walked to the edge of the truck, and
as if struck by some irresistible urge, broke out all over in a
big grin, reaching the cup of water down to the head of
Rosemarie. Sheila saw the whole gesture, saw Layton and his
eyes. He handed her the water and quickly got another. This
one he reached to Rosemarie, and when he looked in her face
he knew that he would never come to the cotton field again.
He would go to school, get himself a job, maybe go on to
college and. . . .

"Thank you," Sheila said.

"Yes, thank you."

Layton was still smiling. But he did not feel as if he wanted
to smile. He was just embarrassed. He had waited to talk to
her and now he had a chance. . . . He leaned over the side of
the truck and after swallowing a cup of water, he managed to
feel his chest.

"I got to talk to you, about a job . . . Mrs. Hooper, she
say I got to talk with you about that job."

"What job?" asked Rosemarie.

Layton felt himself slipping. He hoped the side of the
truck would hide how he looked. "Mrs. Hooper gettin us
jobs with the government."

More people dragged sacks and hollered, gathering around Sheila and Rosemarie.

"Mrs. Hooper is working with us."

"What's you think you writin in that book about us niggers?" Layton asked.

The girl continued writing and sat on the fender of the truck. "You must be Layton Fields," she said, after a long silence. She was filling out some forms, the same kind of forms that his mother had filled out the night before.

"That's right. What you think about it?" He clenched his hands, grinding his toes up into his shoes, digging his knees into the sides of the truck, letting the prick of the thorn sting him, and sting him, letting the sweat gather into a little dam and then leap into his eyes. . . .

He didn't know why he was doing it. He wanted to jump down and hit her and hug her. He couldn't figure out what made him get all messed up over a pretty brown gal. She wasn't pretty. Maybe to some people, but not to him. He let the thorn stick his chest, and he let the image of the figure of Old Lady Rusmaker coming across the field to gossip and stick her nose in business hang in his eyes. He did not look down at her. He still smiled, but it was not like a drink of water.

"Your mother has signed up for the pre-school course. She's going to make more money doing work in town than you will make here in the field."

Layton jumped off the truck and came around to face the girl.

"What you think you doin comin down here to mess with niggers? I bet this the first time you ever see a cotton field."

"Well, I certainly didn't come out here to talk with no dirty mouthed mannerless thing like you." She folded the last

sheet of a form and went to the next one. Layton walked
straight toward Old Lady Rusmaker slowly walking in the
sun. When he got to the sun, he felt himself rise up, struck
by the heat, and then rise up and trot and when he got to the
first row of cotton, he leaped over it.

Floyd Moss saw him and hollered. He waved Floyd off,
but circled in that direction. The sun was heavy on him. He
liked the way it felt. He knew he was going to pick some
cotton today. He was going to get that money, oh yeah, he
was going to get it, and he was going to go to school. He
might even buy him some clothes. That's right. He looked
over his shoulder. All those Negroes picking cotton. He'd
show them how to pick.* Look at that black gal Florence
over there. He ought to throw a rock at her. Laughing at
him. Hell, he knew what he was going to do. When he got
home. . . . He thought of his mother's pinched face, the other
night. A pain had knotted there so long that it was part of her
look. He wanted to change that face. He wanted his mother
to smile. He knew what he would do. He might even apolo-
gize to that gal. She was too old for him anyway. He picked
up his sack, slung it over his shoulder, grunted "*Ummph*,"
and dragged the weight of the sack. He saw his hands move,
and he said, "move hands," and every time he said *move
hands*, they moved, and then he said *move once for my mama*,
and he kept on picking, with the fields all under his power.
There he was, and he said, "I'm gonna pick till it stick. I'm
gonna finish this field so clean, people'll forget what cotton
look like."

And he saw Florence coming toward him. He saw the
Parker boys bring her water and she drank it and across the
dust field, over the rows, Layton saw her, and he knew his
mother wouldn't mind receiving a rose either.

* Author's note in Ms. margin reads: "Why all of a sudden" [Eds.]

Double Nigger

"Yeaah!" said Grease. ". . . and evah time I grunt, that damn peckerwood, he say to hisself, 'Damn if you ain't the workinest nigger I ever seed.' "

We laughed at Grease, but we won't payin him no mind. He was the onliest one who done taken his shoes off tryin to keep off that hot pike.

We was makin it back to New Hope, Grease, Blue, Fish and me. We had just got done with bustin up some road for a white man, helpin out his constructin gang.

We was feelin good, headin back home with four dollars apiece. We'd all take out them bills evah mile or so, count 'em and match 'em up to see whose was the newest. They was the prettiest damn dollar bills we evah made. Totin rocks and stumps for that white man almost busted out natural backs.

"Shet up, nigger," Blue said to Grease. "Your mouth runnin like a stream." Blue was walkin along on the other side of the road even with me. We were fanned out a bit. Fish was ahead. Grease, he was behind him, jumpin off and on to the hot pike to cool his feet.

"Yeaah," I said. "Put your shoes on. Ain't you got no civilization?"

"Yeaah!" said Grease, wavin his greens back at me and Blue. "He say, 'Niggah,' and yall know what it mean when a white man call a nigger a niggahhh, don't you?"

"Naw," said Blue. "What it mean?"

Old Grease, he half fell over laughin, but then he

straightened up and posed hisself like he was a preacher givin us a lesson.

"Nigggahhh. That mean whatever you can do, it take *two* niggers to keep up with you. Then you a Double Nigger," and he fell to laughin again.

We moved on, payin Grease little mind, but glad he wasn't gettin tired. He funny sometime, but he nevah know when to stop clownin.

We come to a hill. The road turned around the hill. It was really hot. Your spit almost boil. We stopped under a shade tree. "I'm so damn thirsty," said Fish, "I could drink my own spit."

We all agreed.

"If yall come on," said Blue, "we be in Rock Hill less'n hour."

Grease said, "I bet that peckerwood there'll let us buy soda water with money look this pretty."

"Naw," said Fish, lookin over the hill. "I think we oughta cut yonder ways, hit the Creek and be home fore dark."

"Boy, you crazy!" shouted Grease. "Tired as my feet is, and full of snakes as that creek is . . ."

"What you say, Tate?" Fish asked me.

"All I want is one bucket of water now," I said.

"What bout you, Blue?"

"It don't matter one way t'other," he said. "We done come this far, we might as well walk the rest."

"Well, yall go ahead," said Grease, pretendin he wasn't payin us no mind. "I'll be drinkin soda water and snatchin on that black gal Lucille as soon as I gets to Rock Hill, and then I catch a bus or a ride with some niggers comin through."

"Yeah," said Blue, "you little squiggy nigger, and you get home tomorrow mornin too. Ain't no more bus comin through Rock Hill."

"Yes it is."

"Naw," said Fish.

"Yeah," I added. "If you do get home messin round down there, you have a rope around your neck. Ain't no colored people livin out here."

"The hell there ain't."

"Come on," said Fish. Blue and me broke off with Fish cross the field.

We knew that Greasemouth was only playin, but he had worked over this way once with some white man sawin lumber. It was just before school started. I member, cause Grease ain't come to school hardly that whole year.

We climbed through the barbed wire fence settin way off the road. There was a creek over that way somewheres. If we went this way, it would cut off five miles, goin over the hills stead round them.

"Creek is yonder way," Blue said. We stood lookin over the area. We hadn't looked back to see if Grease was followin. We didn't much care. He had stopped laughin at us, and when we turned around, we didn't see him.

"Let that greasemouth nigger go," said Blue. "One of them razorback peckerwoods'll catch him sniffin round down over yonder and they'll saw that nigger's lips off."

"If the grease don't stop 'em," said Fish.

We laughed. We always had fun with Grease when he was with us or not. We called him Grease cause whenevah he ate anythang, he let the grease pile up in the corners of his mouth and all over, like he nevah chewed his food but just slide it down with grease and lard.

We all come together now, walkin down the slope, watchin for bulls, dogs, wild hogs, crazy peckerwoods, devils and anything that moved. We might be trespassin. After a while we got deep into the trees. All we saw was a few birds and a rabbit.

"As ugly as Grease is," said Fish, "them peckerwoods'll wind up sending for us and then they pay us to take that nigger outa their sight."

We doubled over laughin. I tripped on a rock and sat there, catchin up on my wind. Blue was just ahead of me. He walked under a shade tree. He was so black that everybody called him Blue. Fish, he wasn't too much lighter. He was about my complexion and they called him Fish cause he could stroke good. Natural fish, he was. They called me Tate cause my head shaped like a potato. I nevah could find no damn potato on my head, but they just keep callin me that anyway, and so I do like everybody else and tease ole crazy Greasemouth. Then I can stand them better teasin me. I stopped laughin and got up. I picked up a stick and thought about throwin it at Blue, but kept it and went runnin on down to catch up.

I don't recollect what I thought it was at first. But all of a goddamn sudden! there comes this wild-buck thang chargin at us from behind a bunch of trees, yellin.

Blue broke in front of me, screamin somethin I ain't nevah heard, and before all three of us knew anythang, ole Greasemouth was doubled over laughin at us.

Fish was the first to holler at him, cause Fish probably saw him fore any of us, and he wasn't taken aback by him jumpin out like that.

"Get up, boy. You ain't scared nobody but yourself," Fish said to Grease.

But he kept wallerin there on the ground, laughin.

"Scared all of you!" he hollered. He began rollin down the hill, still laughin.

"You shoulda seen that . . ." And he pointed at Blue, who was standin just shakin his head as if to signify on Grease for makin a fool out of hisself. But Blue was really scared a little bit. Me too, a little.

". . . that nigger get ready to run. Did yall see that?"

Blue swung his arm on a limb and chunked some leaves at Grease.

"Ah, get up, boy. As ugly as you is, the trees leanin over away from you."

Grease got up and kept on teasin us. We moved on now through the patches of trees and washed out ditches and holes. Grease had put on his shoes now and was way up front, call hisself singin.

Then he hauled off and stopped singin.

"Hey, yonder's a well!" We all ran over and looked where he was pointin.

"Ah, now damn!" said Blue. We stood there lookin.

"Told yall niggers live up here," Grease said.

It was a house sittin beside a busted-in barn and a old wellshed. About half an acre of shale dirt full of weeds was behind that house. Nothin grow on dirt like that but scorpions and mean peckerwoods.

"Dammit, Grease," hollered Fish, "you know it ain't no niggers livin there . . ."

"That's right, and I can't drink that damn house," said Blue.

"Hell," I said, "don't think a peckerwood mind givin four niggers some water."

"Who's gonna ask?" said Grease.

"You, nigger," said Fish. "Didn't you find the place?"

"Yall said I was ugly," he said, "and I don't want to scare nobody, as thirsty as I is."

"Just whoever do the askin, leave the gate open and watch for nigger-eatin dogs," I said.

As we moved toward the house, Blue said, "Ain't nobody livin there. Look, ain't no smoke in the chimney."

Nobody said nothin to that, but we didn't trust it for gettin us water. We moved in slow, waitin for a dog to smell us and start to barkin.

When we had come off the hill into a ditch that run up longside a little dirt road that run in front of the house, sure nough a damn dog caught scent of us, and come runnin. But it wasn't nothin to get scared of. That dog was a sissy-puppy, a fool dog, we called them. It was still a pup, but it was jumpin and switch-tailin round, lickin at strangers so fast it look like it was chasing its tail.

"Toe fleas got that damn dog," said Blue.

"Hey, get away, dog!" Grease stomped his feet. "Toe-fleas got 'im itchin to beg." We headed for the well. "Up his ass and down his legs."

The place did look like nobody was home. We ran to the well. Fish hollered for somebody and then went round back. Me and Blue snatched that rope and let the well bucket down. Grease was throwin sticks for the fool dog to run after. "Sic 'em," he was shoutin, "sic 'em!" But the dog liked us too much. She just wiggled her tail, lickin Greasemouth's feet.

"Look here!" said Grease. "I found somethin worse'n a nigger."

"What's that?" Fish said, comin back.

"A nigger's dog."

"Shet up, boy," Blue grunted. We were pullin up the bucket. The well was old, and the rope was so rotten it shot dust tween our fingers. One of the boards under us squeaked and then that sissy-puppy come up waggin its tail under our feet too.

"Peckerwoods live here," said Blue.

"Ain't nobody home, though," said Fish.

"Les drink and git," I said.

"I want to drink but that dog got to git," said Grease, and he kept tryin to sic that pup off.

Then we heard a loud crashin sound come from inside the well. Blue stopped pullin on the bucket. He leaned over. "I got it," I said.

"What's goin on?" asked Grease. "Hurry and get me some water."

I began pullin again. I could feel the ground shakin under me. The well was fallin, crashin in and givin away. But the bucket was almost up.

"Wait!" shouted Grease. "This is it. Blue, you right!"

I kept on pullin. "Right about what?" Blue asked.

Grease waved us all quiet and he began runnin around the well, lookin at it real close and pointin. Then he ran over near the house and began to study it. He looked dead serious. He almost tripped over a fruit jar, but he kicked it as if he knew it was there and didn't have to look.

He came back to us. I had the bucket up to the top. Grease began pointin at the well. "Don't drink this here maggot water, boys. I know I'm tellin you the truth."

"What's in here, Grease?" Blue asked.

"Look round here. Can't yall smell this place stinkin like a beaneater?"

"Hurry, yall," said Fish. "That nigger's lyin." But nobody was gettin ready to take the first drink.

"Naw, naw, Fish," Grease said. "It's somethin that woulda clear skipped my mind, cept for this here fool-dog. He was a pup then . . . Yall member back last year when I was workin for Tulsom Lumber?"

We ain't say nothin. I pulled the big dirty bucket up and sat it there. Cool water was shootin out the holes. I was gettin ready to plunge my mouth in when Grease said, "Go head, Tatehead. Your head swell up bigger'n a punkin, and when it bust you member my words. Go head."

We ain't say nothin. Then Blue asked him what he knew. He started tellin a long tale about how he was passin by with a white man who knew the peckerwoods that lived there. That's what he meant by Fish bein right, right that white people lived there, not colored. Fish walked off and spit. He nevah believed nothin Grease said.

When we looked in that bucket, we saw pieces of wood in there, dirt and a couple of dead bugs floatin around. Blue smelled it and frowned. I smelled it and Fish came over. The fool-dog was jumpin all over Fish now, and he was wavin it off.

"And here's the thang I couldn't help . . ." Grease lowered his voice. "That white man woulda killed me sure as hell is below high water if he find out what I done to his well. But it won't my fault."

"What happen?" asked Blue.

"It was night, see. That damn fool-dog's mama was a mean bitchhound, then. I was waitin in the truck for this here white man to come out. But he wouldn't come. It started gettin dark. I had to go bad. So I ain't want to bother nobody cause I knowed what he was up to in that house. There was a little ole skinny peckerwood gal in there. I was headin out past the well, see, and no sooner I got jumpin

distance from the well, here come that fool-dog's mama towards me, growlin like she wanted some nigger leg. Hell, I
ain't have no place to run. I jumped up on the well cover and
must've busted it then, cause it's gone now as yall can see,
and jist bout time I got up, the bitchhound was snappin at
me, mean as a peckerwood's dog wants to be.

"I had to go bad, and that damn dog wouldn't let me
down. And that sucker inside wouldn't get off that gal and
come out, to help this nigger.

"So, brothers," he said, as if we woulda all done the
same thing, "I had to crap in that man's well."

"Get this lyin nigger!" Fish shouted, and we all grabbed
Grease. He started shakin his head, but I come right up to
him with my fist drawed back, while Fish locked that devil's
arms. Grease, he started tryin to shake us off. Blue got a hold
on his legs and we started swingin that nigger all round.

"Hold him, yall!" I said, and we all was laughin, but we
wanted to teach him a lesson.

"Go head, Tate," Fish said to me, "git your drink."

I cleared the dirt off the top of the water and got me
some. That water was good.

Then I got a new hold on Grease who was still hollerin.
"Come on now, can't yall take a tale?"

"Yeah, yours," Blue said.

After Blue and Fish got their drink, we drug Grease
long towards the road. He was yellin. That damn sissy-dog
got scared of us and started to bark, tuckin her tail under
and peepin from under that raggedy house.

Before I left, I got that jar on the ground and filled it
full of the dirtiest water on top, rot-wood and all. Then I
stuck the jar in my back pocket and caught up with them
niggers pushin ole Grease long. He kept up a natural plea

with us, but we ain't listen to him. We act like we ain't even know him anymore.

"What we gonna do with this nigger, Tate?" Fish asked me.

"Make him eat a half sack of salt."

"What you say, Blue?"

"I tell you guys. That was the stinkiest water I evah tasted. I think we oughta let this nigger go back and drink a whole bucket full. If he let one drop fall, we tie his ass to the well and let that peckerwood find 'im there."

"That's too good," said Fish. "Les tie his mouth up. This nigger talks too much. Then les pour creek water over his head."

"Naw," I said. "Les lift him up by his big foot to the first low tree we come to and let that sissy-dog lick 'im till he slimes up from dog spit, and his mouth and eyelids stick shut."

All the time Grease was whinin. But we pulled and pushed him along. We got over a mile down the road. We was all sweatin with that squiggy nigger by now, and gettin tired of the game. We figured we was too far now for him to turn around and go back. So we turned him loose and soon as we did, that nigger broke out laughin at us again. He said that while we was tusslin with him he had picked our pockets, and had all that good money. He waved some bills in his hand. Damn, if that didn't get to us.

"Grease, you the lyinest nigger I evah met up with," said Fish, after drawin out his money and lookin at it. We did too, and was about to grab him again when we heard the sound of a truck comin up that dirt road.

We all got serious and pulled together. Round the corner came this beat-up truck with a skinny ole red-necked hillbilly bent over the wheel and a wide-eyed freckled faced gal sittin side him. The truck was goin so goddamn slow that I coulda read a whole chapter of God's Holy Bible by the time it passed us. But it didn't pass.

That peckerwood stopped it and called us over.

Fish stood where he was, but me, Blue and Grease come off the side of the ditch.

"You boys lookin for somethin?"

"Naw, sir," said Grease real fast. "We goin home."

"What you lookin fer around here?"

"We done two days work other side of Rock Hill," said Grease. "We work for a white man named Mr. Nesbit. He paid us and said, 'That's it, boys,' so we goin back to Bainesville . . ."

"You niggers lyin?"

"Naw, sir," said Blue. He looked back at Fish who was gettin mad, if he wasn't already. We coulda all beat that old man's ass, but if we did we'd have to leave the state. Even a poor white man like him could mess over niggers and niggers couldn't do a damn thing about it. Right then I wished Grease's tale hada been true.

"They puttin a cutoff out on the Memphis Highway," I said. "They know bout it in Rock Hill."

"How come you niggers ain't go round through Rock Hill like you ought to? I got a good mind to make yall go back the way you come. We don't allow no niggers over here."

We all just stood there. That young gal was steady twitchin and twitchin. We ain't look at her, but I could see her out of the corner of my eye, twitchin round in that seat like she sittin on a pile of rocks.

All of a sudden that old man hauled off and slapped her.

"Now keep still," he said.

Then he got up a shotgun.

"You niggers come long this road a far piece?"

Fish stood straight now and came towards us. I thought he was gonna say somethin, but Grease beat him to it.

"Naw, sir, we just come off that hill." He pointed. "We tryin to get to the creek, but I tole 'em we passed the creek and best keep on, since . . ."

"How come yall comin this away?"

"We thought we knowed the way cross these hills, but I reckon we got lost."

"How long yall come along this road?"

"We just got on it bout the time we hear a truck comin round the bend, and then it was you," said Grease.

"If I find you niggers lyin, and been in my house, I'm gonna come back here and make buzzard meat outa your asses."

"Naw, sir, we ain't seen no house since we left the highway."

He raced the engine coupla times, then he turned and looked at me. "Nigger, what's that you got in your back pocket? Let me see."

I jerked my hand back there. I done forgot. Fish come over, but Grease beat him to the words. "That's mine," said Grease. I took out the jar of water.

"That's niggerwater for my feet," said Grease. "I got bad feet, and suffer with short wind."

"What you talkin about?" The old man looked like he mighta laughed then, but he didn't. He cocked his head.

"I fell out. Tate, he carryin the water for me." Grease rolled his eyes.

"I ain't never heard of a nigger fallin out," the old man said.

"Naw, sir, it ain't like you think. I was totin a rock weigh three times my size. I come near bustin myself."

The old man looked at each of us. We was all dressed dirty and sweat was pourin off us. He looked at the jar of water, then at Greasemouth, who was showin off how sick he was.

". . . wide open." Grease kinda motioned with his whole self to where he mighta busted hisself, but because that gal was sittin there, Greasemouth didn't point or say no more.

"All right, boy," said the old man. "Thas nough now." He turned to each of us.

"This nigger tellin the truth?"

We all said a loud "Yes Sir." Even Fish said it.

"All right. Yall niggers done missed the creek. You way off, and you better get hell outa my hills. Don't stop till yall hit thet highway. Now git!"

We moved off quickly. That old man still held that shot-gun up in the air. He had braked the truck on the hill, but we never heard it no more, cause when we got round that bend we broke into the woods off the road, runnin fan-wise, cussin, movin down that road like we were four boats in a downriver. We didn't stop till Fish slowed and leaned up ginst a tree, puffin. . . .

"What the hell we runnin for?"

"Gimme my water," puffed Grease.

"What you talkin bout, your water?"

"All right, I'm goin back and tell that peckerwood yall busted into his house, stole his water and pissed and shit in his well."

"Yeah? And that white man shoot the first nigger he see, you first," I said.

Greasemouth must've been really thirsty then, because he was chokin. He was gaspin for breath.

I took out that jar of water and almost put my own mouth to it, but Grease was on it like a rat on cheese.

We all watched. We wanted some of that water so damn bad.

Then old Grease do somethin we ain't expect him to do. He saved back nough for each of us to have one swallow, and then he twisted up his mouth. "I ought not to give you lyin niggers nothin."

"Go head, boy, and drink your water," said Fish, but he didn't mean it. Me and Blue took one swallow each.

Grease took that jar and gave it to Fish. "I knowed a Christian was livin in that devil heart of yours," he said, and he finished it.

We went on, pullin together, and not laughin anymore.

"You just watch," said Blue. "You just watch that nigger Greasy when he gits back. He gonna tell everybody how he did this here and did dat dere. You watch. He be done run a white man down, took his gun off him, whopped the white man's ass and then climbed upon the white man's well and shit in it just for devilment."

We were puffin a bit still, and everytime Blue took a step he puffed and dragged his words.

That fool old man wasn't comin after us. We knew that. We slowed down and Blue kept on teasin Greasy.

Fish was movin longside me now.

We laughed and kidded about what Blue was sayin.

Grease wasn't payin no mind to none of us. He kept movin long, puffin as much as any of us. Then he hauled off and stopped, scratched his head like a mosquito had stuck him one.

"Listen up, you niggers," Grease said. "I know the truth now. Goddammit, I know it."

We ain't paid too much attention to him, but we did slow down.

"I got it all right here." He touched his heart. "You see how that peckerwood jump at me when I tell him the truth. That was God Almighty truth what I told him. But that sucker, he ain't hear me, uh?" He grunted like Rev. Weams do when he windin himself up.

"The truth is the thing. May a dead dog draw red maggots as sure as you niggers hear me. I swear fore livin God, may cowshit stand up and walk, I swear. You niggers listenin? I swear, I ain't foolin round no more. No more lies for me. The truth for me!"

"Aw, you a damn lie," said Fish. "You a lie and don't know why. Shet up and come on."

"Yeaah," said Blue. "Double Niggaahh!!"

A Harlem Game

M<small>ACK</small> and Jayjay stopped at the stoop and while Jayjay bounced the basketball around for practice, Mack slumped down on the concrete steps and fingered an iron spike jutting from the metal rail on the stoop. Up the street the block lights came on and the glow blended with the drugstore's orange-red neons. Mack looked up at the broken lamp in front of his stoop.

"Let's go to the show, Jay."

"I ain't got no money."

"Don't punk out. I can get some."

"You can't," said Jayjay, "You can't get nothin from them if they're playin cards."

"Don't punk out. If my old lady's got even a dollar, half of it's mine."

"Look, she just gave you fifty cents this mornin', didn't she?"

"So what? Come on, go with me upstairs again."

"No."

He watched Jayjay dribble the ball. Then he got up and his shadow formed on the sidewalk beside Jayjay.

"Look, she just gave you fifty cents this mornin, didn't you enough to get in."

"I don't know," said Jayjay. "It's gettin late and I got to take Frisky's ball back." He faced up the street as the ball slapped the sidewalk *pow pow pow pow* across Mack's shadow.

"Then wait two minutes. If I'm not back . . ." He turned and ran up the stairway. At the top a familiar odor came at

him from the darkened hall. Beer cans sprawled near his door
and a blood stain streaked the top step where somebody had
been cut in a fight.

He hesitated for a minute against the knife-carved wood
of his door, his sweaty hand gripping the handle. He leaned.
The door opened. He moved in. He was panting.

Down the hallway in the kitchen he saw the back of the
hunched figure in the usual position at the card table in the
center of the kitchen floor.

He eased into the room. His sneakers made no noise but
the loose floor boards gave his presence away.

The big man shifted his shoulders and poised himself as
if he were listening for footsteps. But he didn't look at Mack.
He continued to watch the woman, Lola, deal. Mack stood
there panting. No one spoke.

Lola sat opposite Jim Davis. Mack glanced at her. She
was pretty and Jim Davis was saying she was a queen of
hearts.

Mack looked at his mother as she picked up her cards.
She held them in her left hand and brought a can of beer to
her mouth with her right. She glanced at him over the rim of
the can. He hoped she would say something.

He looked at the pile of change in front of her. She was
winning a lot. No one else had much except maybe Jim Davis
and Lola. He sensed the vacant table in front of his father. He
could feel the big man breathing like a bull. Jim Davis grunted
and scratched his stubbled chin. Mack moved toward his
mother.

The big man shifted himself in the seat.

"Punk," he said to Mack, "where you been all day?
What you want now?"

Mack stood still. He saw a lone dime in front of his

father. He opened his mouth to speak but only grunted something.

"How much bread you got?" the big man asked.

"I'm broke," Mack said. He looked at his mother. She was opening a can of beer. "I'm broke and I was sorta needin . . ."

"I didn't ask you what you needed," the big man said softly, staring at the center of the table.

Jim Davis wiggled his chair and hastily glanced at Mack. "Say kid, it would be good if you would lend your old man here some coins. He's been losin kinda heavy. We all been losin to your old lady here." He chuckled at Mack, but Mack didn't know whether to smile back or to say, yes, it would be good, or just to come right out and ask his mother for show fare.

He looked at her steadily but it was a long time before she looked at him.

"What you standin there for, Mackie?" she asked. Then she turned to her cards again.

"I . . ." He approached the table. "Jay and me want to make that last show. He's waitin for me downstairs."

The big man cleared his throat and raised a can to his mouth. There was a sound of gulping and the can was empty.

"Stop rubbin them things," Lola said to Jim Davis, who was scratching his chin.

Mack watched his mother. She smirked a couple of times as if deciding what to do. Then she plucked two quarters from her pile and jammed them into Mack's palm.

He felt like running. He turned toward the hall door.

"Punk, you forgettin somethin, ain't you?"

Mack paused.

"Don't you like potato chips?"

Mack wanted to say yes, but he didn't. He trembled and watched the fat arm flex on the table edge. The twist of muscles looked like twin ridges of metal stripping bent back to a rebound point.

Lola was frowning at Jim Davis. "Can't you stop that damn noise? It makes my flesh crawl."

Jim Davis said something about how rubbing his chin brought out the man in him and made him think fast. He wiggled his chair, snickering at the same time.

Mack glanced quickly at all of them and stepped off again.

"I said somethin to you, punk."

Mack clenched his teeth. "Yeah, maybe I could use . . ."

"What about that wise kid, Jayjerk? He eats chips, don't he?"

"Guess so."

"Okay then," he said, looking at the cards dealt out by Mack's mother, "give 'im four more bits."

Mack looked at his mother. She hesitated and smacked her lips, making sounds of disgust with her tongue.

"How much is it to get in?" she asked.

Mack didn't know what to say. He just stood there. He tried to mumble something, but he caught a sudden movement of the arm on the table.

The big man stood up. His body pushed the tiny table and a can of beer fell. He laid his cards down and leaned slowly over the table. His body was like a steel beam bent by some force. It was ready to snap back when the force was released.

"What did I say give 'im?" He looked at the pile of coins in front of Mack's mother.

"This here's enough," Mack said, looking from face to face and holding two quarters out in his hand.

No one spoke. The sound of Lola blowing smoke over the table surface mixed with the sound of the big man breathing. That was all. Then Mack took two steps toward the hall. Lola smashed the butt.

"I thought I said somethin." The big arm flexed.

And Mack's mother, weakly shaking her head at her pile, pushed two more quarters to the edge of the table.

"Okay," she snapped, "but I want my money back."

It all happened so fast that Mack was still standing poised to retreat down the hall.

"Now, punk," the big man said, grinning, "you got nough coins, right?"

Mack said yes, and looked at the extra quarters.

"So looky here," his old man continued, "sposin I told you somethin." He grabbed Mack's wrist and jerked him to the edge of the table. He sat down and smiled at Mack.

Mack's mother said something about leaving the boy alone, but she was draining a can of beer and her words were swallowed.

"Like I was sayin," and he squeezed the wrist. Mack began to feel the sweat gathering up in him. "Like I was sayin, if you was playin a gamblin game here, see, like all is, and your old lady over there just kept on winnin, see, and then I comes along with a pocket full of coins, what do you think I'd do?"

Mack's mother got up and went to the refrigerator where she began gathering and opening beer cans.

"Okay, son, what do you think would happen to me if I had bread like that and didn't want to lend you a few pieces?"

Mack frowned and took a deep breath.

"Well . . . I don't know, I don't know . . ." He felt tight inside and began to try to wrench his arm free.

"What the hell you mean?"

Jim Davis studied the cards after shuffling them; as he dealt he looked at the beer being opened.

Mack stopped struggling and clenched his teeth. He looked into his old man's eyes. But words wouldn't come.

"Son, son, son, son, don't you know that if I was to do that you'd haul off and knock the blue hell outa me, wouldn't you?"

Mack lowered his eyes. The big man gently tugged his arm for an answer. He glanced around at the others. They were busy and did not see him, and before he knew what he was doing he was putting three of the four quarters in front of the big man.

"Thank you, son. You're a smart punk. Now let me see." He pretended he was counting his money. "How about lendin me two bits?"

Mack frowned. He felt the lone quarter in his palm and wondered if he should try to break away and run. He looked at Lola lighting a cigarette. Jim Davis was rubbing his chin and Mack's mother was mumbling something about anybody wanting cheese with the beer. Her face was searching the refrigerator.

"But I . . ." He felt a squeeze and his wrist throbbed. He wanted to punch out at the big man or use a knife.

But he was alone. Looking at the arm digging into his wrist like a steel clamp, he tossed the last coin on the table. Lola's cigarette was jarred from the ashtray to the floor. "Maybe I'll lend you some show fare." He grabbed Mack's arm again and flicked a quarter into it.

Mack stared at the floor. "I ain't goin," he said.

"What the hell you mean?"

Mack stepped away from the table. "I ain't goin."

"Look here, punk, I don't want to hear none of that

jive talk." He stood up again, hunching over Mack. "What did you want with that two bits in your hand?"

Mack took in a breath and gritted his teeth.

"Okay then, punk, let's get this all straight right now. Who did you just borrow a dollar from?"

Mack turned his head in the direction of his mother.

"You damn right. Now, who did you borrow that last quarter from?"

Mack looked at Jim Davis. Jim was dealing cards with a cigarette hanging so that the smoke made his left eye squint. Lola and Mack's mother were now talking about something.

"Who?"

"Maybe you," he gasped.

"What the hell you mean?"

"You, I guess."

"How much you owe all together? You heard your old lady say she wanted hers back, right?"

"But I ain't got . . ."

"Huh? Huh? Huh? Huh?" The big man leaned closer to Mack.

"Buck and a quarter." He stepped toward the hall.

"Now what you goin to do with what I lent you?"

"I was goin to the show."

"Then get the hell out of here. We're playin a game of cards, can't you see?" He sat back down and hunched his shoulders. He gripped the sweaty coins in his hands, then slowly stacked them in a neat pile in front of him.

Mack went out the door and down the steps. Along the street the block lights made shadows of people. He did not see Jayjay.

He slumped to the stoop, wiping his face. Punk, punk, punk, punk. When he got bigger. . . .

He stood up and touched the iron spike. He wanted to scream out and curse, but he didn't. He jerked the coin from his pocket and stared blankly at it. Then he slammed it down at the spike, which momentarily dug at the metal, then skidded off and gouged deep into his palm.

Blood spurted from the hole and he ran off up the street beside his shadow. And the neon night swallowed him up.

Will the Circle
Be Unbroken?

A̲t̲ t̲h̲e̲ edge of the spiral of musicians Probe sat cross-legged on a blue cloth, his soprano sax resting against his inner knee, his afro-horn linking his ankles like a bridge. The afro-horn was the newest axe to cut the deadwood of the world. But Probe, since his return from exile, had chosen only special times to reveal the new sound. There were more rumors about it than there were ears and souls that had heard the horn speak. Probe's dark full head tilted toward the vibrations of the music as if the ring of sound from the six wailing pieces was tightening, creating a spiraling circle.

The black audience, unaware at first of its collectiveness, had begun to move in a soundless rhythm as if it were the tiny twitchings of an embryo. The waiters in the club fell against the wall, shadows, dark pillars holding up the building and letting the free air purify the mind of the club.

The drums took an oblique. Magwa's hands, like the forked tongue of a dark snake, probed the skins, probed the whole belly of the coming circle. Beginning to close the circle, Haig's alto arc, rapid piano incisions, Billy's thin green flute arcs and tangents, Stace's examinations of his own trumpet discoveries, all fell separately, yet together, into a blanket which Mojohn had begun weaving on bass when the set began. The audience breathed, and Probe moved into the inner ranges of the sax.

Outside the Sound Barrier Club three white people were opening the door. Jan, a tenor sax case in his hand, had his game all planned. He had blown with Probe six years ago on the West Coast. He did not believe that there was anything to this new philosophy the musicians were talking about. He would talk to Probe personally. He had known many Negro musicians and theirs was no different from any other artist's struggles to be himself, including his own.

Things were happening so fast that there was no one who knew all directions at once. He did not mind Ron and Tasha coming along. They were two of the hippest ofays in town, and if anybody could break the circle of the Sound Club, it would be friends and old friends of friends.

Ron was bearded and scholarly. Thickset, shabbily dressed, but clean. He had tried to visit the Club before. But all of his attempts had been futile. He almost carried the result of one attempt to court. He could not understand why the cats would want to bury themselves in Harlem and close the doors to the outside world. Ron's articles and reviews had helped many black musicians, but of all of them, Probe Adams had benefited the most. Since his graduation from Yale, Ron had knocked around the music world; once he thought he wanted to sing blues. He had tried, but that was in college. The best compliment he ever got was from Mississippi John or Muddy Waters, one of the two, during a civil rights rally in Alabama. He had spontaneously leaped up during the rally and played from his soul. Muddy was in the audience, and later told Ron: "Boy, you keep that up, you gwine put me back on the plantation."

Ron was not fully satisfied that he had found the depth of the black man's psyche. In his book he had said this. Yet he knew that if he believed strongly enough, some of the old cats would break down. His sincerity was written all over his face. Holding Tasha's hand, he saw the door opening. . . .

Tasha was a shapely blonde who had dyed her hair black. It now matched her eyes. She was a Vassar girl and had once begun a biography of Oliver Fullerton. Excerpts had been

published in *Down Beat* and she became noted as a critic and
authority on the Fullerton movement. Fullerton's development as an important jazz trombonist had been interrupted
soon after Tasha's article. No one knew why. Sometimes
Tasha was afraid to think about it. If they had married, she
knew that Oliver would have been able to continue making it.
But he had gotten strung out on H. Sometimes she believed
her friends who said Oliver was psychopathic. At least when
he stopped beating her, she forgave him. And she did not
believe it when he was really hooked. She still loved him. It
was her own love, protected deep inside her, encased, her
little black secret and her passport to the inner world that
Oliver had died trying to enter. It would be only a matter of
time. She would translate love into an honest appraisal of
black music.

"I am sorry," the tall brown doorman said. "Sessions for
Brothers and Sisters only."

"What's the matter, baby?" Jan leaned his head in and
looked around as if wondering what the man was talking
about.

"I said . . ."

"Man, if you can't recognize a Brother, you better let me
have your job." He held up his case. "We're friends of
Probe."

The man called for assistance. Quickly two men stepped
out of the shadows. "What's the trouble, Brother?"

"These people say they're friends of the Probe."

"What people?" asked one of the men. He was neatly
dressed, a clean shaven head, with large darting eyes. He
looked past the three newcomers. There was a silence.

Finally, as if it were some supreme effort, he looked at
the three. "I'm sorry, but for your own safety we cannot
allow you."

"Man, what you talkin bout?" asked Jan, smiling quiz-zically. "Are you blockin Brothers now? I told him I am blood. We friends of the Probe."

The three men at the door went into a huddle. Carl, the doorman, was skeptical, but he had seen some bloods that were pretty light. He looked at this cat again, and as Kent and Rafael were debating whether or not to go get Probe's wife in the audience, he decided against the whole thing. He left the huddle and returned with a sign which said: "We cannot allow non-Brothers because of the danger involved with extensions."

Jan looked at the sign, and a smile crept across his face. In the street a cop was passing and leaned in. Carl motioned the cop in. He wanted a witness to this. He knew what might happen but he had never seen it.

Jan shook his head at the sign, turning to Ron and Tasha. He was about to explain that he had seen the same sign on the West Coast. It was incredible that all the spades believed this thing about the lethal vibrations from the new sound.

Carl was shoving the sign in their faces as the cop, a big, pimpled Irishman, moved through the group. "All right, break it up, break it up. You got people outside want to come in . . ."

Kent and Rafael, seeing Carl's decision and the potential belligerence of the whites, folded their hands, buddha-like. Carl stood with his back to the door now.

"Listen, officer, if these people go in, the responsibility is yours."

The Irish cop, not knowing whether he should get angry over what he figured was reverse discrimination, smirked and made a path for the three. He would not go far inside because he didn't think the sounds were worth listening to. If it wasn't Harlem he could see why these people would want to go in, but he had never seen anything worthwhile from niggers in Harlem.

"Don't worry. You got a license, don't you?"

"Let them go through," said Rafael suddenly. A peace seemed to gather over the faces of the three club members now. They folded their arms and went into the dark cavern which led to the music. In front of them walked the invaders. "See," said Jan, "if you press these cats, they'll cop out." They moved toward the music in an alien silence.

Probe was deep into a rear-action sax monologue. The whole circle now, like a bracelet of many colored lights, gyrated under Probe's wisdom. Probe was a thoughtful, full-headed black man with narrow eyes and a large nose. His lips swelled over the reed and each note fell into the circle like an acrobat on a tight rope stretched radially across the center of the universe.

He heard the whistle of the wind. Three ghosts, like chaff blown from a wasteland, clung to the wall. . . . He tightened the circle. Movement began from within it, shaking without breaking balance. He had to prepare the womb for the afro-horn. Its vibrations were beyond his mental frequencies unless he got deeper into motives. He sent out his call for motives. . . .

The blanket of the bass rippled and the fierce wind in all their minds blew the blanket back, and there sat the city of Samson. The white pillars imposing . . . but how easy it is to tear the building down with motives. Here they come. Probe, healed of his blindness, born anew of spirit, sealed his reed with pure air. *He moved to the edge of the circle, rested his sax, and lifted his axe.* . . .

There are only three afro-horns in the world. They were forged from a rare metal found only in Africa and South America. No one knows who forged the horns, but the general opinion among musicologists is that it was the Egyptians. One European museum guards an afro-horn. The other is supposed to be somewhere on the West Coast of Mexico, among a tribe of Indians. Probe grew into his from a black peddler who claimed to have traveled a thousand miles just to give it to his son. From that day on, Probe's sax handled like a child, a child waiting for itself to grow out of itself.

Inside the center of the gyrations is an atom stripped of time, black. The gathering of the hunters, deeper. Coming, laced in the energy of the sun. He is blowing. Magwa's hands. Reverence of skin. Under the single voices is the child of a woman, black. They are building back the wall, crumbling under the disturbance.

In the rear of the room, Jan did not hear the volt, nor did he see the mystery behind Probe's first statement on the afro-horn. He had closed his eyes, trying to capture or elude the panthers of the music, but he had no eyes. He did not feel Ron slump against him. Strands of Tasha's hair were matted on a button of Ron's jacket, but she did not move when he slumped. Something was hitting them like waves, like shock waves. . . .

Before his mind went black, Jan recalled the feeling when his father had beat him for playing "with a nigger!" and later he allowed the feeling to merge with his dislike of white people. When he fell, his case hit the floor and opened, revealing a shiny tenor saxophone that gleamed and vibrated in the freedom of freedom.

Ron's sleep had been quick, like the rush of post-hypnotic suggestions. He dropped her hand, slumped, felt the wall give (no, it was the air), and he fell face forward across a table, his heart silent in respect for truer vibrations.

The musicians stood. The horn and Probe drew up the shadows now from the audience. A child climbed upon the chords of sound, growing out of the circle of the womb, searching with fingers and then with motive, and as the volume of the music increased—penetrating the thick callousness of the Irishman twirling his stick outside of black flesh—the musicians walked off, one by one, linked to Probe's respectful nod at each and his quiet pronouncement of their names. He mopped his face with a blue cloth.

"What's the matter here?"

"Step aside, folks!"

"These people are unconscious!"

"Look at their faces!"

"They're dead."

"Dead?"

"What happened?"

"Dead?"

"It's true then. It's true . . ."

Strike and Fade

THE WORD was out. Cool it. We on the street, see. Me and Big Skin. We watch the cops. They watch us. People goin and comin. That fire truck still wrecked up side the buildin. Papers say we riot, but we didn't riot. We like the VC, the Viet Cong. We strike and fade. Me and Big Skin, we scoutin the street the next day to see how much we put down on them. Big Skin, he walkin ahead of me. He walkin light, easy, pawin. It daylight but you still got to walk easy on the street. Anytime the Mo-whites might hit the block on rubber, then what we do? We be up tight for space, so we all eyes, all feet an easy. You got to do it.

We make it to Bone's place. Bone, he the only blood on the block got a business. Mowhite own the cleaners, the super-market, the laundry, the tavern, the drugstore, and all the rest. Yeah. But after we burn out half them places, Mowhite he close down his stores for a week.

Our block occupied with cops and National Guard, but the Guard left yesterday. Man, they more cops on the street now than rats. We figure the best thing to do is to kill the cops first so we can get back to killin rats. They watch us. But they got nothin on Big Skin and me. Naw. We clean. They got Sammy, Momo, Walter and his sister too, Doris, Edie, and they even got Mr. Tomkins. He a school teacher. I had him once. He was a nice stud. Me and Big Skin make it to Bone's place. There a lot of guys inside.

We hang around. Listen to talk. I buy a coke. Big Skin take half. I hold my coke. Police cars pass outside. They like wolves, cruisin. We inside. Nobody mess with us. A cat name Duke, he talkin.

"You cats got to get more together with this thang. Look at the cats in Brooklyn, Chicago. Birmingham and Cleveland. Look at the cats in Oakland!"

A cat name Mace, he talkin. Mace just got out the Army. "Don't worry, man. It's comin." He point out the window. "This is raw oppression, baby. Look at them mf's. Raw oppression." Mace, he like to use them two words so he sayin them over and over again. He say them words all the time. It ain't funny cause they true. We all look out the window at the cops.

Bone, he behind the counter makin hamburgers. When he get too many orders he can't handle, then one of the cats come behind the counter and give him a hand. Me and Big Skin light up cigarettes. Big Skin pass them around. I take the last one. I squeeze the pack up so tight, my fingernails cut my hand. I like to make it tight. I throw that pack at the trash can. It bounce in and bounce back. But Duke, he catch it. He throw it in. Not too hard. It stay. He talkin.

"I mean, if every black man in this goddamn country would dedicate one half of a day next week to a boycott. Just don't go to work! Not a black pushin a thing for Charley. Hell, man, we tie it up. We still the backbone, man. We still got this white mf on our backs. What the hell we totin him around for?"

Mace, he talkin.

"Wait. No sooner we make another move, whitey be down on us like rats on warm cheese. It be raw oppression double over. Gestapo. Man, they forget about Hitler after the man come down on us."

Big Skin he talkin.

"They say that the cats in Harlem is gettin together so tight that the Muslims and Martin Luther King got their heads together."

Nobody say nothin. Couple cats laugh. We heard it before. Word been spreadin for all black men to get ready for war.

Nobody believe it. But everybody want to. But it the same in Harlem as anywhere else.

Duke he talkin.

"An organized revolution is what the man can't stand. They say it's comin? Man, when it do I be the first to join. If I got to go I take some Chalk Whitey with me and mark him all over hell."

We listen a while. The cats all talkin. We just want to get what's happenin.

We split the scene. Duke, he split too.

We move down the block. It gettin evenin. We meet some cats comin.

We stop and talk. We meet them later on 33rd Street. They pawin like us.

Duke talkin.

"You cats see Tyro yet?"

We say naw. We heard he back in town, but we ain't seen him yet. Tyro was a Green Beret in Viet Nam. But he back. He got no legs and one arm. All the cats been makin it to his pad. They say he got a message for all the cats on the block.

Duke say he makin it to Tyro's now. We walk on. I kick some glass. We see a store that is burnt out. A cop is watchin us. We stalkin easy, all eyes, all feet. A patrol car stop along side us. The gestapos leap out. I see a shotgun. We all freeze.

The Man is talkin.

"You niggers got one hour to get off the street." Then he change his mind. "Against the wall!" There is three of them. Down the street is more. They frisk us. We all clean. One jab the butt of a gun hard on my leg. It give me a cramp in the ball.

They cuss us and tell us to get off the street. We move on. Around the block. Down the street.

I'm limpin. I don't say nothin. I don't curse or nothin. Duke and Big Skin, they mad, cursin and sayin what they gonna do. Me, I'm hurtin too much. I'm lettin my heat go down into my soul. When it come up again, I won't be limpin.

We see some more cats pawin along the block. About fifty. We join. They headin to 33rd. Some cats got heats, some got molotovs. One cat got a sword.

Tyro on 30th Street. We go up. Three other cats come with us. We run up the steps. We pass an old man goin up. He grunt out our way. We say excuse. I'm the last up. The old man scared. We hear a siren outside. The shit done started already.

Tyro's sister open the door. I know her before I dropped out of school. She know me, but she iggin. All the cats move in. I close the door. "We come to see Tyro," I say. She chewin some food, and she wave with her hand. It mean, go on up front. I watch her walk. "You Tina?" She swallow her food. "Yeah. You come to see Tyro, he in there." She turned and went into a door and closed it. I followed the other cats up front. My ball still hurt.

There were six cats already in the room. Six more come in. Somebody pass around a butt. I scoot in a corner. So I am meetin Tyro. He known on the block for years. He used to be the leader of the old Black Unicorns. They broke up by the cops and social workers.

I look at Tyro. He a black stud with a long beard. He sittin in a wheel chair. He wearin fatigues like Fidel Castro. When we paw into the pad, Tyro he talkin.

". . . the Cong are masters at ambush. Learn this about them. When we fell back under fire, we fell into a pincher. They cross-fired us so fast that we didn't know what hit us. Out of sixty men, I was left. I believe they spared me so that I could come back and tell you. The cat that found me was hit himself, but he didn't seem to care. He looked me in my eye . . . for a long time. My legs were busted up from a grenade. This VC stood over my blood. I could tell he was thinkin about somethin. He raised the rifle. I kept lookin him in the eye. It was one of the few times my prayers been answered. The cat suddenly turned and ran off. He had shot several of my buddies already, but he let me go.

"All I can figure is that one day the chips are all comin down. America is gonna have to face the yellow race. Black and yellow might have to put their hands together and bring this thang off. You cats out in the street, learn to fade fast. Learn to strike hard, but don't be around in the explosion. If you don't organize you ain't nothin but a rioter, a looter. These jigs won't hesitate to shoot you.

"Naw. I ain't tellin you to get off the streets. I know like you know. Uncle means you no ultimate good, brothers. Take it for what it is worth. I'm layin it down like it is. I got it from the eagle's beak. That's the way he speak. Play thangs careful. Strike and fade, then strike again, quick. Get whitey outa our neighborhood. Keep women and children off the streets. Don't riot. Rebel. You cats got this message. Do what you got to do. Stick together and listen for the word to come down. Obey it."

When Tyro finish talkin, some cats get up and shake his hand. Others leave. Out in the street sirens are going. The doorbell rings. Everybody freeze. It some more cats. We all leave.

Down on the street, it like a battlefield. A fire in a store down the block. Cops see us. We fade. I hear shots. Then I know somethin.

The word is out. Burn, baby, burn. We on the scene. The brothers. Together. Cops and people goin and comin. Some people got good loot, some just hoofin it. A police cordon comin. We shadows on the wall. Lights comin towards us. We fade. Somebody struck them. The lights go out. I hear shots. I fall. Glass get my hands. The street on fire now. We yell. 33rd Street here we come! Got to get together!

We move out. Strikin. All feet. All soul. We the VC. You got to be. You got to be.

Fon

From the sky. A fragment of black rock about the size of a fist, sailing, sailing. . . . CRAACK! The rear windshield breaks.

Nillmon snaps his head to the rearview mirror, wheeling the car off the road.

"Goddammit!" He leaps from the car, leaving the door open. He examines the break, whirls around and scans the evening countryside with quinting eyes.

The distant mooing of cattle blends wtih the sharp yap of a dog.

And then he catches a movement.

Through the trees behind him—past a large billboard with the picture of Uncle Sam saying *I Want You,* over and down a rocky incline, toward a final rise at the top of the levee—Nillmon thinks he sees several pairs of legs scurrying away.

"Niggers!" He steps back to the car, leans across the seat, jerks open the glove compartment, snatches up a pistol lying between a half-bottle of whiskey and a stick of dynamite, and crosses the torn asphalt in four quick strides. Pieces of pavement scatter beneath his feet. The road is in disuse except for an occasional car and a few cattle crossings.

He runs toward a path by the billboard. As he loses sight of the point in the distance where he thinks the figures disappeared, he runs faster. He reaches the beams supporting the billboard. The area behind the sign is a large network of angled shafts and platforms. He follows the path, stooping his shoulders and grunting. He lurches through an opening, twisting his way from the entanglement of wooden beams. He curses. Then he slows his pace, realizing that he's chasing children.

He slips the pistol in his belt. He clears his throat and spits at the long edge of the billboard's fading shadow. Then he resumes his march up the hill.

He looks over the countryside. No niggers running. Across a thin stretch of young cotton three shacks lean back on their shadows, and the shadows, bending at every bank and growth of the land, poke at the muddy inlet of a Mississippi tributary. The only movements are the lazy wag of tattered clothes on the back porch of one shack, the minute shifts of what looks like chickens scratching in a bare yard, the illusory tilt of a cross barely gleaming on top of a tiny wooden church far away, and the fragmentary lines of black smoke climbing lazily but steadily higher and higher. Nillmon peers. He thinks he sees a figure rocking slowly back and forth on the porch of the third shack. Probably an old granny. A cowbell jangles in the distance, and from the shacks Nillmon thinks he hears an angry voice rise and fall amidst a scurry of noises, and then trail off in a series of loud whacks and screams. He tries to locate that shack. He is about to descend.

He smothers a strange impulse to laugh and spits down the incline, jerking his eyes toward the road, over the levee cotton and through the trees.

Then he snaps his neck back toward the road for a second look.

It is not the slow motion of the car door swinging to the uneven idle of the motor that catches his eye. Nor the slight movement of leaves and branches.

Somebody is watching him.

A silhouette sits at the back of the billboard. The slow

dangle of a bare leg is the only motion. The mesh of beams looks like a web. The billboard is empty except for the lone figure.

"Goddammit!" He snatches out the pistol. "Git down!"

The shadows in the trees waver and merge like a field of tall reeds marching gently under the steady touch of the wind. Nillmon wipes his mouth with his sleeve.

"Nigger, can't you hear?"

The figure, almost liquid in his giant movements, begins a slow descent, swinging across a shaft of sunlight like an acrobat. He drops to the ground and stands. A muscular black youth. Bands of fading light make imperfect angles and spears across his red shirt and black arms.

"Who else is up there?"

"My brother."

Nillmon attempts to approach the figure. The youth is standing with the weight of his body on one leg. Nillmon stops in front of him and searches for signs of resistance. The youth holds his head level, but his eyes glare outward, always away from the eyes of the white man, as if they were protecting some secret. Nillmon searches the billboard and trees. The nigger is a half-wit.

"All right, move!"

The tall youth slides into motion on the path made by children. But he carefully steps around the beams, over a few rocks, and proceeds toward the road.

"Black boy, I'm goin to see you put every piece of that glass back in place."

Nillmon watches the rear of the figure moving down the path, and he feels a rush of blood to his head when he thinks of the bullet going right through the dark head.

"I didn't break it," the youth says without turning around or slowing his pace.

"Nigger, you in trouble," says Nillmon. They reach the car. The youth is looking straight ahead. "Aside from gettin your ass beat, and payin for that glass, you goin to jail. Git in."

The youth turns slowly—as if in some fearful trance—and is about to look squarely at the other man, but instead he rivets his eyes on the white man's neck.

"Boy, what's your name?" Nillmon asks.

Cowbells sound up the road. The youth shifts his weight, wets his lips, and looks off. Far, far down the road, cows gather at a fence and a voice yells, a dog barks, and then the cattle neck into the crossing, and some are mooing.

"Fon."

"Goddammit, Fon what?"

The sun has almost fallen. The shadow of the car bounces nervously. Then it stops.

"Alfonso."

Nillmon squeezes the pistol butt. This boy ain't no half-wit. Nillmon knows he is going to break him now. The nigger is trying to act bad. Maybe he'd break him later. Maybe Gus and Ed would want a piece of him. He looks at the youth and he can't decide whether he is bad or not. He hates to see a fool-headed nigger get it. No fun in it. He sees a thin line of smoke coming from the back seat of his car. Sniffing and leaning, he sees that his back seat, where the black stone landed, is smoldering.

"Set fire to it, too, eh?" He moves toward Fon.

He swings his foot upward, aiming for Fon's rear. Seeming to anticipate the move, Fon, without moving his legs, twists his back and avoids the blow, which strikes the air.

"Nobody *threw* that rock from there," Fon says.

Nillmon, half-stunned, finding himself kicking the air

when what he wanted to kick was so plain, wipes his mouth in a nervous sling of his arm, and while the sleeve is passing over his face he tries to see if he holds a pistol, feels himself squeezing it and emptying it. But he can't. It is all too easy. This Fon nigger ain't scared. He knows now he has a nigger that needs a thorough job. Nillmon smiles and spits on the gravel in front of Fon. "Git in."

Fon moves around the car, opens the door, and slowly gets in, closing his door carefully and firmly. Nillmon slams his and jerks the car forward. The car picks up speed. Nillmon grips the steering wheel until the blood is cut off from his hands. A thin line of smoke issues from the rear window.

"Yesss, nigger, think you can count them pieces of glass with the tip of your tongue?" Fon is silent. Nillmon relaxes his grip and looks at him from the corner of his eye. "What the hell you niggers doin up on that sign chunkin at cars anyway?"

A cattle crossing. The car, slowing, slowing . . .

"Teachin my brother how to shoot his arrows."

. . . and the car stops.

Nillmon feels himself lunging toward Fon, pushing him out of the car with his foot, and blasting his body till it swells and bleeds black blood like that Huntsville nigger they got last year. . . . He was deputy sheriff then. Hell, if he hadn't been implicated in that case he would still be on down there in Huntsville. That goddam Federal Agent even suggested that he and Gus lay low till things got under control. The nigger civil rights groups were kicking up so much dust that an honest white citizen in the state couldn't see straight half the time. But it wasn't like that up here in Columbia County. He lowers his foot on the gas and the noisy engine stirs the cattle.

Fon seems to watch the rising humps of the cattle. They

pass in quick strides. A brown-skinned boy, about twelve, hollers and whistles and a dog is barking at the heels of a straying heifer.

"You teachin your brother how to chunk at white folks? How long do you expect your brother to live, actin on what you say?"

"I'll take care of him."

Nillmon feels himself laughing, but his anger rises over it. "You bout a bad nigger, ain't you?"

The straying cow, a large black and white with a swinging udder, turns and heads toward the car.

Nillmon spits out the window. The cows are mooing, their bells are banging.

"Hurry up, boy. Git them heifers outa my way!"

The stray cow lopes nervously back to the line, followed by the dog. Nillmon scans the field for the last cow. A hot wave seizes him, and he gives in to the urge to chuckle under his breath. He looks back at the broken glass on the rear seat. He does not see the rock now, only a haze of smoke in the car.

Suddenly, Fon, his movements like those of a mechanic testing a loose door handle, opens his door, slides out, closes the door firmly and quietly, and walks across the road toward the levee which bends around a clump of trees and past the billboard.

Nillmon, dazed by the sudden movement of the car, aims the pistol at the last cow, but the car rolls over a heap of cow manure and he submits to the urge to curse all dead niggers, but he doesn't say anything then. Through the rearview mirror he sees that the sun is gone and the levee is a thin line hiding the river inlet, and on the road a dog is chasing the car, and in the field the cows are mooing and their bells are banging.

Only shadows fall in front of him now. The shadows in the trees are going over the hill with the cattle, and he sees a light far ahead in the road.

Suddenly he slows the car, leaps out and looks over the countryside. "I shoulda taught that sombitch a lesson," he mutters to himself. When he puts the pistol back in the glove compartment, he brings out the bottle and takes a long drink.

After about three miles on the flat straight road, the light becomes a filling station. Nillmon runs in. An old man with one leg is wiping his hands on greasy rags. "And just whar you been last two weeks? Drunk?"

Nillmon hardly looks at the old man, but breaks through the door leading to the rear of the store which is part of a series of rooms. The top of the house looms in the back. "Where's Gus, Pop?" he asked the old man. "A nigger just about ready to git hisself gutted."

"What nigger?" Pop asks, throwing the rags in the corner. "What's his name?"

Nillmon moves toward the house as the old man hollers, "Gus! Get out here!"

Before Nillmon can ascend a long row of rickety wooden steps up to a screened porch, a figure appears in the screenless doorway. Girlish laughter rises and falls, and the figure, struggling with arms around his waist, yells, "What the hell you want?"

"It's me, Gus." Nillmon approaches.

"Who?"

"Goddammit, it's me." He doesnt advance anymore. "A nigger just bricked my car. I'm goin to get him."

As if Nillmon had spoken something he had been waiting for, Gus, a short wiry man of about thirty years, freezes. He pushes the retreating arms away from his body, tosses his left hand in the air as a signal, and begins a slow deliberate descent. Nillmon turns and walks past the old man.

"Call Sheriff Vacy."

"Where's this nigger?" Gus asks. His words are clear and precise.

"Out at Canebrake . . . A nigger named Alfonso, a big black sucker."

The figure of a blonde girl stands now in the doorway at the top of the steps. She straightens out her clothing. Pop limps toward her. "I'm goin call Vacy," he mutters. "Gus, I'm callin Vacy, you hear?"

"Yeah," Nillmon hollers, "and tell him we're pickin up Ed Frickerson."

"Naw we ain't." Gus examines Nillmon's pistol. They both take drinks from the bottle and slam the doors.

"Where's the nigger at?" asks the old man, limping out with a bundle of oily rags. "I'm callin everybody."

"Canebrake . . . nigger name Alfonso . . ."

"Canebrake?"

"You comin?"

"There ain't no niggers livin in them shacks."

Gus looks at the bottle, clears his throat and takes a long swallow. He hands it to Nillmon who finishes it.

"There is now, and there's gonna be one less come sunup."

"Them Canebrake shacks is haunted, I'm tellin you. Niggers ain't live in them since the flood back in . . . you member, Gus?" the old man says, limping toward the car. Then he whispers, "The time the nigger woman put hoodoo on Vacy's papa . . ."

"Shut up, Pop!"

The old man mumbles.

Nillmon races the motor and jerks the cold car off in a cloud of dust. Down the road, just before they turn off, Nillmon flings his arm out the window and the bottle crashes on the road.

They pick up Ed Frickerson about ten miles later at a town cafe. They get another bottle and circle the town picking up two younger men. Then Nillmon aims the car down the road toward the levee. The faint red crown of the sun is the only thing left of day.

"Vacy's over in Huntsville," says Ed Frickerson. He is ruddy-faced, thick-necked, round-nosed, with a permanent smile wrinkling down his whiskered face.

"I'm the goddam deputy, ain't I, Gus?" says Nillmon, spitting out the window.

"I want to see the nigger that'll chunk a brick at a white man," says Gus. He has the pistol in his belt and is patting the stick of dynamite steadily in his left hand. "Gus wants to see that boy."

The car moves fast. The men pass the bottle around. Nillmon describes the last party he attended in Huntsville. They all listen, devouring with fear and a dark relish the exaggerated details that pour out of Nillmon. They all tremble inside as the car turns off onto a dirt road along the levee. All except Gus.

Nillmon drives the car within a few feet of the first shack. The lights illuminate every weather-worn line in the warping boards.

"Alfonso!" Nillmon shouts, standing near the broken step.

There is a silence over the whole night.

The car stalls and cuts off. Gus jumps out of the car, walks up on the porch, pushes once, twice, on the rickety

door which falls as if the light from the headlights had
struck it. Dust travels across the plane of light like legions of
insects. The shack is empty.

The car backs out and then spins out of its own dust. At
the second shack they find the same thing. Nillmon snatches
up the oily rags. The two younger men light them and hurl
them in and under the shack.

"Where'd this nigger chunk that rock from?" asks Gus.
He lights up a cigarette. The car races down the road.

Nillmon spits out the window. "Back up the road by
that signboard." He feels his hands tighten around the steering wheel.

"Lights down the road," says Ed Frickerson.

"Hell, I know niggers live up here cause I saw about five
or six herdin cows."

"What this nigger look like?"

"Like any nigger. Had a nasty tongue. I gotta get me
some of him."

They reach the third shack. The outline of the second
shack a quarter-mile down the road slowly rises in the flames
that leap out of its windows. "Ain't that a crowd of niggers in
front of that church over yonder?" asks Ed Frickerson.

Nillmon does not look. The headlights of the car strike
the doorway of the third shack. A figure stands illuminated
there, his hands behind his back as if he is contemplating
the situation. It is Fon.

"All right, boy!" shouts Nillmon. "I'm back to settle
that business tween us."

Gus is out of the car, advancing toward Fon in rapid
strides. He holds the pistol in his right hand and the empty
bottle in the other. Fon steps off the steps before Gus reaches
the shack, and heads toward Nillmon, who is now standing

right in front of the headlights. Lighted rags fly through the night.

The other men surround Fon. All of a sudden a series of flashes comes from the area of the church. It practically blinds Nillmon. Gus aims the pistol at Fon's head. They shove Fon into the rear between the two younger men. Gus sits in front. Ed Frickerson, who is sitting behind Nillmon, has collected pieces of glass in an oily rag and tosses the mass in Fon's lap. The bright light continues to shine and the men instinctively turn away. Nillmon slows as he approaches the structure which seems like an old church. "What you niggers think you're doin out here?" Ed Frickerson asks Fon.

"Those are my brothers," says Fon.

"What I want to know," says Nillmon, "is who threw that rock."

"It came from the sky."

Gus whirls and strikes at Fon with the bottle, which breaks on the door frame and the glass falls in Fon's lap. "You *are* a smart nigger." He jabs the bottle neck at Fon, and the sharp edges dig deeply into Fon's side.

Nillmon slows the car in front of a column of black people. They murmur and stare inside the car.

"Keep goin!" shouts Gus.

Suddenly they see Fon inside, and a cheer leaps up from them such as the white men have never heard. A sound of distance and presence, a shaking in the air which comes from that invisible song, that body of memory, ancient. A long sustained roar from the bottom of the land, rising, rising. . . .

"Move out!" shouts Gus.

The car jerks forward and the light from the church follows it far, far in the distance. . . .

The headlights strike the billboard. The sign is old and

worn. They shove Fon from the car and push him beneath the wooden structure. The night crowds in around the sharp line of the car's headlights. They make torches with the rags.

"All right, nigger, git on your knees." Gus wraps his bloody fist in a rag.

Fon—slumped slightly, his right hand touching the ground lightly by his right knee—does not blink in the direct light of the headlights. Nor does he look in the faces of the men around him. They are lighting torches and threatening him. Only Nillmon speaks to him. Fon watches the trees and the long shadows of the beams.

"Boy, what you mean, that rock come from the sky? I thought you said your brother chucked it."

"My brother shoots only arrows."

"Goddammit, you gonna let your brother go, while you go to Hell?" asks Ed Frickerson.

"I'm not *goin* to Hell," says Fon.

Ed Frickerson stuffs the dynamite in Fon's rear pocket. Gus lights the last torch.

Nillmon seems confused. He eyes Fon. This nigger still ain't broke.

"Nigger, you mighty popular, eh? You know how to pray?"

"Prayer is for people who want help," says Fon.

A torch is pushed near Fon's feet.

"Where's your goddamn brother now?"

Fon does not answer right away, but seems to watch the flickering of the shadows from the torches. High in the heavens now, a star comes into view from the clouds. A thin glow from a hidden moon peeps ominously from a horizon of clouds.

"My brother is in the trees somewhere, now."

Gus slaps Fon. One of the lights of the car goes out.

Something has broken it. A puff of blue smoke sails away from the dying light. One of the torches falls, and Nillmon, standing next to Fon, thinks he hears a man's voice moan. "Gimme the pistol." Nillmon turns to see Gus—the pistol falling from his hand—stumbling, clutching an arrow which has completely pierced his neck. Suddenly the other light explodes, and the only light is the darting flame from the dying torches on the ground. Nillmon leaps to where he thinks he saw the pistol fall. . . .

But as he leaps he finds that he is falling, grabbing a sharp pain in his neck.

Silence.

In the distance a dog barks and Fon hears the faint sound of a cowbell. He clutches his side and walks deliberately over to each torch, stomps it out with bare feet. He thinks, *That was mighty close. But it is better this way. To have looked at them would have been too much. Four centuries of black eyes burning into four weak white men . . . would've set the whole earth on fire. Not yet*, he thinks, *not yet.* . . . He turns toward the levee where a light in the night reaches out to him and to the great distance between him and the far blinking of the stars. The light from the church reaches out almost to him. They are expecting him back. . . . When the tower is finished. . . . One more black stone. He will be able to see how to walk back. A fragment of the night, kicking, kicking, at the gnawing teeth of the earth.

JONOAH AND THE GREEN STONE

Prologue

Today I see the rain coming over the river again, swirling round and round in long columns, twisting and turning like sheets that are squeezed and wrung out, pumping, whirling in a violent wrestle with the wind, which butts it and drives it. The rain comes, muscling across the river, across the bowing corn, beating against the shield-like and leathery magnolia leaves beside the porch—blasting them the way machine-gun bullets blast through a thicket. It cracks and smashes my face like shouts from the past; but I am not fearful of water like this. No.

Yesterday at the funeral I watched the first drops swing in from the south, and the people had to scurry, getting in their cars, or holding papers or coats over their heads. I did not run. The rain caught me as I looked once more at the gravestone where Mamada is resting. When the rain came like it did, just after Rev Flare had delivered her soul into the hands of the Almighty, I knew the truth: the rain galloping in and out of the past and its thunder-smashes against the cars and the people and the fields of cotton that lay back from the levee were messages telling me that I had lost the best mother any man ever knew. Right then I began to wonder whether Mamada wasnt really my mother. And I didnt fear the rain because there was no hatred in its force. It was holy rain.

Even the water hoses they turned on us in Greenwood last year did not bring back the first fear I had of the river. The pressure of the water tore my clothes off, knocked Gypsy Bird down and struck Hoodoo so hard that he fell back and fractured his skull on the sidewalk. We were not playing in the water like we used to do as kids. No. But still there was something about the act of confronting the white faces that made you defy whatever weapon they used. I was not really a part of the demonstration then but I soon was, and the water was just as impartial as the men who were shouting, "You niggers gonna learn if we got to drown you!" My fear was carried on the shoulders of some kind of a stubborn mule-headed belief that I discovered existed in the breast of just about every Negro peasant in the South and the North. I did not fear the water or the men then, only the gnawing question of whether I myself would be able to stand the pressures.

No. The real fear can be traced back into those years when I was a barefooted boy picking the sun out of the cotton growing along the lazy Mississippi, those years before the river reared up one spring and spread out like a settling blanket over the valley from St. Louis to the Gulf. It covered everything. And it drove what it didnt cover ahead of it. Somewhere during those early years I learned to distinguish between mortal danger and moral danger, between the waters of men and the waters of God. I am not sure when I learned this, but it must have begun with my real mother—whom I only vaguely remember—and it grew with Mamada, who lived her whole life very close to God. As she used to say, "I been walkin with the Almighty since He built my road."

When Jubal and I got lost in the swamp, and I fell in a lake of devil water, I was afraid, not of the water, but of spirits and zombies in the swamp. Some spirits would take advantage of you while you were in some kind of trouble. But Jubal pulled me out, and when he fell in I pulled him out. Together we defied the whole swamp. We actually enjoyed being lost until we could not locate Old Man Red Eye.

I guess I am flooded with good memories of the waters which flowed over me and helped to form me, shape me as the river shapes the land around it, cutting off, digging deeper, breaking into softer ground, and grinding rocks and shells up in its beds. The few times I had swum in it and fished in it only added to the feeling I had for the river: of love and respect for this giver of good things.

But it is by a sharp ache, throbbing as I guess Uncle Bean's rheumatism pains used to do before it rained, that I know the coming of danger. I had no fear of water when Ruby would hold my head under it in the rain barrel or the mule trough; no fear of the hot water leaping out of those fountains in Hot Springs when Uncle Bean took us all out there; no fear of the river at all when we fished in it.

But when I see the long rain coming, when I see a fullness at the banks of the river that was not there yesterday, when I see the live oak leaves drooping from the long rain, the magnolias and the dogwoods thick and dark, then I know the universe is sending a warning in drops that scream and splash like written words, and it is the time when men will think they are solely in mortal danger. But I do not forget that the waters come for a reason, even though I myself cannot say exactly what the reason is. It has taken me many years to be able to see all of this. And I dont mind recalling how the floods first broke me, and then taught me . . .

Fever

WHEN I WAS A KID, the fear of the river rising was always mixed with the fear of going without food. I was little then, too little to remember things the way they happened. The one thing that I always remember knowing was that I was always hungry, and the most pleasant thought I have of my mother is of eating cornbread and sweet potatoes with her in the cotton fields at noon. But then the river rose up and washed her away. It didnt care about nobody. It treated us nice when it wanted to and treated us like niggers when it felt like it. As much as I hated the river, I loved it too. We used to struggle at the edge of the river, planting cotton and corn and peas, as if we were building a great fence to ward off the creeping fear which would always come when the rains came.

Much of the attraction I felt for the river then was due in part to a fear of it. It held a sinister power over the whole Mississippi valley, and every sharecropper around us, including Old Man Hearth (who used to spit on his hands and rub the spit into his mule while he cursed the land and the white man), feared the river. You had to give that old river room because she was the one who called the moves. If it rained in the north country and the mountains, the river told you about it in the south. If the snows were heavy in the north, Papa—in one of his infrequent speeches—would ask Mama, "Old Lady, how you reckon we gwine make it this time?" And all the land seemed to sense a bad year. Rabbits and squirrels ran off somewhere. Mama used to say they went looking for the Ark. People got a bit friendlier, and everybody knew it was because deep down inside no one wanted to move. But there was nothing you could do about it when the river rose. Mama prayed a lot, which never did any good. Not much at least.

It was that combination of love and hate of the river that always gave me notions. I wanted it to flood out everybody—especially the white people—and miss us; wanted it to put the fear of God into their souls as it did in ours, wanted it to drive everybody to us to beg us for mercy, but it never did.

When that river broke over the mud line and climbed up over the levee and headed toward the farms and town, there wasnt much even the Federal Government could do but obey the river and move.

I recall that I was sick in bed with a fever when the first devastating flood came. I had seen it flood before, but it was all vague and mixed up with what Mama used to tell me about the water rising when she was a girl.

It was a terrible time then. I was only a kid, turning seven, and there was a lot of talk about me going to school; but secretly I knew that I would not go to school, because in my dreams and in my sleep, the old Mississippi had told me that I would not go then, that she had something in store for everybody, and it didnt include school . . .

I lay on a cotton sack filled with pine needles. The fever had climbed into my head and was knocking my brains around so much that I couldn't tell if I was dreaming or not. Much of this time between the river rising and my finding Old Man Hearth's johnboat, much of the time is shaky in my memory because my whole body was fevered up. The only thing that I can never forgive the river for is that it took Mama, although I'll never really know if it was the fever or the river that killed her.

Whenever I think of Mama—vague and shadowy as she is in my memory—I try to love the feeling I get by thinking about her, but then I imagine her struggling in the water, beating her arms against the mud, trying to grab onto the porch, and I begin to hate the Mississippi river. I have dreams at night about it, and in each dream I am all fevered up, and the fever rises with the water. I begin to choke. I hear Papa calling Mama somewhere asking her if it will be another bad year, and soon I am diving deep into that river—searching for that hand which used to feed me pieces of cornbread and sweet potatoes.

For the rest of my life, that first flood was alive in my mind, forming me, and driving me. Of all the times that I played and fished on the mud banks of the river, none beat upon my soul and my body as did the times when I had to go down into the water to save my life. Three times it happened, and each time was like the first all over again.

I was standing in the middle of the kitchen. It was dark but still daylight. The rain was beating down on the old tin roof. I stood there, my head spinning. I believed the rain was beating on my head. I kept shaking it, and every time I stopped shaking it I felt something akin to hunger running wild in my stomach like a hound dog after a rabbit. The house smelled funny. Where was Mama? There was no fire, and I could hear the chickens clucking their low close-to-the-feather talk. I stumbled around, looking toward the door of the cabin, and when I moved I realized that I was out of bed. I was fevered up; I was sick; I was alone; I was hungry; I smelled of pee; I was buck na-ked; and I couldnt remember if I was me or not.

The room next to the kitchen suddenly lurched in front of me. I fell. Mama Mama, I was crying. The chickens clucked at the noise from the house, and I thought I saw Papa and Old Man Hearth outside on the porch wringing their necks. Papa Papa, I cried. Then I saw Mama lying on the cot in the other room. Her face was turned toward me, and I eased into the room, lest I wake her, and I touched her hand, crying Mama

Mama Papa's outside killin all the chickens and Old Man Hearth is eatin em up . . .

The rain beat the fever out of my head. I lay there beside my mother, I dont know how long, but when I awoke again it was night and the rain was coming into the house. I could feel it soaking through the quilt which I had crawled beneath beside Mama. I called her and shook her and called her Mama the fire is out the stove is cold Mama I'm hungry. But Mama didnt move. I listened to the rain and fear began to swell under me, lifting my head to stare into my mother's face, began to drive the tears out of my eyes as I struggled to stand up.

I made my way to the door. The floor was very wet and the whole world smelled of mud and dead wood. I opened the door. And that's when I saw it.

The river was moving all around me as I waded through the yard. It was walking up over the bald mound in the front yard where I had made a mud wagon yesterday before Mama made me go to bed with the fever. The river! It had sneaked up on *Mama* and . . .

Mama! I must have run screaming back into the house. The fever seemed to retreat. I dont remember putting on any clothes, but I do remember tugging on Mama thinking that she was asleep. I tried to drag her to the door but I couldnt. So I ran out on the porch. The chickens leaped over each other to huddle around my feet. Poor Dog growled at the river and snapped at one of the chickens. Out over the land I saw things moving between the lines of rain, trees, hills, the land, houses, and the sky . . . and all the time I was yelling Mmmmmama!

Old Man Hearth must have heard me, because the next thing I knew his voice was beating through the rain, coming at me, and after that I was screaming Papa! where is she?

Old Man Hearth was coming through the water wading knee-deep almost, pulling that old cotton boat that he and Papa used to take me fishing in. "Boy!" He kept coming and I stood on the porch shivering while the rain was beating our house deeper and deeper into the flood. A loose board on the porch that always dug a hole in the ground when it rained suddenly swirled in an eddy passing the house, paused, dipped under and was gone. Old Man Hearth staggered through the water, flung himself up on the porch. "Boy!" Scattering the chickens and a tiny field mouse caked with mud. He tied the boat to the rotten post of our shack. "Boy, where's your mama? Maylene?" He staggered through the door. Seconds later, carrying me in his arms, he put me on a quilt in the boat, went back in and returned carrying her in his arms, a sheet wrapped around her, and he was trembling, "Lord Jesus no, God no! Maylene, child, hold on."

Somehow Poor Dog got in, and every time the boat rocked I raised my head and saw Old Man Hearth putting something in it. The rain beat my head under the quilt again, and then he was off, struggling with the boat, then leaping into it beside Mama wrapped in the sheet. And I wondered why she wouldn't wake up and why Old Man Hearth was crying out to the Lord, and how Poor Dog got in the boat, with the chickens too . . .

The river had risen more, and the two feet which separated our porch from the ground was filled with rushing water. Old Man Hearth was rowing the boat, trying to row it toward high ground which was east toward town, but the river was bent on taking us south. I could hear him hollering at people now, and every time the pole jarred the boat it felt like it was going to turn over. A few limbs struck us, and I kept thinking I was back in our house lying on those stabbing pine needles.

"Pole cross current as much as you can! Tell Jake I got his boy!"

And I heard voices pounding with the rain. "Tell em to get the doctor . . . for May . . ."

I tried to raise my head, but the boat rocked me back to where it was warm in the wet blanket, and I was crying, because I knew that something was very wrong, and that the flood had done more than come into our house. It had come in and taken everything, had taken the only one in the whole world who knew when I was hungry.

Fear started to whip me. I have never been beaten like that before. The whole world, the trees and the sticks, the tin cans, old cars, boxes and everything, all the things which made up my world when I wasnt picking cotton in the fields, everything flowed up, joined the evil flood and beat against the side of the boat every chance they got.

Old Man Hearth, sensing that I knew what was going on, tried to console me by telling me that he was taking me to my papa, but I didnt care about Papa then, because I could touch Mama if I wanted to and she would not touch me back. I could see Old Man Hearth's arms working away at the oars and every time he stroked he would grunt, "Be all right, boy. Gwine git yo daddy direckly, God willin,'' and he would grunt on, "Pray she dont rise no more'n she risin now." I could see limbs and boxes passing and cotton stalks and all kinds of trash. "Be all right, boy, jist you pray the Good Lord stop this here rain," and his shoulders would guide the boat while the quilt was soaking up most of the rain now and sending the rest off. The rain was beating the fever out of me, but it was leaving me empty, and a terrible dread like nothing I had ever known was filling up the emptiness. The whole world was pulling me into a whirlpool, sucking me in, off the outer edge, whipping me closer and closer to the hole that was sucked from the other side of the world.

I remember seeing Jesus, or somebody that I figured must be Jesus, and he was reaching a hand out for me, and I was wading in the water, crying, moaning, but going on out into it, deeper and deeper. Mama's hand was reaching for me, then it was Papa's, then it was Old Man Hearth's, then it was Jesus', then it was Fester Whitlock's hand, but as soon as I saw his white hand I drew back and stopped marching in the water.

"God willin, boy, we pole this boat right into Cruscible." And then I saw Jesus again, reaching his hand out to me, and he was saying, Suffer the little children . . . suffer the little children. And I began to wade in the water again, and the flood got higher and drowned everthing and everybody in its path . . .

When I finally awoke from the fever, I knew that both the fever and fear had whipped me so hard that I would have scars on me for the rest of my life.

I dont remember much about what happened to me while I was on that johnboat until the day when the sun came out and woke me up. I dont know what happened to Old Man Hearth—except for what I heard happened later. As far as I was concerned, I was dead too, floating down the Mississippi on a flatbottom johnnyboat which, as soon as it came up against a few swift currents' snags, was going to roll me off so the old flood could get me too. It had got everything else. Now it was after the people. First it takes the land, the ground you walk on, then it gets the crops, and the trees, and the little houses, the barns, the stores, the churches, and before you know it, the river is taking everything it gave you or everything it allowed you to have. That was the fearsome thing about the river before they built all the fine concrete levees and bluffs to stop it when it decided to march. It came like a wild beast, knocking over anything in its way, swallowing up in one second a whole year's labor, ripping through towns without warning anybody, and in the long run taking back what it didnt get from those who lived before us. It was a vengeful river. Or it came slow like a snake. There was nobody who could tell it what to do. Even the white men did not mess with the river, for I saw fear haunting their eyes many times, and it wasnt any different from the fear that drove my second papa, Papa Masterson, to his grave.

What I remember most about the flood, before I woke up and saw it sinking away into the land, was that it had brought something terrible for me. But it followed a strict code. It had come like a thief in the night, and now it was licking and lapping mud like a suck-egg hound does his paws after sneaking around and doing his dirty work. I hated the river then, but my fear of it constrained me some, and made me cry instead of cursing it.

I have never been able to decide whether the river's code is just or not, because I have seen it give as well as take away. Just as it took away the earliest memories of my past, it gave me a series of simple impressions which I—in my later ignorance and shame—thought unworthy but which helped form the thin cloak, the first pair of pants, which I wore proclaiming myself naked before the world. I was protected because of Mama Masterson, Papa Masterson, Jubal, Aunt Lili, Uncle Bean, Ruby, and Lance. And just as much as the river gave *them* to me, it gave *me* to them.

The rain had beat the fever out of my head. But the flood had swirled around me, filling up any little spot that had a memory in it. I somehow managed to cling to the boat. Old Man Hearth must have tied it to a tree while he tried to salvage somebody or something. At any rate he never returned. I learned later that he had been drowned. They found his body several miles south of Cruscible, dangling from a mountain of trees which the flood had swept up against an oak grove.

What a strange code the river lived by. Old Man Hearth was a good man. I remember him vaguely in dealings with my father, whom I barely can recall. Many times we had gone fishing on that river, and once, the only time that is really clear, Old Man Hearth and Papa hooked a catfish that looked to me then like it was the whale that swallowed Jonah, because it was certainly bigger than me. They were dragging it up from the mud line when Papa slipped and fell in the water, which wasnt really deep, but something must have happened because the fish gave a slap with his tail and Papa screamed and went under, grabbing onto the boat with his arm. Old Man Hearth threw the fish line to me, stepped out and grabbed the end of the boat to pull it up into the mud. "Hold tight!"

I thought he was talking to me—and no doubt he was in a sense because we were all river people then—but No. He was yelling to Papa, who was struggling waist-high trying to get a foothold on the bank. When he said hold tight, I began pulling on the fish line with all my might, and I looked at the great fish—its evil fins rigid behind the working of the red gills. Its eyes were looking at me and it was working its mouth. I shuddered because many times Old Man Hearth used to tease the kids about feeding them to the fish if they didnt behave. My papa had even said it to me once, and when I looked at the fish I felt that they meant to try me on it. We would all be pulled back in the water by the catfish, and there, after my struggles, it would devour me, and whatever point they were trying to prove would be proved. When the huge mouth began to open; when its great body started to flop-walk toward me, I bolted and ran. I ran and no amount of yelling at me from Papa or anybody made me stop, until I was across the fields into the house and crying under Mama's hand stroking me in scents of onion and tomatoes.

The picture of that fish looking at me never left, and I learned to fear not only the river but the shadowy creatures lurking beneath the muddy water. God would not protect you in cases like that, because you never knew if it were God who sent the things after you. That's the way I remember Old Man Hearth—connected with that fish and Papa falling in the river. Somehow when I learned that he had drowned in the flood and had been found hanging on those trees, I couldnt help thinking about that fish waiting below, widemouth in the water, waiting for him to fall.

I dont recall when it stopped raining, or when I actually

woke from the fever, or how long I lay in the boat. I dont remember seeing Old Man Hearth leave the boat tied to a tree. I dont recall anything but the terrible fancies the fever gave me and the burning of my lips and the voices. It must have been the following day, because there seemed to be a long space of time in which there was nothing but wet darkness, rain, wind, bumps, and chickens and animals in the boat trampling over me. I thought the rain was Poor Dog licking me with his tongue.

All of a sudden I began to feel a sense of loss and loneliness. I felt the heat on my lips. I tried to look up, tried to sit up, but I was too weak, and my head spun around, and I looked for the sun because something was burning my mouth, and I suddenly knew that the flood was all around me. I lay back down for I dont know how long. I figured I was dead. Like the boy whose funeral we all went to I was dead, and the only thing I thought was peculiar was that there was no preacher there, nor was there anybody to cry for me. I wondered if I was going to find Mama, because I was trying to believe then that she was floating around somewhere in the flood looking for me. Maybe she had a johnboat with a gasoline egg-beater on it. She would come looking for me and find me . . .

Then the voices came.

I had been hearing them all along for quite a while, but now they drifted close and suddenly . . .

"Juuuuuuuuuuuuuuuuubaaaaaaaaaaallllllll!"

It was not just a scream, but a scream and a moan, a very sustained contralto, piercing the membrane of fever that befogged me. A yell like Mama would have given for me to come in, "Joooooooonnnnnnnn!" and she would stand momentarily in the yard wiping her hands on the apron before she was satisfied that I was obeying her. The voices closed in.

Something jarred the boat. It was picking up speed. As the echo of the yell rolled away like circles in water from my head, I bolted up, tried to stand, fell back, and leaned over the boat, looking straight in the eyes of Jubal.

Sitting on a log as large as a buoy, he pushed himself off the bank of a sandbar, all the while swinging a rope over the water. One end of the rope seemed attached to a tree, and Jubal, looking like a tiny dart in the water now, was twirling the rope for another fling. Voices in back of me were yelling, "Grab the line boy! Grab the line! Grab the line! Grab the line!" And the line struck me, swallowed me, tightened as I shook my head and stood up, feeling for an anchor or lock to tie the rope. But I couldnt find it. The line tightened around my chest, and when I stood up again, knocking a chicken in the water, the boat kept on moving with the current, and as I was falling I remember I heard them calling again: JUUUUUUUUUBAAAAAALLLLLLL!

Ark

That's how I was saved from the water in the flood of 1937. That's how it was. I was tied to a rope that was tied to a tree holding firm in a field and the rope was being pulled by Jubal who was floating on a log and all the time their voices yelled in the back, "Pull that line, boy. Hold tight. Hold tight. He gotcha! Hold tight. Pull that line, Jubal. Pull that line."

I dont remember much about how I got from the water back into the boat again. I just remember waking up, mouth full of water, eyes full of water, and I was beating at the water with my arms, trying to shout and grunt but choking on the water, and then grabbing onto the line and holding on for life. Then they were pulling me up into the boat by my arms—I found out later who helped me in, just as I found out later from Jubal what happened getting me in the boat—and then all of a sudden I heard myself saying, "MMMMMMMMMMammmma."

They took care of me. I had brought them a boat and saved them, and they took care of me. There they were, my new family, Jubal Soloman, Ruby Soloman Masterson, Aunt Lili Hawkins, Mamada Masterson, Papa Masterson. I remember being covered with a smelly blanket and looked at by two dark faces. The boat was good and crowded. There were five of them on it, and they brought all their belongings too. They salvaged enough animals to run a farm: there were two pigs; old Poor Dog was still on shivering next to me, gazing at me wistfully as if to ask me why are you letting all this happen. Chickens were all over the place. Nobody had seen fit to coop them up. They were falling off into the water every so often. Too weak and beaten to try to fly to a log or a snag, they just toppled off or jumped out of the way of somebody polin the boat and went over. Once I saw Jubal trying to save one that had jumped off right near where I was lying.

I lay there under the blanket, feeling weak and dizzy. But I had not drowned and I could see things again. The fever was gone. I looked at Jubal. He was a kid about my age, but I thought he was older. He wasnt any bigger than I was, but he acted like a boy much older. I figured him to be ten or more, but he was only seven, same as I was, and if there was anything about him that stood out, it was his silence and his slow movements. I watched him leaning over me. For a moment I thought he was winking at me. I tried to raise up a bit to see him reaching his pole out to guide the drowning chicken to the boat.

"Little bit more," he was saying, "little bit more." And I felt him lunge over me to grab at the chicken. And then the little girl, Ruby, who I hadnt seen good either, came over on her knees to me.

"I fell in off the barn roof this mornin," she said to me.

I looked at her. She was short-haired, dark, and her eyes were filled with wonder. I could tell she wanted to tell me more. Jubal had put the chicken in the bow of the boat where his mother and the aunt and stepfather were polin. Then he had come and stood beside me with a pole. The boat was moving along now in a swift current, and we had to be careful not to hit trees and snags and other objects. Everybody but Ruby and me were polin. I wanted to get up and pole, but I was too weak. The pressure of the blanket wrapped around me was enough to hold my arms to my sides. Ruby, still talking to me about when she had fallen in and Jubal and Mamada had fished her out, began to tuck the edges of the blanket in.

"What you doin?" I asked.

"Lay still." she said.

"I want to get a pole and help."

"You lay still or I'm gonna tell Mamada."

"Who?"

"My Mama."

"Where is she?"

"She polin. See that long pole?"

I could see the outline of the people and the poles. The boat wasnt that big, about thirty feet long and about ten feet wide. It was a flatbottom johnboat built of cypress logs and planks. In the center was the beginnings of a shed, which Old Man Hearth had never finished. It began to come to me then that they had rescued me from the water. I couldnt remember too much before then, except that something terrible to know waited out there in the miles and miles of flood, something that was going to take shape, many shapes, and haunt me for the rest of my life.

I lay there. In the back of my mind was the feeling of Jubal's silence. Ruby sat there, rubbing the blanket, helping me, but I knew that the flood had come and done something very terrible to me.

"Where's my mama?" I asked.

"She must be on another boat," said Ruby.

"This is the only boat she know about."

"There's plenty boats. And house tops and roofs and everything. I fell off the roof this morning . . ."

The boat swirled and dipped in an eddy. The current was getting stronger as the river continued to rise. The tops of trees barely showed now above the vast sea in front of us. I began to get up, trying to see the destruction passing by. The trees that were able to hold to the ground looked like the shaking fingers of a swimmer clutching the air in that momentary period before going down to the bottom, and the floating trees—caught in the muscles of the river current—were helpless ships, drifting toward the edge of the world.

I remember that I was terribly frightened at that time, looking in the liquid pools of Ruby's eyes, eyes which I was to learn how to read later on as my new sister grew older. There was something in the edge of the circles which always made me look, watching for something not there or not apparent. Just as she remained until we grew older, Ruby then, the first day on the river, did not recognize that fearful something in my voice, and if she did, she was just as afraid of it as I was. Crawling on hands and knees over a pile of rags, she turned and went away from me. "I fell off the roof and went under, and Jubal, him and Mamada done fished me out just like they did you." And she was out of my sight. Only her voice whimpered in my ears. I remember that, because it was then that the terrible feeling of being lost and without any clothes engulfed me.

Tears welled up in my eyes. I began to call my mother, calling her even when I called my father, and all of sudden I was looking in the face of Mamada, and she was rubbing me with damp rough hands that I knew so well. Her face was drawn, the blackness was almost drained from it. I could see that haunted look of fear in her eyes. The flood had put fear and death in the eyes of every living creature. When I saw it I burst into tears, and she leaned over the wet blankets wrapped around me, "What's matter, big boy, you let a little ole Sippi water scare you? Look at my Jubal yonder. It dont scare him none," and I could not cry any longer. There was something else in Mamada's face, something that I had never seen before. Her eyes were like Jubal's, slanted ever so slightly upward, and there was a piercing quality about them, not like little Ruby's big round saucers, but a distant gaze, as if she could always see far off. I dont remember what she told me then about what happened to my mother. At that time she didnt actually know, but the rise had taken so much that it was easy for her to surmise that it had taken my folks, just like it had taken Old Man Hearth and all those pigs and cows we saw.

Down the current we went. Somehow she made me believe that I could soon get up and help pole the raft with Jubal. I looked over at him. "You might be a bit taller than Jubal, but you aint ate no meat, cause your muscles low." She squeezed me under the blankets. I wanted to get up and scan the river, polin and polin til I found them safe on a barn top or our old house top. Mamada's strong arms picked me up and put me in a dryer spot under the shed, which was already getting the smell of chicken manure.

"Good for drivin out that fever," she said.

I heard Papa Lem hollering, and Mamada crawled out and got her pole. He keep on hollering and I could see him wave a couple of times. They had spotted somebody in the flood, stranded. And everybody was polin except Ruby, me and Aunt Lili, who was lying quietly in the corner of the shed, shivering and whimpering, as if she were having a chill. If I had not seen the blankets moving, and heard her voice muffled beneath the wet air, I would not have believed she was alive. But when I finally managed to lean my head over to get a look at her face, I saw that she was wide-eyed and that look of terror which had so frightened me when I saw it, was consuming her face as if it were some kind of an invisible flood itself over her dark skin. She was about twenty years old then, but as I remember Aunt Lili she looked like a woman of fifty. Even the shouts from the outside did not arouse her. Something had washed her soul away. About then I struggled out of the blankets and began to crawl, bumping into a pig, which backed away, staring me in the eyes. And when I stood up I saw out over the distance a lighted figure motioning vigorously and seated on a horse—no, he was standing beside the white horse. Both seemed to be standing on the water, but actually they were ankle deep in a floating island, which was slowly breaking up and giving in to the relentless river. All I remember about him at first was that he was holding a white horse, he was little and he was white.

All of sudden Papa Lem was beside me. He was saying something to Aunt Lili, something I will never recall, but whatever it was it didn't make her stir. He looked at me, and said "Son, what's your name? . . . old man Noah must have been your father." And he was pulling out the rope which Jubal had placed under the shed. I could see Jubal now through Papa Lem's arms, and he was trying to steer the boat. I remember telling him my name was John, but he didnt seem to hear; he kept on talking to himself as well as to Mamada, and he was saying that God had sent the ark after them. That's how I got the name Jonoah. My name was John then, but I dont remember what my family's last name was exactly; sometimes I think it was Hearth, then I think it was Barber, or Herbert or Berth. I was too young, and we had never had much cause for last names. I was John. My mother was Maylene, and I think my father's name was Jake. Anyway Papa Lem rushes back, steering the boat now, and calling me little John Noah. Neither he nor I nor anyone else on the boat then knew that we would become a family, and that what we did for the next few months would be the basis for Jubal and me becoming brothers, Ruby and me becoming brother and sister, and Dog Whitlow being the man I hated, the man who later in my life took on the concentration of my hatred, took the headwaters of my fear and loathing, and by doing so helped me to see how utterly helpless a human being becomes in the face of built-in hatred, a tradition-bound hatred, how utterly and hopelessly dependent one becomes, how useless and senseless it is to hate a river, and how terribly easy it is for a human being to pretend to be naked.

How were any of us to know then that the next few months would mold us into a family that would someday accuse America with its blood? How were we even to guess then who our enemy was . . . or real enemy, that is. I hated the river. And I later learned to hate Dog Whitlow in Arkansas. But they were not the real enemies then. Enemies of the body yes, but not the soul, a thing which we were looking for, a thing which river people said would get lost in the swamps if a body stayed on the river too long.

The White Horse

THE WHITE MAN with the muddy white horse! He began to shout when he saw the current pick up the boat a bit and try to swing against the three oars of Papa Lem, Jubal and Mamada, and I remember that his voice was shrill and broken, frantic, as if he were not hollering at us, even though he could see Papa Lem and Jubal working frantically to steer the boat cross current so as not to have to roar in back upstream. He saw. But he kept on hollering, "Bring it left bring it left bring it left brrriinngggitleeeeft" and he was slipping in the ankle-deep water, wet, muddy, looking like a lost rat on a doomed island. The flood was falling off; the way he was hollering was as if he was trying to get back from the dead. He seemed to yell louder as we got closer to the island, and I noticed that it was beginning to disturb Aunt Lili. She sat up.

Papa Lem was hollering at Jubal, who despite his size seemed to be holding his own against the current. "Harder, boy, harder." We were getting nearer the island now, only about a hundred yards away but the current was strong.

"Bring me that line bring me that line niggers bring me that line bring that line." I could hear his voice echoing booming over the raging waters louder and louder, competing in some way with the flood. I became deathly afraid, I remember, because Aunt Lili began a moaning, a deep moaning that I have never heard before or since—except once in a while at a revival meeting . . .

The only feeling of safety I got was in the thin voice of Ruby outside the shed. She was clutching my dog, Poor Dog, by the neck and even though he was smelly and muddy, she was embracing him, and Poor Dog, having no more resistance or strength left in him, stared out blankly, whimpering now and then at the swirling eddies which brought logs and limbs bump bump boomp boomp up against the side of the boat. Ruby talked softly, reassuring herself, more than Poor Dog, that we would not all drown. And just before we got to the island, I remember I heard Mamada's voice—caught between the two currents, the piercing yell of the white man and the half-grunts holding the oar—screaming, "What he saying that for, what's matter with that white man? Caint he see we doing the best we can?" And then we were being rocked by the floating debris close to the island. Papa Lem flung the line, the white horse slipped in the mud and fell, the white man grabbed the line, plunging head first over into the river to get it, came up screaming again and scrambling back on the island. The boat moved in fast, and Papa Lem and Jubal stood in the bow waiting to pull the white man aboard. Mamada came back to us and told us kids to stay still unless we wanted to fall in the water and get swallowed by a garfish. She made me feel good, but somehow I felt at that moment just as I had felt when I woke up with the fever and found the flood coming into the house, coming in as if it belonged there, coming in without asking and taking anything and anybody it wanted to. I felt naked.

The white man stormed onto the boat. I got the feeling that it was dangerous to have him there because somehow I thought of him as the flood. Even though there was a warmth in his voice as he began talking to Papa Lem, it was not a magnetic warmth, but expedient, necessary because men caught up together in a rise always feel something with each other despite the color of their skins or any other difference. Enemies become friends when the Mississippi rises. But this man, thin and covered with mud, eyes that narrowed and looked right through you, spoke loud even though the flood had climbed up to his ankles. He seemed irreverent. At that time Papa Lem was not a strong Christian, but he had a lot of religion, and he seemed helpless in the face of God's will of the flood. The only time he came alive, I recall, was when he had called me Jonoah. I guess that's why the name has stuck. There was more behind it than just the time of the rise. I still get the feeling sometimes when I think about Papa Lem at this early time, that if he had prayed at that moment God would have struck his heart right then, and he would have been filled with the same thing that made him call me Jonoah, and he would never have had to suffer and die the way he did. The white man could not have touched him then . . . When the man climbed into the boat, dripping the Mississippi all over everything, shivering and cursing, when he came in and snatched up a blanket and threw it around himself, a mood—like death—began to hover over the boat as it sailed under the grey sky in a vast sea of mud, defeated earth. I became part of everything. Aunt Lili buried her head in the blankets and seemed to be groaning a low and strange sound. Ruby sat right next to me, and Jubal, standing holding his pole, watched the white man with eyes filled with something more than horror, more than fear, more than awe, something close to a kind of hate dipped in a potion of some kind of love . . .

"What's the matter with you, nigger?" he suddenly boomed at Papa Lem, "You got nough room on here for two horses like that."

Papa Lem stopped pulling in the line, his head held down facing the island where the horse seemed to sense the situation. It was struggling to its feet, whinnying a bit, and looking at the boat. Jubal was twirling a rope to lasso it.

"Dont you niggers know who I am?" He began to grin his Southern white man's grin at Mamada, who was holding her oar in the mud. Aunt Lili let loose a loud groan. "Cant lose any more to this damn rise. This is worse'n the rise in twenty-seven; I been wiped out. Only thing I got left me is that horse."

"Sir," said Mamada, pointing to the horse, "if we take that horse on here, we'll all drown."

"Thas right, sir," said Papa Lem. He stood with the rope still dripping in his big black hands, running down his sleeve. "We reelin too much in the current. She gonna git worse."

The white man began to wrap the blanket around his shoulders, jerking them a bit in a series of grunts, as Papa Lem slowly straightened his back and brought the rope in. Suddenly Mamada and Jubal gave the boat a violent shove with the poles.

"Hate to do it but guess I'm gonna have to give up my religion after this rise. Water gone as far as Cruscible, taking every plantation this side of Greenville. I cussed God fer that. He aint have to do it." He spoke mater-of-factly, seeming to talk mostly to himself, loud and angry, deep anger, and he boomed his voice out over the water in diabolical defiance of the flood, a little man with a big voice. "So you after me now! You bone making snake," and he spat in the river. "Hurry git this boat away from this place, nigger, I thought I was dead there. Let's hurry and git!" He reached and snatched the pole from Jubal and began to oar himself. We were afraid of him, mainly because he was playing with his soul. We'd much rather him stop blaspheming and act like a regular white man. Papa Lem was so afraid that he trembled. But he somehow managed to avoid taking the horse along. The white man was still angry.

We went down the river. We left the starving horse struggling in the water. Nobody said anything to the white man. He was cursing, and as the boat began to pick up speed in a current, he seemed to get worse.

"Nothin like this damn river to bring folks close together. Even if it's a nigger, a river rat know another river rat. Boy, what you people's name?" he asked Jubal. Jubal, holding a broken stick in the water for an oar, did not say anything. He was amazingly perceptive, more so than I was about what to say and when to say it. He knew the man was just talking, and he kept right on stroking the water over the sides of the raft, even though he knew his broken stick wasnt doing that much good. The white man was polin well. Papa Lem had moved to the back and was trying to rudder the stern of the raft. Mamada was still holding her own against the current.

I dont know how long we floated down the river. The sun came out twice. I remember because Jubal had taken to what I thought was crying, but later I learned it was not. He was moaning like church people do; back and forth went his back as he pretended he was guiding the boat, and every time the sun came out (it came out three times) he would stop.

And when he stopped, Aunt Lili's low sound crept out from the shed like a dirge of death.

There had not been much talk except for the white man talking to himself. He kept on cursing the river and God for all he was worth. But soon his engines began to wear down, and he began a flat monotone drawl which we were all familiar with. He told us his name was Whitlock, and that he had lost his farm in the flood. Said he had been on the island for two days, and before that he had driven his car toward Greenville and had run into a steady rise before he reached high levee sight. In no time the car was stalled. He had waded back, climbed several trees, and when things got too rough he took up in an abandoned shack with an old Negro who was blind and who said he was waiting for the Lord to come and help him to wade in the waters of Jordan and into the Promised Land. This made the white man laugh, though he didnt laugh out loud, but I could tell by his voice that he thought it was funny. I didnt. Nobody else either. We knew. The flood wasnt coming for nothing. It was sent.

We passed another boat. They were colored folks and we all waved and hollered. Their boat was worse than ours. There were at least ten people crowded on the boat, which was also smaller than ours. We all knew it was bad when we saw it, but what could you do, push somebody off? We passed chickens, dogs, birds, rabbits, squirrels, coons and possums all hangin onto limbs of trees. Every tree had a few dwellers. Once we saw a family, two girls, two little boys, and a mother, sitting on limbs. They had managed to get some boards and had made a kind of tree house. They waved at us. The river was going down now, and things would be looking up. I cried, "Mama, mama, where's my mama!" as Mamada's strong hand calmed and steadied me.

It was about this time that something strange happened. I never found out what it all meant until many years after my brother Lance was born, and Papa Lem told it to me during the crisis in Little Rock. We found it hard getting out of the river, because the current was swiftest there. You could tell where the river was because there was nothing but a clear sheet of water ahead, moving fast and furious, but on the sides you could make out where the land was, with the tops of trees sticking up, and barns, houses, and things sometimes floating by, sometimes hanging there fighting the flood. When the flood retreated, mud rings would mark the scars of battle. Jubal had made a fire and Mamada was trying to roast pieces of rabbit forked on willow sticks.

"Nigger, you know this water well," Whitlock said to Papa Lem.

"Yes sir," he returned. There was something cautious about Papa Lem now. I could not quite put my finger on it. But it wasnt the feeling I got when they pulled me from the river and I got in the boat. There was something more than just this man being a white man, and whatever it was, Papa Lem was scared to death of it.

We were steering toward an area of trees which grew higher and higher. Somewhere miles ahead would be the first retreat of the flood, and we could probably meet up with some of the rescue people. They were traveling in motor boats, and big sternwheel packet boats. I got up and sat beside Ruby and Jubal, who were watching Mamada roast the meat. Every time she finished forking a piece she gave it to Ruby or Jubal to hold and roast over the smoking fire. The wood was damp and hard to burn. Aunt Lili was sitting up trembling. In her face was the look of despair. She was crying inside. I wanted to ask her what it was that hurt her, but I could see her gaze fixed at some point beyond Whitlock, or maybe it was on him, and then she suddenly clutched her stomach and screamed.

Mamada rushed to her side and began to talk to her. "Lili, the Lord knows your burden, chile. We all in this thang together. Please honey, trust him."

"Noooooooooooooo," she screamed again, trembling.

Somehow I felt the thing that Whitlock had brought to the boat then, in her screams, felt it as if the screams were my own. I didnt know what was going on, but Papa Lem was there beside her too, a look of terror on his face. Jubal got up and got his pole.

"That man's the devil," she screamed, "and I'm carrying his seed. God, Ah aint fit to live no more," she went on, groaning and leaning her head over the side of the raft.

The two men faced each other. Whitlock, a slight frown gathering on his face, began to peer through beady eyes at Mamada then at Papa Lem. "Where you folks from?" he asked. He knew something was wrong, but his manner showed that he didnt know what it was. And for a white man to act that way around a Negro is dangerous. He finds out soon that something is going on that he doesnt know about, and if he doesnt find out, then someone is going to have to suffer. He began to talk now, to ferret out the closed minds of the grownups.

He baited his hook with us, first Ruby, then me, then Jubal.

There was more than the fear of the river and the fear of God on the boat. Papa Lem had showed it when Whitlock stormed on the boat. The white man's curiosity was aroused now, and he was going nigger hunting; first with his nose, like a lick-tongued hound, then with his teeth; and whatever it was, Aunt Lili seemed to sense it all. She began moaning and calling on Jesus. She cursed and then asked repentance; then she screamed and tried to leap off the raft, but Mamada had tied her down. Before we got off that boat that day, I watched a strange and terrifying game of black and white.

First Whitlock tried to get Ruby to talk. We were nearing a cutoff in the river, and the land rose up a bit on the left and began to loom far in the distance. We were heading the boat toward the trees. "That little dog gonna shore like you, little girl, when this flood is gone." he said. Ruby was still holding Poor Dog's neck. "Yes, he shore gonna like you. I be mighty obliged to you myself. I reckon we be runnin into a sternwheeler by and by. I know nearbout every boat this side of St. Louis. We be picked up, and I shore gonna get you niggers fixed up. Now, little girl, what you want me to buy you when that rescue boat picks us up?" Ruby was almost ashed with fear. She took her arms from around Poor Dog's neck and went to the stern of the boat, where Mamada was polin now. As much as Papa Lem and Mamada guided the boat, the current spun it around until first the bow was the stern then the stern was the bow, and the white man, Mr. Whitlock, polin along the sides found himself spinning just the same. Jubal was tending the fire now and roasting some more meat. He brought me a piece. He had cooped the chickens and tied up the two pigs. I was glad somehow that the white man was polin the boat instead of Jubal because I wanted him to come and talk to me instead of Whitlock. As soon as Whitlock began talking to Ruby, she slid off and hid next to some boxes near where Mamada was polin. She stayed there for a long time, almost years it seemed to me, because I dont remember much of what she did any more until after Cruscible. She stood close to Mamada. You would think that she would stick close to Papa Lem, but I soon learned that it was Mamada who held that boat on course and not Papa Lem, even though he was steering it a lot of times. Anyway, that left me and Jubal for Whitlock to mess with. We were kids and didnt know what he was up to. At least I didnt, but Jubal did. I found out later just how much he knew about what was going on. That Jubal dont talk unless he has to; and when he does, he says what is needed and nothing more.

"Well, you younguns know what happened to a nigger johnnyboat yesditty? I seed it all from the island. Couldnt do nothin at all. That boat hit a dip, more'n likely where the line of those hills break off," and the white man pointed with a quick arm, watching us out of the corner of his eye to see if we were listening, "and I could hear em hollerin. Then everything was all quiet and up pops the boat and a few nigger heads, boy, bout your size"—and he looked at me—"kinda favor you too, well, he commenced to strokin toward the island, but it was too far. The current took him and the whole family under and around, and then I didnt see em no more. They coulda held their breaths and maybe come up way downstream—have to be mighty strong for that though, I dont know, but I reckon—I was sorta prayin for that boat to let the current bring it cross to me, but it didnt. Been expectin to see Captain Hillmann come juggin long here any time now. And when he do I bet I get the best welcome anybody ever got. They all know me on them boats, yessir. I reckon I gonna have to take one of you younguns on board and show you off and tell them poor people how yall rescued a poor river-beat white man. Niggers come along in the nick of time. Only thing loss was wife, stock, seed, and crops." He spoke with deep sarcasm. The tone in his voice alone was enough to frighten me. Mamada had been listening to him and she was beginning to slow down her polin. Aunt Lili was still groaning under the shed. "Well," he said to me, "reckon your mama mind?"

I lowered my head and did not answer. Fear of grown-ups

was one thing, but fear of them using you was another. There was something evil about the way he was doing it. I was tongue-tied.

"Smatter wid that boy?" he asked Jubal, "Cat got his tongue?"

"He dont know where his mama is," said Jubal. And when he said it so matter-of-factly, it took possession of me again and I began to cry. The white man started to curse the river then, worse than he had before. He called it the shame of God and in a bitter tone declared that he was going to change his religion, from Christianity to nothing. He announced that the river was worse on niggers than the klan, because he had seen it take the lives of people but in all his life he had never seen the klan harm a Negro, just scare them. All the while he was talking, Mamada was hollering at us. She told me to stop crying and that we would find my mama as sure as her name was what it was. But Whitlock drowned out her talk by telling about the incident he had seen yesterday, and the fact that the river was taking people as well as livestock. He seemed to be trying to instill something beyond fear of the river into us. What it was I did not sense until he began to talk to Jubal again.

"Boy, what's you name?" he asked Jubal. "You mighty plucky to be so small, polin a boat and all . . ."

"Jubal E. Soloman."

"That so? Well, looky here, boy, when we gits picked up by them rescue people, or when we gits to high ground, I want you to promise me one thing, will you?" And he stopped polin to look at Jubal, who was pulling off a piece of rabbit with his teeth. I watched him. Whenever I watched Jubal I kind of lost some of my fear, but not all.

"You have to ask my mama," said Jubal, without the slightest hesitation.

Whitlock grunted in a short almost disgusted manner and proceeded to push the boat away from a clump of logs. He was

obviously taken aback by what Jubal said. His offer had a tinge
of excitement in it that every boy loved. But it had something
else in it too. And Whitlock baited on, for there was something
about the way Mamada and Papa Lem acted when Aunt Lili
screamed out that aroused his suspicions. There seemed to be
someone on the boat who knew more than he did about something, and that something he didnt even know what it was. I
found out much later that the things had more to do with Papa
Lem and Aunt Lili than anybody. But then as a boy, not really
knowing anything except that I was hungry and scared, I
couldnt trust my feelings in dealing with grown-ups, especially
white ones. Mamada must have taught Jubal how not to be
scared, because he was steady chewing on that rabbit meat. We
were nearing the high ground.

"Boy, you mighty plucky to be so small," he kept on saying to me. "Now I aint even told you what I'm gonna do."

"Jubal!"

Jubal stood up and began to move toward Mamada.

"Yes, mam?"

"Come hep your mama."

I found myself following Jubal, because I didnt want to
stand beside the likes of Whitlock. He might throw me over to
the catfish and then knock me back with the pole if I tried to
stroke back to the boat.

With the poles now, Papa Lem and Whitlock were moving the raftboat toward the high ground. We had to steer
around trees and underbrush which was all muddy and shredded
from the flood. It had drowned everything. Birds were flying
overhead, and we saw some crows in the taller trees. Drowned
animals floated by or hung bloated in the underbrush. I began to
wonder if we were going to eat any of that meat. I hoped we
wouldnt. Ever since then I always wondered, when I was eating
store-bought pig or beef, if the butchers had salvaged their meat
from the flood waters of some river. I felt sick. Uncle Bean

would curse the orneriness of white folks and say they'd serve niggers anything and think nothing of it. All of the stock on our boat, even if it was starving, had managed to survive. We had fed them willow leaves, collard greens and acorns and pecans and honey-locust peas that floated up on the water. We'd lost all but two chickens before Jubal cooped them up. There were two pigs, Poor Dog, somebody's nanny goat, a mule, and a couple stray cats we'd picked up. The current was not moving us now, and Papa Lem, Mamada and Whitlock were workin up a sweat pushing the boat toward land.

I stood near the shed where Aunt Lili lay, cowering away from the flood and still wrapped in a blanket. Jubal and me were standing near Mamada as she poled. We felt safe. On the other side of the boat, Whitlock grunted, hollering at Papa Lem about steering the boat correctly around snags and trees. And in between grunts Papa Lem was saying, "Yes sir, huh huh huh huh."

"I vow there aint been a rise like this since twenty-seven," yelled Whitlock. Despite the fact that we all had somehow eluded his suspicions, a thing which seemed to make him more eager to find out about us, he could not help but feel the teammanship on the boat. We were all dependent on each other. And even though he was white and we were Black, some measure of his existence had been allotted to us, however small. I was a kid, but I could feel this thing even if I couldnt put it in words. To him we were Blacks, unequal to anything he was or stood for. But that was in low water. In high water, things began to be equal. The Mississippi was the great leveler.

They took me under their wing. I told Mamada as much as I could about my mama and papa, how Old Man Hearth used to take us all fishing in his boat, how he built the raft himself and oftentimes used to stay on it weeks at a time. I told Mamada everything, and pretty soon it seemed that she knew more about

my mother than I did. She looked at me and told me, "Dont
you worry none, son, The Lord will bring her out this mean
rise. Dont you fret none. Hold tight to Mamada's hand, and we
find them. Say a prayer to Jesus for them." And she taught me a
prayer right there on the spot. She made me say it over and over
again while she was polin, and every time I made a mistake she
stopped polin and looked at me: "Jonoah, you got to believe
stronger'n that," and when I'd get it right, she'd grunt and push
that stick deeper in the water. And I could tell that the man
Whitlock wasnt about to let niggers off easy. He had cursed
God. It would be only like fanning away flies to beat the truth
out of poor bottoms river niggers like we were. He and Papa
Lem were polin shoulder to shoulder.

"That's a mighty plucky scrap you got there," Whitlock
said to Papa Lem.

"He's my boy," shouted Mamada.

"What's his name?" asked Whitlock.

Papa Lem pulled his pole out of the water and poised for a
shove, elbowing the long pole around a clump of brush.

"Which one you talkin bout, sir?"

"That one," and he pointed at Jubal.

"Them boys dont belong to me, sir. That one's my sister'n
law's kid, and the other belong to God. If it aint for him driftin
by in this here boat, we all be—"

"I dont reckon God had anything to do with it," interrupted Whitlock. "After this rise I'm changin my religion. And,
nigger, you ought to do the same. There aint nobody been beat
down more'n you niggers, besides Fester Whitlock. Listen to
me, Lem, boy, I been thinkin. This here rise is the signal that
God aint running thangs any more. Naw. By God, my wife and
my whole plantation's gone, my hands, my neighbors, my
friends, and if it werent for that piece of car of mine, and that
horse you folks left back there to drown, I would be gone too.

This side of Greenville all the way to Cruscible is like the Atlantic Ocean. I cussed God fer that. He aint have to do it. I was just gettin on my feet, and here come the rains, Goddammit, takin the stock and the crops, breakin the levee, risin inch by inch on the hour. Naw, God aint have to do that to Whitlock. He done took everything in this flood except me, and I aint forgettin it. When this rise drops, I'm changin my religion, from a backslider to a nothin. And, nigger, you better do the same."

"He been good to me," Lem said lowly.

"Niggers is all alike when it come to religion," Whitlock grunted.

There was a silence. From where we kids were I could tell that Papa Lem was disturbed, and he was trying to find something to throw back at the white man, but he was afraid because of who the man was. It was frightening to watch. I didnt know what the nature of the battle was, but I knew the stakes were high. And since the boat belonged to me until we found my mama and papa, I felt that the battle was being fought with me right in the middle.

"Well, boy," Whitlock said to Lem, "look like you got yourself a family here. I remind you bout that youngun yonder though. You better watch him."

"Thas my boy," said Mamada again, and she put her arms around Jubal, and then I could see her strong black hand reaching past Ruby's shoulder for my shoulder, and then it was digging into me, and it was a kind hand, and I remembered how that hand felt all the days of my life, and there she was, her arms spread around us like she was a mother hen. She showed an obvious dislike for Whitlock, and her tone of voice was very dangerous. Despite her protecting us, I began to feel scared when she spoke to the white man.

"Well, watch him," said Whitlock.

"Dont worry, I will."

"You know, nigger," Whitlock said turning to Papa Lem, "you got a mighty plucky crew on this boat. I dont reckon I like it too much."

Papa Lem, his youthful face contorted in grunts as he steered the raft, was obviously left with the next word. Mamada was under the shed now. She had hustled us kids into a safe corner, and she was scrambling around under the shed whispering to Aunt Lili, who was stirring about as if she was about to get excited again.

"Mr. Whitlock, sir, I dont reckon they means any harm. God knows we all just want to get out of this water safe and dry. We been holdin up for three days now, same as you."

Whitlock looked at Papa Lem. For a moment we thought he was going to let things go. There was a strain in his voice, and his tiny face, reddening up a bit, took on a sudden grimace of despair. "Same as me?" he repeated almost inaudibly, more of a statement than a question.

Downstream I could make out a line of smoke. It must be a steamboat! It was a thin line that spread out and inclined westward just above the line of trees which had begun to rise into sight on the other side of the river. I guess it was about eight miles off, maybe more, and the rise of trees to the east—where we were headed—seemed to have people there. There was a vague outline of wagons and a truck, and shacks, all of which fed into the glare of the high water. The sun was beginning to come out more and stay longer. The currents were slacking, and the earth—sucking in the water like it was the bitter medicine handed to a sick child—began to raise signs of life again. Trees begged to be seen. Every tree was a roost for animals and birds. And as the flood began to turn to mud, the fear that had hugged the eyes of every creature seemed to sink away. But it was not so with people.

"Same as me! Yah ha ha ha ha! Same as me, eh? Yah ha

ha." All of sudden he broke out. "Nigger, you pretty plucky yourself. Aint nough for you to have women and chillun barkin at you. Naw, I must look like a nigger to you, eh?"

We were desperately trying to get near the land now. Whitlock had stopped polin.

"I knowed there was something about you niggers when I come on his hunk of logs. Now I know, nigger," and he turned full to Papa Lem, "what you hidin on this boat from a white man? Huh?"

"Nothin, sir, nothin, The Lord—"

"Damn the Lord! I'm talkin to you and that woman of yourn."

"We just poor bottoms people lost in the flood," said Papa Lem in a beseeching tone.

Mamada crawled from the shed. Jubal picked up the stick he was rowing the boat with. Ruby began whimpering and holding my arm. As hungry and beat as Poor Dog was, he began to growl. Aunt Lili was trying to untie herself.

"You from Mississippi?"

"Yes sir."

"You better act like it."

"Who you work for?"

Papa Lem hesitated.

"Who you work for, nigger?"

"Well, me, my wife, we—"

"We from Yazoo City workin for the Wainrights," said Mamada.

"Wait a minute! Woman, I'm talkin to your man, not you."

"And I'm talkin to you. You asked a question . . ."

She never finished. That white man swung his pole around and knocked Mamada in the water. Aunt Lili screamed, Jubal leaped on the man, whaling him with the stick, screaming, "Dont you hit Mamada, dont you hit my mama!" Papa Lem swung his pole around but it slipped and fell in the water. Then he jerked the stick out of Jubal's hand.

"Nigger, you come any closer to me and you better stay on this river for the rest of your life," Whitlock said.

Jubal began pounding him with his fist, and before I knew what I was doing I was beside Ruby, all of us crying, pounding on Whitlock's back. But with one sweep of his arm Whitlock knocked us back. We had felt Mamada attacking him and we had felt free. We were Black against white. It was terrifying because somehow I felt as if I was dying. I felt naked and lost even though Jubal and Ruby were getting knocked around too. Papa Lem, half-defeated, helped Mamada back into the boat, which had begun to drift.

"White man," Papa Lem said, "you ought not to have done that."

"All right, let's begin where we left off. You teach that woman of yours some manners, and we all get along fine. You the wildest niggers I ever seen. Act like you got loco fever. What's the matter with her?" He was pointing to Aunt Lili. Papa Lem hesitated, the stick still in his hand. "Throw it away and act like you got some sense, boy. We all in this together. Dont make sense for me to have to put yall off your own boat, now does it?"

Mamada was weeping softly, but when Papa Lem threw the stick over into the river, she grabbed a pole and began to pole the boat again, silent, Jubal and Ruby and me right beside her. She began to hum softly, prayerfully, and tears came down from her eyes. Her dress, sticking to her skin, was covered with bits of twigs and debris. We all began to wipe them off, and Poor Dog started to bark.

"Lemech," she said. "if you dont act like a man, I swear fore livin God, I gonna do it for you, I swear . . ."

"Boy, you'd better shet your woman up. Now, I want you to talk sense to me. What you hidin from me?"

"Nothin, sir, nothin."

"Nigger, you lyin." He came toward Papa Lem, who backed up and began shouting, "Dont hit me, cause I have to hit you back, Mr. Whitlock, please dont, we dont want no trouble, I swear we dont. I'm a man. I got to protect what is mine. My poor wife, she has lost her mind and the Lord . . ."

"I told you once about what you better do about the Lord," said Whitlock.

"I caint go against the church."

"Damn the church! Look, what good has God done to you poor niggers? Why, hell, he aint even give you enough backbone to defend yourself. Dammit, nigger, cant you see that God done short-changed you? Gave your woman and your youngun more pluck than you. Hell, now he got you between a rise and starvation . . . Damn God . . . Nigger, let me tell you something! There just aint no God!"

Papa Lem hesitated. In a little bit we would be back of a clump of trees that seemed to lift right out of the river. There would be land in back of them, because about a mile down to the east was that site which looked like a landing. The steamboat was coming closer, but it was a long way off. We would be better off getting to land, for most likely the boat would try to reach the landing anyway. It was a rescue boat.

"Thas blasphemy," Mamada said to Lem, "thas worse'n not protectin me and these kids. Thas worse—"

"I know what it is, Ada," he shouted, and he was crying.

Aunt Lili suddenly hollered at Whitlock, "There just aint no God!" Then she came toward him.

"Git back, Lili! Git back!" shouted Mamada, running across the slippery floor. "It dont do no good, honey."

Aunt Lili, her wild eyes and unplaited hair making her look crazy, staggered and fell. "Just one lick at him," and her clenched fist struck the floor.

Papa Lem reached to pick up a pole.

"Boy, you see what I mean? I aint never seen a nigger protect his woman yet. I aint never. Nigger, you a coward."

"I aint gonna blaspheme, but, white man, if you push me too far . . . I dont want to die, but I believe . . ."

"You threatenin me, nigger?"

"I pick you up, Mr. Whitlock, and we all tryin to scape the high water . . . I pick you up cause you was stranded, not cause you white."

"Dont beg me, boy, please. I aint never been sweet on a nigger, and I dont intend to start with you. All right, then, what you hidin from me?"

Aunt Lili began to scream. She began to weep and fling her arms. "Kill em kill em please Lord. Tell em and then kill em!"

"We got nothin to hide from God, and we aint scared of the truth," Papa Lem said.

"Where you niggers from, and what you know?"

"The Lord knows, and I—"

"Damn the Lord! There aint none!"

"Yes there is."

"You callin me a liar?"

Papa Lem held his pole. We kids were so afraid that I dont recall what we did except cringe under the dress of Mamada, who was steady polin the boat toward the land.

Papa Lem would not say whether he was a liar or not.

Then Aunt Lili yelled. "You a devil, just like your cousins. You a white devil," and she broke off into a groan.

Mamada suddenly clutched her pole and advanced.

"Yes, white man, you're a liar, and besides that you're on our boat. Git off." She came, weeping, toward him swinging her pole. "Lem, I cant stand it no more. Either he gonna kill me or git off cause I'm gonna fight." And Jubal had grabbed a brick.

All of sudden we were bumping into trees and the high ground. The water wasnt too deep here.

Mamada swung at Whitlock, but he easily knocked her

into the water. He swung at Lem and knocked him off, and they both tried to get back on but Whitlock began cursing them and striking their hands with the pole. "If you come back on, I gonna put you right back off," and he began to steer around the shrubs.

We were terrified. Even Jubal was cringing, but Aunt Lili began yelling. She seemed to come alive all of a sudden, and she began to yell at Jubal to kill Whitlock. "Kill em kill em before he kill the baby. Kill em Jubal kill em." I remember that Whitlock turned and jumped off the boat into the water and waded the rest of the way to high ground through a field of ruined corn. He was cursing and cursing, yelling that we niggers were lucky that he didnt kill us all, and before he got up the incline, he turned and looked back at the boat drifting and Mamada and Papa Lem wading in water that was chest high, and he yelled:

"Nigger, you see what God do for you! You damn lucky I dont feel like messing with you poor Black bastards. I tell you one thang though, I better not ever catch you all in Cruscible. If I was you people I'd ride this high water out of Mississippi . . . You hear me, nigger?"

He was looking at us kids when he said it, or so it seemed to us. Suddenly Jubal reared back and threw a brick at Whitlock.

He was so small that the brick didnt go too far, but it went far enough to reach the mud line, and Whitlock, turning, saw it coming. I'll never forget the look on his face when he realized that somebody had thrown at him. He looked at the spot where the brick had landed, looked up—as Jubal and I were trying to pole the boat away toward Mamada and Papa Lem struggling in the water and hollering at us—looked down again, looked up at us and then as if studying what to do he looked off downstream where the big stern-wheeler was chugging near the shoreline. He watched it for a second, then turned and headed toward the place which I later learned was Terrain's Landing, now all washed out and flooded.

He turned and looked back again.

"If you aint outta this water by the time I get on the Sprague yonder, your asses are goin down to count clams."

I didnt know what he meant then, but I did later. He was a desperate white man. We watched him hurry away, a tiny wet little red-faced man, who if it had not have been for the flood would have killed us all. We kids struggled to pole the big boat, but we couldnt. It began to drift, but not too much. We got scared. Ruby began to cry and Aunt Lili, untying herself, began to sing:

Oh Mary dont you weep
Martha dont you moan
Pharaoh's army got drownded
in the Red Sea one day
Jesus is calling me
Lazarus wade in the water
Oh Lazarus
I'm old black Lazarus
old black Leper
Oh Mary dont you weep
I'm comin down
to the sea with you Jesus

Wandering in
the Wilderness

Even though Aunt Lili's singing sounded sinister, I guess God must have heard her and knew what she was singing about, because He got Mamada and Papa Lem back on the boat soon, and we managed to get the boat out of deep water before the aftertow of the Big Sprague sunk us. The aftertow can do that sometimes. Old Man Hearth used to tell about his brother Ed selling catfish out of Lake Providence, a small river town on the Arkansas side of the Mississippi. His brother was sleeping on the boat after a fog lifted, and a larger boat came churning upstream almost full steam, and the aftertow rocked and spun him till his craft toppled slightly and went under. He swam to shore but lost all of his fish and his boat.

There is one thing that has lasted with me, one sinister and foreboding thing about that experience on the river. And that is the way Whitlock's image began to form in my mind. For years after, I dreamed about him coming after us. It was true that we had to run from him and that some strange guilt began to take shape around Aunt Lili more and more. But I would be getting ahead of myself if I told how I learned about what actually was happening there with the grown-ups, so I will stick to things in about the order that they happened. The main thing about that river and flood experience is that it made us all know each other and have something to talk about in the years to come. That is the good and the bad about the old Miss Sippi. She take life and she can give life.

Every time we saw a boat or people we looked for my mother. When we were out of danger of the Sprague, we managed to anchor to some trees near shore, and Mamada said she was going to find out where we were. We were below Greenville, but how far toward Cruscible we werent sure. I think the town I was born near was called Holly something, but I cant remember the name. There were plenty of Hollys, Hollyridge, Hollyknowe, Holly Springs, Holly Bluff, Hollandale, and little spots on the river with names, local names, like Holly Bend, Holly's Mocassin, Holy Smoke Baptismal, and Holly Hill . . . but these I learned after I grew up naturally and came to the point in my life where I could understand things and places. Then I was a kid, and I didnt remember anything except the things that made impressions on me.

It didnt take me long to realize that I wouldnt see my mother again. The experience on the river had already qualified Mamada to be my other mother. Jubal was my brother, and Ruby was my sister. Papa Lem, always a vague and soft-spoken person in my mind, did not qualify for my father. Indeed I did not think that I had a father at that time, after the flood. After the water went down, and the states counted their losses, counted the millions of dollars swept away by the flood and the lives lost, the thousands of homes lost, after the wrath of the river was spent, the people had time to reflect. Always we kids would have something to remember.

To Mamada and Papa Lem and Aunt Lili the issue was fairly simple. They were terrorized. They were cast adrift on the angry waters of two floods. One had to escape them both. The flood of wrath from the Mississippi, and the flood of hate from the river of the past flowing through the whole South and breaking the surface in the state of Mississippi. But to us kids, and especially me, it was not so simple. For little Ruby it was facing the floods and also facing the terror and despair in the face of her mother and uncle. It was the time of delta making, the time when the rivers would make permanent marks, lines, etchings, and heaps on the soul. For Jubal I think it was the same, except he was to bear the greatest burden of all in the family. He came out the floods with memories—for we talked about them later—that leveed his soul and made guidelines along his journey. He knew what was happening even though he could not tell us nor could he change it. It was the will of God. We were kids but we knew we were naked and at the mercy of the world.

To be alone, lost, at the mercy of the elements, is one thing, and it is terrible. But to be lost and at the same time be overcome by the feeling of having lost all that you ever had is like dying. When the full realization that I was going to be without my mother and father hit me, I felt as if I was dead. I wanted to find them. I vowed to myself that I would spend the rest of my life hunting for them in the flood, because somehow I believed that they werent drowned. The flood could not have taken them from me. But this was my innerward attempt to hold on to something like a hysterical kid fighting to hold on to his coat in a fight. To be a Negro, a Black peasant in these bottoms lands of the world was no asset either, for the entire scope of our world of experience was defined by color, and the color was upon us: Black. AND BLACK WE WERE. The only one not Black was Aunt Lili, who was brown, light brown, and she was very pretty, but it must have gone to her head, because she never seemed to recover from the floods. I did not know exactly what was wrong with her, but I knew that she was not normal.

It was May. I'm not sure of the exact dates, but Mamada told me it was a spring flood, a flash flood that broke way above Greenville and spread out clear to the Gulf. Every river was flooded—the Arkansas, the Big Black, the Yazoo, the White River, and even the Missouri in the north, which Papa Lem said poured into the side of the Mississippi like a stream of water off a muddy hill. The flood lasted for a month, but when it started to fall, the people were already rebuilding and relocating. A small government boat picked us up before it got dark. We didnt stay on it long because they put us and several colored families off at

Cruscible. They told us that all the homeless and everybody had to go to a place in town. I remember that we had a lot of bundles and somewhere along the way they got lost, and we had to leave Poor Dog. Even the chickens and hogs and all the animals were left at the landing. Mamada said we would come back, for unlike the case with other colored families, there was an urgency about our journey. We had to get out of Mississippi. I thought at first that it was because of what happened with Whitlock, but later I learned that when they left El Dorado and came through Cruscible they were headed toward Arkansas. But what the reason was for their flight I did not know at that time, as I have told you already. It was just above the Holly place that the flood caught them.

After they put us off the boat at Cruscible, Papa Lem and Mamada were at different ends of the river concerning where we were going. Papa Lem was for taking a boat, any kind, and getting as far away from Cruscible as possible; Mamada was for staying over there until the flood let down enough for us to travel west and out of the state. We were gathered in a church with a lot of people. It was late at night. A white man outside in a motorboat had a loudspeaker and was giving directions to people. There were a lot of sick people, and the rescue people had set up a hospital, but the hospital was for the white people. If you were colored and you were sick with spreading fever or anything, you got treated by a colored doctor wherever you could find one, or you didn't get treated at all. This place we were in was an old rock church, very small, and there were a lot of boats outside. The flood line inside the church was way over my head, near the ceiling, over everybody's head. I was hungry, scared, and cold, but I didnt mind that much after looking at that high mud line in the church. Jubal and I said that if we had got caught in that church we would have broke the doors down as soon as we saw the first line of water seeping through the floor.

Around us were people just like us; maybe except for one

or two, they were all river people or farmers. There were a lot of
kids like us too, but mostly we all were too scared to talk with
them. In flood time the best thing to do is to stick close to something whether it is your kin or your boat or your log. If the
flood has no feeling for the levee, it sure wont have any for anybody crazy enough to go wandering off. One woman was talking to Mamada, and while they were talking Papa Lem was trying to talk to Aunt Lili, who was sniffling, and moaning, and
acting strange. She was still thinking about something because
she kept crying:

"Kill em, Lem. He takin me, he takin me, and what
you think about it, Lem? Kill em, I dont want to carry no Black
devil . . ."

"Yall can come stay with us," said the woman talking to
Mamada. The woman was very large, so large that I wondered
how she managed to fit into a boat. It would take a johnboat
like we had to carry her. Her skin was dark brown, and there
were water stains all over her legs. Jubal and I were seated right
in front of her on a bunch of burlap bags filled with sand. I could
see that same look of fear in her eyes, but it was not as alive as it
was in some of the other people. She apparently had made her
peace with God. The flood was sent and she would ride home if
it were her time. The faith of the old folks has never ceased to
amaze me.

"Chile, it's a blessing from the Lord," said Mamada, "that
you got a place."

"We stayed til the last," said the fat woman.

"All we can do is pray now, honey," said Mamada looking
at Aunt Lili.

"She gone need the care of a sure hand," commented the
fat lady.

Papa Lem was putting a blanket around Aunt Lili's shoulders. He looked scared and we felt estranged from him. Jubal
and I sat as close to Mamada as possible. Papa Lem was talking

to a group of young men and some old ones but he soon left them. Aunt Lili, every time he would come near her, would begin to ask him for something, like a pot or a sack or a spoon or a hoe or a line, but he wouldnt give her anything, but would just keep the blanket from falling off and would glance at Mamada and once at us boys sitting on a makeshift pew. Then he sat there by her for a while, his head bowed, as if he were in meditation or hiding.

"We all gone need the sure Hand of God to lead us," said Mamada.

She was very handsome to look at in the dim light of the church. I guess it was there that I looked at her and knew that she was my mother; that whatever came, Mamada was going to be my mama from then on. Presently the fat lady began fumbling around in some bundles which lay beside her, and she brought out pieces of salt meat and handed them to me and Jubal and Ruby, who woke up when she smelled food. We grabbed and began gobbling it up.

"Where's your manners?" cautioned Mamada.

Jubal said, "Thank you, mam."

Ruby said, "Thank you, mam."

But I was in the middle of a chew.

"Jonoah, boy, where's your manners?"

"Thank you, mam," I said.

That was the best piece of salt meat I ever ate in my life. We kids remembered it and talked about it for a long time.

"You aint got no manners," said Jubal.

"I got manners," I said.

"Where they at?"

"I forgot," I admitted.

"Hope she gives us some more," he said, "I could eat a whole garfish."

We sucked and smacked our mouths. I vowed that if she

gave us anything else I would say "thank you, mam," as soon as I saw it coming. I had manners, even though they were not cultivated much. The fat lady and Mamada were talking, and people were moving in and around the church. A preacher was talking to some people near the door. I figured he was a preacher because he had a big Bible under his arm. He was dressed in muddy overalls and a jumper jacket, and he was tall and stoop-shouldered. Papa Lem was watching him.

Aunt Lili began to weep now, softly and determinedly, as if she suddenly knew why she should weep. Papa Lem tried to console her, but she paid no mind to him. We kids sat there on the floor, Ruby wide awake now, watching the grown-ups to see what the flood had done and would do and what they were going to do. It was a lesson in terror, because we could watch the eyes of all the men and women and know whether to expect good or evil. We knew it must be good when we didnt see the fear.

"Hush now, Lili," Papa Lem said to his wife, "I'm a man. I take care you. We be gettin on outta here by and by . . ."

"Dont you fill her head with your lies," Mamada said. "We aint got nothin and we aint know nobody down here. I reckon we in the hands of Jesus' Mercy right now."

"She'll come back to sense if she trust in thangs agin."

"Leave her lone with your trust. You aint save her from disgrace, and you ant gonna do it now with a few words. She in God's hands now. Best you can do is pray for her and your own soul."

"I'm takin you all away from here soon as they come with that rescue boat."

"You aint takin me and these kids nowheres, and if I got any say to it, my sister stayin where she can get well."

The fat lady, who Mamada began calling Beulah, began to talk to Aunt Lili, and after a while she said to Mamada that she knew exactly what spirits had taken up with her, and she could do something for Aunt Lili. Mamada interrupted and told her we were really going to Arkansas.

"We got to git outta here, Ada," Papa Lem began to moan. "I just aint know what they gonna think. The Lord knows I didnt mean it, I didnt mean it."

"You better keep you mouf shet about that, fool," she whispered to Papa Lem as Miss Beulah was trying to talk to Aunt Lili. "You oughta meant it. I'm a Christian myself but sometimes my faith is tried, sorely tried. That man Whitlock be looking for us, and I know he wont rest til he break you. As soon as Lili can travel we pray the Lord guide us."

"We got to git way from this here Cruscible, Ada," he whined again, "I dont know what the law gonna think. The good Lord know I aint meant it . . ."

Mamada looked at him then and lowered her head. The look in her eyes was one of fear and hate at the same time. What had Papa Lem done? There was something we kids didnt know. I dared not ask Jubal, and I knew Ruby didnt know. I kept silent and watched the people. Something would happen sooner or later. It was late that night, and most of the people in the church were going to stay there. The place had a damp and sour odor, but because we were hungry, it smelled good to us kids. I remember that years later the smell of a church never equaled the smell of the one in Cruscible then and that I was always searching for the same smell.

I dont remember falling asleep or anything. Most of the time spent in the church was spent in anticipation of some kind of relief, and when it finally came, other things tended to fade away or not mean much at all. All I recall is suddenly being awakened by Mamada. She was shaking us kids violently and telling us to "Blink up, yall, blink up," and I remember seeing her wrapping something around Aunt Lili's shoulders, elbowing her way through the sleeping people and motioning Papa Lem which way to go. He did not need any help though because he was moving very fast. In fact we all practically ran out of the church. Jubal and I brought up the rear, both of us stumbling along in our sleep, trying to wake up, looking for the morning sun but not seeing it, dropping our little bundles several times and having to pick them up, sensing the urgency, not knowing what it really was, but believing it had something to do with the terror of the flood.

The water had gone down enough during the night for mud-walking. With a stick you could do pretty good in mud ankle-deep and over. Mamada gathered us together in the back of the church and told us to hush and not to speak to nobody, especially anybody white. She said the man Whitlock was after us again. "Yall keep up now else that mean devil grab his hand on to you mighty quick. Jist keep up with Mama Ada and she take care of you. Jubal, you and Jon look after Ruby, you hear me?"

"Yes, mam."

"You hear me, Jon?"

"Yes, mam," I said beginning to wake up.

"Your Uncle Lem here's gonna look after your Aunt Lili til I gets back, and you chillun have to look after yourselves." We didnt know why or where she was going. Ruby began to whine. Mamada looked her in the face: "Shet your mouf." And Ruby shut it. Then Mamada, shaking her shoulders as if she were getting ready to go into battle, touched Papa Lem on the arm gently, "Dont let these younguns out of sight. Stay here in the back of this church and keep your head down, you hear?"

Papa Lem was nodding his head. "Go ahead fore they come," he said.

"And dont talk to nobody, you hear me?" she said again, "cept Miss Beulah yonder when she get herself together."

We looked back into the church. Miss Beulah's large form was moving toward us. Behind her came a little cream-colored man whom I had seen sitting beside her but whom I had paid little attention to because he didnt have much to say. It was her boyfriend, and his name was Big Daddy. He was chewing something. They moved through the shadows of the dimly lit church like one single ghost: Miss Beulah being the real thing and Big Daddy her shadow behind. When they passed in front of the kerosene lamp their shadows leaped up on the wall.

"Here they come now," said Mamada.

"I wanna go with you," Jubal said. He stood beside his mother, not asking her, but merely making a statement which he seemed to feel she ought to have known.

"Then who gonna look after yall here?" Mamada suddenly said looking down at Jubal.

"Jon do it," said Jubal, "and Uncle Lem too," he added as an afterthought.

"Aint nough. You stay, you hear me?"

Jubal, his muddy clothes drying now, shook himself and said quietly, "Yes, mam." And Mamada went down the three wooden steps to the mud. She was gone fast.

There was something that Jubal and Mamada understood between them that drew me to them both. Little Ruby seemed mostly too detached from Mamada, but even between her and Jubal there was something that I liked. I wanted to be a part of whatever it was. I needed their love as well as their protection.

Papa Lem sat drooping beside Aunt Lili, who was quiet now except for asking him for things now and then. He ignored her. Miss Beulah and Big Daddy took up with us without any words. They too seemed in on some conspiracy. Miss Beulah took out some beads and told us all to bow our heads for a prayer. I thought Papa Lem was asleep, but his head was merely down while his eyes were roving around the church, especially the front door.

Miss Beulah began mumbling some strange words. She kept her voice down and told us all not to raise our heads until she said so. Before the prayer was over, we heard loud voices, white men's voices, somewhere outside the front of the church. Fear leaped into me, and I could detect a slight shiver in Miss Beulah's words. Papa Lem put his arms around Aunt Lili, who murmured slightly to herself the prayer Miss Beulah was saying.

"Where's Mamada?" I whispered to Jubal.

"She be back," he said, but he didnt say it with enough conviction.

"She say we gonna stay here?" I asked. I was very scared.

"Maybe she gone to find your mama and papa," he whispered to me, but I could tell he was guessing.

"You scared?" I asked him.

He didnt say anything. Miss Beulah began to *sshhhh* us, and Papa Lem reached over and tapped me on the head. Out of the corner of my eye I could see that tall man we had seen the night before with a Bible under his arm. He was talking to a white man who had a flashlight and was shining it around the people who were sitting up, standing, moving around, and grunting. The air was heavy with the smell of clay, stale food, and destruction. A baby began to wail, and the flashing beam lingered on the area a bit, then found us.

"Scared of what?" said Jubal.

"Them white folks coming after us," I said almost crying.

Jubal began to say a prayer, and he told me to say it too.

Papa Lem tapped Jubal on the shoulder, "Boy, you better keep quiet whilst we praying."

When the light did not move from us, Papa Lem looked up, and I could see that look of terror leaping from his eyes. The light moved on, but we heard the white man moving through the crowd toward us.

Suddenly we heard Mamada's voice. She came through the back door of the church.

"Come on," she said, and we all rose from our kneeling position slowly and followed her out the door. If someone had said boo to us then, I believe we all would have turned to stone.

Miss Beulah and Big Daddy brought up the rear. They dragged along, Big Daddy carrying an enormous cotton sack cut in half and filled with belongings. He carried it over his shoulder, and I thought there was a body in it because it was so long.

I found out later that we had nothing to fear at that particular time because the white man was a government man, one of the flood-control engineers. But from then on I became acutely aware of the rupture in the relationships between Black and white. Whitlock's image loomed in my mind like a great phantom riding a horse, storming across the world and trampling over me without any concern at all. When we left that little rescue station there in Cruscible, it marked the real beginning of our wanderings.

We were homeless now and fleeing something which I did not know but which was constantly alive in the eyes of Papa Lem. They could not hide the shadow of their guilt even though the body of facts supporting it was well concealed from us kids. But we kids did not deal with facts that much. Perhaps it was an asset, a saving grace which allowed us to survive the brutalities of the flood better than the grown-ups. Perhaps. At least we were not at the mercy of our consciousnesses. And to watch this demon crush Papa Lem was like watching Thoat Higgins that time when he caught Nathan's dog and tortured it to death by peeling back pieces of skin with a pair of pliers. I couldnt watch. Neither could Hoodoo. And from that day on we kept a distance between Thoat Higgins and us. There was something about him we hated and feared. We didnt know what it was but that didnt matter. We knew. We couldnt explain but we knew. He was the living example of somebody who stayed in both kinds of danger—mortal and moral—constantly and simultaneously. And we were scared of him.

Papa Lem was at the mercy of this thing. Every white man he came in contact with knew that he was hiding something. If they thought it was just plain sneakiness, then that was fine, because then Papa Lem was young and most white people considered him just another nigger, sneaking and grinning, begging and jigging, quickly reduced to imbecility in the presence of a Bible and a tambourine. But if they thought his guilty look came from something deeper, say, some knowledge of something, something that would put him outside the place they had figured for him in their heads, then Papa Lem became a hunted man. No matter how long it took, they would get any colored man who showed himself to be growing out of the boll, as we said, seeding and making a strong plant out of himself. It was and still is the tradition of the American South to cut down all green plants that grow out of black soil. Unless they bow their heads and yield fruit to the master, they must be cut down.

ROPE OF WIND

The Marchers

IN THE DOME the prisoner, alone in the silence of centuries, waited...

And all the people gathered together and began a trek across the land. From every corner of the land they came. Crossing the great rivers and mountains, they came on foot, in cars, buses, wagons, and some came IN THE SPIRIT FROM OUT OF THE PAST...

Their leaders stopped them at every crossroad and made speeches, reassuring them that to march against the white-domed city was sanctioned by God Himself. And the people believed. They went forth in processions, chanting, singing, and praying. Sometimes they laughed and shouted.

All the leaders were men of learning. They were men who believed that a law existed higher than the law of men. They believed that Justice was that law. They were men who believed that Freedom existed when men exercised restraint in doing that which they had the power to do, and courage in doing that which they had never done. In speaking to the people about these ideas, the leaders always spoke of Equality.

And the people believed. They marched gladly. Never in the history of the nation had so many people who felt oppressed gathered in a great multitude to express their grievances.

In the dome the prisoner waited . . . shackled to inertia by a great chain of years...

And the marchers grew in numbers. Work ceased. Factories puffed no smoke. The highways thronged. The past moved forward. And the great white dome in the great stone city became a hub to the troubled mind of a great nation traveling in a circle . . .

In the dome the silence was stirred by the sound of legions of feet marching. The rumble sifted through the years. The prisoner heard . . . and waited . . .

Then the marchers descended upon the city. And when the sun was high in the midday, they gathered together and built a great platform. Their leaders came and stood upon it and made speeches, and the people cheered and roared.

In the dome, where webs floated in the semidarkness like legions of ghost clouds, where echoes from the outside sifted in the dome, the prisoner . . . stood up.

Outside the dome the marchers listened to their leaders:

TODAY IS THE DAY!

And the people cheered.

TODAY IS THE DAY WE WILL SET OUR SOULS FREE!

And the people roared.

TODAY—and the leader pointed to the dome shining in the noon sun like a giant pearl half-buried in the sands of the sea—TODAY WE WILL OPEN THE GREAT DOOR OF THIS NATION AND BRING OUT THE PAST!

And the people cheered.

NO ONE CAN STOP US NOW! NO ONE! WE HAVE SERVED IN THIS LAND FOR CENTURIES. WE HAVE SLAVED FOR THOSE WHO OPPRESS US. WE HAVE BEEN CHILDREN TO THEM! BUT TODAY WE SHOW THEM THAT WE ARE MEN!

And the people cheered.

IF THE DOME-MAKERS SEND THEIR GUARDS, THEIR SOLDIERS, AND THEIR DOGS UPON US, WE WILL NOT FEAR . . . NO. FOR WE MARCH IN PEACE. WE MARCH IN THE NAME OF *HIM* WHO SENT US, AND WE ARE NOT AFRAID . . .

And the people knelt down and prayed.

JUSTICE WILL PREVAIL! FREEDOM WILL BE OURS! EQUALITY SHALL NOT BE TRODDEN DOWN!

Then another leader stood forth. He was very great amongst the people.

NOW . . . NOW IS THE TIME. TODAY . . . FREEDOM CAN WAIT NO LONGER. WE HAVE ACCEPTED TOKENS OF FREEDOM TOO LONG.

And the people cheered.

OUR FATHERS WERE BROUGHT HERE IN BONDAGE. AND WE HAVE FELT THE SAME YOKE LIKE BEASTS IN THE FIELDS. BUT WE WILL WAIT NO LONGER. WE HAVE LIVED IN A TOMB FOR YEARS, AND WHILE WE SUFFERED WE SANG OUR SONGS AND FOUGHT AMONGST OURSELVES BECAUSE WE HAD HOPE. GOD GAVE US THAT MUCH STRENGTH TO GO ON. AND WITH THAT HOPE WE SURVIVED, FOR WITHOUT A VISION, WITHOUT FAITH, A PEOPLE WILL PERISH . . . LET US GIVE THANKS UNTO THE LORD . . .

And the people roared.

THE SUNSHINE OF A NEW DAY AND A NEW FRONTIER IS UPON US. RAISE YOUR HANDS, MY PEOPLE, AND STRIKE . . .

"Freedom Freedom Freedom!" echoed the people.

WE WILL REVIVE THE DEAD AND CONVICT THE LIVING!

"Justice! Equality!"

LISTEN, MY PEOPLE, AND REMEMBER THIS . . . FOR WHEN YOU TREK BACK TO YOUR CITIES AND TOWNS, THE PRESSURES OF LIVING MIGHT MAKE YOU FORGET.

REMEMBER THIS: YOU HAVE SERVED IN THE
FIELDS. YOU HAVE SERVED IN THE KITCHENS,
IN THE WAREHOUSES AND THE FACTORIES. YOU
HAVE SHED YOUR PRECIOUS BLOOD FOR THIS
NATION, AND ALL THE TIME YOU COULD NOT
EVEN ENTER THE FRONT DOOR OF THE HOUSE
LIKE A MAN ... BUT TODAY, WE WILL KNOCK ON
THE DOOR AND WITH THE ARM OF THE GREAT
SPIRIT, WE WILL OPEN THE DOOR. WE WILL
ENTER. WE WILL SIT DOWN AT THE FEAST
TABLE, AND WE WILL REST AND NOURISH OUR-
SELVES.

"Justice! Equality! Freedom!"

OUR BACKS AND OUR SWEAT HAVE BUILT
THIS HOUSE.

"Yes, it's true!" roared the people.

THEN I FOR ONE THINK IT ALTOGETHER
FITTING AND PROPER THAT WE LIVE IN THE
HOUSE WE HELPED TO BUILD, NOT AS CHIL-
DREN, NOT AS SERVANTS, NOT AS MAIDS, NOT
AS COOKS, NOT AS BUTLERS, SHOESHINE BOYS,
AND FLUNKIES! BUT MEN! THIS HOUSE IS OURS!

And the people applauded.

In the dome the words stung the prisoner. He stirred
himself and took a step. But the weight of his chains shook
him ... and he fell.

Outside, the cheers grew louder. The dome trembled.
Specks of dust leaped up from centuries of rest and wandered like souls in limbo. Suddenly a passion seized the prisoner.

From the ground he came up slowly, as if he were a lost
seed in a sunless cave, a seed that had sprouted into a pale

limp stalk trying to suck a bit of precious sunlight into its impoverished leaves.

Riotous cheers heated the day. The sun stood high and hot. Soldiers came. Dissenters and extremists—organized sometimes and sometimes not—jeered at the leaders and threw stones at many of the marchers. More soldiers came. The police rode around in patrol wagons. People fainted. And the great city seethed while its troubles flashed around the world.

A ray of light shot through a sudden crack in the dome. The beam stabbed the prisoner, and he fell back, groaning and moaning as if he had been struck by a great hammer.

"I remember," he wept, "I remember."

Then the doors came crashing open. The people rushed in. And they trod upon the sentiments, the truths, the lies, the myths, and the legends of the past in a frenzied rush to lay hold of Freedom. They cheered their leaders, and their leaders watched the movements of the soldiers and dissenters constantly. And no one knew who was to make the right move.

They lifted the prisoner, as if he were a flag, and carried him out of the dome, rejoicing as if a great battle had been won.

And when they carried him into the bright light of the noon sun, he felt a great pain in his eyes. He blinked, shook his head, moaned . . . for the intense light immediately blinded him.

And the people shouted, "Freedom, Justice, Equality!"

They put the prisoner on the platform and all the leaders gathered around for a ceremony. A hush descended like dust on a windless plain.

Shackled in his chains, the prisoner opened his mouth to speak.

"My eyes," he murmured. "If I could see . . . *see* this Freedom . . ."

The leaders all stood forth around him and hailed the people.

TODAY! TODAY! TODAY IS HISTORY!

"A drink, please," whispered the prisoner. "The heat . . . a drink . . ."

WE HAVE SET HIM FREE! GLORY TO GOD! THE LORD IS WITH US! LET US MARCH AS SOLDIERS OF THE GREAT SPIRIT! WE CAN SEE THE SPIRIT MOVING AMONGST US! WE CAN SEE! PRAISE GOD! OUR FREEDOM IS OUR SIGHT!

And the people cheered. The leader wrapped his arm around the prisoner, and the chains clanked and pinched the leader's arm.

LOOK! echoed the leader, OUR SOUL LIVES!

THAT WHICH WE THOUGHT WAS DEAD IS ALIVE! THAT WHICH WE THOUGHT WAS LOST HAS SURVIVED! And he raised his hand for silence. THE GREAT SPIRIT IS MOVING MIGHTILY AMONGST US. CAN YOU FEEL HIM?

The prisoner trembled. His lips hung open. "I want to see," he said. "Please, these chains . . . I want to walk . . . for I . . . remember . . . I remember when I had no chains . . ."

WE MARCH FOR OUR FREEDOM, boomed a leader. WE MARCH THAT OUR CHILDREN WILL NOT HAVE TO MARCH!

And the people roared like never before.

ALL OF US MUST BE FREE BEFORE ONE OF US IS FREE!

And the people applauded.

SO ENJOY YOUR FREEDOM! GIVE THANKS UNTO GOD, FOR WE HAVE WALKED BY FAITH, AND FAITH HAS GIVEN US LIGHT! WE HAVE

PROVEN THAT WE CAN MARCH IN PEACE AND
NOT IN VIOLENCE. FOR WHO AMONGST US
TODAY DOES NOT KNOW THAT THE SPIRIT IS
STRONGER THAN THE SWORD?

And the people sang and danced around the platform
until all the leaders came down and joined them.

Beneath the sky the prisoner stood . . . alone . . . trembling, as if he were only a thin line of summer heat wavering
in the noonday sun. His chains clanked and choked him.

Suddenly . . . as the people roared in a wild song of joy
and freedom, the prisoner stared into the darkness of his
sight, and except for the intense heat and the pain, he would
have thought he was back in the dome . . .

Then the platform creaked, broke in splinters, and tumbled to the ground. The people laughed merrily and followed
their leaders up the streets of the city. Today was a great
day. Freedom had come to them . . . at least for a while . . .
and the marching of their feet was their song of freedom . . .

The prisoner fell to the ground. The wreckage of the
mob buried him, and the weight was like all the centuries
linked together around his neck. The pounding of the
marchers shook his flesh, and the heat of the day burned his
thoughts away.

The sun beat down upon the great white dome. The sun
beat down upon his head. And the dome was as white as ever
before, and the prisoner was as black as night.

Prologue: Harlem Square

Micheval's bookstore, guarding the northeast like an outpost for over thirty years, has been an important intellectual meeting place for Africans, Nationalists, Reformers, Muslims, and various dissenters. Some people call it Harlem Square. Almost every weekday evening a small crowd will gather to listen to the haranguing of one of a half-dozen speakers who stand on small platforms or ladders. On weekends the crowd has to be watched by the police. Harlem Square is then in some ways the pulse and the barometer of the community. You can tell the mood of the people by visiting Harlem Square. Of course, over the past ten years the mood of Harlem has been the same, and one doesn't have to visit the square to ascertain what it is ... Many Harlemites feel that they are living in hell.

Harlem

THE Lenox Avenue subway shot through its tunnel, shaking the tracks and debris. A hot blast of air leaped from the subway cavity, as if the train had screamed. The train roared into the station, stopped, recharged itself, and waited. Harold Kane, sitting with his head down and his eyes closed, suddenly looked up, peered through the standing people, and pushed his way off the train. Just as Harold was half out, the doors began to close. His leg caught; the train hissed, the doors reopened and Harold stumbled off the train. He looked around, went through the turnstile, and slowly made his way up the steps, brushing often against people, as ants do in a moving line.

Harold was tall and muscular. He looked older than twenty-two. As he came up out of the subway and onto the street, the sunless haze over Harlem showed his skin to be dark but tinged with redness, as if the blood were going to suddenly break through. His eyes were very large and watered a lot, and even though he moved along the street in a glide, a slow, aimless flow, there was a latent quickness about his walk. At the corner, he did not wait for the light as did some other pedestrians, but weaved behind a passing car, around another, alongside another, and then with his head held dreamlike he stepped upon the sidewalk on the other side of the street. There he stood beside a fire hydrant and looked up at the skeletal ruins of the Islamic Temple.

High over the ruins a flock of pigeons circled, arcing off, and then swooping up again, playing in the wind. Harold squinted closely at the building. A man came and stood by him. They both looked up. People passed. A woman stopped at the corner newsstand and bought a paper. The man was young and neatly dressed. He looked at Harold, who continued to examine the wreckage without acknowledging the other.

"Well, Broh," the young man finally said, "I see you anxious to know when the mosque will be rebuilt." Harold rubbed the fire hydrant with his right hand. He looked at the bundle of newspapers under the young man's arms. "Paper?" The young Brother was handing him one. Harold paid for it and tucked it under his arm. The other moved away and began to hustle off the papers to passers-by. The wreckage was strewn all over the sidewalk—bits of burnt wood, debris, and broken glass. The police had erected a barricade around the burnt-out stores. There were several beside the temple, which stood right in the center. On one side was a beauty parlor, dress shop, bakery, and a drugstore. On the other was a tavern, barbershop, poolroom, and pawnshop. All these had been completely burned down. But the temple was the hardest hit. A bomb had leveled the walls and pillars. Harold watched the scene with a curious familiarity. While the young Brother was selling papers, he kept a close eye on Harold. Soon he and another Brother had their heads together. They had seen him gazing every day now for the last week. At a certain time Harold emerged from the subway like a man in a trance, and stared at the wreckage for a long time. His expression, twisted up with some concealed misery, kept the astute young Brothers from questioning him. They expected him, any day now, to break out in tears.

A bus roared past. Harold leaned his head against the newsstand. He slowly brought his right hand around and touched the top as if he were feeling for something very small. Then he looked at his smudged fingers. He put his head down on his arms again. For ten minutes he leaned up against the rear of the newsstand, not moving except for the shaking and shuddering of his body like spasms of pain. The subway roared beneath him. The street was loud and noisy. People darted here and there. Many stood and looked at him. Most of them thought that he was about to vomit. Perhaps he was. But the heaving of his body was far deeper than his stomach. Suddenly he raised his head and walked off toward Seventh Avenue and Harlem Square.

A group of kids was running toward Harold, and behind them was a man in an apron waving a stick. People stopped to look. There were shouts, but the kids soon disappeared, zipping across the street in the middle of traffic. Several cars screeched to a halt. In front of a record store where the music was pouring onto the street like syrup, four teen-age girls and two boys were dancing, and one of the boys was beating out a rhythm on the showcase window with his fist. Harold moved through the crowd. An elderly woman dressed in a long cloak and with a big gold cross around her neck was weaving through the throng, handing out pamphlets. She put one in Harold's hands, but he put it in his pocket automatically, without even looking. A siren sounded blocks away, and a few people ran off in the direction of the siren. A wino was stopping people up the block near Seventh Avenue. He was holding out his hand and leaning forward. When he came to Harold he assumed a different posture, straightening himself up a bit and wiping the dribble from his mouth with his sleeve. Instead of holding his hand out to Harold, he grabbed him by the elbow.

Harold was dressed in a worn suit coat and a pair of khaki pants. His blue sport shirt had sweat and dirt stains overlapping the collar, and his shoes were runover and unshined. The beggar appeared no better off, but he looked Harold over carefully and probably surmised, *Here comes a good one.* "Please sir," he said—a slight affectation slurring his words— "could you help me get a sandwich?" He showed his

hand. "I just need a dime . . ." He was pulling on Harold's
coat. Harold dug into his pocket, brought out the newspaper,
searched around, brought out cigarettes, then a quarter, and
gave it to the man without looking at him. The man, speechless for a split second, thanked him in a low voice and backed
off, inspecting the quarter, squeezing it, and then looking
around the crowd. He looked as if he were trying to find out
who saw him. Then he moved on down the street and began
to beg again, adopting the same pose he had taken before he
had tapped Harold.

A cop stood in the midst of a group of young toughs
across the street. Another cop was crossing the street to
them, holding his hand up to stop traffic. The cop on the
sidewalk was tongue-lashing the toughs, who taunted him
loudly and then scattered. Later, the two cops stood waving
them away. The toughs, moving through the crowd, suddenly began to run, and a bottle crashed against the sidewalk. The cops took off, chasing them. They all disappeared
around the corner of Lenox Avenue. Harold went on toward
Seventh.

At Harlem Square the crowds were gathering. Traffic
moved slowly, and all along Seventh Avenue people were
sitting on boxes, in chairs, on rails, on the ramp in the middle
of the avenue, and even on the roofs. High over the city
heads sprouted, leaning over the roofs, making it look as if the
building was boiling over. And the street received the crowds,
who found that the heat and the boredom were too much to
fight alone in the musty roach-ruled tenements. Men, women,
children, old and young, poured into the streets. Gangs perched
on roofs like vultures waiting for something to happen below.
A small parade ensemble made loud music in one block, and
the music carried up and down the avenue. Conga drums,
timbals, cowbells, guitars, gourds, and flutes harmonized
raucously and shook the streets. Even small children were

infected by the strange malady of hate and boredom. They had formed little squadrons, and went about with sticks and toy rifles, pistols and cap guns, firing and ambushing unseen enemies. They often aimed at the targets on the roofs, and they ducked down into the basements or into alleyways behind garbage cans for protection and concealment.

Harold stood across from the bookstore. At the corner was Goodman's Jewelry Store, with its huge multicolored diamond flashing on and off overhead. Harold looked up at it, squinting his eyes. He rubbed his head and leaned back against the wall. Closing his eyes briefly, he wavered on his feet. Then he crossed the street with the green light amidst a crowd of people who moved along like ants on a march. When Harold reached the other side he stood by a fire hydrant and watched the sojourn of the American flag as it moved from the door of the bookstore to the center of a crowd standing around a platform under the diamond.

Elder Dawud was preparing to deliver his evening message to the people. He walked behind a man carrying the flag. Another man was setting up a ladder for the Elder, and every once in a while somebody shouted a greeting at Elder Dawud. The people knew him. He was one of the many sidewalk prophets who—more than once—had indirectly caused the people to react in concert over some issue of concern to Harlemites. He was a short, dark man, about forty years old, but his thinness gave him the appearance of youth. He was clean-shaven, but his hair—thick and woolly on the sides, but balding on top—stuck out from the sides of his head. After carefully cleaning his spectacles, he folded some papers, put them in his small brief case, and handed the case to one of his aides. They stood around the ladder like a cordon. He shook hands with several people, looked at his watch, and mounted the ladder. When the people saw him, a hush flowed over them. The only noise was the whine of the siren

in the distance, the honk and flow of traffic, and the unidentifiable roar that emerged from all of the streets of Harlem.

Harold Kane began to cough. He bent over, holding his
sides, and coughed into the gutter.

"Many of you out there . . . ." began Elder Dawud, his
voice slow and liquid, as if it were being oiled for something.
From his throat came a slight rattle, and it gave the impression of motion and force. " . . . want to know just how is it
that a black man can live in the middle of the richest country
on earth and be starving like a sharecropper. Heh? Many of
you want to know about that. Now, again, many of you
out there . . ." and he paused to smile and point at the people,
". . . and I ought to know because I lived with a lot of you out
there . . ." and there was a slight stir amongst the crowd.

Harold moved in closer. He was shaking.

"Many of you want to know what to tell your children
when they ask you why you let the policeman hit you, heh?
Now, I am not one to advocate anarchy, no. Brothers, I am
the most law-abiding citizen. But I'm talking about conditions that require careful examination; do you hear me?" and
he looked at the people for a long time, then he repeated his
question, looking around the crowd. "Careful examination, a
close look, a breaking of things down into component parts,
eh?"

The crowd roared its approval.

"Many of you think you know a lot about the plight of
our people in this racist society. You think you know, so you
dont try to find out anything new. You are what we call
complacent, satisfied, pacified. But you're still feeling the
boot of the white man. He kicks you *up* wherever he wants
you to go or sit to be his Uncle and to do his Tomming for him,
and when he gets tired of your weakness, he kicks you *down*.
Am I right or wrong?" The crowd roared its approval. "So,
you see, the white man doesnt like an Uncle Tom Negro,

either. Down South he uses the Toms and lynches bad niggers. Am I right or wrong?" "Right!" the people exclaimed. "So dont think you know all things about this situation until you have done a little investigation. How many of you have done some honest investigation, eh? How many of you out there have looked into the inequities of the system? Huh?" There was a small show of hands. "Good. I can see that there are some seekers after the truth out there."

Harold did not raise his hand. He stood staring at the speaker, but his eyes seemed far away.

The speaker went on. He began a long indictment of Negro leaders, then of the white city officials, then of the rich merchants who made their living off of the Negro ghetto, then he castigated the disunity amongst the Negro groups, particularly the interger factions. He called them white-minded, brainwashed, whitewashed Toms. Then he brought his argument back to the point of knowing something more important about the trouble Negroes were having. He brought it back to unity, and the knowledge of the coming future . . .

"Many of you out there are going to participate in Jihad, is that right or wrong?" All hands went up, except Harold's. Many turned and looked at him. Some grumbled and murmured. Harold wavered on his feet. His eyes seemed fixed on some point in the sky directly over the head of Elder Dawud.

Soon after Elder Dawud had asked for more hands on various matters, he began to concentrate a lot of attention in the direction of Harold. Not once had Harold raised his hand.

". . . and just as there are wolves amongst the sheep, there are spies and Toms among you. Why, I can spot them a mile away," and he was looking directly at Harold, "and you mark this, Brothers, they run as straight to the Man as if he were God Almighty, and give our precious plans away. That's why

whenever we plan anything, there's the white press and police there ahead of us, waiting. Now, aint that a shame? The
black man is not the master of his own destiny. I tell you,
you are still slaves! Brothers, I know it as well as you do, so
dont get mad at me for telling you. You've got spies amongst
you. Get rid of them.

"Now, the point of this meeting, Brothers, is to tell you
where you can learn something about yourselves. Without a
knowledge of yourself, you cant go anywhere. Why, you
cant even integrate with the white man right if you dont
know anything about yourself. That's if you want to integrate. Example. Not that I am advocating the program of the
Internigs! No. But just to show you that the lack of self-
knowledge wont help you to even do the *wrong* thing! Here
you have so-called Negroes running around Harlem wearing
bleaching creams and trying to make their hair look like
Marilyn Monroe's. Is that the truth? Dont deny it!" There
were several women and girls in the crowd, which was growing every minute.

"Listen, Brothers and Sisters, the norm by which a people live doesnt change without some kind of action and force
on that norm. The standard you have been taught all your
lives is the blond, blue-eye standard. Am I right or wrong?
This has been a sin and a shame to a nation of twenty million
black children growing up. Children, black as night, walking
around with little blond dolls! It is the joke of nations. Other
countries do not look twice at an American Negro, because
they know he is hooked on trying to be like his conqueror.

"I want you to tell me what is right. You have a nation
of twenty million blacks who childishly think they can erase
their blackness, the blackness that God gave them in honor
of their beauty and strength, trying to bleach it out so that
they can look like Roy Rogers and Dale Evans. To me this is
a shame. What is it to you! It is nothing short of criminal. I

think the people responsible for this crime should be punished ..."

Elder Dawud had worked himself up into a sweat by now; the crowd was with him all the way. He began to point out other things he disliked. The people approved. Harold began to shudder a bit, and his face was wet with sweat and tears.

All of a sudden, a man leaped forward, his fist open and his face contorted. He glared at Elder Dawud. Quickly he was seized by the cordon.

"We hear you, we hear you, we hear you!" he shouted. "When are we going to stop hearing you and the rest? We hear you, Brother, we hear! Tell us what to do! Tell us! I want to do something! I am tired of hearing and listening, I'm tired and tired and tired," and he folded in the arms of two men. They carried him out of the crowd. Elder Dawud continued, seeming not to notice the disturbance. The man quickly stood on his feet and tried to brush the strong black hands away, but they took him inside the bookstore, sat him down, and gave him water.

"We know you," said one of the men.

Harold made his way through the crowd and stood outside the bookstore showcase. They had the man seated on a box.

A crowd began to gather inside the store. Elder Dawud's voice was driving into a high pitch. The rattle was changing into pistons, and he was fanning the hearts of the people as if he was fanning a fire that had gone out in the night.

"Forgive me, Brother," the man blurted, his eyes darting wildly from man to man, "I didnt mean to disturb the Elder, but I want . . ." He suddenly put his hands over his face and began to sob softly. The Brothers had a huddle together amongst themselves and then—as Harold watched from the doorway—took the man, stumbling, behind a great green

curtain that hung at the end of the bookstore. A man stood
beside the curtain as if he were a guard. But he opened the
curtain for them. Then he resumed his pose in front.

Down the street a man had a portable swimming pool
built on the back of a truck. He was charging the kids twenty-
five cents for ten minutes. A loudspeaker sent carnival music
out with the announcement of the swim truck. A man was
loading kids on the truck. There were squeals and shouting.
The man was West Indian. His heavy accent could be heard
all over the block: "Y'all haf de money reddy, now. I tell
you, chil'ren, haf de money in de 'and."

Elder Dawud directed his attention to the swim truck a
block away. "Now, you all familiar with Tango's swim truck,
eh? If you aint, you kids is. Well, Tango is a black man from
the Islands, and he is serving a need of the people. Am I
right or wrong? What would you think of running that good
black man out of business in order to let a few Internigs go to
the white man's pool, eh?

"Let me tell you something, folks, my friends, and this is
what my message is tonight to you all. There is a conspiracy
going on to deprive you black people of everything you dont
have. Did you get what I said? Everything that you dont
have! We're strivin for something now, eh?

"Not integration. No. The poor Negro doesnt have
enough knowledge of himself to integrate right with the
Man. Oh, you think the Man doesnt want you to have his
daughter. Ha! Wake up, men. He'll sacrifice his mother, now.
He can see the writing on the wall. But this poor Negro still
thinks he can be like the Man. Why, the white man would
more quickly integrate with the African than the poor American Negro! Why? Why? Because the Negro is a caste man.
He doesnt know his total self. He functions in a self-imposed
prison, the prison of his narrow vision. He sees himself as the
white man defines him. Whatever the white man calls him,

the Negro agrees; witness this, Brothers: He calls you Sam, you say 'yes, sir'; he calls you nigger, you argue and fight amongst yourselves and wind up cursin each other out by calling each other nigger! Right or wrong? He tries to be respectable and calls you Nigrah or Negro, and you smile and nod. You repeat it. He rules you. He is your maker. He is your god. You are trying to be like him. Whatever you worship, you try to imitate. Negroes worship Jesus, right? They try to be like him. Now, I see Negroes trying to be like the white man, to me it means they think he is God.

"Justice, eh. But I know for a fact there's forces at work to take it away from you." The people murmured. "That's right. Let me break it down for you. Harlem is the only place on the Earth where so many black people live so close together, and yet are ruled, governed, and manipulated by somebody else, namely the white man. The only place on the planet Earth. I dont know about Mars or Venus, because I havent got there yet. They tell me that the white scientists are planning on getting a man to walk around up there soon and bring us back a piece of the land. Well, if things dont straighten out down here on Earth, then when they get up there they're going to find the place already inhabited, and the only way to get through and take the land is walk over the inhabitants of that land. I guarantee you that if the black man cant get justice on the planet Earth, he damn well aint gonna let a blue-eyed whitey run over him in his own new land, eh? What do you say about it, Brothers?" There was a round of applause. "Now what I want to say is, and mind this carefully, the conspiracy is on. But first, the Afro-American population has got to go and find out something. He has got to do some investigation. He has got to go back into his soul, Brothers, and I know you all know what that is. The black man in this country has first got to look deep into his own soul, and then he has got to travel a road back there and

straighten out the mess the white man has made. Do you
understand my meaning? Listen, the black man has got to
clear out the funk in his own soul. Let's face the truth. The
white man has maligned us so much, has stripped us so thor-
oughly, has whitewashed our minds and ambitions that all
we know is what he tells us on his TV and on his radio and at
his movie and in his newspapers (we do have a few black
papers now, thank you, Brothers) and in his school system.
The truth is that the journey is not so easy. It is not easy
because no man knows where to start, or which way to go
when he starts, or the end thereof . . ."

And he paused, looking at Harold for a long time. Some
of the men in the crowd looked Harold up and down. There
was a slight movement and a rumbling. The buildings where
the bookstore was located seemed to echo the sound of
drums and thundering feet. The police siren came nearer,
and across the street two cars collided. Elder Dawud, sweating profusely, stepped up one more peg on the ladder and
seemed to wind himself up, tighter and tighter . . .

"There is one who knows the way . . ." He paused. ". . . I
come in his name and bear witness that he doesnt let a black
man down. He is the One. There is no other whereby you can
be saved. He has told me that the white man is doomed, and
he who follows the evil ways of the white man is likewise
doomed. He has sent us Brothers out amongst you to bring
you the message of the truth, the Black truth. So long you
have heard the white truth. Now you can hear for the first
time the Black truth! He who wants to find out his soul must
have a map. You got to have a guide, Brothers, if you gonna
travel in a region so long uninhabited. The soul of the Negro
is an unexplored territory. The map. The master has the key
of knowledge, and he will show us how to find out the truth
. . . Here is the . . . If you want to learn your way around
Harlem, baby, you got to get to know the people. Is that

right or wrong? If you want to know what the black man is
like, then you got to get to know the black man's soul. If you
want to know what goes on in Harlem, then you got to
understand what goes on in the mind of the black people
who live in Harlem. Is that right or wrong?" And the crowd
applauded him.

Harold Kane continued to listen with hypnotized attention.

"Am I right or wrong! I say you would gain integration
much faster if you stopped trying to imitate the white man
and stand on your own feet and become a man of destiny. A
black man of the world! The white man is intelligent, and
he would respect you for being what God made you. He
wouldnt love you, of course, but he would respect you. Right
now he neither loves nor respects you. But the Internigs dont
know this. They think if they become the exact carbon copy
of their white master, then he will let them in the back door.
Ha! Whoever heard of a carbon copy being of any value as
long as the original is around. Why, it is a shame, running
around trying to be the shadow of another man. Hell, the
white man doesnt care about shadows. He cares about men.
Not flunkies."

A Brother was circulating around the crowd, passing out
a piece of paper. Harold looked anxiously at the man, and
when he came near, Harold reached out and received his
eagerly. But he only glanced at it, frowned, and put it away . . .

"Why, I would be ashamed of myself if I didnt have
something to be proud of. The white man boasts of his wars
and his great civilization. He writes histories and books, and
teaches you to bow down and worship his white Jesus on the
cross, while all the time he has you working for him, and he
is paying you to help make his lifestyle into law. The black
man in this country has got to learn one thing: how to use
the key to his soul, for the soul of the black man is an unex-

plored region . . . Who has the map of Harlem? Listen, Harlem has it. Harlem has it. And I speak in the name of One who wants to see Harlem keep it."

Across the street the police were trying to break up a restless crowd that had gathered at the scene of the car accident. There was a bitter argument with several belligerent men. The cops were trying to disperse the people. But the people all stared at the white cops (politely ignoring the three Negro policemen) with a bitter hatred. They called out, "Butchers!" "Klux Klaners!" "Beasts!" "Devils!" "White dogs!" "Mad murderers!" The police retaliated by swinging billyclubs and cracking a few of the slow people on the legs. A bottle thrown from the crowd struck a policeman on the head. He drew his revolver, staggering with one hand on the ground, and fired into the crowd. A youth clutched his belly in a loud scream. The crowd roared and fell back.

A brick struck one of the police cars.

Across the street, Elder Dawud's crowd joined the melee.

Quickly, word spread that the police had killed a black youth.

The police ordered Elder Dawud to close his meeting. Bottles began to fly. The police riot-squad siren started to wail its eerie whine, and the streets around Harlem Square began to clear and alternately fill up as waves of people fell back and then angrily rushed forward, moblike, pursuing the wind with anything they could get their hands on. The police arrived more and more, and soon arrests were being made . . . Harold had moved a block away, watching the disturbance.

Soon he turned his head and headed uptown, walking close to the wall and looking in at the shops and stores of Harlem, as if he were watching the reflections that moved to and fro in the glass, fading and fleeing like ghosts.

The University
of Man

Tyros, the American, looked up from his watch table one day, spitting away a speck of dust.

"Ah, phff!" he said. "Is there nothing else to do but set the flow of time?" He stared at the dismantled watch in front of him. "There is not much more to be learned about the inside of a watch than I have learned in these twenty years. I am an uneducated man," he concluded. "I am run down, tired of chasing the same speck of dust away, weary of winding myself up each morning, tired of squeezing time into metal boxes."

"What can you do?" his wife asked him that evening.

"Twenty years I have labored in my shop. What I learned years ago I know now. I can do my work in my sleep."

"You are getting senile," his wife said, not willing to admit to herself that a strange malady had affected Tyros.

"*This* I am not sure of," he said, "but now I am sure that I must find out. If I am uneducated, what is to stop me from getting an education? I rebuild old watches every day in my shop."

"An old watch can get a new spring," his wife warned, "but you cannot get another heart or a new set of bones."

"True," said Tyros, "yet even an old watch, when all the dust is removed from its parts, when good oil is lubricating the little wheels, when the worn parts have been readjusted— even an old watch will perform well for a long time," and saying this, he went out to the village to announce his decision.

. . .

After the news had spread, the whole village gathered to say farewell to Tyros. His wife begged him not to go, but the priest, seeing the light in Tyros' eyes and recalling his own years of training, said, "It is the quest for knowledge that is holy, and not the knowledge itself."

The villagers presented Tyros with three gifts. The old judge, who knew the history of the town and the ancestors of most of its inhabitants, handed Tyros a book. On the cover was written *Book of Our Town*. The librarian presented him with another book. It was blank. "Write your education here," she said, "so that we will learn from it when you return." The third gift was given to him by the village musician. It was a finely wrought pen of gold filled with dark-blue ink.

"You must go to the best university," said the judge. "Go to the one farthest east, where I went."

"Go to the one in the South," said the librarian. "I graduated there myself, magna cum laude."

"The University of the North," said the musician. "It is great for every field of education. Go there, Tyros."

"The very best university is in the west," said some of the people. "We have sent our sons and daughters there."

Tyros decided to go to each university to see which one he would like.

"You are all very kind," he said, and he kissed his wife. He got into his automobile and drove away, waving back at them until they were only dots on the hill.

Soon the car began to sputter. He stopped at a gas station in a town and had the tank filled. But no sooner had he gone a half day's journey than the car again had to be filled up at a gas station. In the next three days, Tyros discovered that the car had a strange magnetic attraction for gas stations. If he were going to the University of the East, he had better stop spending money on gas. So far on his journey all he had met were gas-station attendants who wiped his windshield and took his money. The car was no companion at all. He would much rather be alone.

"I want to sell this car," he said to a used-car dealer whose lot was at a large intersection.

"Ah," said the dealer, rubbing his head and squinting at Tyros' old car. "Not worth much, not at all. I'll give you thirty dollars."

"It's worth more than that."

"Thirty-nine," the man said with finality.

Tyros took the offer and was about to leave when the man turned to him and said, "Where are you rushing to, friend?"

"To get an education," Tyros said.

"Perhaps you do need a little, but if you are going without transportation, then you need a friend."

The man began pointing to the big sign that advertised his little lot: HAPPY HOP, FRIENDLY SERVICE, FRIENDLY CARS.

"I have just the little one-owner coupe for you, sir. See her sitting over there. Look at the rubber, go ahead, start her up."

"Why do you try to sell me a car when I just sold you one?" asked Tyros.

"Ah, my friend, you cant resist this little baby." He took out a wad of money. "Look, I'll give you twice what you have if that coupe doesnt run ten times better than your old car."

Tyros began walking away.

"Look, friend, dont be sore. I'll make a real deal with you. You get in that little coupe, drive it round the block, on the highway if you want, take your time, check it out good, and see if a blind man cant drive it."

"I'm not blind," said Tyros.

"Of course you're not, my friend, but you'll need a companion on your journey to get an education, true?"

"Yes."

"Then for just a few dollars more than what you got for your car, you can have that coupe."

"Why are you trying to sell me a car when I just sold you one?" Tyros asked again, walking away.

"A blind man can drive our cars," barked the man.

Tyros approached an intersection. A car came screeching around the corner and struck a bus that was stopped.

Tyros turned and asked the dealer, "Is that one of the blind men driving?"

It was only a minor accident, and Tyros got on the bus and rode to the next town.

A group of young boys were sitting in a park, watching for girls to pass. One laughed at Tyros' suit. Tyros recalled that he had done similar things when he was young. He sat down on a bench a few yards from them. No girls passed, and they began to play and punch among themselves, laughing and watching Tyros out of the corners of their eyes.

"Hey," one shouted, "there she comes!" He pointed at Tyros. They all laughed.

Tyros stood up. "If I were a young girl," he said, "I'd be ashamed to be seen with a bunch of silly boys. Dont you know that by now?"

The young men dropped their heads and tried to regain their confidence and flippancy, but they could not. Soon Tyros had engaged them in conversation and was fixing the wrist watch of one of the boys. They crowded around him and asked him where he was going and other questions.

"I'm an old man, but I want to get an education. I am going to the universities." And after he fixed the watch, which had only been wound too tight, the young men said, "Maybe we will go with you!"

Tyros welcomed them, and they all walked along, very excited. But once out of the park, a group of girls passed on the other side of the street, and the boys ran off. Their confidence had suddenly returned, and it blew their chests out like wind does balloons.

The next town was much larger. A river flowed near it, and there was a bit of industry going on there. He bought a meal at a community recreation center, and after the meal went into the recreation room, where groups of men and young boys were playing pool, checkers, cards, and table tennis. He sat down at the refreshment counter and ordered a fruit drink.

"You play pool?" an unshaven young man asked him.

"No."

"Want to learn?"

Tyros thought to himself, What can I loose? Maybe I stand to learn a new game. "Perhaps I'll try," he said.

Tyros did not know that there was money involved. Before he realized what had happened, he had lost half of the money he had saved for tuition fees. Tyros left the center, but a young-looking boy followed him, and when they were only a few blocks away the lad began to call after Tyros, begging him for directions.

"Sir, I am lost and hungry," he said.

Tyros looked at him. "I saw you back at the center," he said to the lad.

"Oh, yes," the boy readily admitted. "I've been staying there, but they dont want me any more. If you could buy me a sandwich, I would thank you." Tyros looked at the boy and wondered what the boy would have said if he had asked him where he was staying. He knew that he should learn to examine his own apprehensions. Often when he fixed watches, he could just tell what was wrong with it by both the person who wore it and the style and make of the watch. He had learned to follow most of his suspicions about watches; now he would have to do that with people.

"There's a place," said the boy, and led Tyros into a tavern. Before Tyros could object, the boy had ordered a sandwich and beer, was drinking the beer and talking to the bartender.

"How do you serve beer to a boy?" Tyros asked the man.

"Oh, that's little Georgie, he drinks here all the time. And besides, his father is an important man."

The boy ate the sandwich, thanked Tyros, and was about to leave. "Why did you lie to me?" Tyros asked.

"I'm not a boy, you old fart!" And the boy left the tavern, wiping his mouth.

A group of young men came into the bar. They looked like factory hands. They all sat around Tyros and ordered drinks. They were loud and talkative.

"What're you drinking?" the bartender asked Tyros, who was sitting pensively on the stool, thinking about the boy. But before he could tell the bartender that he was not drinking, one of the young men shouted, "Give'em a drink on me. Damnit, my wife just had a baby!"

"Boy or girl?" asked Tyros.

"Girl, but the next one's gonna be a boy!" He passed out cigars, and the rest of the men gathered around him laughing and joking.

The beer sat in front of Tyros. He had had beer several times, but it was always at picnics and holidays and other special occasions. Well, he thought, the birth of a daughter is an occasion. He drank the beer slowly. The bartender watched him.

"Give'em another," shouted the young man. "Drinks on me!"

More beer. Soon Tyros was conversing with the young men.

"We will go with you to get an education!" several of them shouted after many more rounds of beer. Tyros had five full glasses sitting untouched in front of him. They tried to make him drink, but he smiled and said he had to go.

"Wait!" they shouted to the ceiling. "Wait, and we will go with you."

But Tyros paid the bartender and left.

By now he was nearing a very large city. Its buildings leaped up to the sky, and he thought that it had been years since he had seen the city. How it had grown. Large avenues and expressways spun and twisted overhead like a maze of race tracks. The noise stung his ears, and something in the air stung his eyes. He knew this was the place described in the catalogues. The University of the East was near here.

He took a bus along the Avenue of the River. He got out and walked along the river until it broke and turned toward the outer limits of the city. He passed several factories squatting on the banks of the river. Soon the river forked, and the tributary poured into a bay and the ocean. Tyros walked along the river, content to enjoy the strange sights and the crowds of people. Soon he discovered that a canal was hugging the side of the stream, which went into the ocean. They have built a canal, he said to himself. Men have built a river. He stopped and began to watch the silent march of the green fungi floating everywhere in the canal. Much of the city used it as an alimentary canal, whereas the factories dumped much of their wastes into the river. Up ahead Tyros saw policemen and a crowd of people. He walked faster. Beyond this point, way up the river, he could make out several huge buildings nestled comfortably on a wide stretch of land between the river and the canal.

When he reached the crowd he could see that both the policemen—who seemed to be there more as a precautionary measure than anything else—and the crowd of people carrying signs were all watching the solitary figure of a man down below on the land between the river and the canal.

The man was stripped to the waist, and over his shoulders were hooked huge ropes. He bent over, pulling heavy wooden structures through the water. A thin rope was attached to both sides of the bank like some kind of a dredge. The man was moving so slow that it looked like he was standing still, but when Tyros looked closer he could see the muscles in his legs and shoulders bulging. A smaller boat, picks, shovels, nets, and a pile of boards made up a tiny site, yards down the river from where the man was working.

The people buzzed and talked among themselves. Apparently some were against what the man was doing while some favored it. The policemen sat in the patrol wagon with their hats slightly cocked. They would occasionally walk to the slope, look down at the man, smile, and motion the people back. Tyros drew near and watched.

The sun shone bright in the afternoon.

"What is he doing?" Tyros asked a man.

"He's a fool! I represent a council for the city ordinance—"

"He's no fool!" interrupted another man. "There is no state law against fishing in the canal."

"They should lock him up. He's a nut. Dragging the canal for a body or something."

"If there was a body, the police'd know it."

"If this isn't the last month he's out there, I pity him in the winter."

"How long has he been there?"

"Since March."

"Where are the fish?"

"Nobody knows! Ha! He's a fool and we want him locked up."

"He must eat the fish raw!"

Tyros looked up the river and down the river. He saw no more figures on the long stretch of land between the river and the canal. A duck and a gull were the only signs of life. The buildings up ahead leaped high in the evening of shadows as the sun began to fall.

He asked the policemen, "What is the man doing?"

They shrugged, and said that their orders were to maintain order. As long as the man didnt break any laws, then they didnt care what he did.

"But what is he doing?" asked Tyros.

"Look, why ask us? If you want to know, go and ask him."

"What are these people doing, then?" he asked them.

"Look, mister, those people dont know what *anybody* is doing, and if I were you I'd move on."

Tyros went to the edge of the slope. The man was digging at the bank of the canal. A long hill of mud almost hid his movements.

Tyros remembered that whenever he wanted to know the truth about the ailment of a watch, he could seldom rely on the notions of the owner. Usually he had to take the watch apart, or he had to examine it very, very closely, and then he himself could tell what it was. If he wanted to know what the man was doing, perhaps he had better go down. As he went down the slope, he remembered that his wife had warned him, "An old watch can get a new spring, but you cannot get a new heart or a new set of bones."

He walked alongside the canal, watching the man mend a shovel. Tyros didnt know how he was going to introduce himself or get the man's attention, to say nothing of getting across the canal.

"Excuse me, sir," he said clutching in his hands his note-book and pen, "the people at the top of the hill could not tell me what you are doing. I came down to ask you."

The man looked over the mound of mud. For a moment Tyros thought that he was going to smile, but he didnt.

"I'm doing my work," he said in a clear voice. "You are the first person except for the children to come this far down."

Tyros looked upstream toward the buildings. He knew that the university was located near here somewhere.

"What is your work?" he asked the man.

"This river and this canal, as you can see."

"Is that the university up there?"

"What university are you looking for?"

"The University of the East."

"That one has that name."

"Are you working for the university?" asked Tyros, thinking that the man might be doing some type of excava-tions for the university, since he was so near their property.

"I do my work," he said and began digging in a long trench aimed toward the river. He sloshed around in the mud. The water followed him as his shovel dug away at the bank of the canal. "The university I work for has no name."

Tyros was silent for a while. He could not determine exactly what the man was doing. If he continued digging, he would eventually widen the canal until it became a part of the river. But it would take years for one man to do that.

"You are looking for the University of the East?"

"Yes. Have you been there?"

The man nodded.

"You have? Tell me, how are the instructions there? I am going there now." He took out his two books and pen as a sort of visual proof to the man and a source of confidence to himself. "Why do you say that the University of the East has no name? I do not understand."

The man was silent. The sun was resting on the edge of the buildings, as if getting one last look at the world before it plunged into the night below the horizon.

"See how the river flows?"

"Yes," said Tyros.

"Who is it that can name the source of a river?"

Tyros thought a minute. "It is a mystery," he said.

"Then, I do my work that I might gain more understanding of that university that is a mystery."

Up above them the people began to shout and yell. Tyros felt their anger.

"Why do they dislike what you are doing?" he asked.

"People dislike what they do not understand. They do not understand anything that makes them ask questions of themselves. The children used to come and ask questions, and they would help me."

"How long will it take you to finish your work?"

"How long will you spend at the University of the East?" he asked Tyros.

"After I learn all that there is, I will go to the Universities of the West, North, and South."

"Then after going to all the universities of the world, what will you say?"

"I will say, Tyros, you are educated. Go home! Then I will go back to my town."

The man nodded, as if he understood everything Tyros was saying.

"How long did you spend at the University of the East?" Tyros asked him.

Without answering the question directly, the man said, "I learned to ask this question at the university: What have I learned here?"

Tyros reflected. "One gains an education at the university."

"What is 'education'?"

"Knowledge," said Tyros.

"Knowledge of what?"

"Need education be knowledge of a particular thing? Is it not just knowledge?"

Tyros could tell that the man was deep in thought. The people and the policemen were leaving. The evening hung over the river with a strange mixture of lights coming from the blinking neons of the city and the quiet appearance of the first stars. The luminous engagement of the sun and the moon below the sky held the shadows on the water.

"Then what need is there for a university? Can I not gain knowledge here beside the river?"

"That seems true," said Tyros, "but I have spent twenty years repairing and rebuilding watches and clocks, and my knowledge has come to an end. All there is to know, I know."

The man handed Tyros a rusted watch.

"Then you should be able to repair this watch, which was lost in the river and no longer runs. I found it when I dragged the water."

"No," Tyros said, "I would need my tools for this. But the watch is probably finished."

"You are saying that one needs tools in order to utilize knowledge?"

"I would need tools to take it apart and clean it."

"Then what is education?"

Tyros thought for a while. "Perhaps there is more to education than knowledge."

"Is it not true that without tools one's knowledge can become useless?"

"Perhaps it is true."

"Then what does one get at the university?"

Tyros thought again. "Knowledge and how to use it."

"And then after you have gained the knowledge from the Universities of the East, West, North, and South, what will you do?"

"I do not know."

"There is one more university. And the tools of its knowledge are learned all through the flow of one's years."

"What is the name of this university?"

"It has no name. It is a mystery."

"What happens to those who graduate from this university?"

"Very few ever finish . . . The weight of the tool is usually too heavy."

Tyros reflected. "What is the tool? I would like to attend it someday. Where might I find it?"

"If one's own weight is not too heavy a burden, if you can bear to look into the mirror of the river, you are very close to it, then. The greatest tool of education is the soul. The truly educated man is like a giant stylus etching in the sands of the earth. As he walks, words and songs flow behind him."

"Who might be writing with the stylus?" asked Tyros.

"Who can name the source of a river?"

"It is a mystery," said Tyros.

"Who can name the source of a canal?"

"Any man with knowledge of where it begins and ends."

"With the knowledge gained at the university with no

name, one does one's work and there is no end to it. Knowledge flows as time flows.

"This is my work," he said, "this canal and this river." And he went back to digging at the bank of the canal.

Tyros went up the long stretch leading toward the University of the East.

As he moved out of the line of the trees and buildings, he could see the top edge of the sun capping the horizon with an orange arc. He stood and watched.

He knew what he would do from then on. He would go to the university and get the tools of his mind and soul sharpened, and then he would come back to the place on the river and he would help the man. And if the man were gone or dead, then he would gather up all the tools of his soul and he would do the man's work.

Rope of Wind

AINT NO water wave, he thought, that's a baby cat bitin my line. The cork in the water danced against the tiny waves, and the waves moved it toward the shadow of the cypress log that stretched like a cannon out from the bank. He waited. The cork began to sink, slowly . . . He held his breath, balanced himself there on the muddy bank as if waiting for the right moment, and jerked the pole upwards. The line hung in the water for seconds, but carried upwards as the wind caught it. He slung the fish with the wind . . . breathing out . . . *got him*! Becha even Hoodoo Brown cant catch this many fish.

He got another worm, hooked it, and threw his line into the water. Overhead, clouds moved across the sun. Where you hurryin off to, Sky, he thought, and watched as the clouds seemed to dip in over the acres of September cotton, brush the land, and hurry away. We bout need some rain. Papa be glad if it do come a rain. Mr. Westland, too, with all that new land he got.

Watching the cork and the slight movement of the tall cotton and the trees that sat here and there along the road, he thought that if he were a speck of dust in the wind, he could easily sail around and see everything and everybody, and then come back even before he got another bite. Wouldnt he have a lot to tell, and besides nobody would ever know he was there, being a speck of dust on somebody's shoulder. He'd like to ride Hoodoo Brown's shoulder and one day see why Hoodoo told so many lies.

Maybe then he'd get on Jubal's father's shoulder, and Mr. Westland would show him how he made the white men sell him that land. Then he could go and tell his Pa how Mr.

Westland did it, and his Pa would get some land; even
though his Pa was too old now to think bout workin any land.
But that wouldnt stop him. He and Jenkins and Coalnite
would work that land. While crazy Roscoe was off getting
drunk; but then, with him helpin and doin Roscoe's part, and
even Coalnite's sometimes, since Coalnite was married to
Honeysue. And then sometimes when Jenkins was helpin
round the house and all, he, just him, Johnny B, would do
everybody's part, and he'd clear that land, plant it, work it,
and drive off any white suckerhead that come lopin around to
take what a poor nigger aint never had. Yes, he would.
Johnny B do that . . .

      And he slung up another fish.

      A narrow thread leaped up into the sky miles across the
fields and spread out slowly, racing along the edge of the sky
like a string unraveling from a rag. He watched it and noted
that it was somewhere in the vicinity of Hoodoo Brown's
house. Must be John Brown. He the only one got a car go
that fast down here, he thought. What you hurrin for, John
Brown? The sun fell, and seemed to roll along the rim of the
sky like a great ball as the clouds passed . . . in black and
purple, he thought, orange and red, blue and true blue, and
that one looked like violet . . . and he stopped watching the
sun, for the faint glow of headlites lifted over the top of the
cotton. The narrow thread was a rope now, curling in the air,
spinning out from the car like that car was a fat spider running along and making itself a web. Johnny B waited before
rebaiting his hook. Then he climbed the bank to the levee
road, and watched the approaching car.

      It zoomed past him. The dust came in fast. He ran a bit
to avoid it, laughing at his game. He was beating the dust
too. He raced along the levee, looking over his shoulder, not
letting the low loop of the dust reach his neck, and he was
laughing, racing everybody, Hoodoo Brown, Jubal E, Lance,

Naomi, Neppie, and even Carstairs Jackson, who could beat everybody from the churchyard to the creek, or from the Frog Dip to the Stink Place, where all the sinker-eaters lived that only came out at nite, and he was beating everybody too, and he thought that if they started to gain on him, if Carstairs started to gain first, then he would make sure he couldnt go any faster, then he would say a coupla magic words, like he heard ole man Red say that time when Jubal and him went up to see him and that ole man reach out his hand and that old dust turn into a rope in his hand, then he swing out on it and sail . . .

The car was stopping. Johnny B stopped running and leaped down toward the river. He didnt know that car. He thought he shoulda known it, but then he didnt know the car. No tellin who was drivin in it. Especially that fast. Might be white.

He headed back to the first clump of trees just before the area where he was fishing. As he swung, panting, behind a tree, hiding, a cloud of dust fell over him. He coughed slightly, not taking his eyes off the levee.

A man appeared there suddenly. A white man. The man walked along, deliberately, coming toward Johnny B. But Johnny B knew that he didnt see him. The sun was half gone. Everything was a shadow. He wondered what the man wanted. No tellin. If there was any more white men in that car, then the devil only knew what was in their minds. Fish or no fish, he'd better set a pace that no man could follow. He took a deep breath. If he ran, it would have to be daylite or hound-dog nitetime for them to follow him.

He ran. The sun was gone. But he prayed there were no dogs before the river!

Voices! He heard voices.

"You! Boy! Wait a minute!" The man had seen him.

He could tell why. Maybe it was the way the man said

wait a minute, as if he just wanted to talk about something that meant nothing between a black boy and a white man. Johnny B stopped and turned around. He wasnt afraid of the man. He tried to tell himself that he wasnt. He breathed rapidly. The man was still quite a distance away, and he began talking to Johnny B.

"Wait a minute, boy," he said, pausing to see exactly where Johnny B was located beneath the trees. "I'm lookin for somebody . . ." The man stopped. Another man was calling him from over the edge of the levee.

"Come here, boy," the man said softly, as if to set up some bond of communication between himself and Johnny B despite the loud calls of the other man at his back. "Come here. We want to ask you a few questions." He came toward Johnny B.

Johnny B held his breath. He saw how far away the man was, how far he had to run before reaching the river. He knew he could reach the great log before the man, and it was darker now, and it would take a bloodhound to follow him. He didnt like the man. They plannin something, he thought. Something gonna happen . . . and he started panting . . . and it aint gonna happen to me . . .

"I'm gonna run," he said to the man. He was surprised at how calm the words sounded. Maybe he wasnt afraid. "I'm gonna run."

"Dont run, boy, I'm not going to hurt you. My name's Jackson, I'm Asa Jackson's new deputy, beside being his nephew. Now, you . . ."

The other man was coming. "Ask him if he knows 'em, and come on! We aint got all nite!"

"Looky here, boy, where bouts is the house of an old colored man by the name of Eastland? You know, boy? Now, where does he live?"

Johnny B leaped forward and was gone into the nite. It

was like he was thinking. They're after somebody . . . Eastland? Johnny B didnt know him. The man was hollering at
him. Johnny B looked back. He thought he saw one of the
men aiming a gun at him . . . he dropped to the ground, still
running on all fours . . . They aint coming, he thought, they
aint running after me, might send a bullet, dont hear no dogs,
might send a bullet. He slanted in and out, past where his fish
were strung in the water, past his pole in the water, up the
log, bowing his head . . . holding his breath, letting it out,
leaping along the log, feeling the fat trunk sink a bit in the
water, raising arms . . . balancing, bowing down, reaching the
spring-off point at the top of the fallen tree . . . Johnny B held
his breath, and leaped high, high into the sky, like he had
practiced time and time again, until he could clear the distance and land on the bank . . . Only Jubal could do it now
without falling in the water . . . A good jump . . . The men
were coming down near the water . . . He wanted to laugh
out loud. Didnt they know they couldnt catch him, not him,
not Johnny B. If they couldnt bring their hounds, then they
neednt come at all. He stood, panting, then fell on his stomach and listened for them.

"Where'd he go? Ed? Where'd he go to?"

"Come on! Leave the nigger be. Caint you see you
scared him?"

"But where'd he go, goddamnit? Where'd he go?"

Johnny B raised his head off the ground. "Here I am."

"Come on, Zack!" The other man had started to climb
back toward the hill. "That nigger done swimmed the river."

The other man turned, muttering to himself. "Ed, I'll be
damned if I believe a boy like that coulda stroked across . . ."
and he turned and motioned to the wide dark water ". . . in
such a short time."

"Did you hear 'em strokin?"

"Naw. Forget it. Come on."

They went. The car sped off into the darkening sky, and Johnny B broke into a trot, watching the spiraling rope of dust fade into the coming nite.

He wanted to laugh! He breathed hard. God! He wanted to laugh, but he didnt. He kept running . . . Got to get home . . . Why, they might be after Jenkins, or even crazy Roscoe, for somethin or the other. No, he thought, maybe they werent after nobody . . . What you runnin for, he said to himself, and immediately stopped, held his breath, looked back at the sky, saw the fading spiral of dust in the air . . . That car might of been filled with white men, might of been full, and him all alone by the river! Shucks, no tellin what was in their heads, and him just a boy. If he was as big as Jenkins he could fight 'em off, but . . . Then he let his breath go, and raced off . . .

When he reached the road that led to the church, he began to think that he was running for nothin. Those two men just lookin for a way outa—He saw headlites far, far over the fields . . . near the old Yickson farm, and the lites were traveling fast. He knew it was them. Be here in five minutes, he thought, be here in five minutes. Got to get home . . .

He had to pass the Westlands before he got home. He would tell them . . . He thought about Mr. Westland, and wondered if they were after him, but what would white men want with Mr. Westland? He was a preacher now, and was probably at church right at that moment. Johnny B strained to see if he could make out the church thru trees and the dust. He raced on.

Always after somebody, all the time trying to mess with folks. Johnny B frowned and spit. Thas why I stay away from 'em, he said. Just like Papa say.

They just got thru killin Ukie Dodds, cause Ukie talked back too much. Johnny B could remember just like it was yesterday. Ukie had a store, and had to buy most of his stuff from a white man named Olsen. Lot of people say it was Olsen that put the others up to lynchin Ukie, but that didnt matter. Ukie Dodds was found shot fifteen or twenty times on his storefront veranda, and the blood ran all the way out into the yard . . . Johnny B knew, because that's when Lance and Jubal started calling him Johnny B, because when all the people were standing around there at Ukie's place after the funeral and Mrs. Dodds was inside crying and Rev Westland was talkin, some of the kids, mainly him, Lance, Nadine, Jubal, were foolin around outside when Hoodoo Brown came up and said that Johnny was standin in the place where Ukie lay and all his blood soaked into the ground . . . They all looked, and there was a few dark stains still there, but the rain had washed that blood right down into the ground, or maybe some of Ukie's family had come out and covered it over, out of kindness to Ukie, because nobody should die and have their blood layin around on the ground so that everybody's foot could trample in it. Johnny B knew that, because that was in the Bible. And they all looked at it, and a funny feeling came over them. While the older folks were standing around, some talkin about the wrath of God falling upon them wicked white folks for killin poor Ukie, Johnny B was sitting on the porch, wondering how that blood flowed, looking at the porch, seeing those stains, and looking closer until he saw thru the cracks to the ground beneath, saw that blood upon them crossed planks, saw it black and blue, red all gone, but blood, Ukie's blood, and it was him who told Jubal and Jubal come and bent over lookin at it with his big eyes and he said it was red blood and Hoodoo Brown said it was Ukie's blood and everybody said it was Ukie's blood and Johnny B felt kinda proud and sad that he had found Ukie's blood but he didnt tell none of the old folks and Lance told Mr. Westland that Ukie Dodd's blood was under the steps . . .

He ran on . . . The church loomed ahead. It was lit.
Prayer meeting. Mr. Westland be there . . .

The car was still coming.

He ran up the steps of the church. "Rev Westland!" he
shouted. "Some white folks comin in a car."

John Westland raised his head from the Bible. He was
the only one there so far, except for Mrs. Harrison, the old
lady who never missed a prayer meeting or Sunday service.
Then he stood up as Johnny B stumbled down the aisle
toward him. "And they up to something Rev . . . I know."

The man and the boy faced each other. Johnny was
gasping, his eyes fixed first on the older man, who seemed
prepared for all this as if he were expecting the men . . .

"Rev—"

"Son, would you do something for the Rev?"

"Yes, sir."

The older man came to Johnny B, put an arm on his
shoulder briefly, and whispered, "I want you to go home to
my son, and tell him his papa is gone."

A strange calm enveloped Johnny B for seconds. He had
caught a strange look from Mrs. Harrison, and now he was
getting the same look from the Rev. He had no time to think
about it. Maybe they didnt hear me, he thought. "Them
white men is after me," he said. "They was chasing me back
at the creek, and I jumped it . . ."

Johnny B saw that the Rev wasnt really looking at him.
He was looking thru him, out into the churchyard, even beyond that, maybe, further, past everything . . . And Johnny B
was frightened by the look. But somehow it gave him
strength. When he spoke again, he was calm and his words
came easy. Yet inside he was trembling.

"But they after somebody, Mr. Westland, they after—
here that car comin now!" Johnny B was surprised at the

calm in his voice. He moved toward the door, still waiting for the older man to say something.

"Go on, boy, and do like I told you," the man whispered.

Then it hit Johnny B.

They was after Mr. Westland!

He was out the door, squeezing past Mrs. Harrison as she was standing up.

The old woman was silent . . . but Johnny B heard a sound of suppressed moaning and weeping such as he had never heard on the moaning bench, such as he had never heard at revival, such as he had never, never heard. And that look in her eyes before, and the look in Rev Westland's eyes . . .

The car was stopping in front of the church . . .

Johnny B went out the back . . . running. He didnt know why, but he knew he didnt belong there, somehow.

He ran around the side of the church. Two men were walking toward the church. Johnny B ducked and hid behind the oak tree, which stood over the church like a great canopy . . . the tree where Jubal fell and broke his arm that Easter . . . and Lance got whipped by Mr. Westland for telling a lie . . .

Now he could see them. There were two more men in the car. One was getting out and coming around the side of the church. He was walking slow and looking around to see what he could see. Johnny B held his breath. The huge tree could hide him if he wanted it to. Better run, he thought, better run and get to Lance. Tell everybody white men gettin Mr. Westland for somethin . . . But he didnt want to run . . . Spose they shot him, he thought, spose they shot him.

But they wouldnt shoot him, not him, Johnny B. What had he done? He moved from behind the tree. He hadnt done anything. Or had he? He went back in his mind. But he knew it was useless. There never was any reason why a white man wanted to git a nigger. He remembered Ukie, how they had come and shot Ukie, and what had Ukie done? They say that Ukie was always having meetings . . . Even Mr. Westland use to go to them meetings . . . The white folks had come to the church before . . . But Ukie had kept on having meetings, and then they just shot Ukie because Ukie was getting a store, and they say he would buy meat from this here white man that . . . Johnny B grabbed his chest!

A pain shot through him. I'm shot, he thought. They kilt me. But he was holding his breath. He was holding his breath, thinking about Ukie's blood drying up under that porch . . .

And then he saw them. The men. Mr. Westland. They had him. They were pushing him toward the yard. They were laughing. The man who was walking around the side of the church turned around and headed toward the car. They all got in. The door slammed. And Mr. Westland was sitting between them. It was all very calm. Too calm. And Johnny B began to shiver.

He ran to the edge of the road. The red lites of the car bounced behind a film of dust that leaped up. Johnny B looked, and then he knew that something about the car had reminded him of a spider. And the spider was coming to get Mr. Westland, when all the time he thought it was after him.

Mrs. Harrison came out of the church.

She was mumbling, ". . . The Lord will repay, He will repay. Yes, He will, yes, He will . . ."

She looked over at Johnny B when he moved out from the shadow of the tree hanging out into the road.

"Go git Deacon Hines," she said to him. "Run tell Mrs. Westland and Deacon Hines. Go tell, boy. I'm just a poor old lady. Cant run," and she began to sing softly.

Johnny B didnt know what to do. Tears were gathering in the old lady's face, but her voice was stern and deliberate. He glanced up the road at the car and then at her again. She was leaning against the church steps. "I'll make it," she whispered. "I'll make it."

And car lites danced like two red eyes. Johnny B reached out to touch them, to bring that car back, to snatch Mr. Westland from that back seat, but he only choked on his own sob. Then it all dawned on him. They were going to do him just like they did Ukie. That was Ukie in that car. That was Ukie. And them red lites, those red balls jumping in the back of the car, they were Ukie's blood. Johnny B took a few running steps after the car. He had to see that car. Mr. Westland was going to get kilt like Ukie.

He ran some more, stopped, ran, stared after the car, ran again, and then kept on . . .

As long as he could keep the car in sight. As long as Ukie's blood was there, he could follow that car. He could follow it. He heard somebody calling him. Sounded like Hoodoo Brown. He did not turn around. The two red eyes were growing smaller, and he had to keep them in sight. Behind him they were calling him. The people were gathering at the church and on the road. And they were calling him. He kept running, and the road dipped and headed north. The red lites were fading. And he felt his chest paining . . . He stumbled. And when he looked again, he could not see the red lites. A strange sob gathered in his chest. He wanted to cry. He fell in the road. They got Mr. Westland and they gonna kill him. I know it, he said. I know. I can see Ukie's blood again. Them white men gonna kill Mr. Westland for nothing, just like they did Ukie, just like they woulda did to me if I hadnt run and got away. He held the sob deep in his chest. It rolled around like a giant ball, rolled against his sides, his heart, and his stomach, doubling him over in the road, making him stumble and moan. He held the sob deep

inside him. It would not come, but the tears did. He couldnt
hold them back.

So he ran and he ran and he ran, and suddenly he came
to the Yickson cutoff in the road. He saw the moon ahead of
him, sitting above the horizon and looking at all that was
going on. He wondered if the moon knew which way that car
had taken Mr. Westland. He looked at the moon. A thin
cloud of dust was coming at the western edge of it. He took
the fork to his left. He wished Lance and Jubal were with
him. It was their father and they would never let nothing
happen. He knew that. But the moon was his witness. The
moon was his witness. It was up to him to follow that car. His
chest was burning and his limbs felt heavy. The dust seemed
to clog the air now, and a wind was blowing across the fields.

How could he ever tell them how he saw them come and
take Mr. Westland away? He had to follow that car. If he
could just ease up on it now, and he looked thru the stream of
tears and the road was dark.

But he kept on. And the moon was his witness.

Time spun in Johnny B's head as a dizziness closed in on
him. He increased his pace when he thought he saw the red
eyes looking back at him miles ahead, but it was only the
pain of blinking and the heaviness in his chest. His heart
pounded louder and louder.

He should stop and rest, he thought. Gain some strength
and then go on, then maybe he could draw in closer to them.
He knew they wouldnt go thru town, but town was fifteen
miles, and he had only just started running.

He thought about his pockets. What did he have in them
to help Mr. Westland when he caught up with the car? When
he faced them, what would he do? He'd have to watch them,
and if he saw that they were going to hurt Mr. Westland,
then he'd have to do something. He'd . . .

He felt in his pocket, and the matches felt wet against

his thigh. I got matches, he thought, I got matches! And he stumbled in a ditch, never went down, heaving and swinging himself up, and ran on . . .

Then he saw them again, the lites, the red eyes. But they looked like tiny specks of blood far in the distance. He knew he had taken the right turn-off. The moon was his witness. The moon wasnt gonna let them get Mr. Westland.

A wave of dizziness closed in on Johnny B and lashed him to the ground. He lay there in a heap, breathing out of every opening in his body, gasping, holding his stomach . . . Thoughts hovered over the air of confusion in his brain, hovered and then fell upon him, bringing him quickly to his feet and tracking along the rutted road in the nite. Lance aint here. Jubal aint here. It's only you, Johnny B, you and the moon is your witness. And so he ran on and on into the nite chasing a vanishing pair of red eyes . . .

And the car appeared and reappeared like some phantom teasing him, and soon his mind lost track of time and his body became fixed, rigid, in step with some ultimate purpose that he had ordained for himself—indeed, that had been foreordained for him. Johnny B was to be the messenger of the blood. The spirit surviving in each generation and appearing in the young. He ran on, and the lites of the town shone ahead of him. He forgot about who he was. Everything passed out of his mind except the vision of the red eyes in front of him. What was he running for? He forgot, because his chest was bursting and his mind was spinning and his legs were falling off and he had no arms, no tongue, for it was beaten off by the wind, and his eyes were swollen, and every now and then a twist of wind would crash against his face and a stream of water would leap from his eyes. What were the tears for, or were they just tears of joy?

Once again the car turned off, but this time it drove to an abandoned farmhouse, parked . . .

The men sat there for a minute. Mr. Westland, his long face poised and fixed, stared straight ahead. They had been asking him questions.

"Listen, old man, you think you're smart, dont you?"

"We know who you is . . . Thought you could git away, eh? You black bastard!"

Somebody struck him. The blow sent his head thudding back against the rear of the car seat, and before he could straighten up, the fat man next to him was dragging him out.

"They make 'em all kinds," said one of the men.

"Yeah, but this nigger gonna talk if I have to cut each word out 'em with this here poke iron," and they led Mr. Westland to a clearing beside the barn.

"Listen, old nigger, you got five minutes to live."

Mr. Westland never opened his mouth.

"Wait, Mule, this nigger's different. Caint you see that? Let me handle him."

The moon had risen. It shone clear and round. It was rising higher. The fields and the town miles off began to sparkle under its glow.

"All we want to know is one thing, old man. Did you once live in Mississippi, in Crucible, Mississippi, and did you kill a white man? Did you? Now, aint that nice of me to ask you like that, aint that nice that I didnt call you nigger and slap your face and kick your ass, now, aint it . . ."

Mr. Westland never said a word.

And the other man swung a fist and knocked Mr. Westland in the mouth and he fell backward . . .

"Answer me, nigger! Aint your name Eastland? Aint you killed a white man, aint you the nigger that sneaked up behind my father and shot him, aint it the truth? Cause if it aint, you'd better start talkin."

And Johnny B fell in the grass, panting like an enraged

animal. He saw it all with his eyes, thru the grass, laying on his side, holding his stomach, and feeling his chest explode . . .

They were gonna string him up. Johnny B could see the others tying him. They were gonna kill him.

Then Johnny B saw Mr. Westland open his mouth, and his eyes had that same look they did in the church, the same look that Mrs. Harrison had . . .

And he spoke: "Since when does it matter to white men bent on murder who they murder? It doesnt matter to you who I am. Yes, my name is Eastland, a pity I ever changed it. Yes, I am called by my father's name, John, the man from the East . . . and if—"

They didnt let him finish. His speech was too much like an attack, and no black man attacks a white man and lives.

They fell upon him like wild men. With sticks, rocks. They put him in a large white cotton sack, they tied the sack to the bumper of the car.

They shot the sack, once, twice . . .

Johnny B counted them . . . five six seven times . . . and the silence of the nite gathered in upon his sobs. The red-eyed spider rode beneath the moon . . . spinning a web of madness . . . and round his neck Johnny B felt a ring, a ring of sweat and blood . . .

He wept beside the blood of Mr. Westland and the moon was his witness and all the days of his life swam across his mind like a legion of soldiers and he swore by the moon and by the nite to overtake that car and to cut Mr. Westland free with his knife . . .

His heart was hurting, but he ran . . .

The men drove the car in and thru the town, around and back, and were coming toward Johnny B again. He fell into the road and waited for them to pass. But they stopped at a house. Todd Henson used to live there. Todd Henson sent all his kids north and stayed on down in Arkansas to work and die. He worked a lot and then died and left the house to the ghost and the land. And both inhabited it.

The moon was high. It was getting late.

Johnny B was a long way from home now, maybe ten miles, maybe more. He approached the house at a slow, even trot, his head cocked to one side, his tongue laying flat against the bottom of his mouth to let in the most air, his eyes staring at the place where the headlites went off and house-lites made a shadow to the car . . .

He could hear them laughing. They were drunk. When he got to the house the windows were all barred. He saw Mr. Westland in the sack, still tied to the car. He fell down, shocked, to his knees, crawled toward the house, got up and ran to the sack, and slit it open.

The blood flowed all over him, and he could tell that Mr. Westland was dead, and his tears fell into the blood, and he wanted to be with Mr. Westland, for when he told Lance and Jubal what had happened, then they would all want to die, just like him. He filled the sack with weeds and rock, and every time he heard them laughing inside, he stumbled, fell to the ground, and stopped what he was doing. He hid the body in the weeds. He remembered the license plate . . . and just before he broke into the road again, he saw that the moon was still his witness.

He ran. As if he were making a river, he ran. As if behind him flowed a river of blood and tears, he ran, slow, like a phantom in the nite, black Johnny B, the running spirit, breaking the silence of the nite with his breathing, the only sound that kept his feet pounding the road, running, running, and running . . .

He would tell them just where the men were. But he knew that if he did, Lance would want to kill them, and the whole town would have to either move or declare war. Lance was crazy, but what could anybody do in a case like that? It was his own father that they killed. And he, Johnny B, saw it, and they would want to kill him for not stopping them. And they should, for he could have, or how . . .

He ran.

They saw him coming at dawn.

They saw human spirit coming out of the past.

They saw their own souls age before their eyes. Johnny B came like a ghost, wavering in the road, stumbling and falling.

Lance ran from the house, leaping over the dogs in the yard. Jubal was close behind. Hoodoo Brown and Coalnite ran as far as the gate and trotted from then on. Mrs. Harrison came out of the house and managed to get into the yard. And by the time Lance had scooped Johnny B up in his arms and was bringing him down the road, the yard was filled, the house was emptied, and an electric tremor seemed to spread throughout the neighborhood as kids darted up and back with news—Johnny B was comin, Johnny B was comin!

They laid him in the spot over which Ukie's blood had flown. They laid him on the porch in the morning.

He opened his eyes, stared fixedly at them all . . .

"Where you been, Johnny B?" asked Lance, with his lips touching the boy's ears.

Johnny B looked at Jubal, who knelt beside him. He looked at them all. They were waiting to hear him, just like they waited to hear Reverend Westland preach . . . they were waiting on him, and so he would tell them . . .

"Mr. Westland told me to come get you . . . I . . . follow them . . . they got him . . . go to Todd's old farm . . . I follow him . . . they . . . I cut him outa that sack . . ."

And the blood burst out of his mouth . . .

And they covered him, lest the flies pollute his blood.

Devil Bird

I THINK it was Satan the Devil who came first. I was sitting just inside my grandfather's room, reading a comic-book story of David and Goliath. My father heard the knock at the door and let him in. My father must have been expecting someone, because he didn't ask who it was. I heard the door open, heard a scuffling, and felt a rush of hot air. When I looked up from the comic book, I looked into the eyes of a very tall man. He wore bright carnival-looking clothing that shone iridescently. He paused at the door of my grandfather's room, and a shadow fell across my knees, extending to the edge of the bed. My grandfather, who had been quiet all day and who seldom moved, suddenly sat upright, his eyes popping and his thin chest heaving. His groan filled the whole house.

Then the Devil—I am sure it was him now, because of the things that happened afterward—bowed slowly, almost imperceptibly. In his gloved hands he carried a tapering rod shaped at the smaller end like a key. As he passed by the door, his eyes rested on me, and I think I heard him chuckle. At the same time, my mother, who had heard the scream of my grandfather, rushed past the visitor and entered the room. I had stood up, unable to do or say anything. My father followed the visitor into the front room, which we called the Game Room, and there they began to examine carefully our family Game Book.

My mother and I tended to my grandfather. It must have been the sudden rush of air that choked off his breath. Soon he was resting as before. His eyes were half closed and he lay still, making only little grumbling noises now and then, which I had learned—after listening to my father and mother discussing Grandfather's activities in his younger days—were fusses and fights he had had with his deacons. My grandfather was a famous Negro minister in his day, and there were many who were jealous of his closeness with God and his influence as a Christian.

My mother gave my grandfather some medicine and sent me out of the room. Then she turned out the light and tiptoed out.

We were all in the Game Room now. I sat in the corner, watching the tall visitor thumb through the Book. Every now and then he would pause and look up at my father, who would study the page and shake his head. My father called my mother to his side, and they examined the pages together. After looking through half the Book, the visitor closed it and took out a long, narrow cigarette. He touched the end of the cigarette with the key, and instantly flames sprang up. The smoke smelled like burning weeds.

Soon there was another knock at the door, and my mother got up. She asked, "Who is it?" There seemed to be no answer.

"Who is it?" she asked, louder.

There came a voice: "I am here."

My father stood up, and the visitor, laying the lighted cigarette across the Book, also stood up.

"That is my partner," said the visitor.

"Your partner?" asked my father.

"Yes, oh, yes. Didn't you know?"

"Well . . ."

"You were expecting someone else?"

"Well, according to the Game Book, we . . . are partners . . ."

The visitor laughed. "You *are* a partner," he said. "Are you like the old man in there, who thinks a god is his partner?"

"Let him in, Grace," my father finally said.

I looked at the Devil. He was smiling. He pranced around the room now, and his footsteps shook the floor. I don't know what got into me, but I got mad at him. I could feel my comic book tearing under the pressure of my hands.

"My father doesn't want anybody to put their cigarettes on the Book," I suddenly said to the visitor.

He faced me and blew a smoke ring. I pointed at his smoking cigarette. "And besides, it stinks, and Grandfather is sick."

He looked quizzically at me and pranced about heavily. But when I fetched an ashtray from the Game Room supply closet and placed it on the table where the Book always rested, I noticed the cigarette was out and the visitor was waving the key rod around as if he were writing in the air. He then smiled at me, bowed, and continued marching around, stepping so loud I thought the walls would fall and the floor would give way.

Then entering the room was another tall man. He was dressed shabbily, as if he had been in an accident or a fight. His eyes were dreary and his head bent over. He came in, my mother following closely behind him. He sat down at the table and began looking through the Book. In the sick room my grandfather moaned. My father and mother came over to me now, and I could tell that they didn't know exactly what to do.

When the second visitor had finished looking through the Book, he looked at my father and said, "Do you have any good cards?"

"I don't know," my father said, going over to the supply closet. "What about these?"

"The Book says a game of cards," said the second visitor, "and may the good man and woman of the house accept their hands."

The Devil began to clap his hands and dance around the room. He grabbed God by the shoulders and hugged him, calling him "Partner! Partner!"

Every time Satan the Devil touched God's shoulder with his long gloved fingers there was a sizzling sound. A cool wind was blowing the smoke out of the room. Suddenly a light came on in my grandfather's room. My mother hurried to the room. I could see my grandfather's thin arms wavering across the sheet, as he was trying to reach and pull it over his frail body.

"The Book is right," said the Devil. He prepared the table for a game, ushering my father around as if he was a child. I didn't like the way he did things, but then, a person isn't supposed to like the Devil. It doesn't matter whether or not he really is the Devil, or whether he does good or bad things. If he looks like what you think the Devil is supposed to look like and if he acts like the Devil, then you are supposed to fear him and hate him.

Soon God Almighty and Satan the Devil were sitting opposite each other at the card table. They were partners. My father was sitting opposite the vacant chair. Our family played cards often. I had seen my father and uncles, aunts, and relatives play late into the night, often sending me to bed before the games were finished. There was something about the way they played that made me stand for hours, watching the plays and the expressions on their faces. They played as if everything counted on the game. Sometimes I believed it did. When I played with my friends, I found myself putting on the same expressions and acting with the same intensity, whatever the game was. I went to the table. God was still studying the Book. My father had his head in his hands. When he heard me climbing into the chair, he looked up.

"Little fellow, that's not your seat."

"But who's gonna play with you?"

He looked at God, fumbled with the Book, and cleared his throat as my mother turned out the light in Grandpa's room.

"But I want to play," I said.

"I know, son, but when Mother comes you'll have to get up."

"Why?" I asked. "She's taking care of Grandpa."

The Devil, reaching out for the ashtray, looked at my father and said, "Do you want to play or forfeit?"

"Let him choose," said God. "Let him make sure he wants to do what he does." He looked at my father. "I will allow you another chance."

My father began to shiver. I wanted to help him. Here were God and Satan, playing against him. It was against everything I had learned in Sunday School. I got mad at both God and the Devil, but I felt ashamed and tried to keep quiet. I was waist high to my father then, and I wasn't supposed to know as much as he did. Yet I remember everything that happened as if it were only yesterday.

Father thumbed nervously through the Book.

"There are some mistakes," he began, "because, according to the Game Book—"

The Devil cut him off. "Is it not true that he is your father and that for twenty years he was the spiritual leader of ten thousand Negro Christians from all over this nation?"

"Moreover," added God, "you and she have played the game of cards. You know the game, and it would be unfair for us to use another method. Am I not true?"

I heard my father whisper "Yes" under his breath. He withdrew his hand from the Book and watched as my mother took the seat opposite him.

"And so," said God, suddenly seizing the deck of cards. After shuffling them deftly three times, he handed them to the Devil, who looked them over and asked, "Why are you giving them to me?" Still holding them, God reached and touched the extended edge of the key rod to the deck, and immediately there was a flash. Then God shoved the cards in front of my father and said, "You shall deal your hand."

It is the rule in whist that the opponent to the right of the dealer shall cut the cards. My father, forgetting this rule —although he was an expert whist player—began to deal out the cards. As soon as my father had given God and my mother their first cards, the Devil held up his hands. "Halt."

"What is wrong?" asked my mother.

"The Book says that I have to cut the cards."

My father looked dumbfounded. He knew the rules, and he dropped the cards on the table and prepared to reshuffle them.

"No, no," said God. "Let him cut as they stand. You will learn that you get no second chances in this game. Mistakes are costly."

The Devil cut the cards, and I am sure that the cards he got from then on were better than the ones he was going to get, for I could see his hand from where I stood and it was a very good one.

"But the Game Book doesn't say you can cut after the cards have been dealt," protested my mother. She was angry.

Then God and Satan the Devil put their heads together, whispering and thumbing on the table as if they were in deep concentration.

From Grandpa's room came a stirring about and a series of grunts.

The Devil took out his key rod and waved it. He touched the Book with it several times, pointed it around the room. When he pointed it toward my father's clothes closet, the door opened and a hat fell out. Before anyone could react to this, the Devil jumped up and seized the hat, putting it on and stomping around the room, growling and fuming as if he were the meanest Devil in hell. While he was doing this, God was thumbing through the Book, making funny marks in the Book with his right finger.

Then the game resumed, and when my mother brought up the same protest, she was allowed to examine the Book to find the rule she was quoting. While she searched, God toyed with the hat the Devil had been wearing, twirling it around and around in his right hand.

When my mother found the rule she read it:

Upon the failure of opponent to cut cards before the commencement of dealing, the opponent shall halt the dealer and perform the ritual of cutting as prescribed without the reshuffling of dealt cards.

When she finished reading she gasped, for obviously the rule was different.

"He did something to it!" I said, pointing at God. "He did something to it!"

"Now, now, young man," the Devil said to me, "when your turn comes to play a game of cards with us, I hope you have learned the rules yourself." He smiled and turned his back on me.

My father frowned at me.

Mother looked at her cards now in wonder and fear. My father dealt out the entire deck.

"Love," said God, "is the ultimate rule. If you love the game, there is no rule."

"The Book speaks in many languages," said the Devil. "A lifetime can be spent in the worthwhile pursuit of the wisdom of the Book. There are special situations with no rules, and special rules for no situations."

The game progressed. I could not tell who was winning, but the Devil and God had two private conversations. My

parents looked at each other rarely and kept their heads
down. On each hand they looked at their cards with less and
less enthusiasm. And I guess I can say that since they had no
enthusiasm in the very beginning, their faces were vacant
and without hope. I was not only sad, but scared. I had never
heard of folks playing a game with God and the Devil.

Then the two visitors seemed to get into some kind of an
argument. They were on their third private conversation in
the corner by the supply closet when their voices grew loud
and vexed.

"Let the father," screamed the Devil.

"Let the son," persuaded God.

"And what about the other?"

"She will come in time."

"No."

"I want them all. Did we not make an agreement when
he arose?"

"That was for their sakes. Even he knew that. How many
more races do you think we can afford to the Promised
Land?"

"Ask him if he really loves her."

"Let the son do it."

"Why should we tarry over this issue? Did not Jesus
prove they cannot live without grace and there would be no
grace unless he died?"

"Then we will take him?"

"It is written. He served his purpose. His love shall justify their hate. He has overstayed."

They went on like that for some time. I sat down with
another comic book, because I had begun to believe that the
visitors were imposters. But all that changed soon enough.

Suddenly from the sick room my grandfather appeared,
standing in front of the table like a ghost. He heaved and
wavered, a stack of bones held together by withered black

skin. He had wrapped a sheet around himself, and under his arm he carried a replica of the Book.

"Blasphemy! The smell of blasphemy is abominable. In my own house my children curse me and Jesus."

"So," the Devil said, turning to my grandpa and smiling at him, "Uncle has arrived and can speak for himself."

"Let him speak," said God.

My grandfather seemed not to see them. He directed his whole attention to my parents and me.

"You allow this young one to learn the vocabulary of evil. For twelve years I have pastored this flock, and never have I heard anyone blaspheme against the Holy Ghost! God is no respecter of persons, and His love is free to Negroes as well as whites. When we get to heaven there won't be any racial trouble, because those risen in Christ are free of the flesh."

While he preached the Devil motioned to God. They both tiptoed out of the room and then turned shortly. At first I didn't notice anything, but when they took their regular seats I noticed something peculiar. The Devil was twirling the hat with his left hand and God, smiling wryly at my grandfather, examined the key rod. There was no mistake. They had changed clothes.

Soon my grandfather was down on his knees, witnessing and beseeching God and Jesus to save the souls of all the Negro Christians who had gone astray. My mother was down on her knees, trying to get him back into bed. But he was wild. My father sat in his chair, his head in his hands, shuddering. I thought he might be crying. I hoped not.

Then the Devil cracked the key rod on the table. When he did that, a long-beaked bird that cawed like a crow flew from the hat God was twirling. It flapped around and left droppings on the Book. Finally it balanced itself on the shoulders of my grandfather and began to bow, repeatedly, at

its audience. I hated that bird. It was funny, but the moment
I saw it I disliked it and what it was doing. It was bad
enough for Grandfather to be wallowing on the floor, but to
see the bird make fun of us was too much.

"How beautiful is the dove of peace," smiled Satan.

The next thing I knew, my grandfather was sitting on
the chair opposite my father, and my mother was trying to
get him to rest. Then they began another game.

This time, after my father cut, God dealt. The Devil lit
up a stinking weed, and the smoke began to fill the Game
Room.

My grandfather tried to hold his cards, pleading with
God to forgive him.

"Lord, forgive Thy servant. My daughter has just informed me that you are here. Lord, Lord . . ."

No one spoke. Several times the Devil made quick, angry
motions with his hands, pointing to the center of the table for
my grandfather to play his card and stop running his mouth.
The game was on, and that was all there was to it. You play
the game or you get out of the seat. I knew that much about
it myself. My father was getting restless.

The smoke got thicker, and all that could be heard in the
room was the whining of my grandfather and the cawing of
the silly bird. It was flying all around the place now. Once it
tried to light on me, and I slapped it all the way across the
room. I watched the table. I was planning on getting a hold
of the Devil's key rod, and if that bird came again, I was
going to set it afire.

The game went on. "Please, forgive Thy humble black
servant, Lord, for sin did lurk in the innermost parts of his
soul, but Lord Jesus, with Thy cleansing power he shall be
washed white as snow . . ."

Somebody's voice came through the smoke—"He is not
here, Reverend."

My mother coughed and went out of the room. I couldn't see anything except that silly bird flying around the room. I looked for the key rod that God had been playing with. The bird cackled and screeched, as if it were making fun of my grandfather. And even if my grandfather did sound a little crazy then, I didn't like any silly crow making fun of him.

The smoke got really thick. My grandfather coughed every time he said two or three words. Nobody was talking except him and that bird. Every now and then I could hear the two visitors snorting. I couldn't tell whether they were laughing or emphasizing some point in the game. I could hear the cards hit the table. My father wasn't saying anything. I rolled up my comic book as tight as I could so I could hit that bird if he tried to settle on my head again, and I eased my way toward the game table.

"Lord . . . aggh . . . if I had only . . . aggh . . . known You were coming . . ." My grandfather's thin shadow showed itself through the smoke. When I eased a bit closer, I saw the craziest thing. That bird was hopping around on the table. My grandfather's head was bowed. He was on his knees, holding onto the edge of the table with his hands.

"Lord God, I have been Your servant nigh unto seventy-five years. Why are Your ways still mysterious to me, Lord? I fast. I pray, Lord. But I must still have a little sin lurking somewhere. Your will be done."

He kept on like that. And all the time he was talking, I could hear the game going on. I saw the cards hit the table, WHACK!

"What have I done, Lord? What have I done? At least I thought that my onliest son here would deserve Your blessings?"

The cards were hitting the table more now, WHACK! The smoke got thicker. And I came right up to the edge of the table.

Then I saw what **was** going on. My father was leaning over his hand, shaking. I got scared just looking at him. He was playing cards out of his hand. The Devil was playing cards from his own hand. God was playing cards from his own hand. But that crow bird was playing from my grandfather's hand, which was face down on the table. He was kicking the card into the center of the table with his beak and then on the next play, he'd use one of his feet. He was showing off and strutting about. I raised the comic book to knock him off.

"Boy! What you doing?" It was my father.

"Look at that bird! He's messing up Grandfather's cards! Grandfather! Grandfather!" I yelled.

Before I could say anything, one of the visitors said something to me through the smoke. I couldn't see their faces any more.

"It's all right. It's part of the game. All you have to do is to be careful when we come back again."

I didn't hear them. I was furious. I called my mother, and I could feel tears swelling up. It wasn't fair. I called to Grandfather, who was still talking. Suddenly he seemed to get angry at me, at Father, at everybody except that bird and the visitors.

"Blasphemy! In the House of God! I won't stand for it, Lord! I have told them. I have told my son and my daughter ... these children. They have strayed, Lord. Forgive me, Lord. I waited so long for You to be my partner, Lord. We are partners, aren't we, Lord Jesus? We are partners, aren't we? Ask me, Lord. Command me. I want to be in Your name ..."

I shook Grandfather and told him that my father was his partner, and that he should play. "Please, Grandfather." But they laughed at me.

It was funny, listening to them laugh. It sounded far away. Then I could hear my grandfather moaning. The

smoke got in my eyes, and all I could hear was my grandfather asking God to change places with my father. He tried
to make everybody change places so he and God could be
partners. And when this happened, I felt a hot rush of air,
then a cold one. Then the smoke cleared.

I saw the Book, burnt, and the key rod lying there—
which I quickly snatched—and I saw the visitors leading
Grandfather away past his room. They looked over their
shoulders at all of us, and just before they went out, one of
them said, "I'll be back."

We sat tight, but nobody ever came back.

I think it was Satan the Devil who said it, but I'm not
sure.

I had a lot of fun chasing that bird around the house,
trying to set his tail afire with that key rod. Finally I caught
up with him, and just before I set him afire he cawed,

> To profit by what is heard,
> You must remember that
> I am a prophet,
> And not a bird.

I didn't pay any attention to it. I jabbed him, and when I
did he burst into a stinking smoke.

My father took the key rod out of my hand, and I think
he was getting ready to say something to me, but we heard it
again:

> To profit by what is heard,
> You must remember that
> I am a prophet,
> And not a bird.

I have been trying to figure it out since. Whose voice did
that bird's sound like?

The Distributors

"W<small>E START</small> at eight sharp," the foreman said to me, "but you and your friend be here at seven-thirty tomorrow so we can sign you up." We shook hands and I left.

A job at last. Kenny and I had spent the last three weeks looking. I found a phone in the corner restaurant to call him. He would be excited, even though it was only construction work. We had both wanted to spend the summer in the sun. School had drained all the blood out of us, anyway.

The line was busy, so I ordered a cup of coffee and sat down near the phone. Halfway through the cup I called again. Still busy. He must be calling ads in the paper, I thought.

A neatly dressed woman came into the restaurant. She and the waitress began talking.

". . . and it's saved me so much work. Honest, Sue, I just dont know what to do with all my time."

"Where's your father-in-law?" asked the waitress.

"It's amazing, Sue. That's taken care of too. And maybe he's better off. Even the baby rests good now." And she whispered in the waitress's ear: "They call it acceleration or something."

"Well, what's Fred think?"

"Oh, he's too crazy about the automatic memory cells to worry about that. You know it tells you everything you were thinking all day!"

"Yeah," said the waitress, "I've heard about it, but we cant pay for one right now."

"They're cheap," whispered the other woman.

"How much did you pay?"

"They have a special credit plan, and you dont have to pay unless you like it."

As I dialed Kenny's again I wondered what it was they were talking about. The line was still busy. I decided to take a bus, because Kenny might be talking to Edna and on the phone a long time.

Mrs. Waspold came to the door.

"Hello, Carl," she said. "Kenneth is on the phone."

I knew he would be. I told her about the job possibility and that the foreman had said he could use two men for the summer. "Well," she said, "I dont think Kenny will like it. They just called him up for a job a little while ago."

I sat down in the living room, wondering who Kenny was talking to. From the kitchen Mrs. Waspold stirred about. A pot dropped and she became irritated. As I sat there I could hear a heavy wheezing coming from old Mr. Waspold's room. Kenny's grandfather was very sick and helpless. The chortling of his chest sounded like the dying sputters of an engine.

Just then Kenny came into the room.

"Hey, Carl, listen! Great news! How would you like to be a representative for American Dynamisms Incorporated?"

"What're you talking about?" I asked. His enthusiasm had taken me by surprise. He moved like a guy rushing to catch a train.

"Come on," he said, running to the door. "I'll tell you all about it on the way."

He got the keys to the family car. "Mother, if Edna calls tell her I'll be by to see her after the interview."

I followed Kenny out. We were halfway across town before he could settle down.

"Listen," he said. "Carl, baby, we're in!" We stopped for a red light, and among the people crossing was the same woman from the restaurant.

"I got both of us interviews."

"Doing what?" I asked.

"Well, I dont know exactly . . . using our college training," he told me. I talked with a Mr. Mortishan, and he promised us jobs making over a hundred dollars a week to start. Man, oh, man!"

"How certain is this, because I've already made arrangements for us to start at the construction company down Canal Road."

"Forget it, Carl. We're in. Mr. Mortishan said for us to come down immediately, and he'd sign us up for the whole summer. With raises!"

"Sounds too good to be true," I said. "But I'd like to know a little more about it."

"Well, what's the difference what we do? If we can make that much money starting out—"

"Wait," I interrupted. "Suppose we get hooked doing something we dont want?"

"Dont be silly. This is a big outfit."

"Who was the guy you talked to, and why cant we know what kind of a job we're being considered for?"

"Listen, Carl, I talked to the guy. He sounded okay to me. I'm not going to tell them how to run their business."

"Yeah," I said, "but I'd like to know what's the job."

Kenny became defensive. Ever since taking that course called "The Sociology of Management," he seemed to be tolerating me. Once he said that the course I was taking was totally useless.

"Where'd you get the tip about this place?" I asked. I had heard of American Dynamisms, but I couldnt remember where.

"Remember the guy who came around during exam week, sending kids places for jobs?"

I did recall a well-dressed, efficient-looking guy around

the campus before graduation, recruiting seniors, but for what, nobody knew.

"This is his card," and he handed me a card. "Mr. Mortishan said to see no one but him, under any circumstances."

The card was the folding kind. On each section were bold letters in the center and small ones at the bottom.

STAY UNDER CARE KINDNESS EFFICIENCY OF R
Processing Card
DISTRIBUTING AMERICAN DYNAMISMS ABROAD
Rek-cording Card
SEND THE WHOLE FAMILY TO CAMP
Human Factor Card

Mr. Mortishan's name was not on it. I handed it back. Kenny parked the car in front of a deserted store three blocks from the river, behind a factory. Closed Venetian blinds hung at the windows. We checked the address. No mistake. This was the place. The lettering on the door was plain and neat, just like the card.

We went in. Down a narrow hallway in front of us were double doors. They looked tight, but noises drifted through the place, as though coming out of the walls. A thin haze of cigarette smoke mixed with a stronger odor, possibly of cigar or burning wood or incense. Off the hallway were doors; the first one was extremely wide, as though it contained a gigantic piece of equipment that could not go through an ordinary door; the rest were shut. We didnt see anyone at the huge desk in the first room.

Strange music penetrated the walls. We heard voices, then a roar, as if people were cheering. The tempo of the music was one degree faster than any human could keep up with.

"What can I do with you?"

Standing in the hall behind us was a neatly dressed man with close-cut hair whose ready smile was wide, even, and precise.

"We have interviews with Mr. Mortishan. I just talked—"

"I'm sorry. Mr. Mortishan is very busy now. May I help you?"

"I have an interview at eleven," said Kenny.

"Fine. I'm Mr. Mortishan's assistant. Come down the hall to my office."

Kenny stood still. "I just talked to Mr. Mortishan on the phone a few minutes ago, and he warned me not to talk to anyone else, under any circumstances."

"Oh." The young man laughed. "I'm sorry, but you must forgive me. That was our Rek-cording. Mr. Mortishan is on an extended visit out of town. He will process in later. Wont you step into my office?"

Kenny looked at me, shrugged his shoulders, and went into the room.

"Not you." The young man halted me. The door slammed. From behind the double doors down the hall came the continued rise and fall of unintelligible sounds, like some kind of a meeting.

I went up the hall into the open room and sat down. I didnt know how long Kenny's interview would be. I looked for something to read. But there were no books, magazines, or pamphlets, only a picture hanging almost to the ceiling. I looked at it. What an odd place to hang a picture, I thought. Even more, what an odd picture. I couldnt tell if the thing was a multicolored machine or an Expressionist painting of an elongated peanut.

Just as I was beginning to examine the rest of the room, the picture began to move. I was not scared at first. What kind of a gag is this? I wondered. For a moment I thought the room was some kind of a psych testing lab, and if it was, Kenny and I were going through the test for hiring.

The picture moved down the wall, and as it moved, the wall opened in back of it, unzipping itself. I stood up. The noises increased, and before I could think of moving out of the room, the picture was touching the floor—flat on its face —and stepping out from behind it was a very fat man.

"Sit down, Carl," he said to me. He waddled around to the great desk. "I'm sorry to keep you gentlemen waiting."

"What kind of positions do you have open?" I asked.

"Stop," he said, lighting up a fat cigar. "Stop." He reached into his drawer and handed me a stack of forms, saying, "Fill these out first, then ask questions."

He picked up the phone and began dialing. I wondered if he were Mr. Mortishan. I didnt have a chance to say anything. He was talking and blowing smoke. After looking at the application, I knew that it would take almost two hours to finish. I wondered if Kenny was going through the same ordeal. The questions were routine, and as I hurried through them I could hear the fat man talking in a low voice on the phone about demonstrations and appointments and camps. He was watching me out of the corner of his eye. I hadnt noticed, but the picture was back in its place and the wall was closed.

All of a sudden I heard voices in the hall.

"Stop writing," the fat man said. "Go into the hall."

I got up and went out. The double doors were open, and the hall was filled with young men dressed in shirt-sleeves and ties, milling about, drinking from cups. I saw Kenny just as the assistant was shoving a cup in his hand.

"Hey, Ken . . ." He didnt hear me. The men were moving back through the double doors. Behind me came several more, and I was swept into the room through the double doors. Inside was like an arena. I lost sight of Kenny. In the center of the floor was a large area that seemed like a thresh-ing floor. It was sunken and worn in a circle. Around the room were hundreds of chairs. Some of them were occupied by fat-looking men sitting like dignified spectators. Their weights seemed to spread out over the seats, as though in a moment they would turn to lard and flood the floor.

"Selling is the business of every salesman! But our men distribute rather than sell. Rekcus sells himself! Rekcus Rekcus we adore! Rekcus Rekcus nothing more!" It was the assistant. He ran to the center of the floor, holding a metallic-looking suitcase in one hand and a torch in the other. He raised the torch and shouted, "Every person you meet is a potential customer. Consider him already owning a Rekcus. Never cross him off until—"

A bright light suddenly shone from the ceiling on the assistant; otherwise the place was still dim.

"—until we demonstrate and deliver him—"

A roar came up from the men, a frenzied sound, as if they were drunk.

"—Rekcus! And remember: D-A-D, Deliver American Dynamisms to your home! your job! your place of play!"

Someone shoved a cup toward my hand. I didnt want it, but rather than let it fall I received it, since the person was letting it go. I was about to taste it when the odor of some chemical hit me. I put the cup on a table and sat down in a chair, feeling a bit dizzy. The crowd was forming a circle around the speaker. I tried to spot Kenny. He was lost in the crowd, which began a mad chanting after periodic shouts by the assistant. It was crazy. I looked for the door.

Two men came over to me. A light shone in my face.

"We would like to demonstrate at your initiation cere-mony," one of them said. The other one held the light stead-ily on my face.

I tried to dodge the light. "What're you talking about?"

"Dont you believe in the Rekcus principle of acceleration?"

"In the factors of humanoid control?"

"In simuldad?"

"Yes, distribution and demonstration simultaneously?"

"Do you have old parents?"

"Where is your appointment card?"

"Your initiation card?"

"What initiation?" I asked.

"Would you simuldad a Rekcus to your mother?"

"Your father?"

"Have you ever sold anything to a child?"

"Do you understand Rekcus dehumanization?"

"Are you ready to sell?"

"Who is your dadsponsor?"

"What?" I asked.

They looked at each other; then they jerked me off the
chair and shoved me out into the room among the crowd,
which seized me, spun me around, locked arms, and we all
went frantically around the center of the floor. Sitting on an
elongated bulletlike structure in the center of the room was
the fat man. He was grinning at me. Then he pointed at
Kenny: "Get him!"

They all descended on Kenny. He ran. Was he playing
the game? I couldnt tell. One man tackled him waist high,
bringing him down to the hard floor. The shrieks, shouts, and
laughs grew louder and louder. Speeches were begun and not
finished. Hot drinks were flung to the ceiling. Desperately I
tried to find the door.

"Where do you think you're going?" The ready smile of
the assistant greeted me. I coughed. "Well, I was looking for
the other fellow. Kenneth . . ."

He began to laugh hysterically, bending over several

times. Kenny came limping over to me, a big grin on his face.

"Carl, we're in! We're accepted. All we gotta do is sell—I mean, simuldad—I mean—"

"REKCUS REKCUS WE ADORE! REKCUS REKCUS WE ADORE!"

They kept it up, and Kenny, his lips hesitating at first, then catching up with the words, broke away from me and skip-hobbled back across the room with a couple of young men running on either side of him, trying to trip him up. Then Kenny suddenly turned and hollered at me: "Carl! I told him I'll be your sponsor. You have to come to my initiation tonight. Your whole family is coming. At my house!"

"What?" I asked, but he didnt hear me. Suddenly the assistant stopped laughing, came over to me, looked me over, glanced at his watch, and said:

"Get out."

He spoke softly, but his words were like two knives stabbing, one on either side of my chest. The double doors opened in front of me. I stumbled over somebody, felt for the door, and was out. I waited. The doors closed and the shouting went on.

I hurried out to the car, and sat in it, sweating. When I tried to go back in an hour later, the door was locked. I sat in the car for another hour, waiting for Kenny. Then I went to look for a phone. No one was at my house. I phoned Kenny's. No one answered. Mrs. Waspold was probably helping the old man to the bathroom. I ran back to the car. It was gone.

I phoned Edna, Kenny's girl friend, to see if he was there. "Oh, Carl," she said, "Kenny was looking for you. He's on his way here. Congratulations on the job. You're coming to the demonstration tonight, arent you?"

I held the phone away from me and stared at it briefly; finally I managed to say "Yes" and hung up.

Wandering through the park, I watched a softball game. After that I sat near the pond, watching the ducks paddling around. But even when I went home my head was ringing: *Rekcus Rekcus we adore. Rekcus Rekcus nothing more.*

After dinner I drove my folks to Kenny's house. The living room was filled with talking neighbors. Kenny rushed over to me.

"Carl, buddy, how do I look?" He had gotten a crew cut, a new suit, a manicure, had shaved so close he had nicked his chin, and he was smiling in a peculiar way.

"Sharp," I said. "But what's all this demonstration business about?"

"Ahhh," he said, looking at me with a doubtful frown, "then you didnt get *your* appointment yet?"

"I dont think I want anything from that place," I began, but Kenny wasnt paying attention. "What's the initiation for? I waited a couple of hours for you."

"I'm hired, Carl!" he said, racing off to answer the door. "I start selling tomorrow. My first contact will be your house. It has all been arranged."

Coming in and following Kenny to the center of the living room was the assistant. Kenny made a brief announcement. The excitement was high as everybody took seats and waited.

While Kenny was introducing him, Mr. Mortishan's assistant was setting up a metallic tube box.

"On behalf of American Dynamisms I want to thank you all for coming, and especially you, Mr. and Mrs. Waspold, for allowing us to use your home. Today we discovered Kenneth Waspold. D-A-D is looking for loyal, dedicated young men with bright futures and clear minds. We think we found another one in Kenny." He smiled, executed a turn, saying, "Now to the point of the meeting."

He pointed to Mr. Hendy, sitting nearby. "Come here,

sir." Mr. Hendy got up. "Put your hand here." Mr. Hendy did
it. "Squeeze." A narrow tube began to rise from the strange-
looking case. Mr. Mortishan's assistant seized it and put it
close to Mr. Hendy's ear. "Continue squeezing." After a minute of this Mr. Hendy looked astonished, faced the audience
with a look of paralysis, opened his mouth, and speechlessly
turned red in the face.

"Incredible . . ." he mumbled and stumbled to his seat.

The assistant went around the room with the same procedure, next with Mr. Hendy's wife, then Kenny's father and
mother, and after each person had a chance they all were
gasping with amazement.

I sat in the corner. A curious fear held me there. Not
once had he looked at me, and when it finally came my turn
—since I was the last—a quiet fell on everybody.

"You had your chance this afternoon?" He wasnt asking
me a question, as it sounded. Rather, he was telling me.

The guests began asking him questions. My only question was, What had they heard and felt? But he didnt give
them a chance to overwhelm him. "We believe firmly in letting our products sell themselves. That's why we never high-
pressure our customers. Ladies and gentlemen, there is no
product more capable of selling itself than Rekcus! You have
just met Rekcus!"

Kenny was wide-eyed, taking it all in. No doubt he
thought he would use the same procedure at my house. The
neighbors were awed. My folks seemed very receptive.

"Have you ever met a machine like this one?" he asked.
The people shook their heads. "You have seen nothing yet!"
He pressed a button, and the machine began to enlarge itself.
Sections opened and closed, fitting with other parts. It
stopped. It looked like a metallic peanut. When he pushed
another button, the machine began to hum as a handle came

out; the assistant seized it and pushed the machine around the floor for five minutes in a vacuum-cleaninglike motion.

"Examine your floor," he said to Mrs. Waspold.

"Oh!" she exclaimed, after careful examination.

The women began buzzing. The assistant went through several other miraculous demonstrations: cleaning and washing dishes without soap and water, air-conditioning and moisture control, dry-laundering without removing linen from bed, massaging, electric cooking, and more.

"Ladies and gentlemen, there is nothing Rekcus cant do in the home!"

He demonstrated for the men. The machine began ejecting tools, gadgets, and supplies. It was a workshop in itself: a radio, a TV, a phonograph, a fan, a movie projector, and more. I couldnt believe it, and I began looking for him to make mistakes, like a magician does once in a while.

But he was polished in every way, a master salesman. The machine did all the work. Both were perfect.

After an hour of breathtaking feats, the machine began to expand by itself, unfolding like a crib. I could see soft blankets inside.

"Would you like to put your baby in the crib?" he asked a woman with a newborn child. "I assure you, the child will be the better for it."

Smiling, the woman placed the baby in the machine. "He's going to cry," she frowned. Once down, the tiny baby began to whimper, then cry.

Mr. Mortishan's assistant just stood there with a ready, even smile.

The machine hummed and began a liquid motion back and forth. An arm appeared and cuddled the baby. A bottle leaped up. Music and the sound of a woman's voice—very much like the mother's—calmed the baby. It stopped crying and closed its eyes, sucking away.

"Ladies and gentlemen, you have seen nothing! I speak the truth. There is no machine like this one. You cant buy it in the stores, you cant see it in the shops, but you can own one without any money down. You have just seen it *perform*. Now see it *live*."

The machine grew again until it was about six feet, standing on wiry metal legs four feet from the floor.

"I want a volunteer. If you have been suffering from backache, heart trouble, rheumatism, hardening of the arteries, sinus, colds, flu, fevers, high and low blood pressure, gland trouble, liver infections, kidney ailments, lung trouble, overweight, underweight, headache, ulcers, sores, boils, cavities, tumors, and old age, then come. If your spirits are deflated, no pep, no get-up-and-go, no zoom, no desire to do anything but sleep it off, if you have longed to travel to distant shores in search of a utopia and bliss, if you need a doctor, then come, I want a volunteer.

"Ladies and gentlemen, D-A-D will go even further for you. You have heard many hot-line salesmen attempt to force something on you that you dont need. If you are in what you think is good health, you might want a change of disposition. Modern psychology has taught our scientists that there are many of us normal people who desire to experience the difficult aspects of living. Rekcus and our scientists have discovered a unique method: cytoplasmic acceleration of metabolic processes. Through C-A-M-P and psychotherapy we can induce any malady known or unknown to man.

"I repeat: if you're suffering from aches and pains of body and mind, youth, old age, come. I want one volunteer!"

Several people got up, but old Mr. Waspold was being led up by Kenny's father. He was so old and helpless that he had been kept in his room during the demonstration. He mumbled things to himself as Mr. Waspold and Mr. Hendy helped him into the machine. He lay down immediately as if he were back in bed.

"The Rekcus is both a dehumanizer and a humanizer, two-in-one, a truly amazing machine. Right here I hold in my hand the simple program card that will set the vitalizers to charge the patient."

A lid slid over the sleeping old man. The machine looked like an overgrown bullet. He inserted the card. A humming sound filled the room, and the old man's voice could be heard chuckling. Then it grew higher and higher, as if it were going back in time. Soon it was whimpering like a baby. The people buzzed and talked to each other.

Suddenly the lid opened.

The assistant motioned them to come. From where I was I could see the old man's face. It was the same, but the inside of the machine had been dressed up with silk, and the old man's clothes had been changed to suit and tie.

"He's resting well," a voice said.

When it came my turn to look, the lid closed, and the assistant said to me out of the corner of his mouth: "You get out."

Kenny's grandfather hadnt moved. The people were poking him and exclaiming.

"This machine is not only accurate in telling the body's time, it is practical. It *does* something about the body's time. And it is very cheap if you want to get another Rekcus . . ."

I left and sat in the car. Tall buildings blocked the moon. *Oh, you don't have to pay unless you like it. Fred's too crazy about it to think. Get out, get in, get out. Rekcus will help you. Get out, Rekcus will get you.* I left the keys in the car and walked home, thinking I hoped I got there before Kenny.

"Well," said the foreman the next morning, "did the other guy find a better job?"

"No," I said.

"What? Is he sick?"

"Yes," I said. "He's sick."

"Well, I cant wait. I'll have to get another guy in his place."

"Yes," I said. "He's very sick."

Thrust
Counter Thrust

Long black clouds lurched across the sky, bumping into the moon. The November wind, blowing up suddenly, whispered low sounds in miniature whirlwind fits. Saul Newman, his dusty head rising slowly from the ditch where he had fallen asleep, blinked his good eye, stared, blinked, and saw two moons hovering like drunken eyes over the church steeple. The low hiss and swish of dry grasses bowing in quick jerks, mixed with the sifting of sand and dust and a dryness, a burning, converged in his throat. He stumbled out of the ditch and peered down the country road. Maybe this was how Lon got it, he thought. Dark shadows jabbed and retreated down the road like troops of soldiers running in the ditches. Maybe some of them Koreans, he thought, coming to finish me too. He stumbled to the road, raising the wine bottle to his face, feeling the wind thrust deep into his body, hearing in his mind the rumble of the bus that had let him off hours ago. Through the wine bottle he saw the eye of the moon, cold, indifferent, a single force, standing immobile on the tip of the white folk's church steeple. "Watcha lookin at me for? You goddamn . . ." and with his elbow knocking free the flap of his denim jacket, he hurled the empty bottle high, high in the sky, and a fierce grunt followed his arm like the tormented scream of a soldier in pain. When the glass was tumbling piece by piece, like frozen bits of flesh, from the roof, Saul fell to his knees whimpering, cursing, unable to bring into focus the object of his hate, unable to accept the news that his brother had been killed in action in Korea, unable to push aside the memories of him, unable to ask Jesus for forgiveness, because the pain was too much of a reality. The wine, churning in his stomach, burned and gushed through his veins, gushing *thru* him as it probably had done *from* Lon over there in that cold ditch. Who had helped Lon? Who had come? Maybe some buddy. They send you off to war to be killed, and when your own brother tries to enlist they turn him away. O Lawd! he thought, I'll show them white bastards, if I ever git my eye fixed up.

A pair of headlights loomed down the road. Saul fell away from the road. The ditch! Combat maneuvers! The dirt! Hit the dirt! The car stopped. Saul squinted at it from his position. The light was yellow, striking the ground yards ahead of the car, illuminating the dust, which moved like scampering feet.

Saul heard a voice—*sounded like Mr. Vance!*—another voice, and then he heard the skidding of a piece of glass from the church roof. It tumbled and crashed, and Saul held his breath. His head reeled while the men began calling, "Hey, boy! Commere!" And Saul saw the moon, its naked oval appearing from a cloud, staring and throwing a light over the ditch ahead of him. He hid in the shadows of the church.

"Coulda sworn I saw somebody up there, Reverend," one of the men hollered into the night. The car moved on. Reverend Donaldson, thought Saul. That lying bastard. Reverend Donaldson. The men drove near the church and stopped. The service sign shook in the wind. Saul was sure the voice was that of Togart Vance, who held the land that extended from the church all the way back to his house and beyond to Hoesville Pond. He knew them both well.

Reverend Donaldson was pastor of the church. What would this holy white man do if he knew that Saul had just thrown a wine bottle and it had fallen on the church steeple and broken? Saul hugged the dirt. The men went into the church and presently lights came on, and a faint purple light filtered into the night from the stained glass.

A fear gripped him. Sweat gathered on his skin. He began to crawl toward the lighted area outside the church's long shadow, but hesitated, knowing the moon was traveling high into the night and feeling himself ready to bolt across the pathless field toward his house. He waited. A troop of clouds butted across the sky, and he knew that when they struck the moon he would be off. What was he afraid of? He had done nothing wrong. If he had just kept walking along the road when he saw the car, then they might have . . .

"Goin home, Mr. Vance."

"Where you been, boy?"

"Been to town," he would say.

"Sorry to hear about your brother, there, boy," Reverend Donaldson would say out of the corner of his mouth. "Hear your mother's takin it pretty fine, though."

"Yessir."

"He was younger'n you, wernt he?"

"No, sir, older three years."

"You drunk, Saul?" Mr. Vance might ask.

"Well, Mr. Vance, I just was feeling bad and wanted to—"

"Nigger, are you drunk?"

"No, sir."

"You been drinkin?"

"Well, I—"

"Well, dont you have no respect for the Lord? What the hell you mean passin in front white folk's church, stinkin like a damn fool! Git the hell off the road. Now, run! Run, nigger!"

And he would run, and his fear would subside and he would slow, listening, and he would hear Mr. Vance laugh, and Reverend Donaldson would be saying something in a low tone, and then Mr. Vance would probably yell, "Hey, boy! Commere back!" And then he knew he would be in for a

night's trouble, cleaning off the church steps, wiping dust off
their car, all for a quarter, and listening to the stern chas-
tisement of the Reverend. The image of this man hung in his
mind as the figure of the cross, reflected off the church steps,
glinted in his eye.

"That's one-eyed Saul," Mr. Vance might say. "You remember coupla years ago when one nigger brother blinded
'nother in a fight? Well, this here's him."

"Yes, well, what— That's time my stained window was
broke too." Mr. Vance would agree, and the cloud fell upon
the moon. He bolted up, crouched, and ran the wind, bowing
the grass of the field ahead of his sprinting feet. Dirt! Hit it!
He lay panting.

The wine tasted sweet upon his tongue, but his head was
clear. Up! Running! Across the field, back toward the road,
down, leaping over the ditch, eyeing the moon over his
shoulder, his jacket flapping. He stopped, turned. Panting, he
looked back at the lighted church. Another car was pulling
up to it. He watched. The stained-glass windows came alive
with light now. He remembered the day when it had happened.

Lon was taking him over to Mr. Vance's to get the job.
Lon had worked for Mr. Vance for a year, and when he had
been called into the Army, Saul was going to carry on. He
had liked his job, especially because Gloria was cooking part-
time in the kitchen. She was Lon's woman. They had a kid,
two years old, and he had always liked Gloria. She was finely
shaped, small, very black, with hardly a rough spot on her
skin, and her voice always had a smile, as if she was having
some secret pleasure out of talking to you. But Lon had taken
her; Lon was older, bigger, and Lon was good, not like him,
Saul. O Lawd, he thought, when you gonna save me? When
you? Then he bent forward on the road lit by the light of a
cloud-winked moon, and he knew that if he went to Mr.

Vance's house before he went home, Gloria would be glad to see him. He knew she wanted to see him. He knew how she felt since Lon was dead, but maybe he'd go on home and play with Lon's baby, his nephew. Mama would be looking after that little baby. Looked like Lon, too. Mama would be there, but so would that goddamn preacher, Reverend Wiggins, that gold-toothed bastard! waiting for Gloria and making eyes at his mother. If Lon would be there, that dog-eyed, grease-bellied, pig-suckin preacher— Lawd! How he despised that high-yellow sneak, a snake in the grass, layin low to jump when some woman'd pass, the . . .

The Vance estate loomed through the trees. He decided he'd go. He trotted around, out of the woods, back to the paved road. No cars. He walked briskly. "Jesus," he said out loud, "you just aint gonna help me, is you? I been askin you till I'm black and blue. Askin you, you Jesus, to let me help my brother." He stood in a clearing. The moon spilled down upon him. Across the meadow, down into a valley, up and onto a tiny rise, sat his house, the third shack in a clump of dark buildings lit with oil lamps. Him and Lon used to walk that. He remembered that day. The pain came ripping back, a memory that reeled his head down, and he fell upon his knees again, sobs lurching out of him, and the pain was so mixed with bitterness that memories became only tears, like drops of blood cutting through his eyes.

They were climbing the green meadow toward the Vance estate, and Lon was talking about Gloria. Coming up behind them, Richard, the youngest brother, was throwing sticks for the dog to get.

" 'N she more'n a woman than Lucille, man. I'm tellin you," Lon was saying.

"Hell, if I ever catch Lucille's sister 'gin like I did up in Cooty's loft . . ." he was saying.

"Man, thas good stuff, but she jailbait, I'm tellin you."

They jogged along together. Lon was much taller, maybe a foot or more. Saul was stocky, and he moved in a thudding, plodding manner, as if he was still ploughing in loam clods. Richard was only a boy. They had let him come along, but Lon had told him he'd have to wait down by the road because he was sure the white folks didnt want a whole tribe of niggers coming up to get one job. Besides, Mr. Vance was known to have evil streaks. Not like Mrs. Vance, with her petite fingers and dainty voice waving and whispering music in the air. Mr. Vance was quick-tempered and hard on Negroes. He was a graduate of some military school in the North, and he always acted like he was reliving the days when he was a major in the First World War.

They never made it to the house. Richard was playing down the road. He was training that mutt that Reverend Donaldson's son gave him when some white boys, about five, began rocking him. He threw back, retreating up the road toward the white church. They chased him to this point, but always a point where Negroes were forbidden. This was enemy country for any nigger who wasnt able to account for himself. Richard hid behind the church, wondering how the dog was making out. The white boys closed in, yelling, "Hey, you black sonofabitch! Come way from there!" And Richard, trembling beside a shrub, picked up some round driveway stones, filled his pockets, ran out toward the back of the church, whirled, catching sight of them coming, and began a fierce bombardment. He struck two or three boys, but they closed in, shouting insults. A rock caught him on the shoulder. He ran. And another rock crashed into his temple. He stumbled, again, again, knees, hands, ground, up, stumbling, and shook the blow loose. Circling the field, he eluded the boys, who probably were content to have driven a nigger from their citadel.

When Lon and Saul returned, the boys were sitting on

the steps. Saul remembered how he felt then. Every movement, every detail of his life up till that day often appeared
like paintings or voices, clear and exact. Lon was mad.
Richard's dog had come barking behind them before they
reached the Vances' gates.

"Gitta way dog," Saul had yelled.

"Where's Richard?" Lon asked the dog, who was acting
strangely.

Saul peered back through the few trees where the road
bent. He saw no one. Lon took a few steps back, trying to
see.

"Come on, man," Saul said.

"Naw. Wait, Saul," Lon said. He remembered how acute
Lon's senses were for detecting something wrong. The dog
had acted as if it had been hurt. Probably one of the boys had
popped him with a rock. Saul watched his brother.

"I think that's Richard yelling for help."

Saul listened. "Somebody's hollerin," he decided, "but it
soun' like more— Wait, man, reckon . . . ?"

Lon was off. The dog barked and bounded out ahead of
him. Saul leaped behind them and gained at the road. Goddamnit, he said to himself, I'm gonna kill me somebody
today, so help me, Jesus.

They attacked the white boys, who were dressing their
wounds on the side of the church. Richard saw them coming
and circled to join them. Blood was clotting on his shoulder.
He held his head, and when he saw his brothers coming, he
held back tears. "Five of 'em," he said, trotting beside Saul.

They caught the white boys by surprise, and the fight
raged for almost half an hour. The white boys had a whole
driveway of stones, but after Lon was hit and driven away
from the road, Saul and Richard, retreating to the field,
began to run low on stones. Lon knew where an old car was
rusting in a swamp pit. The white boys were attacking them

now. Lon was hit hard in the neck. He kept shaking it now and then to ease the pain away. One white boy whom Saul knew, one of the Donaldson boys, was rushing them. Lon called to follow him. Richard's dog was hit again. The white boys were laughing now. "Hey! Another nigger! Get that four-legged bastard, too!"

Lon reached the car, ripped off a strip of iron and began trying to break up pieces. Rusty pieces fell away. Glass shattered. Saul remembered seeing Lon face them.

Some fear, blazing out of his eyes, seemed to color everything he said. Saul had never seen his brother act like that. "Let's go, man," he said to Lon, who was pounding away at the car. Richard held his head nearby, calling the dog.

"Not till I get me one, just one lick!" he grunted, breaking and bending rusted metal.

"Come on, Lon," Saul remembered he had said. "They coming!"

"You scared them devils?" He glared at Saul, who saw rocks begin to fall near them. One struck the car and bounced, striking Lon.

"See that!" he yelled. "They tryin to kill us!"

And the fight was on again. With the rusted car as a fortress and an arsenal, they had held off four white boys who were cursing and laughing. But before the fifth boy could return with more rocks, they had run out, and Lon, seeing this, leaped forward. When the boys saw him leap up like a jack-in-the-box and come charging across the field, two of them bolted and ran. Saul followed, hurling a piece of iron that must have struck one of the boys hiding behind a clump of bushes, for he yelled and was breaking off a stick for a club when Lon, running toward him, hurled a piece of glass, which curved, curved, and sliced off a piece of bark from a tree.

One white boy was yelling now. "Niggers, you better be

careful! Watch what you—" He retreated. "Better not catch
you niggers again!"

They were scattering now, amidst the careful aim of
Lon, who was bearing down toward them, dodging an occasional rock, and calling for Saul and Richard to back him.
Then Saul, seeing a white boy returning with more rocks
from the church, charged to meet him. He hurled a large
piece of iron. The boy hurled back. Both pieces fell short.
They approached each other.

"Nigger, I'm gonna rock your ass in the ground."

Saul was frightened, but he answered the announcement
with a mighty throw of curving glass. The boy leaned away
from it, then threw. Lon was coming toward them. The white
boys behind began calling retreat. The boy carrying rocks in
his pockets turned and ran back, turning twice to hurl rocks
to slow down the pace of Lon and Saul, who were giving hot
chase.

"Not too far," warned Lon. "I got one shot left."

"Well, I got four pieces glass here, man. Take one."

"Naw."

"What's matter?"

"Richard's hurt bad. Bleedin."

"Let's get 'em fore they can get to the church an get
more rocks," said Saul. He tossed Lon two pieces of glass.

Saul gave chase, but the boys were gathering in the area
around the church and suddenly counterattacked with a
bombardment of rocks. Lon called, "Come on back, Saul!"

"They cant reach us now," Saul screamed.

"Then les' get while we can!"

Saul fought down a torrent of fear and rage. Why was
Lon retreating now when they could have overtaken them?
He fired several pieces of glass and retreated safely across the
field before they had time to gather more rocks. He didnt
know, but he trusted Lon, and . . .

"Dammit Saul, come on, man!" Naw, he thought. He was still running, and he had two pieces of glass. They were his bullets, he thought. He'd split that dog-haired Tim Donaldson's head wide open, the sneaky bastard, always talking religion to him and Lon, always laughing at them with that silent smirk. Whenever he went to Vance's store he had to control his temper. That Tim was a teasin sonofabitch. Callin other guys niggers and fools, but always meaning something deeper, always meaning *him*. He wanted to get one good blow at Tim, but he couldnt tell— Yes! He saw him coming toward him now. Tim was yelling, "Hey, you coons, watch this!" and he hurled, another boy hurled, and Saul ducked, still moving forward, his left arm shielding his face, his right cocked to throw, and he heard Lon hollering.

"Saul! Come on, man! Get 'em tomorrow!"

But he was propelled, and rocks were striking him, one! two! three! and the white boys were yelling, the dog was yelping, and he aimed a piece of glass for Richard. It curved, missed! They closed in on him. But he knew Lon . . . A rock thudded his head. Dizziness. Stumble. Up, down, more rocks, yelling. Up, one piece of glass left. Aiming. Running blindly. He was crying now, yelling himself and cursing, "You white trash! Bastards! Kill you!" Fear was upon him. He saw Lon coming, hurling and hurling, fiercely. The white boys retreated now.

"Hey, you all throwing glass!" Tim screamed. "You nigger bastards!" He advanced upon Saul, pommeling him with stone. Saul fell to the ground.

He recalled all this as if it were happening again. He was standing now near the spot where the road bent and went up to the Vances'. Gloria would be getting ready to come off soon. Perhaps he ought to wait for her. He sat upon a stump. Naw, he thought. I'm not sober. But Gloria wont mind. She's good. She's good. Dammit, my brother had a good woman, and now she gonna be mine, if that white bastard Vance dont rape her. I kill him and all his kids for that. Honest to God, I will. Gloria, you oughta quit that place. Plenty places, other places . . .

Other voices rang in his mind. His mother, Lon, Reverend Wiggins. "Saul, Saul, how come you cant keep a job?" "How come you aint marry Gloria? She need a man take care that child, and you always talkin bout likin her." "Saul, you better come to church. The Lord got a word to say to your soul." "Saul, you drink and you lie too much, Saul, you sawed-off nigger runt. Git your black ass stone. Dont come back to Cooty's but you pay Cooty his money! Man, what kind of friend you tryin to be . . ." Mr. Vance, Mr. Vance, Vance. The nigger-loving killer. Vance, the credit-giver, the sharecropper. Vance, advance. "Goddamnit!" he screamed, and tears came again, just like they did when he got up and fell again, only the next time he fell he never got up under his own power.

Lon was attacking, Richard following behind him. The white boys held their ground, and when Saul got up he hurled the last piece of glass blindly toward the crouching figure of Tim, but Tim leaned, the missile curved, rose, rose higher, and crashed one of the stained glass windows of the church.

Lon fired on and on.

Amidst the melee Saul turned and began to retreat as rocks fell all over and around him. He started to leap toward them, but he never finished. Something took his eye away, a slicing, curving object took his eye, crashed, ripped, dug deep into his forehead, and he fell, the pain blinding him.

Lon screamed. "Saul, Saul, git down, man! I did that! I hit you!"

Tim Donaldson and the rest retreated and watched from the front of the church. Occasionally a stone landed near

Saul, but the war was over. He could tell it in Lon's voice. The dog was sniffing his face. Saul lay, his face buried in the grass, not wanting to think of the pain that was filling up his head. Lon reached him, pulling on his arm. "Saul, what happened? That last piece I chunked got you? Did it?" Saul wanted to say naw. He rolled over, holding his face with both hands. Naw, naw, naw. But Richard was upset.

"Saul, you bleedin worse'n me. Saul."

Lon was carrying him across the field, running now, running faster. "Put me down, Lon. I can walk." Faster, as the taunts of the enemy faded beneath the excited tone of Richard running beside Lon. Saul held his head, held his palms tight over his face. But the blood came on, reddening his hands. "How you feel?" he managed.

"We all right, " Richard answered, but Lon said nothing and Saul knew that he might be crying. He managed to look. "Saul, your eye bleedin bad," said Richard. "Maybe we oughta make it to Mr. Vance's. Gloria be there. She fix it."

"Mr. Vance cant do nothin for this," whispered Lon. He jogged along as Saul asked again and again to be put down, and Lon would say, "Save your strength, bro, you hurt," and Saul felt his strength flowing down his arm and onto his chest and neck.

When they reached home he remembered that he lay on the bed for hours, days perhaps. He wasnt sure. His mother and Lon bandaged, then rebandaged and finally the doctor, Dr. Oaks, the colored doctor from Little Rock, came and bandaged and announced after healing set in, after weeks at the hospital and office, that he was blind in one eye. But he knew he wasnt blind because he could see faint traces of light, and he prayed someday to see with his left eye again.

Hardly before the bandages were removed Uncle Sam called Lon into the service and over to Korea, and Gloria cried, for they were set to get married. "Mama," she would say to their mother, "Lon say he marry as soon as he come home on leave."

"Child, that rusty nigger'll tell you anything. You oughta drag him up. I gotta good mind to really tell him a piece of mine tonight."

"Yessum." Gloria was sweet, and Saul felt that perhaps Lon was taking a bit of advantage of her innocent and easy-going behavior. After all, that girl in Hevysville tried to cut Lon so he would marry her. Even Lucille slapped him, but Lon had been drunk himself and had fought with her. Her sister got a baseball bat after Lon, and chased him across the field, where he turned on her, threw her, and took her right there, and Saul had heard these episodes over and over again until they were a part of his memory, his view of life. He had started going with Bessie, because he had dared her to hit him with a baseball bat. They were hot, tempestuous, and wild.

Saul had lain in the bed for centuries while the fear, the dread of losing that eye, came leaping up at him out of the somber nights and the gray days of fall, out of the stuttering tones of Reverend Wiggins at church, out of the soundless days when the plough cut up the fields, the smell of cotton and the sweet potatoes and greens swirled in his mind like the north wind. The day was like a single shot, a burning picture, never consumed like the bush Moses saw, and he recalled how he never talked to Lon again as they had earlier. Gloria came to his bed after chastising him for moodiness but showing a tenderness she seldom if ever showed to Lon, a tenderness like something he imagined would have explained the feeling of the love that the preacher always lied about, trying to show forth like a light to the world.

Lon was eighteen then and in a few weeks he was gone. Gloria's baby came months later in the spring, and Lon came home for a couple of days to play and bounce it, but his eyes showed something new, something far off and distant. He wore his Army suit around, complaining about the discipline of training but boasting of his new status whenever he got the chance. Saul questioned him and ached to go with him. He dared not ask whether they would take anybody with one eye, but he prayed and begged God or—he couldnt bring himself to believe as his mother and Gloria did—Jesus or somebody to allow him to fight along with his brother.

"Naw, man," Lon said the day he was stuffing his things in a brown duffle bag. "This Army'll break a man. Damn, man, I aint had no woman cept what we pay for. But man, that aint no good."

"How they test you for aimin a gun?" asked Saul.

"Ah, man, it's tough as hell. I'm tellin you. Man, nigger sergeants worse'n the white. Man, this one sucker from Oklahoma. He grab me one day, and I had been on the firin line before too, he grab me, talkin bout, 'Soldier, dont ever let me catch you aim that weapon anywhere but there!' and he hauled off and kicked me straight up the ass. Dammit, I learned."

That night, with Lon and another guy from Little Rock going away, six or seven of them all went out looking for girls at Cooty's Inn, and they all got drunk. He recalled that Gloria met him when he staggered home. She didn't say anything. Lon had gone. Mother was sleeping, the stars were out like frozen tears, he thought, a wind was coming up and the leaves, rustling across the stretches of . . .

He thought a poem:

> The universe shrank
> when you went away.
> Every time I thought your name,
> stars fell upon me.

. . .

and wondered about the sleeping sun:

The lights gathering
on the night lake
sing a thousand songs
of the sleeping sun.

Six Days You Shall Labor

THE FUMES from the solvent can were making me and Big Mo drunk. I wished HyLow would get back with the soda pops we sent him after. Big Mo coughed and went over to the window. He opened it and motioned to me. I stooped down and came around from behind that printing machine. It was a good thing that Big Mo had let me come along with him, because I know he couldnt have squeezed in and out from behind that machine and cleaned it as good as I was doing. I am small and never had no trouble squeezing in and out of things.

Big Mo was coughing out the window. I took deep breaths out the window. I looked down the street, and I saw HyLow talking in front of the shoeshine parlor with some people dressed for church. He got the pops in one hand, and he takin somethin from one of the group with the other.

I say, "Here come HyLow."

Big Mo, he coughed and bring in his head. "He been gone half hour." Big Mo sneezed and his whole body shook. I see his muscles shaking, and I think I know why people called him Big Mo, but then I know why he always got mean when somebody called him fat. Big Mo was like that. He didnt mind you callin him Big Mo, but you couldnt call him anything else except his name, Morris Haynes. They tell me Big Mo almost killed a man once for calling him a fat nigger. The only one I ever hear mess with Big Mo was HyLow. HyLow was a year ahead of me in school. He was one of the craziest niggers I ever run into. Some people say he's crazy. Some people say he's not.

When he got back with them soda pops we could hear him hollering at us like he didnt know where we were. Like

he was bringing back them soda pops, and they werent soda
pops but something better than soda pops, and we were
suppose to thank him for them.

He came in the door. "Hey! While I'm away the Ink
Spots play." He put two pop bottles on the table away from
the rags and solvent can, brushed himself off like he didnt
want none of the dirt from us to get on him, and then sit
down in a chair in the corner, drinking his pop and laughing.
That guy is always laughing. No matter what happen to him,
he laugh. Big Mo, he just the opposite. HyLow pulled out a
pack of cigarettes and pretended he was trying to strike a
match. That just about tore Big Mo up. But we kept on working. With me helping him, this job was gonna be cut in half.

"Hey hey hey?" HyLow laughed, bending over with his
soda in his hand. Suddenly he laughed so hard that he spilled
a little on his suit. "Whoops!" But he keep right on laughing.
"Now see what you Sabbath breakers done made me do." He
finished the bottle. "Now I cant put no money in church with
this stuff on me. People think I been out drinkin gasoline from
under trucks, stinking with that stuff you boys got over yourself." He pointed to the solvent cans. "Naw," he shook his
head. "Think I gonna go into business today." He took something out his pocket and cracked it with his jaw. Big Mo, he
let the top down on the machine, and we shined it.

The church bells were ringing again, and we got ready
to go. Big Mo, he went over, let the window down, and then
sit down in a chair.

"We finish?" I asked him.

"You is, kiddo," he said.

"Hey hey hey, listen to the big boss," said HyLow.

"Shut up an gimme couple of them pecans," said Big
Mo.

HyLow laughed and went into his pocket and then
brought it out empty. He winked at me.

"Now listen, kid. I gotta wait here till she call," said Big Mo. "I dont need you no more. I'll stop by your house and pay you."

I didnt say nothin. I aint want to go. I figured it was because of HyLow. But I didnt say nothing about it. When Big Mo drove pass my house early in the morning, I was sitting on the porch doing nothing. I waved him down. I ask him could I go along with him on the job. I knew he must be going out for some job, because that's how Big Mo made his living. He had an old piece of car full of junk and tools. He would haul or do anything for a little piece of money. Everybody used to say that he was eating that money, because he didnt drink, smoke, or waste himself.

He say he going up to the Collier newspaper office to clean a machine. He ask me if I was going to church, and I told him I didnt have to if I could make some money to show Mama when I got back. About halfway through the job, right after Sunday School let out, old crazy HyLow Walker pass by and see Big Mo's car and found us in that building.

"Dont do it, kiddo," said HyLow.

It was about eleven o'clock. We could hear church bells ringing down the street.

HyLow, he sat over in the corner, cracking pecans and tossing the shells into a trash can beside him. Now and then we'd hear shells hit the inside of a barrel or trash can next to us, and then he bust out laughing again.

"Working on Sunday, same as working on Monday to some people. Yes, sir, you spots got all the money, all the—"

"Gimme some of them pecans."

"You boys know where I got these?" And he took out a handful and shook them like dice. They sounded good, and I could tell that they werent the pea-size kind that tart your mouth.

Big Mo, he raised up, cleaning his hands with the rag,

and looked over at HyLow rearing back in that chair, pretending he been sitting there all his life.

He tossed me one and I caught it.

"All right, lil bits, tell your boss what you got." I looked at it, and I could see that it was a big brown nut, shaped like a watermelon. It even had a few snake lines on the ends, left by the shells. That was a sign that it was fresh off the tree. It was thin-shelled and the meat was juicy. We called them papershells. When anybody got them kind of nuts, they knew they had some good eating. The best ones came from Georgia, but there was one place around our town that had trees and that was on the Collier plantation, which been closed off for years.

"Papershell, right?"

I cracked that pecan open. It fell perfect. I halved it, trying to keep the solvent on my hands from getting on it, and then I ate it. Big Mo, he watched me.

"Shore is," I say.

"Hey hey hey, tell my secret, then it be yours; keep my secret, you look for yours."

"He bought them things over at Yancy," Big Mo said to me.

"Now, aint that just like a jealous nigger. He cant get none from there, so he say they didnt come from there. Now, you look and taste that papershell, kiddo, and tell your boss if it aint just come off the tree last night."

I handed the other half to Big Mo.

He waved it off and went on cleaning. "Dont let 'em fool you, kid. He's tryin to be slick."

I chewed and looked. I wondered if them papershells come from the Collier place. "Where you get them?"

And just about that time the phone rang. We was standing near the door. Me and HyLow. Big Mo picked up the phone. He say, "Hello?"

Then he listen. Then he say, "Yes, Mrs. Collier."

Then he dont talk for a little bit. Then he say, "Yes, Mrs. Collier."

Then he dont talk for another little bit. Then he say, "All right, Mrs. Collier. I want it today. I need it today." Then he hung up.

HyLow began to laugh again. Then he looked at Big Mo. "Look at that, wont you." He punched me on the arm to make me pay attention to what he was talking about. "Just look at that. Old big boss talking to Mrs. Collier. Man, I know he gonna get him some of those papershells out there."

Big Mo was paying nobody no mind now. "Yawl git out." Then he went around the side of the machine, turned off the power, and fixed everything right. He turned out the light and came out the door behind us.

When I got out into the air, the sun was bright. Church was about ready to take in. I could see all the people along the street. Everybody in town came that way to go to the Baptist Church. Everybody in the country went to the Baptist Church too. There wasnt no other kind of church around, maybe except the Methodist Church over in Haleton.

"Big Mo, how bout let a Christian ride in your 'chine for the morning service?" said HyLow.

"Tie your tongue up, nigger, and get in."

We all got in the car, me and Big Mo in the front, and HyLow in the back.

"You know, Big Mo," said HyLow as we headed down the small street, "I thought you wanted to make some money."

"What you talkin about?"

"I thought you were smarter than that. Dont you know where these papershells come from?"

Big Mo aint say nothin. Keeps drivin.

"Out at Collier's," I say. HyLow, he wink at me.

"Kiddo, you smart."

"Where you get them papershells, boy?" Big Mo said.

We had to stop for a lot of people crossing the street. I looked away so as the people dont see me. My aunts and uncles in town, if they see me in Big Mo's car and not in church, they be tellin it before I get one dollar of my money. About that time the car is pulling near the corner where the church is. Big Mo slow down and stop. HyLow, he crack a couple more them pecans. "How much you think you gonna get from them for that job, boss?"

Big Mo, he shake his head. "I dont *think*, I *know* how much I ask for. I work for my living, like anybody else."

HyLow, he laughed. "Thirty dollars?"

When I heard him say that I almost jump out of the seat. I know it aint worth that much, but I was wonderin just how HyLow get such a notion in his big head. Thirty dollars. I know I'd be gettin about five or more.

"None your business, boy. Now get out and go on to church like you ought to."

HyLow, he opened the door and shook some papershells on the ground. A lot of people were looking at the car. They knew Big Mo's car, and some of them were straining to see who it was with Big Mo. "Ah, I cant go in there with the smell of that stuff on me."

HyLow, he lean back and wave Big Mo on like he real mad for having that stuff on him.

"Man, aint nothin on *your* clothes," said Big Mo.

"How come I can smell it?"

"That's us you smell," I say.

HyLow, he winked at me. He slam the door and set back.

"Well, either you gettin out or you aint," said Big Mo.

"Hell, they think I'm one of you guys, working on Sundays for the white man, like you aint got no respect for Christian upbringing at all."

"Shut up and go on to church."

Just then crossing the street was old Mrs. Rankin. She was hobbling along on her cane with a couple of other women. One of the women was suppose to be some kin to Big Mo, but I never knew how. It didnt make no difference, because soon as Big Mo see them he turn his head and look at HyLow. "You gettin out or not?"

Everybody knew that beat-up old wine-colored Studebaker. It had no shocks, no springs, and would just make thirty-five miles downhill. It couldnt go uphill at all. So, they act like they aint see Big Mo at first. Then, just like that, Mrs. Rankin, she stop, turn around, and look at Big Mo.

"Morris Haynes! I want to talk to you!" She came over to the car. I was sitting there wishing I had a place to hide my head.

"Yes, mam," Big Mo says respectfullike. Big Mo is very respectful to old folks. I never heard him raise his voice to old people. But he could cuss you out in a minute if he wanted to.

"Morris Haynes, I been watching you for a long time now. Why dont you do your duty on the Lord's Day?"

Big Mo looked down at something on the steering wheel.

"Your mama and me was good friends when she was living, and when she died I promised myself I'd keep my eyes on that boy of hers. Now, Morris, you been round this town all your life . . ."

We all knew what was coming. HyLow cracked one of them papershells. I heard him chewing and fidgeting.

" . . . and you was baptized, as I recall, along with Sister Tinslow's daughter yonder . . ."

We all knew what was coming, but it didnt do no good. I

guess I felt about as bad as Big Mo did. Big Mo never laughed at religion. He might curse out a preacher, but he never talked about the Church like HyLow sometimes would do.

" . . . you aint got decency and respect enough to set aside one day, the Sabbath, to thank the Lord that He let you live the rest of the week. Son, I been watching you. You know better. That's why I said to myself: 'This time I aint gonna do what others do, pass him by and turn my face. I gonna speak my mind.' Because, Morris, you raised in the Church. Your mother was a Christian woman. She raised you right. Son, you ought to think about your soul."

Big Mo was looking down, nodding his head a little, but he never turned off the engine. HyLow never stopped cracking them papershells. A few people slowed down to listen. I hoped none of my aunts or uncles came by, cause they would jump on me worse than Mrs. Rankin was getting on Big Mo. She looked in at us and called our names. "That goes for you young men too." Then she nodded her head, agreeing with herself like I seen old people do when they know nobody's listenin to them so they got to agree with themselves.

Just before she left she poured it on strong. "I'd be ashamed of myself if I was you. Takin something that dont belong . . . Six days . . . but the seventh is the Lord thy God's. Now, I want to see every one of those young faces back in church next Sunday. And I want yawl to come to the Thanksgiving program we having this evenin."

We all said, "Yes, mam," and Big Mo drove off. The people were gathered in front of the church. It was a bad time. Big Mo couldnt turn around. He had to drive right past the church now. People started hollerin at us. It wasnt too bad, but then Mrs. Rankin was right in the middle of the crowd, and she pointed several times, and people turned.

"Man, Big Mo, your people sure make a fuss over

church," said HyLow. "Last summer when I was in Memphis, niggers went only if they felt the spirit, and nobody said anything."

"Well," said Big Mo, "that's Memphis. This is Bottomsup, and Negroes like to go to church down here. I got to go back sometime too. That woman is right—"

"Now, listen to this sinner," said HyLow.

Somebody hollered at us to stop. Big Mo kept going. It was Russell Moody. He ran across the street and waved us down. Big Mo pulled over. Russell Moody had a truck. And now and then he did a little hauling and such. Russell Moody always did handyman work like Big Mo, but he had people that called him, just as there was people that called Big Mo. I guess the jobs were about split up between Big Mo and Russell Moody, but Russell had another job cleaning the jail and the law building. Plus he had six kids. He was older than Big Mo.

"Tell me you worked on Collier's press," he said to Big Mo.

"What's on your mind, Moody?" Big Mo never had no likes for Russell Moody.

"How much he pay you?"

"How come you didnt take it?"

"I woulda, I woulda," he said in a hurry.

"You scared of that machine?"

"Naw, naw, Mo, you know me—"

"Yeah, I know," said Big Mo. He took his arm off the door frame, away from where Russell Moody was leaning into the car. Then he did a funny thing. He turned and looked at HyLow. "Man, I see why you always laughin."

Russell Moody said, "Any time you get a job you cant—"

"Moody, what's wrong with you on Sunday morning? There aint no job Mo cant take care of."

"Well, I just want to ask you about what . . ."

Big Mo started shakin his head. I didnt figure it out until pretty soon Big Mo and HyLow were laughing. I never seen them laugh together. It looked so funny that I laughed too.

Big Mo drove on out of town. We ate up all the pecans.

HyLow said, "Looky here, kiddo, why dont you and me get out the car before Collier Road, and make it along the wet side of the levee till we come to them pecan trees other side of—"

"Boy, you gonna get us all shot," said Big Mo. He looked at me. "Kid is working with me."

"Listen to this preacher, will you, kiddo? Jack of all trades and that's about it. If you make a little money, you'd have a fit. Big boss, hey hey hey. Mo, you as good as Russell Moody."

"That nigger's a fool and a ass-kisser. He lick the white man's ass so shiny he can see how to grin in it." I had heard HyLow say that in school one day. Big Mo was pickin up things HyLow says.

"Yeah, but at least Russell'll jump at a chance to get thirty dollars' worth of pecans."

"Thirty dollars?" I said.

"That's right, kiddo. Now, if you asked Russell Moody, he would say, 'Naw, naw, they got dogs, dogs.' All I have to say to that is, 'Now, whoever heard of a nigger scared of a dog that's tied up?'

" 'Naw, naw, I'm talkin about—'

" 'And who's gonna let a dog aloose?'

" 'We might run into one of them peckerwoods live out there.'

" 'They be doin the same thing we doin.'

" 'But them dogs . . .'

"Then I say to him, 'Listen, Mr. Moody, I guarantee you we'll be safe, because I guarantee you two things.' "

And then HyLow leaned over like he was really talking to Russell Moody.

" 'What's them two things?' Russell Moody would ask.

" 'Number one, I ain't going to go up to that Collier place and ask them white people to let me turn their dogs aloose...' "

Then he laugh like he knew he was gettin to Russell Moody, and it sounded just like Russell Moody, and I was laughing, and Big Mo, he had to grin.

" 'And number two, I know you aint either...' "

And he laughed like Russell Moody, and we all laughed, and then HyLow, he said, " 'Right?'

"And Russell Moody, he laughed out loud and said, 'That's right, that's right.' "

"So then, what're we waiting for?"

That's how we all got headed to the pecan trees.

At the Delta Switch we pull off the road and drive up to Gary's. Mr. Gary was fixing a flat tire on his old Buick. He was dressed for church, and all his kids were standing next to the Buick, waiting for him to fix it. His oldest boy, Clint Gary—he was in my class—was helping him.

We all got out. Big Mo, he ask Mr. Gary if he had any croackersacks. Burlap bags, as some folks call them. Mr. Gary told us to come around to the back, and we went around to the back. He went in his shed, and we go in behind him, and then he turned and say, "I hope yawl aint goin to mess with that man's trees?"

"Just what you think," say Big Mo.

Mr. Gary, he was an old man. Everybody liked him because he spoke his mind and he dont cheat you.

He say, "I'll tell you what I told Russell Moody the other evening. I told him what I know about the Colliers. Just as sure as these bags got dirt on them, they be waiting for you." He handed the bags to Big Mo. "Mr. Collier stopped by here two weeks ago fore he go and say to me, 'Gary, I'll be glad to let anybody that wants to gather him a few pecans, but they'll have to come up to the house like a man and ask for permission.' But he say if he or his man Fane catch anybody trespassing his land, they'll shoot them."

"We aint going in daylight," said Big Mo.

"I'm just tellin you what the man said," Gary said as he closed the door to his shed and headed back to his car.

"But you know he lyin," said Big Mo.

Mr. Gary, he just looked away. "That's right."

"Well, on Sunday aint no niggers or crackers down in them fields, so we got to make it."

Mr. Gary, he aint say nothing to that. He just half nod his head and walk on. Then he turned and say to us, "That crazy fool Fane, he patrols round on a horse and couple of dogs. But he always do it around lunchtime and late at night. Sometimes the sheriff and him come out to talk with Mrs. Collier. The best time is at dusk. They're eating dinner, and the dogs have to be fed. Save me a few of those papershells. I aint had any since they closed it off."

Then Mr. Gary looked at me. "Boy, you stay close to Big Mo, you hear?"

"Yes, sir."

I see him get in the car, and I could see Clint Gary in that car. I know that Clint Gary knew what we was doing.

We drive down that Collier road. Their plantation is spread out. But you can see for miles and miles in places. Over to the east was corn and tomatoes. He had a tomato factory at the edge of it. Them pecan trees run along the edge of the cotton, which was in the west, along the river. We could make out the levee pretty soon, and old HyLow, he lit up a cigarette and cursed imaginary niggers and white people out in the cotton fields. "Look at yourselves, stinking and rotten, all weighed down with the white man's cotton."

He kept it up for a long time. "Shet up," say Big Mo, "cause I saw you in that patch once or twice."

"Hey, now!" And then HyLow broke into a laugh. It was something so funny he was just doubled over laughing. He took off his sports jacket and laid it on the seat. Then he raised up. "Did you hear that, kiddo? Did you hear that?"

"Yeah," I said, but I didnt know that I was playing into HyLow's hands. He sure was a trickery nigger himself. I had picked so much cotton myself that I aint think it possible for me ever to lie and say I didnt.

"He saw me in the cotton field. Yes, he did. But Big Mo, you know me good enough to know one thing . . ."

HyLow, he looked at me. I wanted to ask what it was, but I figured this time I'd keep my mouth shut.

"One thing. And I tell you just like I told Russell Moody the other day. I know, but you dont know what I was doing there. I was in the cotton field, but I didnt pick no cotton. But I sure know what Big Mo was doing whenever I seen him in the field. Old Big Mo got a big, long, strong back, walking in the mud with a cotton sack."

"Shet up, boy. Least I work honest for what I get."

"Except when?"

"Always."

I wanted to laugh myself, cause HyLow had him again. And Big Mo didnt even see it. We drove the car onto this gravel road that was wide. It led to the pike, which we would take to the center of the plantation.

Big Mo was driving fast and the car was overheating. I looked at the heat gauge. It was broke, but I could feel the heat coming in and hitting my legs. I opened out the vent on the window. The window of the car was broken out, but Big Mo had managed to have a vent. And I guess that was about the only thing on that car that wasnt broken. We reached the plantation. Big Mo, he knew where to drive around to the back. I could just see his old raggedy car, now, parked in front of that big house. We looked over it, and HyLow, he hollered, "Nigger, nigger, in that house, come on out and look for the cat! White folks, white man, nigger sucking louse, why you treat a nigger like that?"

"Dont holler," I say.

"You scared, kiddo?"

"Naw."

HyLow knew I was scared. But I told him I wasnt. I wanted to go.

"Stay close to me, then, kiddo."

"Leave the kid to me," Big Mo said. He pulled the old Studebaker up to an old trough where they water cattle and stock. We hear dogs barkin, and across the road is two parked cars. One looked like the one Mrs. Collier drove sometimes, and the other we knew was Fane Paxton's.

"If you want to get straighten out, kid, you listen to me, hear?"

I say, "Okay."

Big Mo, he get out and walk to the house. Now, this aint the big house. It was down the road. We could see it from where we was. Big Mo, he walk to the house. And me and HyLow, we hear the dogs barking, and then Big Mo, he turn and walk around to the back of the house. We dont see much of him, as he is standing up on the steps of the house. Then we see Big Mo come back to the car. He wave at me to get out.

"Come on, kid."

"What for?"

"Just come on. You helped me, didnt you?"

I got out and went with Big Mo. HyLow, he hollered at us. "Man, you mean I didnt help none?"

Big Mo, he looked at him, and then all he could say was, "Come on."

Big Mo stood on the steps and we stood in the yard behind him. When Mrs. Collier came to the door, I aint expect to see what I see. Big Mo rang the bell about five or six times. We was gettin ready to leave.

She opened the door. "Oh, Morris! I just forgot about you." She laughed a little. Her hair was loose and all around her back, and she was wearing one of those loose see-through dresses. "You know that Mr. Collier is away, and Mr. Fane has your money."

"Yes, mam," said Big Mo. HyLow nudged me. Mrs. Collier was swaying in the doorway. "But there's something I'd like to ask you. Walker and young Neal, they gave me a little hand, and I was wonderin if we could have your permission to pick up a few pecans."

She laughed and waved her hand. Then that redneck Fane came to the door. As soon as we see him pushing her out of the way, we all stiffen. Big Mo, he dont move.

"You Morris Haynes?" He opened the door and came down the steps. He was drunk.

"That's right," said Big Mo. He didnt move none.

"Well, fore I pay you for the job you sposed to have done for me, I want to see it. Now, what you bring all these boys along with you for?"

Big Mo huffed himself. Mrs. Collier was laughing. "Give them the money. Frank does business with Morris all the time, doesnt he, Morris?"

Big Mo said, "He always pay me too, Mrs. Collier."

"Well, I aint got nothing against a nigger. I just want to see the work before I pay him."

"I cleaned up the presses, the ink rollers, that's all. Here's the key."

Big Mo showed the key to Fane, and then dropped his

hand. All he was doing was showing Fane that he had the key, but I felt that he had made a mistake. HyLow did too. He nudged me. Big Mo asked Mrs. Collier was there anything else she wanted him to do, and she said no, and Fane, he reached in his pocket, leaning up against the wall. He was very drunk. "I say I want to see the work."

"Frank, you cant see the work," screamed Mrs. Collier. She was not mad, but laughin. I knew she was going to let us get some pecans, then . . .

Fane gave Big Mo the money. "Three dollars, right?"

"No, Mr. Collier always give me five for the job."

Fane, he squint-eyed at Big Mo. That red-faced white man was so drunk, I bet he thought we all was one nigger. "Day's Sunday, and these niggers dont stop workin."

Mrs. Collier came out. "Please, yall go now."

"I come for my money, Mrs. Collier, like you said."

"Oh, Frank, this is silly. Give them the five dollars."

The drunk man, he just looked out at us, staring from one to the other, trying to make things out, I guess, then he grunt, and start mumbling something about giving us a minute to get out of his sight and letting loose them dogs. And then he took the five out, and he handed it to Big Mo. Big Mo gave him the key.

We turned and went to the car. But we could hear Fane cussing and laughin behind us. Then we heard the dogs barkin.

We got in the car. Big Mo drove fast again. He was mad. I could tell. HyLow, he was shakin his head, grinnin.

I couldnt tell what HyLow saw funny. I figure he sometimes lose part of his mind, crack his brain or something, and laugh at anything. Big Mo ask him what he laughin at, but HyLow, he dont hear. He got tears in his eyes. I dont know what made me start laughin, but pretty soon, I just laugh, and Big Mo, he gettin madder and madder. We all laugh so hard that Big Mo stop the car. Me and HyLow get out and fall on the ground. It was just too much, and I tell you that is one of the first times that I think I found out what make HyLow laugh at everything. I'm tellin you I think I looked at everything different from that day on.

We couldnt wait till dusk, like we said. No. We head for North Bend, where the river turn and straighten out and come along about one quarter of a mile in from the plantation. Cotton grew all along there. Come Monday morning, you still find a few niggers out in some of those fields, pickin the last of it. We head for the bend. Big Mo drivin fast. We meet a car. It looked like somebody going out to the Collier place. Nobody say nothin. We know we had one thing to do. Big Mo wanted to wait till dusk, but HyLow was against it.

"How we gone to frail a tree at night and no lights?"

When we heard that we didnt say nothin. I hadnt figured on frailin a tree, but just picking a few and gettin out. HyLow must know more about it than he told us. We parked the car under a row of trees and headed for the levee. The best way to keep out of sight would be to hit the levee, get on the wet side of it, and then go back downriver, keeping out of sight on the low side. HyLow said by the time we got there it would be dusk anyway. It was about three o'clock in the afternoon then, the sun was far away, but it was hot. We started out. Big Mo, he in the lead, walking with his croaker-sack over his shoulder. HyLow next, and he always looking back at me, winking. I say to myself, That nigger is crazier than a coon.

We march along for a while. If anybody come along and see Big Mo's car, they'd know. But it would take them to be doing the same thing to see the car. The river was moving along like a big snake. We could just make out the other side good. Twice we saw people on the other side. Nobody say nothing. After a while, Big Mo slow down. He way ahead of us then. He hold up his hand for us to hurry. We get to him, and we see we reach the first of the pecan groves, but it aint papershell.

We pick up a few, crack them and eat them. But Big Mo, he didnt mess with them. They were them pea-size pecans, real hard, and if you get any of the hull in your mouth, your mouth draw up like it was gettin smaller. It was a funny feeling, and we mostly used the pea-size nuts to chunk at people. Nobody would eat 'em. You couldnt sell 'em to store-keepers, and you couldnt make no money yourself. Only poor people and squirrels ate 'em. So as I was cracking one open HyLow say, "Kiddo, you know what happen to you if you mix peas with papershells, dont you?"

I spit out them shells. "Naw," I say.

HyLow, he shake his head. Every time he open his mouth, he either laugh or makin rimes. That's the way he was.

"Man, if you dont know, then I have to school you, cause I dont want nobody to fool you. There's an old saying my mother taught me. It go like this:

> Whiteman work him
> cause he cant figger.
> He run and eat pea-nims
> and turn to a nigger.

"Then there's another one:

> That's an old story
> about an African slave.
> Brought 'em to America
> but he wouldnt behave.
>
> White man wonder
> what's in his gut.

They cut him open.
They find a pecan nut.

Black folks bury 'em
in the middle of the night.
African scare 'em
and the nigger turns white."

Pretty soon we come to the clearing. HyLow, he tell us we can see the papershell trees from there, and he point. They about a quarter mile away, running along the edge of the cotton to our left. Every now and then we hear a dog bark. Big Mo, he steady watching in the direction of the big house.

"If we get spied," said HyLow, "I'm going south along the river. I know a place down there, I can get across. Mo, you take kiddo and make it out."

Big Mo didnt say nothin. He was just ahead of us.

"We stick together," he said.

"Like hell, man," said HyLow. "If them dogs come after us, we split."

Big Mo, he think about it, then he say, "We stick together unless we hear dogs comin."

"Well, if the dogs come, you know where Nadley's cotton gin used to be? Well, I meet you there one hour after we split."

"I think about it," said Big Mo.

"Man, there aint nothin to think about. When somebody spy us, then we dont have no time for thinkin."

So we went on. I was spose to stick with Big Mo. HyLow would go downriver to draw them off us. Nobody said anything, because we hoped we wouldnt have to do anything like that.

One thing in our favor is that we knew what was going on back there at the Collier house. At the big house there probably wasnt nobody there except Mr. Collier's old grandmother and grandfather and their nurse. Maybe one of the sons home from college, but that was all.

When we reached the papershell grove, I could tell that nobody had been picking those pecans. Sticks and limbs, leaves and nuts, were scattered on the ground. We fell into the first tree like crazy men.

For about half hour we filled the sacks, all the time we were gruntin and thankin Jesus for such beautiful nuts. We picked up under five trees, and then Big Mo said we should move on to the next ones.

"Aint no more like these," said HyLow. "That one yonder is stunted this year. Worms in every other nut. Something got them. The other ones down the line are the same. If we want any more nuts . . ."

Big Mo, he come over to us and examine our sacks.

Now, a croakersack can hold a lot of nuts, and by this time we had filled each of them with about thirty pounds of nuts. HyLow said we ought to get as much as we each could carry. And Big Mo said he could carry two sacks, and with that we just kept on pickin them up. Now, huntin pecans is not as simple as it looks. When there's grass and brush around, you have to know how to look for them. Some people, after they have cleaned from right under the tree, think there aint no more on the ground. But most of the time if there is a little grassy spot right outside of where the tree's shadow falls and when the wind or a storm hits, as one hit the night before, then you can bet your hammer hand that you can pick up a couple of pounds of nuts from there.

So on, it was almost dusk. We looked along the edge of that cotton. HyLow started climbing a tree. He had a long stick, and leaned it against the tree.

When you get ready to frail a tree, then you pick out the one with the biggest and the sweetest nuts and then climb it with a bamboo stick or something, and then just sit out on a limb and knock that tree till all them nuts are on the ground.

Now I saw HyLow get up in that tree. "Man, we better get out of here!" said Big Mo.

"I thought you could carry two sacks," said HyLow.

"Yeah, but if you get shot up in that tree, I might have to carry you too."

"Nigger, you know if I get shot you'd run," and he was knocking down so many pecans that they were raining on us. "Listen to him, kiddo, listen to this big old ink spot, so black that aint nobody know we even out here."

"Well, I aint never seen but one dog climb a tree," said Big Mo. He was laughing himself now and filling his sack.

"Whose dog is that?" I asked, cause I aint never heard of a dog climbing a tree. Big Mo, he laughed.

"That one that's in one now," and he hollered up at HyLow, "Man, you see any possums in that tree?"

HyLow, he was grunting. Then next thing I know, Big Mo was climbing the big tree next to the one HyLow was in, and his big self was sitting out on the first branch, and he was shaking it just like a wind had hit it. I kept looking because the limb sounded like it was cracking. I dont think there was one pecan left. Then he came down and got up in the one HyLow was frailing. "When you do a job," he said to Hy-Low, who was climbing down, "do a good job."

"Listen to him, kiddo, will you? Braggin. You better hurry up. We cant come out here every night."

We frailed three trees so good there wasnt no pecans left except for stunted ones. Our sacks were loaded. Big Mo had two croakers on his shoulders, and HyLow had one. I carried the two twenty-pound flour sacks.

Just at dusk we heard the dogs barkin. They sounded close. We started back the way we came. We saw a car coming. Looked like the same car that had passed before.

When we reached the car, we could still hear dogs barking. They must be loose cause we was a long way from the
house.

We loaded the car down. Sweat soaked our backs, but
we hadnt stopped for nothing. Big Mo drove. We got back on
Collier Road and headed toward town. All the way back we
laughin and eatin them papershells.

If you aint never had no pecan nuts right off the tree,
then you ought to try some, because when you do, then you
dont want no more of the ones that dry out in the store and
the ends crack. Fresh pecans got all the good-tastin oil right
there in the shell. The best time for papershells is right after
they come down out of the tree. The shell is thinner than pea-
sizes and the other kinds. If they stay around too long, they
dry out.

HyLow, he say we ought to go by the church.

"Them people dont want to see us," said Big Mo. I felt
he was right. HyLow, he come to shake his head. He put on
his sports jacket.

"Listen, Brother kiddo," he said to me, "I aint got time to
mess with thick-headedness. You want to make some money
or not? What you make with Mo today? One dollar? I fix it so
you can make ten dollars, what you say?"

I didnt know what to say. Big Mo, he driving the car.
Pretty soon we in front of the church. The people were having some kind of Thanksgiving program.

"Well, you know damn well we aint gonna eat two
hundred pounds of pecans by ourselves. Let's go to that
Thanksgiving program," said HyLow.

"You crazy, man, I aint ready for—"

"You promised Mrs. Rankin you be back."

"That be next Sunday," said Big Mo.

"You make your contribution while its still in you, or you
wont make none at all. I know what I'm going to do. I going

in just before the services are over. I wont have to sit long, and then they'll know I'm there, and I can pass out a few papershells, and then that's it."

"You bout the lowest Negro I know, and—"

"Listen to this big old nigger." HyLow started to laugh. When HyLow laughs, his laugh just make you think, and when you hear him, you know he aint foolin. If there was one thing that never told a lie, that was the way HyLow laughed. He had a slippery tongue, but if he laugh and you listen, you find something there. He was laughin, and then I found myself grinnin. Big Mo he aint say nothin, but I could see him figurin out. Suddenly the car started making a loud noise, and then it jerked. The car suddenly stopped going and steam was popping out of it.

Big Mo jumped out. While me and Big Mo were looking under the hood, HyLow disappeared.

Pretty soon we could hear the people turning out of the church. Big Mo and me, we get back in the car, but the hood was still up. Before we could hide, here come HyLow, bringin some people.

"The best papershells this side of the Mississippi. We sellin for not one hundred for ten pounds, like Yancy do those dried-up things he ship off up North. But we selling them for twenty-five cents a pound."

Russell Moody was there. The Gary kids crowded around the car, and before we knew it we were digging into those sacks, selling the papershells to the whole church.

While we were tryin to shorten the line of kids and people, I see Mrs. Rankin coming along. It was my job to hold onto the money in the front seat and pass out change. This time, Mrs. Rankin with some of the old ladies. I figured she wouldn't stop, but I was wrong.

She come over to the car, look in at me, and watch HyLow and Big Mo sellin the pecans.

"Well, Morris, I can see you worked the whole day. You know the Lord said six days was allotted for work—"

"Yes, mam," Morris said. He was always respectful.

"And on the seventh Thou shalt steal," whispered HyLow to me.

We all knew Mrs. Rankin knew where them papershells come from, because she used to work daywork for the Colliers. She come over to the sacks. "Papershells?"

"Yes, mam."

"Here, try some," said HyLow. He gave her a free sack, but she shoved his hand away, ramblin in her purse. "Those are good pecans," she said. "I cant chew like I used to."

But she handed HyLow a coin, anyway. "I want to see you young men in church next Sunday." She looked at Morris. "Morris, you need to lose a little weight."

"Yes, mam," said Big Mo.

"And you, young man." She pointed at me. "Better stay away from these older boys, you hear?"

"Yes, mam."

Then she came over to HyLow. "And you, I bet you can smell when pecans are ripe . . . Comin round here, acting like you from somewhere. Why, all of you ought to thank the Lord that man aint shoot you . . . Now, save some of them papershells for your own people."

"Yes, mam," we said. Then she went on down the street.

"Now, how she know where we get them papershells?" asked HyLow.

"That old lady know the day you was born," said Big Mo.

"Hey hey hey," said HyLow. But it was the first time all day I aint heard him laugh. He didnt have to laugh. The truth was the truth anyway it come.

The Voice

We WERE KICKING around down near the river, just walking off the feeling that came when Spencer died. We just walked around, silentlike, our hands stuffed in our pockets, mainly for style. It wasnt that cold. We were just kicking around down there, me, Willie, and Blake, trying not to think about Spencer, but knowing all the time that we were lost without him, knowing that we would never sing the same again, knowing that something had died within us as a group.

We named ourselves the Expressions. We sang gospel and blues all over Harlem. We had been together only a year, but our reputation was good and we were starting to make a few coins. It seemed the more we sang as a group, the better Spencer sang alone. He was a lead tenor, and his voice was like one you never heard before. The guy could sing. Girls, they fell out when he sang. But then one day he just got sick, and in a week he died.

We had been kicking around ever since the funeral. For a while we were spending a lot of time at Spencer's house. But after a couple of weeks we stopped going regularly. A lot of Spencer's kinfolks were still coming to the house. Some were coming from Virginia and Georgia, where Spencer's mother and father came from, and even though the funeral was over people were still dropping in. We felt that some of them couldnt understand why it had to be Spencer.

After a while things started to drift back to the way they were before it happened, like everybody going to work and school. This is what made us kick around a lot. We felt things would never go back to the way they were. How could they? The Expressions. We were the Expressions, not singing any more, not even wanting to harmonize or anything, just wearing our group jackets, which werent very warm. They were red, with the group's name in blue letters on the back. Our individual names were written in fancy letters over the left front. But all we could do was kick around down by the river.

Willie scraped a handful of snow from a piece of metal sticking out of the shore like it was a cross. He began to make a perfect round out of it, packing it slowly and neatly.

"Arnold wants to come in," he said.

Blake kicked at a rusted can and walked closer to the edge of the water. We all knew that Arnold just couldnt sing. Arnold was Spencer's brother, but he had no tone or color in his voice. Once or twice when we first got together he messed around with his guitar, but Spencer began to sing him out. Arnold couldnt sing, and Spencer was doing more with his voice than Arnold was with his guitar. He just faded out and never was around much when we practiced, but we knew he was getting better and better picking on that guitar.

We didnt say anything about Arnold. Willie suddenly took a quick leap and hurled the snowball far out over the river. It broke in the wind and splattered the water. We watched, then moved on down the shore. A seagull dipped in front of us, swung upwards in an arc with the wind, and faded into the haze over the city.

Blake walked a few feet ahead of us like he was looking for something in the sand. He was shorter than the rest of us, but he was wide and strong. Even Blake's mustache was fuzzier than ours. He had shaved once, but all of us—except Spencer, whose mustache had never started—were letting ours grow a bit more, at least to where it could.be seen. Blake's mustache stood out well against the brownness of his skin. Since we were all darker than him, we would have to let ours grow. Blake told us that if we shaved, ours would grow back much faster, but me and Willie didnt do it. We just shaved around ours.

"You know what?" Willie said.

"What?"

"If I was God ... if ..."

"What you mean?" I asked. Willie and me were walking together now. Blake trudged ahead of us. I looked at Willie. I had never known him to talk about God except to curse.

"You know what I mean, man, you know."

I mumbled something and plunged my hands deeper in my pockets. Maybe I felt the same way. Why had God let it happen?

The river curved and we took to the streets, shifting along three abreast, not looking at the people, and crossing the streets without waiting for the lights. We had a silent pact. We dared anybody to hit us. The Saturday traffic was heavy too. A lot of people were getting ready for Easter, buying things and going places.

We didnt say anything for several blocks. We were nearing St. Nicholas Park, which slanted off the side of a cliff on top of which ran Convent Avenue. The park lay beneath a fluff of snow. The rocks—some buried deep in the ground—seemed to peep from peaks of ice and snow. Bird tracks on a few benches, the tracks of a dog and somebody walking, were the only signs of life in the park. A wind blew up from the spaces in-between the Harlem buildings, and we began to feel cold.

The park was a big place and we liked to come there. Every time we used to come, a funny feeling would get us. Once in the fall we tried to practice, but the wind and the leaves made so much noise that we had to cool it. Spencer, though, he kept on singing by himself. He just kept on singing, making up the song as he went along. We gave a low harmony, but the wind was blowing so hard. When he finally finished, we patted him on the back and told him how boss it was and that we all had to learn it. The song was so good that we were kinda scared of him.

The wind whistled every now and then. We were kicking up a path in the snow ahead of us, walking through the park that we knew so well but that had taken on a strange quietness. All of a sudden Blake stopped in his tracks, stared at Willie, and said, "Only the Devil would do what's been done to Spencer."

We stopped near a bench. I brushed off the snow.

"Think maybe Spencer made it to heaven?" asked Willie. He didnt know what Blake was talking about.

"Remember that!" said Blake, pointing a finger at Willie for emphasis. "Only the Devil."

"Yeah," I said. "Ole Spence is in heaven, and he'll be singing to the angels up there and get up a group—"

"What kind of a God would let him die? Answer me that!" Blake walked off a piece and kicked at the snow.

"Maybe God didnt have nothin to do with it," said Willie.

"That's what I'm sayin, Willie. Didnt you hear me? There *aint* no God, man. There aint *nothin.*"

"Except the Devil?" I said. "You just said the Devil did it, man."

Blake was silent. Maybe he didn't believe in the Devil, either. We watched him.

"Well, man," said Willie. "Somebody has to be up there in the sky. I mean, God made us and everything in the world. Aint that right, Al?"

"Yeah," I said.

"You just like the other suckers," said Blake. "Man, dont believe everything some preacher spits in your face. There aint no God, no nothin. When you dead, you dead."

"Ah," said Willie. He turned to me for support. "I mean,

I dont know about where I'm goin myself, but I believe Spencer's in heaven right now."

Blake frowned. We all moved on a bit.

"If there's a heaven, then there's got to be somebody in it," I said.

"Why so? Why so?" Blake shouted at me. "What kinda talk is that?" We had trapped him, and he was trying to think his way out. We got kinda scared of him. "If Spence went to heaven, then there must be a heaven, and if there's a heaven, then there's got to be a God to run it, right, Al?"

"Yeah," I said.

"Have you ever seen God?" asked Blake.

I was silent. We were going up a hill. A man walked ahead of us, and a big brown boxer loped among the shrubs and rocks.

"Man, you're crazy," said Willie, picking up a handful of snow. "You cant *see* God. Not even Moses could see him. But maybe you can see Jesus Christ. He was God too, you know."

"Well, I aint never seen Jesus Christ, God, and none of the rest of them people. Look here, Willie," Blake said, scooping up a handful of snow, "you see that dog over there," and we looked at the dog. "Well, man, I believe in what I can see and what I can feel." He patted the snow into a round ball. "I can feel this snow and I can see that dog. I believe in both of them." And he threw the ball. It thudded off the side of the dog. The dog jerked and turned around, sniffing the snow and the air, but it didnt yelp.

The man turned around. He was an old white man. We had seen him a few times. He lived somewhere over Convent Avenue near the other side of Manhattan. Once when we were practicing he stopped and listened.

We slowed, but he waited for us, the leash swinging in his hand. "He's only a pup," he said as we were still far away. "He wont try to bite."

We had prepared inside ourselves to fight. We moved on cautiously and the dog began ranging off again. The man reminded me of a rabbi. He had a funny-looking beard and he wasnt too tall. Even Spencer was a bit taller than he was. The only thing we were really afraid of then was maybe having to outrun a dog.

The man began to talk to us, very softly, as if he had known us all his life. We didnt speak to him. Blake wouldnt look at him. And then, as all four of us moved along the path, the man said that he had heard us singing several times and had enjoyed it.

We were cautious. We thought he was lying about seeing us. How could he enjoy our singing? We were singing soul. He was white. How could he even pretend to understand? We didnt say anything. Maybe we were better than we thought, if a white man liked our sound. We tried to walk ahead of him and get out of his way, but suddenly the dog loped in the middle of the path in front of us. Blake was up front, and instead of going around the dog, he slowed and let the man pass, and we all three lingered behind.

"Let's go see Arnold," said Blake. We stopped. The man was putting the leash on the dog.

"Come on, man," said Willie, "let's all go up on Convent Avenue."

"For what?" I asked.

Blake wasnt going to go up on Convent. He was always the leader of the group in things like knowing what to do and all that, but it was always Spencer who led us when it came time to sing. It was late afternoon, and pretty soon it would be getting dark. The man was passing us now. He was going back down the hill.

Then he shook us up.

"Did you fellows ever resolve your debate about whether

there was a God or not?" he asked, pulling on the dog. "I heard you as I passed you below."

Willie and me looked at each other, but Blake drifted down the hill, as if he didnt hear the man.

"Where is your tenor today?" He was talking about Spencer.

Blake stopped walking down the hill and looked back. Willie and me stood near the man, staring at him. Then we stuffed our hands deeper in our pockets, kicked around a bit, and shrugged away, the only sound coming from the wind and the panting of the man's dog. What could we say to him? He didnt know us. He should have been afraid of us, but he wasnt. A lot of times guys will gang up on somebody who looks like money. Sometimes we'd stomp a guy just because we didnt like the way he looked. We had done it a few times, but usually on other guys.

"He got sick," said Willie, but he was looking at Blake. The man stopped. "And he died," said Willie, looking at me.

And before the man could finish expressing how sad he felt about it, Blake came running back up the hill.

"Hey, mister, you Jewish, right?"

The man nodded slowly.

"Then tell these stupid guys that there aint no heaven. Jews dont believe in Jesus, right?"

The man pulled in the dog. "Werent you talking about God at first? What has that got to do with whether or not there is a God?"

"I say there's no God. No *good* God gonna kill a guy like Spence." He bowed his head and kicked snow off a rock.

"Nobody killed nobody," said Willie. "It was some kind of disease."

"Spinal meningitis," I said.

"He knows what I mean!" said Blake.

"You're trying to get me to admit that there's no God," said the man to Blake. "I cant do that. I believe in God."

"Tell me this," said Blake. "If God is good, then everything he does must be good, right?"

"Wait, now," said the man. "Let me ask you some questions."

"Answer mine first! Do you believe in a Jewish God? Yeah, I guess you do!" Blake wouldnt give nobody a chance.

All of a sudden, Blake burst out laughing and he wouldnt stop. "Look, *Reverend*," he said, "these guys here are my friends, see, and havent seen God, but they believe in Him. You're a preacher, so I guess you *seen* Him?"

Slowly but surely the man breathed and said, "Yes."

Oh, no, we thought, Blake had trapped him.

Blake cocked his head in doubt. He smirked and turned around to go on down the hill, still laughing.

"Wait, man," said Willie. "Why you runnin away? He said he seen Him—"

"What do you mean?" I asked the man.

But he didnt answer. Instead he started walking down the hill. He unleashed the dog and it began to range all around. Suddenly Blake turned around and asked, "Where?"

And the man said, "Here." He pointed with his arms, sweeping the whole landscape.

Blake broke out into a fierce laugh. He bent over and groaned his guts out.

Then he started picking up snowballs and hurling them at the dog. One missed, but another one hit, and then he turned on the man, hitting Willie once by mistake, me twice, and the man several times. He was crazy.

We started to rush him, but we retreated, not because we were scared of getting hit, but from the same feeling that hit us since it all happened. We couldnt dig what this feeling meant. I guess I kind of envied Blake for doing something.

He was letting it out, even though it was scaring the hell out of us.

We left the man in the park. He had shouted at Blake and us too. We fled him and finally caught Blake in the streets.

Something kept us from saying anything to him. We walked along abreast until he stopped and faced us. We were standing in front of a church, and a priest was coming out.

"So, did he tell you where *he* saw God?" laughed Blake. We kicked around. Snow was falling slowly from the sky.

"Ah, man," said Willie. "Stop being so messed up. I mean, nobody knows where Spence is except Spence."

Willie shouldnt have said that, because Blake turned on him all over again. The priest was listening to us.

"If you can see God, tell me what He looks like. Tell me," said Blake.

We were silent.

"What color is He, huh?"

"You cant see a spirit," said Willie.

"You stupid m.f.," said Blake. "You believe what that white man told you?"

"You cant see a spirit," said Willie.

"That rabbi was talkin about *his* God. *His* God is a white one. We're black. What color is that snow?" Blake pointed.

We tried to laugh and argue Blake down, but he pressed in on us. The priest was coming near now.

"Every time I see a picture of Jesus, he white, right?" We were silent. Willie shook his head.

"What you mean?" Blake turned on Willie.

"You're sayin there's a God now!" I pointed at Blake.

"Shut up, Al!" he shouted at me.

We were standing there as if we were going to fight. I got mad at Blake.

"Man, you didnt have to snowball us," I said.

"You a crazy fool," said Willie, but Blake cut him short.

"I aint admittin nothin. All I want Willie to do is to tell me what God looks like."

The priest was standing near the curb now, as if he was going to cross.

"Man, aint you never seen no picture of Black Jesus?" asked Willie.

Blake broke out into a laugh that even made me ashamed. "Dont be a sucker, man. Just because some white man come along with a bucket of paint and paint Jesus' picture black so he can get your money, dont make me fall for that jive. Not me, baby." Blake laughed.

"What bout Black Marcus?" asked Willie. "He said God is black."

"Black Marcus aint believe that jive," said Blake. "He only say that because he know niggers are stupid. You cats are suckers!"

"Ah, you crazy, man."

Blake grabbed Willie by the sleeve and spun him around. I thought his fist was going up beside Willie's head. "Sucker," he said. "Father Divine is your daddy of Grace." Willie shoved Blake off.

I guess we had never really thought about things too much. When Spence was here, all we did was sing and go to parties looking for girls. Willie felt it like I did. He looked back at the priest who was coming toward us. Blake was talking loud about everybody having their own different gods. The same difference between people was the same between gods.

"I aint got no God," he said.

The priest was near us now. We had heard kids call him by name—Father Wilson. Blake walked away slowly, stuffing his hands in his pockets. A few people passed and turned their heads toward us but kept going. Once an ambulance screamed down the avenue and drowned out what Father Wilson was saying. We thought about Spence.

". . . the Creator is invisible, like the wind," he was saying. "He cannot be compared to a man."

Blake turned. "What about Jesus Christ? Wasnt he a man?"

The father nodded and looked over at Blake. Blake walked near a garbage can and sat down on the lid after banging off the snow.

We followed the priest over. He asked us what had started the argument, and we told him that our friend had died.

"Yes," he said, nodding his head. We knew he probably knew about Spence. A woman carrying shopping bags passed between the priest and Blake. When she had passed, Blake's eyes were following the path of her feet in the snow.

We didnt say anything. The priest was waiting on Blake.

There was something funny about the way we were silent. I felt that Blake was thinking about Spencer. He was frowning. If there was no God, then Spence was dead and gone forever. If there was, then Blake was wrong. All of a sudden he turned on the priest and asked, "Okay, tell me, what color is God?"

"I once saw a painter," the priest said, "after he had labored weeks on a painting. It was a painting of a summer sunset over a lake. There was a house where a man sat playing a guitar. When I looked at the painter's hands, I saw all the colors that I saw on the painting . . ."

Blake didnt say anything. He stuffed his hands in his pockets and drifted on up the street. We couldnt tell from his back if he was laughing or not. Willie asked the priest something, but I watched Blake.

Then we heard him yelling: "You guys comin? What's the matter, huh?"

The priest stood near us, but neither Willie or me dared look into his face. We waved at Blake to leave us alone, but there was something in his voice. We kicked off up the street behind him, leaving the priest there. We didnt worry about the priest. Religion was his business.

We thought we were mad at Blake, but deep down we sorta respected him.

"Man, what's the matter with you?" I said.

"Yeah, man," said Willie. "You scared of gettin made to look like a fool?"

Blake walked ahead of us, crossing the street against the light and telling us to shut up. But he didnt seem to be mad, only confused. We believed in something but didnt know how to say what it was. Blake believed in something and was saying it. He must have done a lot of thinking about all those things, but he still couldnt figure them out, especially since he liked Spencer as much as we did.

"I'm goin to see what Arnold's doin," he said.

We followed behind him. He knew we would come. Going through the streets toward Spencer's house was like coming back to places we knew before. Right then I thought I didnt want to hear Arnold's nowhere voice. And I didnt want to be thinking about all the good days of the Expressions. Willie was feeling the same way. He pulled me aside, and we stopped for a couple of minutes for an orange drink in the candy store a block from Spence's house.

"You goin up?" he asked.

"You?" I asked.

And neither one of us answered. We walked on down the street. When we came to the stoop where Spence lived, we just went up the steps and on up the stairs. Spencer lived on the top floor. Blake had already gone up and was almost up the last flight. We stood looking up from the first floor for a while.

We heard the bell ring and the door open. I thought I heard a few guitar chords, but it didnt last. We heard the heavy voice of Spencer's father from the back. When me and Willie got up the steps and into the house, we could hear a lot of voices. Spencer's father shook our hands like he always did. He liked to treat us like men. We went in and his mother began kissing us. She wasnt crying, but there was a strain in her voice. Several people were seated in the living room. All three of us were introduced as Spencer's friends, the singers. They made us sit down, but we didnt want to.

"You boys sit down," said Spencer's father. "Arnold be right up here— Arnold!" and he leaned his head toward the hall and the back rooms.

"Arnold! The boys are here!"

I glanced around the room. The two women and a man were looking at us. One of the women I had seen before. She was Spencer's cousin. I didnt know the others, but the man and woman on the couch had something familiar about them. Blake was moving toward the hall. He stood looking at Spencer's mother as if he was asking her permission to leave. She was a short, dark woman, with a sparkle always coming out of her eyes. She was quick to cry and quick to be glad over anything that she liked. We liked her. Sometimes she called us her children.

"If my children dont sit down," she suddenly said, "I'm going to have to ask them to sing us a blessing before dinner." And she stood up smiling and went out of the room.

"In my church," said the man, "I have a group like you boys." So he was a preacher, I thought. I knew there was something familiar about him.

"I need a drink of water," Blake said, going back toward the kitchen.

Nobody heard him, because Willie was talking about the priest.

"Well, what I really dont understand is if all the religions believe in one god, why there isnt one religion," Willie was saying.

"There *is* one religion," said the minister with a smile. "But everybody has his own private interpretation of God's word. We all have to worship God the way our conscience tells us. If you got a clean heart and you can ask a good, honest question, God will answer you. He never failed yet. Dont worry about all the confusion of religions and the babel of tongues. They're all man-made. God has one religion and He's always on time."

He was a pleasant sort of a guy. Not like a lot of the ministers we'd seen. He had a Southern accent, but it was pleasing and he wasnt too old. I kept looking at Willie every time he would ask a question. He was *really* trying to find out things. The minister was talking about the young man who came to Jesus, asking Him what he must do to get into the kingdom of heaven. I thought about Spence.

I got up and went back to the kitchen, where Spencer's grandmother was cooking. The smell of roast chicken and dressing filled the hall. Memories of those feast days at parties and church affairs filled my mind. From the kitchen came the sound of a guitar. I could hear Spencer's mother saying, "Go on, go on," and the grandmother saying, "Hum. The Lord blesses good singing," and I came into the kitchen. Blake was standing there beside Arnold, and Arnold was picking that guitar.

Soon the women went back up the hall, and we didnt say much. Some feeling was pulling us. Arnold was picking loosely at the strings of the guitar as if he was inspecting them. Blake just stood there for a while, his big chest puffing out and his eyes blazing. Then he broke off into a chorus. I couldnt help but follow, and Arnold was right there and it was a good sound. We were singing "The Hills of Love," the song that Spence got that day in the park.

Then, coming in from behind us, was Willie.

We sang from our souls, and before long everybody was standing round listening. Spencer's mother was trying not to cry. And then all of a sudden Blake caught a note, and we all heard it and we came to his aid. We got to feeling good, and the people backed us up with some hand-clapping. Spence should have been there then, because we were all singing and making one voice.

GOODBYE, SWEETWATER

Rain God

CUD AND ME are running so fast that the two birds over Ned's head are slowing down in the sky and now they are passing behind the low cloud, which must be the one sprinkling these few raindrops on us, but we are still running faster than the drops, me and Cud. They know where the Devil is at.

Cud is ahead because he ain't afraid of the Devil, but I am, and we are running along the fence and Cud is leaping over. I am sliding on the little slope beside the fence, catching myself on the leaning old fence post, pulling up, and then I am standing high on the fat fence post, looking at Cud as the big hole in the seat of his overalls shows his black skin and his legs roll away over the field. Ned is standing near the stump waving at us like he found the greatest secret in the world, and I am standing higher on the post, puffing, stretching out my arms like a bird so that I can see if I can *see* the Devil beating his wife. If I can see from here, I am staying here.

I am a waterfall flying off that post and I must be a river because the fence is shaking like the dead trees did in the stream when we were fishing. A waterfall can put out the Devil in a hot Hell, so I am running faster, and then the sun stands on top of me and then hides his head again and you should see my shadow leap away from the side of myself, just like when I was swinging from the oak limb on Cud's rope yesterday, and higher and higher! and I'm gone. . . .

Look at Ned. But I am looking only at Cud when he slows down. What's he slowing for? He must see something. Ned stops waving me on. If I really see this Devil I'm gonna be scared of *everything* for the rest of my life.

But Cud he sees something and he keeps seeing it and now he's waving and it is my turn to see but I am slowing. Then I am running faster and faster as the sun comes out over the center of the field, like a fat pillar of golden air and the rain is catching up with me and I can see it on the grass and feel it climbing over my muddy bare feet, cleaning the stink off. . . .

"Hurry, Blue!"

"You missin it, man!"

What they yelling me on for? They see I'm coming, and while I'm coming I strain to see what they see, but I don't see nothing but the sun shining down from the sky and the dark field all around shaking in the wind and the rain striking across the light. And on the grass I slide and I am there!

"Look!" Ned is crazy.

"They dancin!" Cud, he crazy too. He leans in on the stump, squinting at two figures, like little carved dolls, on top of that old stump. It's an old stump, rotten, and a hole is right in the center. The rings for age are around that hole, which is a rot hole, and the rings are like little ditches. Splinters and twigs stick out of that stump, but not like the two figures dancing in the light around the center hole, and when I see it I close my mouth shut. Then my mouth drops open on its own, and I feel the rain spirits soaking into me.

Ned is whispering:

If in the rain you find a snake,
The Devil's will you sure can break.

But if in the rain you find the sun.
The beating of the Devil's wife's begun.

Turn the snake on its back,
Lay the snake out on a fence.

The Devil sure to loose your track,
And you bound to keep your sense.

And Cud is whispering a little, and I am shivering because the sun *was* hot, but now it is rain-cold, and the little dolls on the stump are dancing faster.

I see the Devil dressed in red, swinging a whip around his head, snorting smoke when a rain drop strikes, striking the other on the back. The Devil's wife is dressed in white, and the Devil's wife is falling, and she falls. . . .

into the hole. But she catches the edges of the stump and the Devil pulls her up, and gets on top of her and I am watching him straddle her, and then I hear a scream and the wind is slashing me with rain. Sun is gone, just like that! and in the field I am alone. Cud and Ned are racing away, yelling, and when I look at the stump, only the twigs dance in the wind, slow, back and forth, growing bigger and bigger as the sun flicks off and on, off and on, clouds running, and both of them are getting taller and taller, giants with hands so big that the fingers are reaching for me now, and then I am stumbling over my legs, leaping with my heart which I can feel driving a river all over my body and I fly.

They are way ahead of me and I don't know what's in back of me and don't see anything but the Devil chasing me, and at home I am puffing out everything, watching Cud's eyes and Ned's eyes when we all climb on the back of papa's wagon, which Papa is driving into the yard, and I know it's my turn to feed the mule, but I still am puffing when Papa gets down and that's my papa, he knows everything.

". . . Yall git your chores did 'fore it start lightnin."

I am puffing and Cud and Ned climb down, but I cannot stop puffing and Papa hears me puffing and I can't talk because the Devil is still chasing the road, and I point into the sky where the sun is setting and where the rain is still coming and going.

My papa don't care nothing about it and he is saying, "Boy, that ain't lightnin!" and I am still puffing and then I have to get off the wagon, and they all looking at me.

"Rainin and sunshinin at the same time," says Ned, and he whispers something to Cud, who don't say nothing except work his mouth. And Papa says, "Rain under the sun, you stick a pin in the ground, and put your ear to it and you can hear the Devil beating his wife."

"We know it," says Ned. I tell my papa I know it, and my head is nodding up and down, up and down, dizzy, and I have to say it.

I have to say we didn't hear the Devil beating his wife this time because we see him do it and my papa is looking at all of us. He is going to holler at us but he don't because he sees something . . . maybe over our heads he sees him coming . . . and maybe out of my eyes too, raining, and I have to tell him, but I don't right then. . . .

"How come he beating her?" I ask. My papa is unhitching them mules and we all around him, and he tells us the truth, and the truth is because it is raining and sunshining at the same time.

The rain spirits are coming strong now, and my papa, he says, "All you got to do is to stick a pin in the ground or a stump and put your ear to it and you can hear the whole thing. Now y'all git and do them chores!"

But we are standing there, dripping, which is a lot of rain by now, and I feel a river rising up in me and I see Cud's eye and Cud, he looks at Ned, and Ned, he looks at me, and I am licking my bottom lip with my tongue, tasting the sunny salt in the rain, and I am going to be the first to tell him. . . . I'm going to tell my papa we see the Devil.

Thalia

The mind knows only what lies near the heart.
—Paraphrase of an old Norse saying.

SOMEHOW I HEARD the snow begin to fall even before it began its slow feathery descent. I thought of the sweater of wool you made for me. I was sitting upon the damp tree where we always sit, the tree with the notches carved from the first limb down to the roots. You know the tree, the tree where I wrote to you and you cried. And afterwards the tree broke the silence of winter that year, and shook away the fist of ice that paralyzed it. Remember how my knife bit into the bark and the tree bled, and you sang warm verses? The same tree I sat beneath, and I heard the wind, hoarse from barking all winter, but cold and ruthless. Maybe it was the wind that told me that the snow was going to fall. I cannot say, for I was listening for your voice. Everywhere I turned I saw you, and whenever I reached to touch you the touch of passion told me the truth, that you were gone and I must bring you back. Thalia, every moment you were gone has been like time racing backwards into a darkness I care not to try to remember.

As soon as I felt the snow I rose up and crossed the field to your house. And there I stood for an hour looking in at the empty house, recalling how you always looked inside, and how you came from it to greet me and how you departed from my vision and my arms to the warmth of the house. Soon your father discovered me standing outside. I looked like a pillar of snow, a snowman sprung up out of the yard, I imagine, and he hurried me inside, chastising me for inviting a chill. Inside you embraced me, and I never heard a word your parents said until your brother came downstairs putting on his coat.

"Let's go over to the Club."

I asked him what was over there because I didn't want anything or anyone to take your closeness away, but he begged me
to come, if not for my sake for his, because he anticipated being
bored by the discussion and wanted to have some reason to
leave. You know your little brother, and for you I rose up and
we went out together.

"I am writing Thalia a book of songs tonight," I said, "and
just as soon as you are bored I want to leave."

As we drove along the streets the snow increased. "Take
me quickly to my house, only for a second."

He didn't ask any questions but drove to the house and I
went upstairs into my study and shook the snow away from me.
How close you felt to me then. I closed my eyes and searched
around the room like a blind man. I had not forgotten where I
kept the sweater, but I wanted to discover you. Thalia, how I
miss you, and I touched blind fingers against the window. (Oh, if
your brother saw me I know he would confirm his suspicions of
my lunacy, and yours for loving me, but he never said anything,
caring only to observe us, as you well know, with his impartial
botanical eye. Sometimes I think he believes that we are plants,
trees entangled, I hope.) And my fingers found you, warm! I discovered you. And I put the sweater that you made with your
hands, I put it on and pressed it so hard that the woolen sparks
went into my flesh and burned my skin. I covered you with a
warm coat and went out into the snow.

There was a crowd at the club. I looked at the great face of
my watch. It said 1:00. But I remembered that the club never
opened until 12:30, so all the people standing out must be gathering for something special or my watch was fast.

We went in and found several friends at the Lounge, waiting for the activities to begin.

I watched them all in the great mirror that hung over the
blue ceiling. I began to feel cold and distant. I wanted to leave,

but I had promised your brother, so I ordered something hot to drink and drew you closer around me. The big clock on the wall showed the time to be exactly 12:30. I looked at my watch. It was very fast. I was about to set it when a group of girls came into the Lounge and, after briefly talking to several others who were all drifting off to the activities, they came over to me.

There were eight of them and they asked about you.

I closed my watch and watched them through the mirror. The warm drink slid down inside of me and drove out the cold, and the sweater pressed in close locking out the cold forever, and I looked at them waiting there and I felt you tickling me, and I opened my eyes very wide and they looked into them. Suddenly they were gone and I saw you in the mirror briefly, and I took out my pen and wrote a song to you.

Your brother was delivering a speech to some group, and while he spoke I listened to you sing beneath the tree. I am so peculiar sometimes that I don't hear people unless they speak of you or quote your verse to my ear. I think perhaps this is unfair to other people, Thalia, but I do not care. If I could not find you somewhere then I would depart outside the universe and search for you everywhere.

With all the songs I am making for you I will make one great song and sing so loud and so sweet that you will come back to me, for the world of reflections is hard to bear sometimes. I do not know how long my mind can deceive my spirit, nor how long my body can remain warm. Thalia, my beloved, when I sing my song, time will stop to listen and his racing feet will bend to the ground. The sea will blush and turn a thousand colors and breathe glass spheres that hold your image. Thalia, my beloved, and I will come down to the sea singing you up out of broken glass.

The eight girls suddenly entered the room and sat down together in the back. Your brother seemed not to notice them, but others in the room turned to glance at them. A discussion period began after your brother finished speaking and soon people began to leave, but the girls stayed. I dared to listen to the discussion.

"We live in a world which has made love a beast that stalks the mountains and valleys of earth seeking whom he might destroy."

But this is only a phase which is a part of the dissolution, the evil which affects us.

"What evil?"

In my speech I spoke of the transformation of power, from the gods of power to the god of power, that power is none other than the obsession to creation. Man is obsessed, not toward creating but toward creation. The gods of power were worshiped in early times and man was inspired toward creating. He created everything to the gods of power, not because he loved, but because he feared. Then the god of power, the force which united the strivings of man, began to breathe upon man, and he became obsessed toward creation. By this unity man began to see himself and love himself, and love God and respect God.

(Thalia, if he was saying that since that time God has loved us, then I will make a song to God also.)

The discussion went on.

". . . The evil that has returned to the earth is the evil of the death of the god of power. What will follow, no one can say, but I am sure it will be a terrible time. Man will be obsessed again to create, and there will be chaos and destruction. Instead of another transformation, there will be a dethroning. The force that drives man to discover creation will no longer exist, and man will be driven by the evil powers of imitation.

"How is this evil?"

The beast which stalks us now is not driven by a desire to understand himself, but to satisfy his hunger, which is not one hunger but many. He has no respect for the diversity of crea-

tion. His end will come when he devours that which is poison to
him.

"Love?"

I did not hear the answer to that question for I was leaving
the room. When I got outside I saw that the eight girls had also
grown bored and were filing out. They mingled with several
young men at the Lounge. I watched them through the mirror.
Then I went outside and sat in your brother's car. "We live in a
world which has made love a beast that stalks the mountains and
valleys of earth seeking whom he might destroy." The voice
echoed in my mind and I wondered what your brother was
thinking about this. When he came out I asked him, but as hard
as I tried, I could not bring myself to listen to him. Every time
the snow struck the windshield I watched it cling, thaw and melt
into spring water. A warm sensation hurried from the arms of
your sweater and churned inside of me, and while we rode I
sang song upon song to you, upon the dead explanation of his
treatise.

I looked at my watch. It was 2:00.

"I'll buy you a drink," he said.

"Only if I pick the place."

"Okay, where?"

I guided him to the little place outside of town where they
play music that haunts you in your sleep. Remember? That place
where we discovered a book of songs in the one solo of the
bassist?

After your brother had had one small drink he wanted to
go. I tried to persuade him to stay until we heard the song you
liked, but he insisted. The atmosphere was too wet and loose,
too slimy and too incoherent. I felt cold suddenly and told him I
would go.

Thalia, how impossible it is for even those who are close to us to know how it was with us. Forgive me for that thought of wondering if they are supposed to know. My watch was running fast again, how fast I do not know. Again I was watching the snow melt into rivers that flowed down like your hair spreading in front of my face, and I breathed, you came, I was warm.

I took my watch to a watchmaker.

"You have broken it," he said.

"I know," and I saw your face in the crystal.

"You will need another watch," he said.

I looked at it. "Yes, this one runs too fast or too slow."

"No," he said, "it does not run at all."

All day long I wrapped myself in the sweater you made for me. I began to study the design in it and the red trimming traveled around me like a river of blood. There was fire in you, and when I looked at my broken watch again I knew that the wool shaped by the touch of yor fingers was turning into my skin. I lay upon a bed of tears and sang a song that Thalia might know wherever she was that I loved her only, that I was obsessed by the creation of love, that none would ever touch me if I climbed outside the cell of time and slew the beasts with every song that you gave me. All the day long and all the night through I sleep in the shell of your kindness, and I could hear the armies of the sea roaring up out of the mist of time and my eyes were opening in the dream that brought you close to my bosom, where I made you as warm as you made me.

There was a crowd gathering on the shore, a crowd of shapes like children running. They paid no mind to me as I approached them. The games engrossed them so that when the mist began to creep in from the sea they did not notice.

First they made war against the sea, leaping and charging naked into the green waves. Then they dragged a great fish from the sea and up onto the sands and danced around it. When they saw me they hailed me to join in. I went to look at the dead fish. They built a fire. But they sang no songs and their voices were like the croak of dying frogs. Soon they began to play in the sand. One muscular boy carried eight great stones; from off the land they all built a fortress. They hailed me and invited me to join in. The mist hung over our heads like a curtain about to fall. I went to the edge of the sea and listened, but I could not tell them that I heard you singing out there. My heart leaped, for as naked as they were, so was I; but on me there was the touch of fingers designed upon my skin.

They looked at me and began a discussion and I could not bear to listen at their croaking. My ears were tuned to the sea, and whenever I stooped down I could peep through a line of separation between the sea and the mist of the sky, and along the line was a bright light dancing into shapes and colors. How beautiful was the specter out there. No one noticed it but me, and while the children played their games of life and death, I scanned the horizon with my eyes and leaned my ears out to sea.

Beneath the rumble and the roar of the vast blue expanse I thought I heard what I was trying to hear, and what I was trying to hear was what I wanted to hear. Then I could not hear anything but the croaking, and no song grew louder in my ears until I went to the edge of the yellow sands and waded out into the water. The waves roared in under wings of foam, and Thalia, I knew your ship was coming over the line in the sky, but the children were calling me and their voices were angry.

I watched them build a fortress and make war. I watched them tear it down and dance around it. All the time I leaned my head out to you.

Up the beach the children ran. They passed me by and locked my arms to theirs, dragging me for a mile. They laughed and squealed and their voices began to cut my ears away. I heard a sound of breaking glass inside my mind. They were drowning out the rumble and the roar of the vast sea, and driving you further and further away from me.

When I could not stand it any longer I took my watch and flung it at them and stood to watch. But their games engrossed them more than me, and they played on and on, up and down the shore, and the mist hung lower and lower.

Goodbye,
Sweetwater

HIS ARMS flapping like a bird, Layton Bridges stood on the porch of the shack and listened to the distant whistle of the freight. Its long sustained peal told him that it was carrying a heavy load, maybe enough cars for the sun to set before the last one passed. He rolled up the frayed ends of his jeans above his bare legs so that the air could get to them. Sometimes after a long freight passed, all he could see was the shadow of the last car streaking across the fallen sun, plunging through the dusty evening, leaving behind only an echo and a hush of loneliness.

The little back country district of Sulfur Springs, Arkansas, sits upon a series of bauxite and sulfur layers. The mineral richness below the surface has transformed the once cotton and tobacco lands into little pocket mining communities, sticking like hardened sores beneath the white dust. A cement factory adds to the gray haze that has become the shroud over every village and rural town.

Holly Springs, where Layton lived, got its name because it has spring water untouched by chemical hardness. Most of the well water in the area was known for its hardness and the taste of sulfur, but this one district erupted now and then with fresh spring water. The spring played a hide-and-seek pattern, going underground and reappearing later.

The only source of soft water in Sulfur Springs was a tiny spring in the middle of a stretch of land closed off by the federal government. Located a mile south of the road near Layton's shack, this land was once part of a rich cotton plantation. Now it was broken up and leased to planters and corporations. The rural people, like Layton Bridges and his grandmother, thought of themselves as living on the edge of a great burnt-out plain, thirsty and bitter, cracking daily under the malice of men. Eventually the land would swallow them up. The big companies would move in and buy them out. Already Sulfur Springs was depopulated, as if overnight the earth had reclaimed or frightened away the people. Besides Layton and his grandmother there were five other families. None of them could claim any young people, except for the kids, too young to move out on their own.

Sixteen-year-old Layton went out into the bare yard where the chinaberry tree stood. The hot afternoon dust leaped up between his toes like fire. He put his arms out as if he were going to dive. Then he leaped, caught the limb of the chinaberry tree and swung himself up. The freight train, like a fleeing worm, crawled atop the horizon of distant trees and hills. It was about a mile away, and Layton wanted to get close to it now. He had believed that any day his mother would come for him or the man she had written about, her friend, Mr. Stubbs, would drive by and take him away. But he had been waiting long months now. He would leave soon, he knew, if he had to make a way himself. The only thing Layton could not reconcile with this joy of leaving Holly Springs was the gnawing feeling that his grandmother was not going. She did not want to go. She would shake her head and say, "Son, I reckon the Lord know best what your grandma gwine do. He been keepin me here on this land now since 'fore anything flyin in the sky 'cept the birds. . . . You go on wid your mama. You go to your mama up there in New York. Go on and finish school. Go in the army. Go to college. Get yourself some learnin. Take care of your mama. You do that and your grandma be happy." Layton always felt and trusted the deep faith and nobility in her voice.

Somehow his grandmother was bigger and stronger than the land. No matter how many factories they built nearby, or how many highways they proposed, or how many mines they dug, his grandmother's strength would last when the rest had crumbled to dust.

He climbed to the top of the tree. The freight still passed, its many-colored, many-shaped cars looking like the curious shapes of a puzzle.

Down the road Layton saw his grandmother coming. Beside her walked Mrs. Fields, who lived in the cabin with her ailing husband and his mother, Granny Lincoln. Nobody knew how old Granny Lincoln was except Granpa Fields. He claimed that his mother was born a slave and when she was a girl had seen Abraham Lincoln campaigning for the presidency. The two old women wore wide straw hats, which cast long boatlike shadows in front of them. Their aprons bulged with vegetables as they approached in the dust, an ancient silence walking beside them, a part of them, and yet, like them, a part of the land.

Leaning out from the tree with his feet firmly set in the notch where the limb sprung from the body of the tree, and holding to the neck of the tree with his left hand, Layton raised his right hand at the train. How many times had he waved at trains? If he could live as long as the number of times he had waved, he knew, without counting them, that he would live to be as old or older than Granny Lincoln. But there was something about waving at a freight train that seemed dry and meaningless. He lowered his hand. He had always waved at the swift passenger trains, and many times when he went across the river and sat by the tracks, people on the train would wave back. He never knew if the white faces waving at him would ever make the engineer stop the train for him. His brother had ridden on a train when he had gone off to Vietnam. But that was two years ago and his brother had been killed over there. They said he had been missing in action. He thought of himself in a few years riding on a train or maybe even an airplane and being a soldier somewhere. He would fight in his brother's place. He would save up all his money and come back to New York, give it all to his mother to help her. Yes, he would do all that and then he would buy a car, come back to Holly Springs and take his grandmother to Illinois where his uncle Joe lived. Uncle Joe had said that he wanted her to stay with him, but she had always refused.

Layton watched the last car on the freight. The hot white dust clung to the smooth hard surfaces of the tree like powder.

Long before the cement factory was built several miles down the road, Layton had fallen from the tree, but it had been because he was careless. Now with the dust from the trucks and cars and the factory, all the trees and shacks in Holly Springs took on the look of the blight. Granny Bridges called it the blight. It had come with the bauxite mines years before and now it had spread over the land like a creeping fever. A dry fever. One that made you sneeze, cough and choke. It killed the trees, the grass and gardens. There were certain vegetables that his grandmother could not grow anymore. Something about the land refused the seed, as if the land was sick, and didn't know any longer what its nature was.

Once he recalled, when Granny Lincoln was brought out to sun, some big trucks loaded with ores stopped in front of the house. The men had heard about some sweet water around somewhere in the area and wanted some. Granny Lincoln had wanted to know what the men were doing carrying away her yard, and when Granpa Fields tried to console her, she refused to listen. Finally she had taken consolation in the Bible, saying that all of those trucks and men were signs. She said it was written that in the latter days, Satan and his angels would come forth from the earth seeking whom they might devour.

He began to climb down, the deadly powder making his descent as treacherous as his ascent. He had seen no sign of life on the freight. He had only shaken white dust into the air. It was a three-o'clock afternoon sun, hot, direct, lapping at the wounded earth with a dry merciless tongue. Layton did not feel angry at the sun, not really. He had learned somewhere in school that the sun was the source of all power. It was the sun that made the gardens grow, made the fields of hay, and cotton, corn and sorghum. It was the sun that drew up the rain from the ocean and sent rain down to make things green. Yet he knew it was by some terrible agreement, something beyond his comprehension, that allowed the sun and the whitemen to weaken the land. It was the same feeling which took his joy away when he thought of his coming new life in New York. It was like waving at a freight train. Somewhere he felt betrayed. Perhaps he was betraying the land himself. He felt that it all was a part of a great conspiracy . . . with the sun in the center. He did not like to think of leaving her to the mercy of the heat and the dust. And yet . . .

The only thing that gave Layton any real consolation was the fact that his grandmother was indestructible. He watched her slow pace up the road, her blue apron bulging with vegetables she had gotten from Granny Fields. She would sit on the porch in the evenings and the white dust never settled on her. Sometimes, he would think, gwine live forever. . . .

The two old women entered the bald yard in front of the shack. Their heads were bent as if they were watching the direction of their shadows, but Layton felt instinctively that his grandmother knew that he was in the tree. She never had to look at things to recognize them. She knew because it was the same to her as her bones telling when it was going to rain.

Layton was about to swing down to the last limb above the ground when he turned his neck to get a last look at the horizon where the trains passed. The 6:00 P.M. passenger would be the next one on the line, and he imagined that in a few more days he himself would be on it or maybe riding in the car with Mr. Stubbs. They would cross the tracks in Mr. Stubbs's car at the Sulfur Springs Greyhound station and he imagined telling Mr. Stubbs just what time the trains came by. . . . When he recognized the swirling dust as a car in the distance, he was already swinging down to the last limb. He never touched the ground, but swung, toes over head, back up onto the limb, grunting, his mouth open, his stomach flopping down on the limb. Upside down he saw the two figures climb wearily up on the porch. Mrs. Fields sat down in the rocking chair that was especially padded for her, and his grandmother rested in hers. He climbed back to the top. The car he saw had not taken the road which led to the cement plant. It was headed toward their house. He knew that no mistake could be made. There had been signs posted on the road for years. A screen of dust leaped from behind the car as it came like a racing beetle.

He almost blurted out the news of the car, but suddenly felt his throat dry up; in a careless movement of his foot, he slipped. . . .

Even the chinaberry tree, in its struggle with the land, had grown spiteful. It had not produced any berries in two years now, only a few scrawny pits that even the birds would not eat. He fell against the next limb, shaking the tree as if a wind had blown through. Before he caught himself he heard his grandmother's voice, calling him, warning him. He knew she had seen him fall, and in her voice, he could tell that she was saving him. His arms hooked the limb and he held it.

"Grandma," he said, swinging out of the tree and feeling grit in his throat, "yonder come somebody."

The old lady, as if she had known not only that someone was coming, but that her grandson would report it just that way, looked up from her lap where she was shelling green peas. "I reckon, your grandma and Mrs. Fields, 'bout to die of thirst, son."

By her voice he knew that the car was another betrayal. Yet there was no reason why it couldn't be Mr. Stubbs. The letter had said as soon as school was out and school had been out for weeks. He had not told Mr. Purdy at the cement plant that he was leaving, but he had told everybody else. No more night walking and night working. No more sleeping in the daytime and walking the dark roads at night with a flashlight. No more breathing the rock dust and chemicals, breathing them so much that you thought you were going to choke to death. No more looking in that cracked mirror at the plant and seeing a face covered with white dust, a black face underneath covered with a dry white fever. No more of the loneliness of walking to school and finding one less face there each day. . . .

Willy Strom, he gone off to Chicago with his brother. Maybelle Davis, she pregnant and gone to live with her cousin in Little Rock. Jesse Higgins, he left last night with Odell Miller and Claude Sykes. They all goin to the Job Corps in New Jersey. Louise Watkins, she getting married to a guy some kin to the Lawrences. They goin to Los Angeles.

Layton walked across the yard and stood in front of his grandmother. "I get you some sweet water." He paused. "Grandma, who you reckon comin yonder?" He couldn't really believe that his mother's letters were also betrayals.

Sarah Bridges, her long silver hair tied neatly in a bun, stopped shelling peas and lifted the straw hat to her face to fan. The brim slapped a fly into her lap and Layton watched as the insect regained its wing power and buzzed off.

"Reckon it nothin but somebody lookin for somethin to get, son. Every empty truck and car or wagon come into Holly Springs nowadays, always roll out full. It the change of the seasons, son. You get old as I am and you learn when to see the change of the seasons."

Granny Fields, her black face shining in her perpetual silence, looked up from her lap of peas. Her short arms continued to work as the round peas fell from the shove of her thumb. The empty hulls fell with their brothers on the floor beside her ancient high-top leather shoes. After years of working in the earth, her shoes had taken on the color of the dirt.

"I hear your mama want you up there with her, boy," she

said to Layton. She leaned out over the porch and spit a brown
stream of snuff.

"Yes mam," Layton said. Something began to ring in his
head now, like a kind of church bell. He looked out over the flat
land. He could not see the car now, but he picked the point in
the distance where he knew it would come into view. "But I
reckon if she don't, then I'm gwine go visit her and maybe work
for the summer. . . . I might even go to school up there next
year."

"You stay outa trouble, you hear. And mind your mama,"
said Granny Fields. She returned to her accustomed silence now,
having gathered up all the forces of her intellect to deliver her familiar warning. Layton liked Granny Fields because she spoke
only when she thought it necessary. Almost in his motion to go
back into the shack there came the deep and respectful, "Yes
mam."

He went through the shack. On his bed he saw the dusty
brown suitcase which he had put there every day since he got
the word from his mother. Even if she didn't send for him, he
was going to use that suitcase.

On the back porch he went to the earthen jug. It was the
vessel which he had filled every one or two days since he could
remember. He had gone with his mother when he was only a
tiny boy, to fill it, and he had gone with Granny and Mr. Fields,
and once with a man who Granny had told him was his own father. He couldn't remember his father because it was only that
once that he had seen him.

His mother had gone off to get a job, and even though she
sent money to his grandmother, Layton felt a kind of dryness,
an emptiness, whenever he tried to imagine her living way up in
New York. He wanted to go himself, and as he stirred the dipper around in the dark inside of the jug, he could hear the ringing of the train whistle, and the roar of sounds he knew he

would have to learn to identify. New sounds. New smells. New sights. No more picking cotton. No more dragging the long sack of cotton over sunbaked fields of dusty stalks, kicking up the red dirt. No more choking on cement dust. No more squinting at the distant death-smoke which began early in the morning as a haze but which by afternoon had become a cloud, a cloud of white gray dust, catching the sun, and choking off the rain and smothering the land. He did not drink. He would have to go out to get some water. There was just about two dippers full left.

He could see the sulfur-water well half hidden by the clothes on the line between the shack and the well. He checked the two sulfur-water buckets at the far edge of the porch; they both were full. A yellowish scale clung to their insides. Layton dipped up some of the water with the dipper, held it in his mouth for a short while, rinsed his mouth as he had seen the old people do after dipping snuff, and then spat. The taste of the water was intensified because the sun had broken through cracks on the porch wall and heated the water. It was not for drinking anyway, only for washing.

He poured the water from each bucket into a large bent tin tub which leaned against the rear of the shack. His grandmother used it to wash and collect rainwater. He would fill both buckets with sweet water at the spring.

When he lifted his head, he could see the pillar of dust swirling like a miniature twister. He went to the earthen jug and poured the contents into one of the buckets. The he went through the house and stood looking beyond the front porch, beyond the sound of his grandmother humming softly, beyond the almost silent flick of thumbs shelling peas, beyond the china-berry tree, obstinately clinging to the land, and beyond the edge of the young cotton, that Mr. Fields and he had planted and chopped, to the point where the car now appeared.

His grandmother lifted her head and squinted toward the

road. Mrs. Fields in her silence lifted her head also, as if she had waited for the other woman to make the first indication that the car was drawing close enough to look at.

"Granny Fields, you want a dipperful now?" Layton asked, watching the scale from the bucket shine from its slakeness and wondering how it was that sulfur got into the water, and how was it that the sweet water managed to escape the sulfur.

"I can wait for the fresh, son," she said. A pea popped from a shell and rolled off the porch. Layton saw it disappear in the dust, and the neck of a chicken shot from under the porch and struck the pea. He knew his grandmother always waited for fresh water too.

He stepped off the porch around a feathered form of a chicken asleep in the sun, its wing fanned out in the dust as if it were taking a bath. His bare feet slapped the baked clay in a familiar rhythm.

He stepped in a hole, where as a small boy he had played with wooden blocks and tin cans nailed together by his brother for trucks, cars, tractors, airplanes, or anything they wanted them to be. They had played bauxite and coal mining, cement hauling, gold digging and war.

Who would go and get the sweet water from the spring? The trip was too long for any of them to walk. Old Mr. Fields could not walk that far every day for water. They would all have to drink sulfur water, and he knew that was a bad sign. He stood there, paused beside the house watching the rapid approach of the car now, prolonging his own thirst. When he heard his grandmother's call, he felt the same feeling when he slipped on the tree. She did not call him but once, softly, as if she knew he had not gone very far, as if she knew that he was watching the car from the side of the house.

He saw a tailspin of dust rise up and then fall forward over the car. It had stopped in the yard. A whiteman emerged from the dust, wiping his face with a handkerchief. Layton climbed up on the porch and watched the man. He was Yul Stencely who came now and then to collect money, and Granny Bridges always paid it without question, as if it were her duty. He knew that the money he made and the money his mother sometimes sent finally went into the whiteman's hands. He watched the man approach. Yul Stencely looked around the yard expectantly. Layton knew he was looking for a dog to rush out at him.

"How do, Mrs. Bridges," the whiteman spoke, mopping his blond head and then resetting the straw hat he wore back on it. He drew near the steps. Particles of dust floated and settled on the porch. "Mighty hot today."

"How do, Mr. Stencely." She had already put aside the peas in her lap. Now she brought out a paring knife and began to peel a large white potato. "Yes, 'tis hot."

The whiteman drew out a notebook from his bosom pocket. Layton watched him. The man did not once notice the presence of Granny Fields nor did he look at Layton.

Tall, thin and straight, he wore a coat that was too large. Layton looked closely but he could see no signs of sweat, although the man was constantly wiping his face. He would look at the dirty handkerchief, blow his breath into it as the cloth passed over his mouth and then look at his notebook with silent appraisal. He stepped into a tiny shaft of shade near Granny Bridges at the edge of the porch.

"Who told you I had anything for you this time, Mr. Stencely?" There was no real anger in her voice, but Layton could tell that there was a determination, a kind of defiance which always made him feel that his grandmother was indestructible. She kept on peeling potatoes, without looking at the whiteman. He cleared his throat and continued his scrutiny of the notebook. Then he looked around the yard again.

"Well, Mrs. Bridges, aint no harm in comin. Is there? Sides, I reckon you owe since the last time I was here. . . ." He paused. Layton studied the man. Granny was right. He had

come like the rest. They come empty and leave full. Layton suddenly wanted to know the reason for this continued payment to
the whiteman. Why was it that it was always Negroes who paid
money to the whiteman? Yet he knew the answers, but asking
the questions over again made him feel a fire rise up from his
toes and churn away in his stomach. And the fire gave him direction. "Well, I reckon there aint no harm in comin, Mr. Stencely, and I reckon there aint no harm in me askin you to come
again next month. I speck my daughter-in-law gwine send a bit
of money . . ."

Layton set the bucket down. It made a noise. The whiteman turned and looked at it. Then he looked away around the
house toward the well. Layton felt as if she had said something
then to take away all the years of his faith in her strength. If his
mother had sent some money, it would go to that man. . . . He
knew that. But it just shouldn't. . . . Over and over now he
heard the ring of the tin bucket on the ground. . . . The settling
of the dust was millions of tiny bells.

The whiteman laughed. He couldn't go any further than
the old woman would let him. He knew that they were poor,
but that was not his fault. He collected from poor whites as well
as poor blacks. He even had some Mexicans he collected from.
He was hot and he needed a drink.

"Well, Mrs. Bridges, I tell you what I'm gonna do. You let
me have a drink of your good well water and I'll be obliged to
come agin when you able . . ."

Granny Bridges flipped a long curled potato peeling out
into the yard where a chicken neck grabbed it and fled beneath
the house.

"Layton, give Mr. Stencely a drink of water. . . ."

When she called his name, Layton was already in motion.
He left the bucket with the two dippers of sweet water from the
earthen jug and went to the back and to the sulfur-water well.
He let the long aluminum cylinder down into the well shaft. The

ringing of the rusty wheel which rode the chain up and down was a kind of music which Layton associated with dryness. The water from the well never really quenched your thirst. Only the spring water could quench your thirst. He felt the cylinder strike bottom, fill, and grow heavy. He coughed and began to pull. His muscles burned and the sun struck him through the hood of the well right in the face. He frowned, and his frowning made him hot. The whiteman would drink what he gave him. He would drink, but he would not lose his thirst. His stomach would swell and almost burst, but he would still be thirsty. Hours after drinking this water you would belch it and want to spit, but your tongue would be dry. Your throat would crack, and you would sweat.

He returned to the front porch with a bucket and a glass from the kitchen. He took the dipper from the sweet-water bucket and watched it sink in the freshly drawn sulfur water. Then he stood in the doorway, motionless. He expected the whiteman to reach and fill the glass and drink. He didn't hear his grandmother's voice calling him. He lifted the sweet water pail and stepped back into the doorway. . . .

"Layton."

The truth still rang in her voice. It halted him. He heard the slosh of the remaining bits of water in the pail against his bare leg. "Yes, mam?"

"Aint you got no manners?"

He returned to the doorway and saw his grandmother lifting the bucket of sulfur water and aiming it out to the yard.

She slung it. "This water aint fit to drink." Layton felt as if the water had been splashed in his face. A shiver went up his legs. He quickly looked at the whiteman, then set down his bucket.

"There be enough for one drink left," announced Granny Fields. She looked up at Layton as if she had suddenly come out of a cave after a long time.

Layton watched as the whiteman carefully drank two full glasses of water. Not one drop fell. He mopped his face again. "Mrs. Bridges, that's the sweetest water in Holly Springs. You sure you aint got a softener hidden out in that well somewheres?"

"The Lord provides." She was not receptive to flattery. She set the bucket down in front of Layton and then sat back down in her chair. Yul Stencely stepped into the sun. He looked at Layton. Their eyes met.

"That's your youngest grandchild," he stated rather than asked, without taking his eyes off Layton.

Layton came out on the porch, picked up the other bucket, walked off the porch in front of Yul and went around the side of the house slinging the two buckets violently. He did not hear what she said anymore. He passed the sulfur well, passed the old grassy area where their hog pen used to be. They could not afford to raise hogs anymore. They had a few chickens. Even dogs would not stay. Dogs would roam and die off, getting run over on the highway or killed by other dogs. Layton could hardly remember when he had a dog. It was his brother's dog that Yul Stencely had seen on his last visit, but that was months ago. His brother had gone off to Vietnam.

Layton felt funny thinking about that whiteman coming to get money when they didn't have any. The few pennies he made at the cement plant would not keep him away. He even began to wonder if his grandmother's sturdiness could keep the dust away any longer. His brother had gone. . . . And yet Layton knew that staying was like dying. He could not die. He would go off and take his chances. At least you had a chance. But staying here trying to finish school, by alternating it with chopping and picking cotton or with pit work at the plant, was sure death.

He pictured one day a whiteman coming after him. But it burned him inside to feel that. He had seen the fire in the eyes of the kids in Holly Springs last year in the marches and demonstrations. He would join in the voter drive, he would get out and work against the dryness.

He moved along a path toward the spring. It was a grassy path. When he reached the sign and the high fence which read GOVERNMENT PROPERTY KEEP OFF, he scanned the fence for a weeded spot, then broke over, throwing the two buckets over ahead of him. The spring lay a half mile within the boundary of the fence. He had to hurry.

When his grandmother threw out that water, it was like seeing her fall down in the dust on the road. No. He rebuked himself for a thought. Even the Bible . . . He didn't know much about the Bible. He could not quote it like she could. The Bible didn't hold that much interest for him. It was those preachers who always came looking for sweet water. He didn't want to distrust the Bible, but then he could not give it all of his trust. She did not really want him to leave and go North like she said; she wanted him to stay. There wasn't nobody around Holly Springs anymore. All gone. And his grandmother wanted him to be like Granny Lincoln and the rest of the old ones. The thought choked him. He reached the spring.

The cool clear water bubbled out of the little opening in the ground near an encirclement of trees. A slight depression in the ground marked the spot. The water flowed for a very short distance and then disappeared again in the earth. His bare feet moved over little stone steps. The spurt of the water from the ground was about seven or eight inches. Layton drank.

Well, maybe she didn't really want him to stay, but then who would take care of her . . . after she couldn't do it herself? But he could not picture her ever reaching the point where she could not take care of herself. When all the rest were down, Granny would still be there.

He noticed that the spurt was thinner than it was yesterday. He wondered if anybody else besides the Negroes who lived near the spring had discovered it. It wouldn't be long before the government found out that it had sweet water on its plantation. By then the spring would disappear and come up again somewhere else.

Or maybe the spring was tired of feeding the sulfurous earth and was going to return to the deep darkness forever. Layton filled the buckets and drank again. . . . When he bent over he felt his head spin as if stars were falling on him. . . .

When he returned to the shack, the sun had gathered itself into a kind of orange brilliance and was aiming toward a line in the distance. Layton filled the earthen jug, letting the water fall to make bubbles like the sound of the spring. He took the women a bucket and a dipper. But before his grandmother drank she called him.

"Son, I reckon you see a lot of things in town and out at that plant that your granny don't see. I reckon you got a right to get mad like the young people these days. I'm all for that, but I aint for you gettin mad like a mad dog. You 'member when your brother's dog got the rabies, don't you, son?"

Layton nodded. He figured he knew what his grandmother was going to say. . . . But he could not run from it. Somehow he wanted to hear it even if it cooled him. The taste of the sweet water seemed to linger in the air. . . .

"A mad dog will bite anybody, son. It don't matter who it used to belong to. It even bite the man what raised it. A mad dog will bite its own mother, son. So I'm sayin, son, be mad but not like a mad dog. Be right first. Be truthful first. And when you get mad at somethin then you got all *that* to back you up. Don't spite that man cause he thirsty and white. That's wrong. Give 'em your best at all times. When you give 'em your best when you don't like him, he be the first to know it. God on your side then."

It never mattered whether he really agreed with Granny or not, because she seemed to be right. Mrs. Fields, in her silence, had only glanced at him, and he knew that she was backing up his grandmother. It was a conspiracy. It was a bond which he could not understand nor defeat, and nothing in his experience seemed full enough to satisfy him. His mother was not sending for him. She too was trapped. In the North she wasn't doing as good as she said. He had heard how that in cities up North they were having race riots and killing Negroes. Then what good was his trying to wait till she sent out Mr. Stubbs? There wasn't no man. His father was dead and that was it. He felt himself now ready to cast off the dreams and things people said. He would believe no one, and if he dreamed something, he would not believe it were true until *he* made it come true. . . . If he were going to leave soon, then it would be because he wanted to. Even if his mother sent a ticket, it would mean nothing unless he wanted to leave. His grandmother would not drink sulfur water unless she had to and he knew that as long as there was sweet water coming out of the ground, she would be strong. . . .

A long whistle broke the late evening heaviness, and Layton stopped packing his suitcase and went out to the bald yard. . . . If he climbed the tree to see the passenger train, he knew that he would not fall.

About Henry Dumas

THE CULT OF HENRY DUMAS has continued to pulsate with ever-widening life since his premature death by gunshot in a New York City subway on May 23, 1968. By the time of his death at age thirty-four, Dumas had completed a Ulyssean journey, beginning in his hometown of Sweet Home, Arkansas, taking him to New York City, where he finished Commerce High School, to City College and Rutgers University, into the U.S. Air Force where he spent a year in the Arabian Penninsula, through tent cities in Mississippi and Tennessee, into civil rights activities and the little magazine circuit, through Hiram College as assistant director of Upward Bound, and, finally, to Southern Illinois University's Experiment in Higher Education, in East St. Louis, where he served as teacher-counselor and director of language workshops. Throughout his journey, Dumas wrote heroic tales and poems, publishing in small magazines like his own *Black Ikon* (founded in 1963) as well as in *Umbra, Trace, The Anthologist, The American Weave, The Hiram Poetry Review*, and *Negro Digest (Black World)*. Since his death, Dumas's reputation and following among students and critics have mushroomed. His poems and stories have appeared in more than a dozen anthologies, and four collections of his works have been brought out by major publishing houses. These volumes—*Poetry for My People/Play Ebony Play Ivory, Ark of Bones, Jonoah and the Green Stone*, and *Rope of Wind*—were all edited by Eugene B. Redmond, executor of the Dumas estate. Redmond is also guest editor of a special summer 1988 issue of *Black American Literature Forum* dedicated to scholary and critical examinations of Dumas. Currently, the late writer's works are being taught in public schools and universities where they have also been adapted to stage and set to music. Dumas's widow, Loretta, and his son, Michael, live in Somerset, New Jersey.

—E.B.R.

About Eugene B. Redmond

EUGENE B. REDMOND, Poet Laureate of East St. Louis, Illinois, has authored or edited 15 books of poetry, fiction and literary criticism. He has taught at California State University—Sacramento, University of Wisconsin—Madison, Southern University—Baton Rouge, and Oberlin College, and is currently Poet-in-Residence for the public school system in his home town.